ALSO BY MICHAEL ROBOTHAM

When She Was Good
Good Girl, Bad Girl
The Secrets She Keeps
The Suspect
Lost
The Night Ferry
Shatter
Bombproof
Bleed for Me
The Wreckage
Say You're Sorry
Watching You
Life or Death
Close Your Eyes
The Other Wife

WHEN YOU ARE MINE

— *A Novel* —

MICHAEL ROBOTHAM

SCRIBNER

New York London Toronto Sydney New Delhi

Scribner
An Imprint of Simon & Schuster, Inc.
1230 Avenue of the Americas
New York, NY 10020

First Scribner hardcover edition January 2022

SCRIBNER and design are registered trademarks of The Gale Group, Inc., used under license by Simon & Schuster, Inc., the publisher of this work.

For information about special discounts for bulk purchases, please contact Simon & Schuster Special Sales at 1-866-506-1949 or business@simonandschuster.com.

The Simon & Schuster Speakers Bureau can bring authors to your live event. For more information or to book an event, contact the Simon & Schuster Speakers Bureau at 1-866-248-3049 or visit our website at www.simonspeakers.com.

Manufactured in the United States of America

10   9   8   7   6   5   4   3   2   1

Library of Congress Cataloging-in-Publication Data

Names: Robotham, Michael, 1960–, author.
Title: When you are mine : a novel / Michael Robotham.
Description: First Scribner hardcover edition. | New York : Scribner, 2022.
Identifiers: LCCN 2021033879 (print) | LCCN 2021033880 (ebook) |
ISBN 9781982166458 (hardcover) | ISBN 9781982166472 (ebook)
Subjects: GSAFD: Suspense fiction.
Classification: LCC PR6118.O26 W48 2022 (print) |
LCC PR6118.O26 (ebook) | DDC 823/.92—dc23
LC record available at https://lccn.loc.gov/2021033879
LC ebook record available at https://lccn.loc.gov/2021033880

ISBN 978-1-9821-6645-8
ISBN 978-1-9821-6647-2 (ebook)

To Monsignor Tony Doherty

BOOK ONE

Extinguish my eyes, I'll go on seeing you.

Seal my ears, I'll go on hearing you.

And without feet I can make my way to you,

without a mouth I can swear your name.

Rainer Maria Rilke

1

I was eleven years old when I saw my future. I was standing near the middle doors of a double-decker bus when a bomb exploded on the upper level, peeling off the roof like a giant had taken a tin opener to a can of peaches. One moment I was holding on to a pole, and the next I was flying through the air, seeing sky, then ground, then sky. A leg whipped past me. A stroller. A million shards of glass, each catching the sunlight.

I crashed to the pavement as debris and body parts fell around me. Looking up through the dust, I wondered what I'd been doing on a London sightseeing bus, which is what it looked like without a roof.

People were hurt. Dying. Dead. I spat grit from between my teeth and tried to remember who had been standing next to me. A tattooed girl with white earbuds under hacked purple hair. A mother with a toddler in a stroller. Two old ladies were in the side seat, arguing about the price of movie tickets. A guy with a hipster beard was carrying a guitar case decorated with stickers from around the world.

Normally I would have been at school at 9:47 in the morning, but I had a doctor's appointment with an ear, nose, and throat specialist who was going to tell me why I suffered from so many sinus infections. Apparently I have narrow nasal passages, which is probably genetic, but I haven't worked out who to blame.

As I lay on the street, a man's face appeared, hovering over me. He was talking but he made no sound. I read his lips.

"Are you bleeding?"

I looked at my school uniform. My blue-and-white-checked blouse was covered in blood. I didn't know if it was mine.

"How many fingers am I holding up?"

"Three."

He moved away.

Around me, shop-front windows had been shattered, covering the sidewalk and roadway with diamonds of glass. A pigeon lay nearby, blown out of the sky, or maybe it died of fright. Dust had settled, coating everything in a fine layer of gray soot. Later, when I saw myself in the mirror, I had white streaks under my eyes, the tracks of my tears.

As I sat in the gutter, I watched a young policewoman moving among the injured. Reassuring them. Comforting them. She put her arms around a child who had lost his mother. The same officer reached me and smiled. She had a round face and brilliantly white teeth and her hair was bundled up under her cap.

My ears had stopped ringing. Words spilled out of her mouth.

"What's your name, poppet?"

"Philomena."

"And your last name?"

"McCarthy."

"Are you by yourself, Philomena?"

"I have a doctor's appointment. I'm going to be late."

"He won't mind."

The police officer gave me a bottle of water so I could wash dirt from my mouth. "I'll be back soon," she said, and she continued moving among the wounded. She was like one of those characters you see in disaster movies who you know is going to be the hero from the moment they appear on-screen. Everything about her was calm and self-assured, sending a message that we would survive this. The city would survive. All was not lost.

Standing in front of the mirror, sixteen years later, I remember that officer and wish I had asked for her name. I often think about bumping into her again and thanking her for what she did. "I became a police officer because of you," I'd say. "You were my childhood hero."

I laugh at the thought and stare at my reflection. Then I pull a face which is supposed to reduce my chance of wrinkles but makes me look like I'm busting for the loo. My mother swears by these exercises and recommends them to all her clients at the beauty salon, most of them older women who are desperately clinging to their looks, while their husbands get to age gracefully or disgracefully, going to seed, without a care.

Leaning closer to the mirror, I consider my face, which looks heart-shaped when I bundle my hair up into a topknot. I have gray eyes, a straight-edged nose, and an overly large bottom lip, which Henry likes to bite when we kiss. My eyebrows are like sisters rather than distant cousins because I refuse to let my mother near them with her tweezers and pencils.

I am working early today, with a shift starting at seven. Henry is still in bed. He looks like a little boy when he sleeps, his dark hair tousled and wild, and one arm draped across his eyes because he doesn't like to be woken by the bathroom light. Henry could sleep for England. He could have slept through the blitz. And he doesn't mind when I come in late and put my cold feet on his warm ones. That must be love.

I glance at my phone. It's not even six and already I have four voice-mail messages, all of them from my stepmother, Constance. I don't normally refer to Constance as my stepmother because we're so close in age, which embarrasses me more than her, and my father not at all. What a cliché he turned out to be—running off with his secretary.

I play the first message.

"Philomena, sweetie, did you get the invitation? You haven't replied. The party is two weeks on Sunday. Are you coming? Please say yes. It would mean so much to Edward. You know he's very proud of you . . . and wishes . . . ." She doesn't finish the statement. *"He's turning sixty and he wants you with him. You're still his favorite, you know, despite everything—"*

"Despite everything," I scoff, skipping to the next message.

"Philomena, darling, please come. Everybody will be there. Bring Henry, of course. Is that his name? Or is it Harry? I'm terrible with names. Forgive me. Oh, let me check. I've written it down . . . somewhere . . . yes, here. Henry. Bring Henry. No presents. Two weeks on Sunday at four."

Constance has a posh, braying voice that makes every utterance sound like "yah, rah, hah, nah, yah." She is the granddaughter of a duke or a lord who gambled away the family fortune a generation ago and "doesn't have a pot to piss in," according to my uncles, who call her "the duchess" behind her back.

Henry stirs. His head appears. "What time it is?"

"Nearly six."

He raises the bedclothes and peers beneath. "I have a present for you."

"Too late."

"Please come back to bed."

"You missed your chance."

He groans and covers his head.

"I love you too." I laugh.

Outside, a dog begins furiously yapping. Our neighbor Mrs. Ainsley has a Jack Russell called Blaine that barks at every creak and cough and passing car. We've complained, but Mrs. Ainsley changes the subject, pointing out some act of vandalism or petty crime in the street which is more evidence that society is unraveling and we're not safe in our beds.

It's an eighteen-minute walk from Marney Road to Clapham Common tube station, along the northern edge of the common, past sporting fields and the skate park. I am wearing my "half blues," with my hair pinned up in a bun. We're not allowed to wear our full uniform when traveling to and from work. Periodically, a politician will suggest the policy be changed, arguing that police officers should be more visible as a deterrent to crime. Cops on the beat. Boots on the ground.

I can picture my morning commute if I were in uniform. Random strangers would complain to me about schoolkids putting their feet on the seats or playing music too loudly. I'd hear how their neighbor doesn't recycle properly or has a dog that keeps crapping in their front garden. If trouble did break out, how would I call for backup without a radio? And if I made an arrest, where would I take the offender? Would I get overtime? Would anyone thank me?

I catch a Northern line train to Borough, which is six stops, and walk two minutes to Southwark Police Station, stopping to buy coffee at the Starbucks across the road. The skinny barista is called Paolo and he keeps up a constant patter as he presses, steams, froths, and pours. He offers the ladies "extra cream" or a "sticky bun," making it sound like a sexual proposition. His brother works the sandwich press and occasionally adds to the banter.

While I wait for my order, I think about my father and his sixtieth birthday party. I haven't spoken to him in six years and haven't been in the same room with him for nine. I can remember that last meeting. Jamie Pike, the coolest boy I knew, was fumbling in my knickers in our front room. One moment he had his hand down my pants, acting like he'd lost a pound coin, and the next he was flying backwards and slamming into an antique sideboard, where a William and Kate wedding plate toppled from a stand and shattered on the floor next to him.

My father marched him out of the house and spoke so sternly to Jamie that he never so much as looked at me again. A few years ago I bumped into him at a cinema in Leicester Square and he literally ran away. He might still be running, or hiding under his bed, or checking his doors are locked. My father has that sort of reputation. He is steeped in myths and stories, many of them violent, hopefully embellished, but all of them spoken in whispers in dark corners because nobody wants to discover if they're true.

Jamie Pike isn't the reason that I'm estranged from my father. My parents' divorce set us on separate paths. I chose to live with my mother, and Daddy chose not to care, or care enough to fight for me. Yes, he sends me birthday presents and Christmas gifts and makes overtures, but I expect more from someone who broke my heart. I want him to grovel. I want him to suffer.

When I applied to join the London Metropolitan Police, I knew it was going to be difficult. Not just the job—policing a city of nine million people—or the other responsibilities of counter terrorism and protecting foreign embassies and the Royal Family. I was up against history, tradition, misogyny, and the baggage that comes with my family. The form asked me to list my connections with any known criminals. I named my father and three uncles. I watched the recruiting inspector read my application and felt as though the oxygen were being sucked from the room. He laughed, thinking it was some sort of joke. He looked past me, searching for a hidden camera or whoever had put me up to this. When he realized I was serious, his mood changed and I went from being an applicant with a strong CV and a first-class degree to being a fox asking permission to move into the henhouse and set up a barbecue chicken joint.

His face changed color. "Money laundering. Extortion. Racketeering. Theft. Your family is a pox on this city. Are you seriously suggesting I allow you to join the police service?"

"I cannot be held responsible for the past actions of my family members," I said, quoting the regulations.

"Don't lecture me, lassie," said the inspector.

"I'd prefer not to be called 'lassie,' sir."

"What?"

"That's the name for a dog or a young girl."

My mouth, running off again.

My application was rejected. I applied again. Another rebuff. I threatened legal action. It took me four attempts to gain a place at Hendon, where the instructors were harder on me than any of the other recruits, determined to have me fail or drop out. My classmates couldn't understand why I was singled out for such brutal treatment. I didn't tell any of them about my father. McCarthy is a common enough surname. There are twenty-eight thousand of us in England and almost the same number in Ireland. A person can hide in a crowd that big. A person might even disappear, if only her father would let her.

At Southwark Police Station, I get changed into my full kit: my stab vest, belt, shoulder radio, body camera, collapsible baton, CS spray, and two sets of handcuffs. My hair bun fits neatly beneath my bowler hat, so that the brim doesn't tilt down and restrict my field of vision. I love this uniform. It makes me feel respected. It makes me feel needed.

Although only five foot five, I'm not frightened of confrontation. I teach karate two evenings a week at Chestnut Grove Academy in Wandsworth, and occasionally on weekends. I can block a punch and take a fall, but more importantly, I can read a situation and stay cool under pressure. I don't practice karate because I'm mistrustful of people or frightened of the world. I like the discipline and improved fitness and how it speeds up my reaction times.

Twenty officers gather in the patrol room for the briefing. Our section sergeant, Harry Connelly, has a quasi-military bearing and weight around his middle that puts pressure on his buttons. Certain jobs need to be followed up from the night shift. Crime scenes guarded. Prisoners escorted to court. A suicide watch at a hospital. Outstanding warrants to be served.

"We had a confirmed sighting overnight of Terrence John Fryer, a violent escaper, wanted for drug use, supply, and manufacture. He tried to break into his girlfriend's house in Balham. You have his mug shot. He's dangerous. Call for backup if you see him."

Paperwork and follow-up calls are the bane of a copper's life. Every LOB (load of bollocks) from an MOP (member of the public) generates a report and a response. Forms in triplicate. Statements. Updates. Liaising with other services.

"Morning, partner," says Police Constable Anisha Kohli, falling into step beside me.

Kohli gets called "Nish" and is the station heartthrob. Tall and lean with milk-chocolate skin, he was born in East Ham and has never been to India, but he still gets peppered with questions about arranged marriages, the caste system, and cricket.

"Why do people treat me like I'm fresh off the boat?" he once asked.

"It's because you look like a Bollywood star."

"But I can't sing or dance or act."

"Yeah, but you got the looks, baby."

We sign out a patrol car, which doesn't smell of piss or vomit. I'm grateful for that.

Nish gets behind the wheel and I radio the control room. Our first jobs are a reported burglary in Brixton and a series of cars that were vandalized near Peckham tube. Nish and I work well together. Instinctively, we choose who should take the lead in asking questions. Some of the more experienced officers aren't sure how to treat female constables, but things are getting better. One in four officers are now women, and the ratio is even higher in management.

The morning is a mixed bag of accidents, burglaries, a bag snatch on a Vespa, and a dementia patient missing from a nursing home. Nobody on patrol ever says, "it's quiet," because that's considered bad luck, like an actor naming that "Scottish play."

After three years I can plot my way around South London based on the crime scenes that I've attended. A hit-and-run on this corner. A jumper from that building. Cars set alight on that vacant block. Some locales are more famous or infamous than others, and some crimes are so shocking that the victims' names are seared into the history of a city: Damilola Taylor. Stephen Lawrence. Rachel Nickell. Jean Charles de Menezes.

Most people look at London and see landmarks. I see the maimed, broken, and the addicted, the eyewitnesses, the innocent bystanders, and the bereaved.

At midday I'm picking up coffees from a van near London Bridge when the control room radios about a domestic in progress. A neighbor can hear a woman screaming. The address is one of the newer warehouse developments near Borough Market. Nish pulls into traffic and gives a blast of the siren to clear an intersection. He looks at the dashboard clock. "This one kicked off early."

Nish presses a buzzer on the intercom. The neighbor answers and unlocks the main door. She is waiting on the fourth floor, an elderly black woman in a brightly colored kaftan and slippers. Her ankles are as wide as her toes.

"Mrs. Gregg?" I ask.

She nods and points along the hallway. "I can't hear them anymore. He might have killed her."

"Who lives there?" I ask.

"A young woman. The boyfriend comes and goes."

"Owner occupier?"

"The owner works in Dubai. Rents the place out."

"You said you heard screaming," says Nish.

"And stuff breaking. She was yelling and he was calling her names."

"Have there been other fights?" I ask.

"Nothing like this."

"OK. Go back inside."

We take up positions on either side of the door. I have one hand on my baton and my legs braced. Nish knocks. There are muffled voices inside. He knocks again. A chain unhooks. A lock turns. A woman's face appears. Late twenties. Dark hair. Attractive. Frightened.

"Hello, how are you?" I ask.

"Fine."

"We had a report of a disturbance. A woman sounded upset. Was that you?"

"No."

"Who else is in the flat?"

"Nobody."

Nish has braced one foot against the door to stop it being shut.

"Can we come inside?" I ask.

"You must have the wrong address," she says. "I'm fine."

"What's your name?"

"Tempe."

"Is it short for Temperance?"

"No, it's a place . . . in Greek mythology. The Vale of Tempe."

"What about your last name?"

"Why?"

"It's a question that we have to ask."

Tempe's eyes go sideways.

"Who else lives here?" asks Nish.

"My boyfriend. He works nights. He's sleeping."

"You said you were alone."

She hesitates, trapped in a lie.

"Can you open the door a little wider?" I ask.

"Why?"

"We have to check on your welfare."

Tempe edges it open, revealing her swollen left eye, which is filled with blood, and a split lip that has twisted her mouth out of shape. Even with a damaged face she looks familiar, and I wonder if we might have met before.

"What happened to your face?" I ask.

"It was an accident."

Her gaze shifts to the left again. There is someone standing behind the door.

I motion with my head and mouth the words "Is he there?"

Tempe nods.

I cup my ear in a listening gesture.

Another nod.

"Maybe you should wake your boyfriend and tell him we're here," says Nish, speaking more loudly.

"No. Please. I'm fine. Really, I am."

She tries to shut the door, but Nish has his foot in place and matches her effort. Tempe backs away. The front of her dress is stained with blood and her lip looks like a large marble has been sewn beneath the broken skin.

A man steps from behind the door and shoves Tempe out of the way.

Shielding her. He's shirtless and shoeless, wearing a pair of gray tracksuit pants that hang low on his hips. Late-thirties. Smiling.

"How can I help you officers?"

"We had a report of a woman screaming," says Nish.

"Screaming? Nah. Must have been the TV."

"The young lady has injuries."

"That was an accident. She ran into a door."

"What's your name, sir?"

"Let's not go there," says the man, who has a Roman centurion tattooed onto his shoulder and scars on his chest and stomach. "I'm a copper, OK? This is all a misunderstanding."

I glance at Nish, looking for guidance, but nothing has changed in his demeanor. He asks the man to step outside.

"What for?"

"My colleague is going to speak to Tempe alone. You're going to stay here with me."

"That's not necessary."

"She has a black eye and a split lip."

I step past the man, who throws out his arm to block the doorway. I duck underneath.

"You don't have permission. I know my rights," he complains.

The hallway has a broken bowl on the floor and a smear of blood on the wall. Tempe is in the living area, sitting on the sofa, with her chin resting on her knees. She has found a bag of frozen peas in the freezer and is pressing it to the side of her face. She has long, slender feet that are calloused around her toes from wearing high-heel shoes.

Her boyfriend is still arguing with Nish.

"What happened?" I ask.

"I made him angry."

Her accent is Northern Irish. Belfast, maybe, but softer. She is two inches taller than me, with almond-shaped eyes that are pale green. Again, I feel as though we might have met, but I can't place her.

Voices are drifting from outside, where the argument continues. I distract Tempe with a question.

"You live here?"

She nods.

"Is your name on the lease?"

"No."

Tempe lowers the frozen peas. Her left eye is almost completely closed.

"Your cheekbone might be fractured. You'll need an X-ray. I'll take you to hospital."

"He won't allow that."

"He'll have to."

I take a photograph of her face. "Lift your chin." I take another. "Pull back your hair." And another.

"Any other bruises?"

"No."

"Change your clothes. Put the dress in a plastic bag."

"Why?"

"It's evidence."

"I'm not pressing charges."

"Fine, but I'm taking you to hospital."

Tempe goes to the bedroom and I look around the apartment, which is tastefully decorated, although everything looks like it came from a furniture showroom, one of those places that puts fake books on the shelves and empty bottles of wine in the bar fridge. There are no personal items like photographs or souvenirs or knickknacks. Nothing that creates a signature or gives an insight into the occupants.

Tempe clears her throat. She is standing in the doorway wearing a modest woolen dress with a cowl neck. She collects her handbag from the table, making sure she has her phone.

"What about your passport?"

"Why do I need that?"

"It's good to have proof of your identity—in case you don't come back."

"I'm coming back," she says adamantly.

I take her forearm as we walk along the hallway. Nish is still arguing with the boyfriend.

"Why are you writing stuff down? I told you, nothing happened."

"Why does the young lady have blood on her dress?"

"It was an accident."

"Yeah, so you keep saying."

"You won't be writing this up. I'm a detective sergeant stationed at Scotland Yard. The Intelligence Unit."

Nish sounds less certain than before. "I need your name."

"Fuck off!"

Tempe tries to step around him, but the boyfriend grabs at her hair. I knock his arm aside and push her behind me, before bracing my legs, one forward, the other back, letting my hands hang ready at my sides. This time he lunges at me. I dance back a step and perform a rising cross-block with open hands.

Suddenly, enraged, he swings a punch, but I grab his attacking arm from inside and back-fist him in the jaw. Dropping to one knee, I trip him backwards, turning him onto his chest and twisting his arm high up the middle of his spine.

All of this happens so quickly that Nish hasn't had time to unholster his Taser or extend his baton. Taking cuffs from my belt, I snap them on his wrists.

"I am arresting you for assaulting a police officer. You do not have to say anything. But if you do not mention now something which you later use in your defense, the court may decide that your failure to mention it now strengthens the case against you . . ."

The man has blood on his teeth. "You're finished! You're both fucked!"

". . . a record will be made of anything you say, and it may be given in evidence if you are brought to trial."

"I am Detective Sergeant Darren Goodall. I want my Police Federation rep."

I glance at Nish, who is taking notes but looks dazed. "Can you arrange transport to the station? I'll take Tempe to the hospital."

He nods.

Feeling calm, almost weightless, I lead Tempe along the hallway to the lift.

Goodall shouts after her. "Not a word, bitch! Not a fucking word!"

Inside the lift, Tempe pins herself against the mirrored wall, wrapping her arms around her thin frame.

"How did you do that?" she whispers.

"What?"

"You dropped him like a . . . like a . . ." She can't think of a word. "He was twice your size. It was like something you see in the movies. What are you? Five six? A hundred and thirty pounds?"

"On a good day." I laugh, the adrenaline starting to leak away.

"Do they teach you that in the police?"

"No."

"You were so fast. It was like you knew exactly what he was going to do before he did it."

"I knew he was right-handed."

"How?"

"That's the hand he used on you."

Tempe touches her swollen eye, making the connection in her mind.

We've reached the patrol car. Tempe sits in the backseat and I get behind the wheel. We can see each other in the rearview mirror on the windscreen.

"Is he a detective?" I ask.

"Yeah."

"How long have you been seeing him?"

"A year. He's married. Does that shock you?"

"All part of the rich pageant," I say, but instantly regret the comment because it sounds flippant and condescending. I shouldn't be mocking an institution that I'm about to embrace.

Tempe pulls at the collar of her dress. She's fidgeting, wanting to busy her hands. We've stopped at the traffic lights and I take a moment to study her face, not the bruising, but the half which is undamaged. Thoughtful. Sad. Lonely.

Ten minutes later we walk into the Urgent Care Centre at Guy's Hospital. The waiting area is full of the broken, beaten, and accident-prone. A black woman with her arm in a sling looks at me with undisguised hatred. She has two small kids clinging to her skirt. What have I done to deserve such loathing? Put on a uniform? Kept the streets safe?

A triage nurse takes down Tempe's details and then we sit side by side in the waiting area. A different nurse gets Tempe an ice pack, which she holds gently against her cheek.

"Has he hurt you before?"

No answer.

"Will you make a statement?"

"No."

"Why not?"

"I'm not stupid."

I don't blame her. If Darren Goodall is a police officer, he will know exactly how to handle a complaint like this one: what to say and who to call and how to twist the details. He'll claim that Tempe hit him first or that he was trying to protect himself. It will be her word against his. No contest.

"You look so familiar," I say. "I could swear that we've met before."

"I don't think so," says Tempe.

Then it comes to me—the memory of a pretty girl with dark hair who was three years ahead of me at St. Ursula's Convent in Greenwich.

"We went to school together," I say. "But your name wasn't Tempe."

"It's my middle name. I hated being called Margaret."

Maggie Brown. I remember. "You were school captain."

"Vice captain."

"And you had a sister who was older."

"Agnes."

"You didn't stay. You left before your finals."

"We moved to Belfast."

I have a vague memory that something happened—some scandal or incident that people talked about for a few weeks—but I don't recall the details. My friend Sara might remember. We were besties at school together and her appetite for gossip is insatiable.

What can I recall about Maggie Brown? She was pretty and popular but not an extrovert or a queen bee. She didn't "own" the corridors or mistreat anyone or compete for attention or call shotgun on the backseat of every bus.

"Do you keep in touch with anyone from St. Ursula's?" I ask.

"No," she replies dismissively. "I hated that place."

"Oh!" I feel a little hurt.

There is another long pause. I watch the triage nurse examine a new arrival—a drunk man with a mouth full of broken teeth and a T-shirt that says "Trophy Husband."

"How did you meet Darren Goodall?"

"My girlfriend and I witnessed a crime. A guy on an electric scooter snatched a handbag and took off, but as he ran a red light, he was hit by a lorry. Killed him outright. Maybe it served him right." She doesn't sound convinced. "The police made us wait around to give statements. Darren took down our names and addresses. A few days later he called me."

"Why?"

Tempe laughs. "Do I have to spell it out?"

I feel the tops of my ears grow warm.

"How did he get your number?"

"He's police," she says, as though it should be obvious. "I didn't know he was married, of course. He let me think he was single. When I learned the truth, I tried to rationalize it—telling myself I wasn't hurting anyone."

"You thought he'd leave his wife."

"No. Well, maybe. But he has two young kids. I'm not naive."

"Is there somewhere else you can stay?" I ask.

"Not really."

"I can take you to a refuge. It's a safe space until you find somewhere else."

"He'll have calmed down by now."

"Has he hit you before?"

"Not like this." She looks at me defiantly. "I'm not some battered wife."

"I didn't say you were," I reply, wishing I had a tenner for every time I'd heard the same thing said by wives and girlfriends with bloodied faces and bruised limbs who didn't see themselves as victims but as strong, independent women who would never let a man beat them . . . until they do.

"I have to ask you a series of questions," I say. "If your answer to any one of them is yes, then you should think about whether your relationship with your partner is healthy."

Tempe laughs bitterly. "I think we both know the answer to that."

"Are you frightened of him?"

She doesn't answer.

"Do you fear injury or violence?"

Again nothing, but I don't expect or need a response.

"Is this the first time that he's hit you?" I ask.

"You asked me that already. Twice."

I rattle off more questions. "Is the abuse happening more often? Is it more extreme? Does he try to control everything you do? Do you feel isolated from friends and family? Does he constantly text or call or harass you? Is he excessively jealous? Has he ever attempted to strangle or choke you? Has he ever threatened to kill you?"

Tempe lets each query wash over her without comment, but I know that she's listening.

A nurse calls her name. She's taken to an examination room, where fresh white paper has been rolled across the bed. A young Asian doctor appears, wearing green scrubs and showing the tiredness of a long shift. She asks Tempe questions about her age and height and weight and medical history, before telling her to get undressed behind the screen. "This is a rape kit. I need to take a few swabs."

"But I wasn't raped," says Tempe.

The doctor looks at me. "I thought . . ."

"No," I answer, glancing at Tempe to make doubly sure. "I was worried about her cheekbone."

The doctor asks Tempe to sit up straight and shines a penlight into her right eye. Her left has closed completely.

"Any blurred vision?"

Tempe shakes her head. The doctor moves the torch from side to side, then up and down.

"Any headaches?"

"One big one."

She touches Tempe's swollen cheek and runs her fingers over her eyebrows and the bridge of her nose.

"I don't think you've fractured a cheekbone, and your eye socket is intact, but that's going to be one ugly bruise."

"How long before the swelling goes down?" asks Tempe.

"If you keep it iced—twenty-four hours."

Tempe looks aghast. "But I have meetings. If I don't work . . ."

"Maybe you could hide it with makeup," I suggest.

"Or put a bag over my head," she replies sarcastically.

The doctor peels off her latex gloves. "I'll write a script for painkillers. Keep up the icing until the swelling goes down."

I wait for Tempe to complete the necessary paperwork before escorting her through the waiting area.

"I'm obliged to give you this," I say, handing her a tear-out form with four pages of information. "If you sign here, I can give your details to a support agency."

"I'm not signing anything," says Tempe. "I won't be making a statement and I don't need a chaperone."

"I understand, but this report will be given to the local Safeguarding Unit. Someone will be back in touch with you."

"I don't want to be contacted. I don't give my permission."

We are outside the hospital. A group of orderlies is smoking and vaping near the doors, standing in a patch of sunshine that illuminates their exhalations. Tempe lowers her head, not wanting anyone to see her face.

"This is a number for the National Domestic Abuse Helpline," I say. "Like I said, I'm not judging you, but I don't think you should go back to the apartment. Not today. Give him some time to cool off."

Tempe bites the undamaged side of her bottom lip and contemplates an answer.

"I'll go to the shelter," she whispers. "For one night."

The large freestanding house is in the back streets of Brixton and has no outward signs or identifiers apart from the extra security of barred windows and a CCTV camera covering the entrance. As we approach, I notice a child standing at an upstairs window. A girl. I wave. She doesn't wave back.

The intercom sends a jingle echoing through distant rooms.

"Can I help you?" asks a woman's voice.

I hold up my warrant card to the camera and give my name and rank. "Do you have room for one more?"

"Won't be a tick," says the voice.

We wait another minute until the twin deadlocks turn and the door swings open on creaky hinges. A large woman smiles and ushers us quickly inside, checking the street before locking the door again.

"Call me Beth," she says in a no-nonsense voice. "First names only in here. Cassie is upstairs with another new arrival—a mum and two kiddies. The little boy is a doll."

We climb. She talks. Tempe's room has a single bed, a wardrobe, and a sink in the corner. The bedspread looks like something from a motorway Travelodge, but everything is clean, with cheerful touches like the colorful prints on the walls and a small vase of flowers on the windowsill.

"You'll be sharing the other facilities," says Beth. "We have a laundry room downstairs and a secure garden. The kitchen is a busy area, but you're allowed to prepare your own meals. We have a cleaning roster for the communal areas." She ties back the curtains. "Do you have any other clothes?"

"No."

"We have a pool clothing system. Nothing fancy, but you'll find something that fits you."

She puts a set of sheets on the mattress, along with a pillowcase.

"Spare blankets are on the top shelf." She points to the wardrobe. "Once you're settled, come downstairs and we'll fill out the admission forms."

"I won't be staying long," says Tempe, glancing at me.

"Makes no difference. It's the protocol. You'll have to fill in a Housing Benefit form and sign your license agreement. I'll also give you a copy of the house rules."

"There are rules?"

"No visitors, no alcohol, no drugs, no bullying, no threatening staff. I'll be your support worker. We can have a session once you're signed in."

"I told you, I'm not staying," says Tempe, even more adamant.

"Give it a chance," I say.

Beth looks at her face and clucks sympathetically. "I'll get you some ice." She has one hand on the door handle. "Is he looking for you?"

Tempe doesn't answer.

"Don't tell anyone where you are. This is a secure address. We have mothers and children who finally feel safe. We want to keep it that way."

My phone pings. Nish has sent me a text: *You should get back here ASAP.*

"It's all right, you can leave," says Tempe.

Halfway down the stairs, my shoulder radio squawks. "Mike Bravo 471, this is control, are you receiving?"

"This is Mike Bravo 471, go ahead, over."

"Where are you?"

"I'm leaving the shelter in Brixton."

"Report to the custody suite."

"Received, out."

Tempe and Beth are on the landing.

"I'll call you," I say, but Tempe doesn't reply.

Outside, a bank of dark clouds has cloaked the sun and the temperature has fallen five degrees in the space of a few minutes. Unlocking the patrol car, I slide behind the wheel and feel a hollow emptiness in my stomach. All is not well.

2

The walk through the station is a strange one. I sense that people are watching me, peering over computer screens and pretending to read reports, but nobody wants to make eye contact. I have tried to call Nish, but he's not answering.

Two shaven-headed men wearing army surplus clothes are being processed in the custody suite. They've been arrested for fighting and are still hurling abuse at each other. I wait outside Sergeant Connelly's office, sitting opposite a narrow window that gives back a watery reflection. I touch my hair and nurse my hat on my lap.

There are male voices drifting from inside the office, but I can't hear what they're saying. When the door opens abruptly, I jump to attention, fumbling my phone before putting it away. Connelly motions me inside. Nothing on his face.

Another officer is waiting, a stranger, who introduces himself as Chief Superintendent Drysdale, a short, square man with a pale face and deep-set eyes. His hair is receding, and port-colored capillaries are shading his nose. I glimpse a small tattoo on the inside of his left wrist before he tugs down the sleeve of his jacket. Three letters. MDM.

"Sit down, Constable McCarthy," says Connelly.

The men remain standing.

"Explain to me what happened."

"Regarding what, sir?"

"You arrested a serving police officer."

"He assaulted me."

"That's not what he told us."

"If you look at the bodycam footage."

Drysdale interrupts. "Darren Goodall distinguished himself with the Specialist Firearms Command. Eighteen months ago he won a George Medal for chasing and tackling a knifeman who had killed three people. He was stabbed twice and almost bled to death. The man is a Goddamn hero."

The memory crashes into me. The headlines. The TV coverage. It was at Camden Market, a busy Saturday morning. A mentally disturbed man went berserk with a butcher's knife, attacking shoppers and stall-holders.

"You arrested a police officer without due cause," says Drysdale.

"He assaulted a woman. Her dress was covered in blood and her left eye had closed."

"Did she call the police?"

"No, sir."

"Has she provided a statement?"

"A neighbor complained—"

"*Has* she provided a statement?"

"No, sir."

Drysdale takes a seat and leans back, his plump hands linked across his generous stomach.

"Detective Goodall says her injuries were sustained before she arrived at the address."

"That's not what she told me."

"You entered his apartment without a warrant or his permission."

"I was concerned for her welfare. PC Kohli will back—"

"We've talked to Constable Kohli. He said it was *your* decision to arrest DS Goodall."

"We both—"

"DS Goodall clearly identified himself and offered an explanation, but you refused to listen."

"That's not what happened. If you talk to Nish—"

"Are you calling Detective Goodall a liar?"

"He attacked me, sir. He was abusive and aggressive and he tried to prevent me speaking to the victim."

"His informant."

"What?"

"Tempe Brown is a registered police informant. She is also a prostitute who was beaten up by her pimp and came to Goodall seeking help."

I feel like someone has suddenly tilted the floor and I risk sliding sideways. "Tempe Brown lives at that address. I saw her clothes in the wardrobe."

The comment lights a fire under Drysdale. Flecks of foamy spit are clinging to the corners of his mouth.

"You're not listening. You went off half-cocked and embarrassed yourself. You took the word of a prostitute over a police officer. DS Goodall has filed a complaint against you. He has accused you of using unlawful and unnecessary force."

"That's ridiculous."

"Did you use martial arts to effect his arrest?"

I don't answer, but Drysdale fills the silence. "Under the Met guidelines you are required to use only those control and restraint techniques you were taught in your training and no greater level of force than necessary."

"I didn't use excessive force," I say, less sure of myself.

"DS Goodall wants you charged with misconduct."

"This is bullshit," I mutter under my breath.

"What did you say?"

Connelly is trying to calm the situation, raising his hands as though quieting a skittish horse.

"Let's all take a deep breath and settle down. I'm sure this can be sorted out without any further ructions."

Such an old-fashioned word, "ructions," but he's that sort of man. I bet he wears flannelette pajamas to bed and calls his wife "queenie" or "dearest."

"Have you filled out your domestic violence arrest form?" he asks.

"Not yet, sir. I still have to do the intelligence checks."

"I will handle that. What about your body camera?"

I point to my chest.

He holds out his hand. "Give it to me."

I hesitate. "The footage hasn't been downloaded."

"The Safeguarding Unit will take it from here."

Reluctantly I unclip the camera and hand it over. I glance at Drysdale, wondering where he might be from—what department or section.

"Go home, Constable McCarthy," says Connelly.

"But the paperwork . . ."

"Your shift has ended."

"Am I suspended?"

"You will stay at home until this is sorted out."

I am so stunned by my rapid fall from grace that I don't notice Drysdale following me out of the office and along the corridor. He touches
my shoulder. I react instinctively, dropping into a defensive crouch.

"You're quick," he says, smiling wryly. His lower teeth are over-
crowded and yellowing. "I know you think it's unfair, Constable, but we
have to protect our own at times like these."

"What times are those, sir?"

He doesn't respond.

"Will Goodall be investigated?"

"That's not your concern."

"That's a no, then."

His smug, self-satisfied smile grows fixed. "Let this go, McCarthy. No
good can come of it."

I want to come back at him with one of those killer one-liners that
always occur to me when it's too late, but my mouth is my worst enemy.
Karate has helped me to control my temper, but my tongue still needs a
hand brake or a dead man's switch.

I turn away and jog up the stairs to the locker room, where I get
changed into my civvies, locking away my stab vest and duty belt and
putting my hat on the top shelf. I can taste my anger in the back of my
throat and wish I could spit it out and gargle mouthwash.

I want to give Darren Goodall the benefit of the doubt because he
almost died saving people at Camden Market—and maybe that trauma
left him with PTSD or acute stress or some other behavioral problem—
but I can picture Tempe at the shelter, making up a single bed, shower-
ing with a threadbare towel, nursing her bruises. He called her a sex
worker and one of his informants. Even if it's true, it doesn't give him the
right to beat her up. My father always told me that any man who raises
his hand to a woman is a coward with the devil living in his heart.

I close the combination lock and shrug on my jacket, checking that
I have my keys and wallet. Outside, I bury my hands in my pockets and
make my way home, knowing that the world isn't any safer or cleaner or
fairer because of what I've done. Good never prevails. It simply treads
water and waits for the bad to show up again.

3

Henry is in the kitchen constructing a sandwich that looks like a work of art. Every jar in the fridge is on the counter, as well as two chopping boards, assorted knives, salad vegetables, and sliced meats.

"What are you doing home?" he asks, smearing Dijon mustard on a slice of sourdough.

"I could ask you the same thing."

"Archie has a toothache. I'm taking him to the dentist."

"Where's Roxanne?"

"She has a meeting."

"With her hairdresser or her therapist?"

Henry makes a meowing noise.

I wrap my arms around his waist and press my face into his back. "You love me being jealous of your ex-wife. It makes you feel wanted," I say.

He points to the sandwich. "Want me to make you one?"

"I could have half of yours."

He pouts, aggrieved, but slices the sandwich diagonally and plates up. We sit side by side at the kitchen bench, needing both hands to eat.

"What time are you picking Archie up from school?" I ask.

"Four thirty. Roxanne suggested he spend tonight with us."

"The Wicked Witch strikes again."

"What do you mean?"

"We have Margot and Phoebe's housewarming."

"Oh shit! I totally forgot."

"Roxanne didn't. She'll be planning her evening as I speak."

"We'll get a babysitter."

"At four hours' notice? Good luck with that."

I don't mind that Henry has been married before—or that Archie, aged six, comes with the package. He's a sweet little boy who sleeps over three nights a week and crawls into bed with us each morning, clutching his battered teddy bear. He doesn't call me "Mummy," which is good, but he does introduce me to strangers in the supermarket as "Daddy's girlfriend," announcing it in a booming voice.

I didn't meet Henry until after he and Roxanne had separated. And we didn't have proper sex until his divorce came through, although we did everything else. We were like teenagers steaming up car windows and getting hot and heavy in the back row of the cinema. The no-sex rule was important because I didn't want to be accused of being a home-wrecker or stealing someone else's husband. I know women like that, including my friend Georgia, who treats sex like a sport and happily sleeps with married men. I once accused her of being an anti-feminist, but Georgia replied that sisterhood and sex weren't mutually exclusive.

"It's not my fault if some women frump up after they get married," she said.

"Frump up?"

"You know what I mean."

I have tried to befriend Roxanne, and I would never bad-mouth her in front of Archie, but she is the sort of ex-wife that comedians make jokes about—"the good housekeeper who gets to keep the house" or "the hostage taker who stays in touch after collecting the ransom."

My main complaint is how she uses Archie as a weapon of mass disruption. Whenever I arrange a weekend away or have concert tickets or (case in point) a housewarming, Archie will be dumped on our doorstep with his overnight bag and strict instructions about what he's allowed to eat, wear, watch, and do.

Henry tilts his head to one side. "So why are you home?"

"I think I've been suspended."

"Is there some doubt?"

I make a humming sound. "You want a juice?"

"I'd prefer an answer."

"I'm prevaricating."

"I can tell."

Eventually I tell him the story. Henry asks all the right questions and makes concerned noises, which is why I love him.

"You're saying this guy beat up a woman and attacked you, but nothing will happen to him."

"Tempe didn't give us a statement. She was too frightened."

"Who is he—Harvey Weinstein?"

"Not quite."

I take my laptop from its case and type in a Google search for Goodall's name. The screen refreshes. There are dozens of stories about the knife attack at Camden Market. A paranoid schizophrenic called David Thorndyke stabbed seven people, three of whom died, before Goodall intervened.

I find the bravery citation:

Sergeant Goodall was off duty, shopping with his family, when he responded to screams for help. Despite having no personal protective equipment, he tackled the knifeman and sustained life-threatening injuries as he wrestled with the attacker and held him until help arrived.

There are more stories and profiles, including a YouTube clip of Goodall on breakfast TV, sitting on a sofa looking stiff and uncomfortable.

"Do the events of that day feel real to you now?" he is asked by Piers Morgan.

"No, it feels more like a dream."

"What do you mean?"

"Sometimes I wonder if I really did those things. And what could have happened. My wife might be a widow. My children might not have a father."

"You're lucky to be alive," says Morgan.

"I guess so."

Pushed to unbutton his shirt, he shows the scars on his stomach and chest. I recognize the gladiator tattoo and remember the smell of his sweat.

I call up more stories. One has a photograph taken outside Buckingham Palace. Goodall, dressed in a dark suit with his hair gelled into place, has his arm around his wife, a pretty brunette about my age, who is wearing a hat for the occasion and balancing a baby girl on her hip. An older boy, school age, is holding her other hand.

I don't know what I should feel. Admiration. Sorry for his wife. Angry. Goodall is doubtless a hero. He saved lives that day, and almost lost his own. It's also clear that he's become an important asset for the London

Metropolitan Police, to be wheeled out on TV talk shows and featured on recruitment posters.

Henry picks up crumbs with his wet forefinger.

"Where is his girlfriend now?"

"At a women's refuge."

"How long are you off work?"

"A few days, maybe."

"It's a shame I can't get time off. We could go away."

Henry is a firefighter stationed at Brixton, a thirteen-year veteran, who is now a crew manager. He works rolling shifts—two days, then two nights, before a three-day break.

He's tidying up the kitchen, putting jars away and wiping down the benches.

"You're almost fully house-trained," I say.

"Where do I fall short?"

"Occasionally you leave the toilet seat up and the top off the tooth-paste and you put empty milk cartons back in the fridge."

"Capital offenses."

"And you yell at the TV when you're watching football when the referee can't possibly hear you."

"I'm passionate."

"Yes, you are."

I put my arms around him. We kiss. I feel him grow hard.

"What time do you have to pick up Archie?"

He looks over my shoulder at the oven clock. "Twenty minutes."

"We can do it?"

"Are you giving me permission to hurry?"

"Just this once. Quick march."

4

Henry is the fifth most beautiful man I have ever met. I don't count film stars and boy band members on my list because I don't know any of them and some—like Ryan Gosling—are so handsome they could be aliens. My desert-island top five are normal people who I've bumped into at parties or at school or at university.

In chronological order they are:

Rodney Grant
Patrick Hamer
Paul Crilly
David Sainsbury
Henry Chapman

I've only ever slept with one of them. The others were luxury cars in a showroom—high-end models that I wasn't allowed to test-drive in case I lost control on a bend and damaged their bodywork.

Rodney Grant was the first. He fancied me for a week when he heard that I used my tongue while playing spin the bottle at Bridget Maher's twelfth birthday party. I can't remember what boy I kissed, or whether I used my tongue or not, but that was the sort of rumor that spread like wildfire at our primary school.

Later, playing hide-and-seek at a birthday party, Rodney followed me into a cupboard beneath the stairs, where it was pitch-black. He finished up kissing his mate Chris, thinking he was me. This led to much spitting and wiping of mouths, but strangely, many years later, Rodney turned out to be gay. I don't think I played a role in his coming out, but who knows.

Patrick Hamer worked at the local hardware store, part-time on weekends and during school holidays. I used to make excuses to buy lots of stuff that I didn't need like masking tape, gloves, and a shovel. He probably thought I was disposing of a body.

Paul Crilly was my English Classics professor at university. He was only thirty-five but dressed like a young fogy, in tweed jackets and corduroy pants, and he smelled of books and Old Spice aftershave. God, he was gorgeous. I used to leave love poems in his pigeonhole, quoting Keats and Elizabeth Barrett Browning and Byron, but Professor Crilly showed zero interest.

The fourth most beautiful man was David Sainsbury, my long-haired, motorbike-riding rebel without a cause, who had wine-stained teeth and smoldering eyes and a thing for college-age girls—all of them except me. He slept with at least seven girls I knew at university, including the Oakdale twins. There were also whispers about boyfriends, which didn't surprise me because David had that sort of androgynous beauty that appealed to men and women.

Henry rounds out my top five. Last but not least. Before he came along, I had dated a dozen different guys, all of whom had something nice about them—their eyes or their laugh or their smell. Maybe I was setting the bar too low, but if they showered regularly, picked me up on time, and ate with their mouths closed, they tended to get a second date. Make me laugh and they'd sometimes get lucky. That makes me sound überconfident, with clearly defined rules, but nothing could be further from the truth.

My mother thinks Henry rescued me from a lonely spinsterhood, or from becoming a weird cat lady, even though I'm allergic to cats and I was quite happy being single and financially independent. I was twenty-five when we met, hardly old, but I am rather pleased that he came along, with his dark curly hair, his piercing blue eyes, and the cleft in his chin that he has trouble shaving. He has a world-class bum and I keep telling him he could be a butt double in the movies and do those scenes where Ryan Gosling or Chis Hemsworth have to step out of the shower.

"I don't want people looking at my bum," he replies.

"What about me?"

"Except for you."

I met Henry two years ago on one of those humid, heat-heavy summer evenings where London is transformed into an incubator for madness, racial tension, and sexual mores. People were spilling out of pubs onto sidewalks and dining at open-air cafés or taking in a stroll.

The air-conditioning had broken at the academy where I teach karate, and I had taken my junior class to a nearby park. Barefoot on the grass, my students looked cute in their uniforms, like miniature ninjas. I had them jumping over and sliding under things and dodging trees. I teach Goju-Ryu, which is a traditional Okinawan style of karate that means "hard-soft" and reflects the closed and open hand techniques. It's the same style that Ralph Macchio learned in the *Karate Kid* movies and teaches in the Netflix spin-off *Cobra Kai*.

I was packing equipment away when I noticed Henry watching me from beneath one of the trees. He was dressed in black jeans and a T-shirt and had a small boy with him who had an identical haircut.

"Looks like you need a hand," he said as I wrestled with the mats. "We'll help, won't we, Archie?"

I led them back to the studio, where we stacked the mats against the wall and put away the rest of the gear. Henry wiped his hands on the back of his jeans and introduced himself. I blew a strand of hair from my forehead and tried not to fall into his eyes.

"You made that look like fun," he said. "How do we sign up?"

"I can give you a form and a timetable. How old is Archie?"

"Four."

"He could start in our junior program. We have classes on Tuesdays and Thursdays."

"What about private lessons?"

"For Archie?"

"Both of us . . . together, I mean."

"That wouldn't work. You're too big. He's too small."

"I don't want to fight him."

"Sparring is an important part of karate training."

"But it's mainly defensive, right?"

He had a nice voice, low and sexy, with a London accent that swallowed the occasional consonant.

"I was hoping we could do it together—a father-and-son thing. We only get to see each other on certain days."

Ah, a clue! He was either divorced or separated, or maybe it was a drunken one-night stand and a broken condom. He didn't run away, which was a good sign.

"I could ask around and see if one of the other teachers are willing."

"What about you?"

"There are better teachers than me."

"Yes, but I know you. We have a connection."

Please don't blush. Please don't blush.

I found myself agreeing and wondered later if my ovaries had made the decision for me. They sometimes jiggle when I'm around a man I fancy. Some people get butterflies in their tummies. I have jiggling ovaries.

That's how it began. The private lessons, the first date, the second date, the first sleepover, the day that Henry said, "I love you." Now we're engaged, but no date has been set. September would be nice. I don't believe in long engagements. Too much can go wrong. I'm the sort of person who can talk herself out of things if I spend too long thinking about them. It's like when I was buying a new car. I spent months doing the research, looking at reviews and pollution ratings, talking to salespeople, taking test-drives, until eventually I had so much information that I couldn't make up my mind. Henry called it "decision paralysis."

Thankfully I didn't overanalyze his marriage proposal. It was the day after I graduated from Hendon Police College. I had been away for thirteen weeks, living in a dorm, coming home on weekends. During that time, Henry had been working on the garden, planting flowers and shrubs. On the morning after my passing-out parade—and the party—I woke up in his arms and he asked me to open the curtains.

"What do you think of the garden?"

Standing in the upstairs window, I looked down and saw a flower bed with a message spelled out in purple pansies on a deep carpet of green. It said: "Will You Marry Me?" The question mark hadn't quite worked and it looked like he wanted to marry someone called "Meg" but I got the message.

"Are you sure?" I asked.

"Of course."

"I'm very normal."

"I've lived with neurotic."

"And I'm bossy."

"In a good way."

We went back to bed and began filling the jar—the one where you add a marble every time you make love before you marry and subtract a marble when you make love afterward. I don't know how long it will take to empty ours because we are going to marry with a rather big jar.

5

Early morning, trapped in a dream, I wake suddenly and seem to levitate off the bed, my heart pounding and mouth open in a soundless scream. Henry holds me, whispering, "You're safe. We're home," but I'm fighting at his arms, desperate to escape. It's like I'm piloting a plane that is plunging towards the ground, while a mechanical voice is bleating monotonously, "Whoop! Whoop! Pull up! Pull up!"

Slowly, my chest stops heaving and my breathing returns to normal.

Henry is still holding me, stroking my hair. "Was it the same one?"

"No."

I'm lying. This is the third night in a row that the nightmare has woken me. Normally, I'm wrenched awake by bombed buses and flying body parts, but this dream is different. I'm in a basement room where a young woman is hanging from the ceiling. A thin nylon washing line is looped over a lagged water pipe and wrapped around her neck. A set of aluminum steps has toppled onto the floor beneath her bare feet. In the dream, I notice her painted pink toenails and the bruises on her ankles below her skinny-leg jeans, which are soaked with urine. I try not to look any higher but can't stop myself.

Tempe Brown's head is tilted slightly as the rope presses against her jaw. The pink tip of her tongue peeks from between her blue lips and her eyes are open, looking puzzled or disappointed.

Henry has fallen back to sleep. Awake now, I slip out of bed and change into my gym gear. Minutes later, I'm sitting on the front step, lacing my trainers, feeling the cold concrete under my buttocks.

"You're up early," says Mrs. Ainsley, who has taken Blaine for a walk. Dog and owner are wearing matching neck scarves, a Liberty print, and she's carrying a plastic bag of dog shit like it's her favorite handbag.

I nod and smile, avoiding a conversation because of her deafness. Blaine sniffs at my shoes and I'm terrified he might cock his leg.

"He made a lot of noise last night," I say.

"Pardon?" she shouts.

"He was barking."

"Yes, the parking is terrible. No point having a car in London."

"I mean Blaine."

"Shame. You have a lovely day too," she says as she unlocks her front door.

At least I tried.

It is one of those smoked-glass spring days, all sky and clouds and patches of heavy sunlight. I begin jogging towards Clapham Common, waving at several local residents who I recognize, including the green-grocer, who has been up since four, and the local newsagent, who is unbundling the day's papers.

At the park, I run through my drills, working on my speed, strength, and flexibility. Soon I'm fighting invisible shadows beneath the trees, crouching and kicking and punching at the air. My first instructor told me that I would never be a great martial artist if I only trained alone, but the academy is closed at this hour and my usual sparring partners have jobs to go to or beds to keep warm.

After forty minutes of drills, I pause to drink from a water fountain and check my phone. There are more messages from my stepmother about the party. Why is she so eager that I attend this one? Other birthdays and anniversaries have come and gone. Perhaps my father has learned about my engagement. Edward McCarthy wants to walk his only daughter down the aisle and give her the sort of wedding that *he* has always dreamed of; something suitably extravagant, with vintage cars, ice sculptures, and a celebrity chef doing the catering. That's what his birthday will be like, a celebration of his newfound respectability.

Whenever a newspaper or magazine does a profile on my father, he is portrayed as an East End barrow boy made good. The seller of knock-off perfumes and toiletries who rose from Petticoat Lane to Mayfair, creating a property portfolio worth a hundred million pounds. Rags to riches. From the gutter to the stars. All down to hard graft, sixteen-hour days, and the "luck of the Irish," he tells them. But that's not the whole story. It's not even good fiction.

The perfumes and luxury goods weren't cheap knockoffs from Taiwan or South Korea, and they hadn't "fallen off the back of a truck." They were the genuine articles, stolen from lorries that were hijacked at truck stop cafés or motorway service centers. During the eighties and nineties, the McCarthy Brothers were the most notorious criminal gang in southeast England.

From hijacking trucks, they branched out, controlling the movement of goods through ports like Harwich and Dover, collecting fees to load and unload every container. The racket was finally broken in the noughties and three of my uncles went to prison, but not my father, the oldest, the Teflon man. While the others were languishing behind bars, Eddie McCarthy reinvented himself and made himself a fortune. London had won the bid to host the Olympics and the East End was being carved up for venues and an athletes' village. Parlaying his connections and reputation, he bought into companies that serviced these building sites, providing concrete, scaffolding, formwork, construction workers, and security guards.

Every week he'd visit Daragh, Clifton, and Finbar in Wormwood Scrubs. Sometimes I'd go with him, listening to these big, hard men talking in rhyming slang and strange codes. I didn't regard them as being bad men. They were my uncles. They were husbands and fathers. They were family.

At some point I have started running again, skirting Clapham Common and following Abbeville Road towards Brixton. The dew-covered pavement is drying under my feet and salty tidal air fills my lungs. I know my destination, but I'm not sure what I'll say when I arrive.

A different woman answers the intercom at the house and remotely unlocks the front door. An older child is pushing a sibling on a tricycle in the entrance hall, knocking paint off the walls.

"I'm looking for Tempe Brown," I say as the woman appears from an office.

"She's gone."

"When?"

"Yesterday."

"Did something happen?"

"A policeman showed up and took her away."

"Did he give you a name?"

"No. Tempe refused to leave at first, but he convinced her to go."

"What did this officer look like?"

"Fortyish. Dark hair. Handsome, I guess." The woman blinks nervously. "Why?"

"He's the one who beat her up."

Her mouth opens and closes several times before she finds the words, but I'm already moving, down the steps and along the pavement. I call Tempe's mobile number. It goes to her voicemail. The image in my dream flashes into my mind and I see Tempe hanging from the water pipe, her eyes accusing me. Picking up speed, I navigate my way towards Borough Market. I know this area. After university, I shared a house not far from the site of the old Marshalsea prison, made famous by Charles Dickens, whose father was an inmate. If you're a reader or a nostalgic, London sweats history from its pores; every road, sewer, building, grave, and open space tells a story.

I'm out of breath when I arrive at the building and press the intercom. Nobody answers. I try Mrs. Gregg, the neighbor. I'm about to buzz again when she answers, sounding annoyed by the interruption.

"It's Constable McCarthy. We met a few days ago."

"You're not in uniform," she says suspiciously.

I wave at the camera. "My day off. Can you let me in please, ma'am?"

The door unlocks and I make my way upstairs. Mrs. Gregg meets me before I reach Tempe's door.

"Have you seen her?"

"She came back yesterday, but I think she's gone again."

"You saw her leave?"

"No, but I found her keys under my door when I woke up this morning."

"What about the man she was with?"

"I didn't see him until an hour ago. I heard him yelling into his phone and calling a plumber."

"A plumber?"

"Yeah."

"You talked to him?"

"Are you crazy! I wouldn't open my door."

"Do you still have the keys?"

Mrs. Gregg disappears inside her apartment and returns a few minutes later holding the keys and an envelope.

"I found this in my mailbox yesterday. It's addressed to someone called Margaret Brown. Could that be her?"

"Yes."

I study the envelope, which is postmarked from Northern Ireland but has no information about the sender. It seems to have bounced between several addresses, chasing Tempe from place to place.

"Will you make sure she gets it?" says Mrs. Gregg.

"I'll do my best," I say, glancing at the keys. One has a fob that opens the main doors downstairs.

I move along the corridor and slide the key into the lock, nudging the door open.

"Hello? Is anyone home?"

I remember the layout of the flat. The lounge room is directly ahead of me, linked to an open-plan kitchen and dining area. The two bedrooms are on the left with a bathroom in between.

Taking out my mobile, I call Tempe's number again. It begins ringing. My heart skips. The sound is coming from the nearest bedroom. I peer around the frame of the door. The queen-sized bed is covered in clothes and rumpled bedding. The floor-to-ceiling wardrobes are open and have been ransacked. Clothes are scattered on the floor, crumpled and trodden underfoot.

Again, I call Tempe's number. The screen lights up in the darkest corner of the room. Pushing aside shoes, I uncover the handset. There are twelve missed calls. Three are from me. The battery is almost dead.

At that same moment, I notice a spray pattern of dark droplets on the pale carpet. Blood. Dry to the touch. There are deeper stains closer to the bathroom. As I step into the doorway, I see a bloody handprint on the edge of the bathtub. Shuffling sideways, I steel myself for what might be coming. A hinged glass partition acts as a shower screen. I peer around the edge of the glass, expecting the worst.

The tub is empty. I breathe. Retreat. Call 999.

"What service do you require?"

"The police."

Several dull clicks follow, before I hear a new voice. *"Police service. What is the nature of the emergency?"*

"This is PC Philomena McCarthy of Southwark Police. I'm at an apartment at Borough Market. There are bloodstains in the bathroom. The female occupant is missing."

They want an address and have follow-up questions. *Are there weapons involved? Is the address hard to find?*

I should wait outside until the police arrive, but I return to the bedroom, avoiding touching any surface. At first glance it looks like a burglary or a frantic search, but as I look more closely, I notice damage rather than absence. The sleeves of business shirts have been cut off and a blue blazer slashed to the lining.

I move to the living area, where the sofa cushions have been disemboweled and foam stuffing covers the floor. Broken plastic crunches under my running shoes. Crouching to get a better look, I find the remnants of a small HD webcam. I notice a power cable tucked behind a row of books, next to a potted orchid, on a floating shelf next to the TV. The camera is one of those small, high-quality models that have an internal memory card, but the slot is empty.

The kitchen has a half-eaten bran muffin in the pedal bin and a broken coffeepot in the sink. A cutlery drawer has been upended and the contents are strewn across the tiled floor. I can't work out if I'm looking at an act of vandalism, a robbery, an abduction, a murder scene.

Retreating outside, I wait for the police to arrive. Sweat has dampened my clothes and I'm shivering in the hallway when two uniforms emerge from the lift. I recognize both of them. I went through training with Stefan Albinksi at Hendon. Tall and thin, he was nicknamed "Horse" on account of his long face, although he says it's for a different reason. His partner is Kevin Boyd, who played league football for Oxford United and is "almost famous," according to Nish, who follows football.

"What are you doing here?" asks Horse.

"I was following up on a callout."

"Off duty?"

I explain how I took Tempe to a hospital three days ago and dropped her off at the women's refuge. Boyd goes into the apartment.

"You think she came back?" asks Horse.

"A neighbor saw her."

"What about the boyfriend—where is he?"

"He lives elsewhere. Married. Kids." I hesitate. "He's a copper. A detective sergeant."

"Who?"

"Darren Goodall."

"You mean *the* Darren Goodall?"

I nod.

Horse laughs nervously. Boyd emerges from the flat. "There isn't enough blood to think anyone was seriously injured."

"What about the handprint?" I ask.

"Could have been a nosebleed."

"You should check the local hospitals."

Boyd doesn't like being told what to do. "Did you bother looking at the rest of the place?"

"I saw the cut-up clothing."

"Someone has poured a bag of flour down the sink, blocking the pipes."

"Sounds like an act of revenge," says Horse. "A woman scorned."

"She wouldn't leave her phone behind," I say defensively.

The constables exchange a glance. Neither wants to get involved in this, but I'm forcing their hand. The questions come quickly. Is Tempe a drug addict? Could she have run away? Was she depressed or suicidal?

"I barely knew the woman," I say.

"Yet here you are," says Boyd.

Another look passes between them. They want me out of here and I have no authority to stay. This is their callout.

"We'll take it from here," says Horse, nodding towards the lift.

I want to argue, but there's no point. Downstairs, I push through the heavy glass doors, out into the morning. Rain has begun falling. A sudden cloudburst. Big drops dance on the road. Shit! My phone vibrates. There are two missed calls from my stepmother. Two voicemail messages.

Delete.

Delete.

6

Ten days pass after my suspension and I am summoned back to work. The email makes no mention of the misconduct charges, but I'm sure they've been filed away, a permanent stain on my record. I return on a miserable day in late May, when wind chases litter along the gutters, pinning it against fences and lampposts and bare legs. Summer postponed.

As I'm picking up a coffee from across the road, a man holds the door open for me.

"Philomena McCarthy?"

I smile, thinking we must have met, but I don't recognize his unshaven face or his foppish brown hair or the slight kink in his nose.

"I'm Dylan Holstein. I write for the *Guardian*. I wanted to ask you about Darren Goodall."

I push past him, ignoring his approach. He matches stride with me.

"A little birdie told me that you two had an altercation."

"Altercation" is such an old-fashioned, almost polite word. A euphemism for a scuffle where harsh words are exchanged but nobody gets hurt. Couples quarrel. Siblings squabble. Lovers have spats. Altercations are for neighbors, who knock on doors at three in the morning, fed up with AC/DC being played at full volume through the walls.

I dodge a street sweeper's barrow, trying to stay ahead of Holstein, who jogs to catch up with me. Foam spills from the spout of my travel mug.

"Have you ever heard of the name Imogen Croker?" he asks. "She and Goodall were engaged to be married."

"No comment."

"She fell from a cliff in East Sussex eight years ago. The coroner said it was an accident, but her family doesn't agree."

Holstein is walking backwards in front of me. He almost collides with a woman pushing a pram. He apologizes and catches up with me again.

"Goodall refused to give evidence at the inquest. He hired a barrister to represent him."

"You're blocking a public thoroughfare."

"Imogen Croker's family thinks she was murdered."

"Please get out of my way."

"Goodall pocketed a payment from her life insurance policy. He also extorted money from a friend of mine. He's a bent copper."

I'm almost at Southwark Police Station. He won't be able to follow me inside.

"You're Edward McCarthy's daughter," says Holstein.

That statement is like iced water being poured down my back. I miss a step and stumble, catching myself, spilling more coffee.

"I once made the mistake of writing about your father. Do you know what he did? He dumped fourteen tons of building waste outside my house in the middle of the night. Blocked the road. My neighbors were furious, but I got off lightly. It could have been so much worse."

I can feel myself slowing down.

"A gangster's daughter working for the Met. That's a good story. Money laundering. Extortion. Racketeering. Theft. That's some family history. Do your colleagues know who you are?"

I turn to confront him. "How did you find me?"

"I'm good at my job."

"I am not my father's daughter."

"Prove it."

I pause inside the glass doors and uncurl my right fist, which has been clenched so tightly that my fingernails have left marks on my skin. My heart is racing and I feel the heat color my cheeks. I am annoyed at being ambushed in the street, but most of my anger is directed at my father. After ten years, I am not free of his shadow. I hate hearing his name. I hate passing through areas of London that remind me of him. I hate visiting markets and hearing barrow boys yelling for trade. I hate the woman he eventually married. I hate his new house, even though I've never been there. I know it's irrational, but I blame him for things he has no control over—when shoes pinch my feet, when traffic lights take too long to change, when days are too hot or too cold. Stupid, I know, but he has that effect on me.

Climbing the stairs, I pass Judy Ellis, another constable.

"All right?" I ask, trying to appear normal.

"Why wouldn't it be?" she replies curtly. Maybe she's had a tough shift.

The locker room is empty. I set down my bag and begin getting changed into my uniform, but I catch a whiff of something coming from my blouse. No, it's the locker. I search the shelves, pushing equipment aside. My hat is on the top shelf, resting upside down. I didn't leave it that way.

Reaching higher, I take it from the top shelf and bring it down to eye level. The smell makes me gag. Inside is a dead, half-gutted rat, crawling with maggots. I glance quickly towards the door, wondering if anyone has come to watch or record the moment. I'm alone.

Holding the hat at arm's length, I carry it into the shower room and dump the lot into the bin, sealing the plastic liner with a knot. I scrub my hands and contemplate the cost of a new hat.

Back at my locker, I search the shelves for more ugly surprises, tipping up shoes and unfolding my towel. I could complain, but that would only make things worse. This is either a one-off statement or a declaration of war, and if I return fire, things will escalate. I close my locker and head downstairs to the briefing room, where I sit apart from the other officers as Connelly issues orders and sets tasks for the afternoon shift. I study the backs of heads, wondering who put the rat in my locker. These are my colleagues. My friends. We are supposed to work together and to watch each other's backs.

I used to think my family had a Mafia mindset, using words like "honor" and "loyalty," but the police are equally tribal. The abiding narrative is "us against them." We are the thin blue line. The gatekeepers. The guardians. Criminals sometimes die breaking the law, but we will die defending it. And while most people appreciate the sacrifices we make, and the dangers we face, few of them want to be our friends. It's why so many police officers socialize together and marry into police families.

Assignments are given out. I am on restricted duties. Deskbound. Paperwork. Another punishment. When the briefing ends, I stay behind.

"Can I help you, McCarthy?" asks Connelly.

"Are we good, sir?"

"In what sense?"

"The other week . . . the incident with Detective Goodall."

"What about it?"

"Has it been resolved to your satisfaction?"

He grunts softly. "The misconduct charges have been withdrawn."

"Thank you, sir."

I wait for something more, but he tucks a folder under his arm and departs, leaving behind a lingering sense of disappointment, or disaffection.

Taking a desk in the parade room, I begin filling out reports. Every incident that an officer attends will generate between ten and thirty minutes of paperwork, even without a complaint being made. Intelligence logs must be updated, facts checked, and phone calls made. In the background, I can hear the radio room, communicating with the foot and vehicle patrols. It sounds like a typical night of fights, accidents, assaults, robberies, and domestic disputes.

Ignoring the distractions, I work quickly and create a window of time for myself when I can look through the custody logs and booking sheets for any mention of Darren Goodall or Tempe Brown. There is nothing. Nobody filled out a "use of force" report and there is no record of interview. There were no background checks for either callout to the apartment. Nobody is looking for Tempe or is concerned for her welfare.

I take out my mobile and call Nish, who still lives at home with his parents in South London. When he doesn't pick up, I try their landline. Nish is the only one of my fellow officers who knows about my family connections. I told him because I trusted him to keep my secret, and sharing it made it seem easier to carry.

Mrs. Kohli answers, sounding posher than the Queen.

"Is Nish there?" I ask, before correcting myself. "Anisha."

"Who shall I say is calling?"

"Work."

She puts the phone down and shouts in Hindi. I hear footsteps on the stairs. Nish's voice.

"It's me," I say.

Silence. I think the line has dropped out. I try again. "Nish?"

"We shouldn't be talking."

"Why?"

He goes quiet. I wait. He breaks. "This isn't personal, Phil. You did nothing wrong—it's just . . . I don't want to . . . People are . . ."

I can't wait for him to get to the point. "Did you fill out a domestic abuse report?"

"I was told not to."

"What about the bodycam footage—was it uploaded?"

"Not by me."

"They've buried this."

"Maybe that's for the best. Goodall has a wife and kids."

"And a mistress."

"Not our business."

"Who he beat up."

Nish goes quiet.

"They wanted to charge me with misconduct," I say.

"I know. But it won't happen—not if they want to keep it quiet."

He's right, but silence won't save me from being ostracized.

"Somebody put a dead rat in my locker."

"Fuckers!" he mutters. "This will blow over. Keep your head down and nose clean."

"I have a very clean nose."

Nish lowers his voice. "Ever heard of the Gladiators?"

"You mean the Roman variety?"

"The modern equivalent. About twenty years ago, a group of trainees at Hendon started a drinking club and came up with the name. They liked to party hard and play hard and pretend they were better than everyone else. Over time it became something more." He hesitates, as if searching for the words. "If one of them had a problem or needed something—a promotion, a transfer, a glowing reference—the others would sort it out. All for one and one for all."

"Like the musketeers."

"All swash and no buckle."

"How do you know this?"

"Every year they recruit a handful of new trainees."

"You were invited?"

"I'm the wrong color, but I know someone . . ." He stops. Starts again. "Like I said, they're more a drinking club, but once a member has proven themselves worthy, they are given a tattoo. Three letters: MDM."

I remember the tattoo I saw on Superintendent Drysdale's wrist.

"What does it stand for?" I ask.

"Maximus Decimus Meridius. Commander of the Armies of the North."

"You've lost me."

"Russell Crowe's character in *Gladiator*."

I laugh because it sounds so foolish. Secret clubs, passwords, funny handshakes—I thought the Masons were a thing of the past.

"If you attack one of them, you attack them all," says Nish.

"I didn't attack him."

"You bruised his pride."

Why is it that men have pride but women have shame?

The silence is filled with the sound of us breathing into the phone.

"Are we good?" I ask.

"Never better," Nish replies, "but you have to let this go, Phil."

"Of course."

Even as I'm making the promise, I'm typing Darren Goodall's name into the CRIS database and searching for past incidents or complaints of domestic abuse. It comes back with a single hit, but the file is restricted. There is a case number and an investigating officer, but all the other details are hidden.

Trying a different approach, I search a separate database called Merlin, which stores information on children. Any domestic violence incident where minors are witnesses or living at that address will trigger a Merlin report, which is shared with child protection agencies.

"Bingo!" I say, too loudly. I glance at the nearby desks, making sure that nobody has heard me.

On-screen is an incident report dated 14 August 2019. An emergency call was made from a private home in West London. There is a recording. I put on headphones and press play.

"You're through to the police. What's the nature of your emergency?"

A child's voice, a little boy. Sobbing.

"Daddy and Mummy are fighting."

"Where are they?"

"In the bedroom. She's crying."

"Is he hurting her?"

"He's hitting her." He takes the phone away from his mouth and begins yelling, *"Stop it, Daddy! Please! Stop it!"*

The dispatcher remains calm. *"What's your name?"*

"Nathan."

"Listen to me, Nathan, where is your mummy now?"

"She's trying to get the baby."

"What baby?"

"My sister." Nathan lowers the phone and starts yelling, *"Please, Daddy, don't do it, don't do it."*

The dispatcher grows desperate. *"Nathan? Nathan? Can you hear me? Nathan? Nathan?"*

I am holding my breath. The boy answers softly, whispering, *"Yes."*

"Where is the baby?"

"He's holding her upside down over the stairs."

"The police are coming. They're not far away. Is the front door open?"

"I don't know."

"Can you open it and come back to the phone?"

"OK."

Seconds tick by. I can hear a woman screaming in the background. The phone is picked up.

"Is that you, Nathan?"

"Uh-huh."

"Where is the baby?"

"She's not moving."

"What do you mean? Where is your mummy?"

"No, Daddyyy. Noooooo! Noooooo! Daddddyyyy."

The phone falls.

"Nathan? Nathan?"

Someone picks up the handset. I hear breathing.

"Nathan? Is that you?"

The line goes dead.

The written portion of the report is a summary of the incident. Goodall was arrested and taken to Acton Police Station, where he was held overnight. He was released in the morning without charge. His wife, Alison, was treated in hospital, but declined to make a statement. Photographs were taken, showing swelling to her face and bruises on her chest. These images should have been enough to bury Goodall, but nothing happened. He wasn't charged or suspended. He didn't accept responsibility or agree to counseling.

Closing down the screen, I glance over my shoulder again, making sure nobody has been watching. Even so, every keystroke and viewed page will have left a digital trace. I can't use the information without risking my own career.

Just before midnight I change into my civvies and make my way downstairs. The shift has changed and there is new personnel on the front desk. One of them signals to me. Warily, I approach.

"These arrived for you," he says, pulling a huge bunch of flowers from behind the counter. Roses and lilies in pinks and peaches are arranged with branches of gray-green eucalyptus.

"Is it your birthday?" he asks.

"No."

I open the card. The handwritten note says: *I'm sorry about what happened. No hard feelings.* It's unsigned.

"Who delivered them?" I ask.

"A courier. Maybe you have a secret admirer."

"I doubt it." I look at the card again, turning it over, hoping for a clue.

Perhaps Tempe is letting me know that she's all right. Or maybe Darren Goodall is sending me a peace offering. Either way, it's disturbing rather than reassuring.

7

Henry is up early, thumping around the kitchen, opening cupboards, grinding coffee, and watching YouTube videos on his phone.

"Did I wake you?" he asks.

"You woke my grandmother and she's been dead for a decade."

"Sorry."

"Blaine barked all last night."

"I'll talk to Mrs. Ainsley."

"She'll pretend to be deaf."

"She *is* deaf."

"Selectively."

He notices my clothes. "Going for a run?"

"Visiting a friend."

I steal a slice of his toast and make my way downstairs, contemplating if I should pick up a coffee because I might have to sit and wait. My Fiat Punto collects more leaves than miles because I drive it so rarely. Douglas Adams once likened driving a car in London to bringing a Ming vase to a football game, and my Fiat already has the battle scars to prove that point. Every time I read those stories about the cost of running a car in London—the insurance, road tax, petrol, parking, congestion charges, etc.—I know it makes little financial sense, but each time I get behind the wheel, it still feels like a badge of freedom and being a grown-up.

I drive north across Battersea Bridge, glancing along the Thames at the string of bridges to the east, which are like loose stitches that hold two halves of a city together. Turning left, I follow the river until the road curves north again, passing through Chelsea, Fulham, and Olympia.

Just before eight, I turn into Kempe Road and park diagonally opposite the semidetached house, which looks like all the others in the street with decorative fasciae, net curtains, and a wrought iron faux balcony above the front door. Ten minutes later, a young woman emerges in a dressing gown and collects two bottles of milk from the doorstep. A cat darts between her legs, making a dash for freedom. She calls after it, but the cat has already jumped onto a wall.

"I'm not letting you back inside. You have to go around the back."

I recognize Alison Goodall from her photograph. She looks too young to be a mother of two. She glances skyward, as though judging the weather, before shutting the door.

At a quarter past eight, it opens again. Darren Goodall is juggling a travel mug and an overcoat. Alison kisses his cheek and helps him into the coat, one arm at a time. He unlocks a sporty-looking blue Saab and waves to her as he leaves. She is standing in the doorway with a toddler on her hip.

More time passes as I debate whether to knock on the door. What would I say? "Excuse me, your husband keeps a mistress in a luxury apartment at Borough Market. And he beats her up as well." Maybe Alison knows about her husband's affair. They could be seeing a counselor or have an arrangement, or he's promised her to be a good boy from now on.

The door opens again. Alison is dressed in leggings and a baggy sweater. The toddler is strapped into a stroller. Alison shouts back into the house and a little boy appears. Nathan. He's dressed in gray trousers and a white shirt and is pulling on a purple sweater. Alison stops to tie his shoelaces and tuck in his shirt.

I remember Nathan's voice on the telephone, his terrified sobs, his pleading, and the worst sound of all—the phone going dead.

The family sets off along Kempe Road but only as far as the next corner where tall plane trees shade the playground of a primary school. I follow them on foot, keeping a safe distance, as Alison turns into the school. Other children are arriving, the girls wearing purple-and-white gingham dresses and the boys dressed like Nathan.

Alison crouches and kisses him goodbye. Nathan wipes his cheek and runs to join his friends. After spending a few minutes chatting with other mothers, Alison pushes the stroller along Chamberlayne Road, crossing the bridge over the railway tracks. Two blocks south, they arrive at a modern-looking sports center. A membership card swipes her through a security gate. She's gone.

"Can I help you?" asks a young woman behind the counter.

"I'm new to the area," I say. "I'm looking to join a gym. Can I get a tour?"

The woman hands me a voucher. "We have an introductory deal. The first three classes are free. We have a yoga class beginning at nine thirty."

I search for Alison in the changing rooms and at the crèche. When I finally spot her she's following a group of women into a studio with mirrored walls and a sprung wooden floor. Barefoot, in an oversized T-shirt, she unrolls a yoga mat near the back of the room. I ask her if I can squeeze in next to her and she moves over to make room. We sit cross-legged on the floor and begin stretching while listening to the female instructor, who has a sculpted stomach and legs that bend like noodles. Soon we're moving through the yoga sequences, being told to inhale and exhale, to breathe into our hips and into the space behind our hearts. I have always liked yoga, but I don't buy into the "deep healing" and "mastery of life" patter. I like the strength and balance exercises, but I don't expect it to miraculously cleanse my liver or unblock my seven chakras. I couldn't name one chakra.

We are asked to pair up and I turn to Alison. Self-consciously, we help each other perform a seated forward bend and a downward dog and child's pose.

"She's very bendy," I say, commenting on our instructor. "I bet she could fold herself into an origami swan."

Alison stifles a giggle.

"Do you find this serene?" I ask.

"I guess."

"I try to empty my mind, but all I keep doing is making lists and wondering if my boobs look lopsided in this bra."

Alison laughs out loud and the instructor shoots us a look. We smile apologetically and we're on our best behavior until we bow, hands together, and bid each other, "Namaste."

"I'm sorry I distracted you," I say as we roll up the yoga mats. "When she told us to go to our happy place, I thought of going home and opening a bottle of wine."

"Bit early."

"True."

Alison reties her hair. "I haven't seen you here before."

"My first time. I'm giving the place a trial run. How about you?"

"I live nearby."

Introductions are made as we walk to the changing rooms. I sneak a look at Alison's arms and neck, searching for signs of bruising.

"Do you fancy a coffee?" I ask.

Alison glances at her phone. "Sure. I have to get my little one from the crèche."

"I'll wait."

We go to a café at the entrance to the center. The yellow chairs and tables are set far enough apart for prams and strollers to fit in between them. I order coffees and buy a juice box for Chloe, who has corkscrew curls that bounce when she swings her head.

"How old?" I ask.

"Almost three." Alison notices my engagement ring, a single emerald on a delicate silver band. "That's pretty."

"And new."

"Congratulations."

"How about you?"

She holds up her left hand. "Oh, I'm well and truly married. Seven years."

"Isn't that when you get the dreaded itch?"

"Only if you have time to scratch."

She has a slight lisp, a sibilant s sound that emerges as a quiet whistle, but only on certain words. Small talk comes easily, but I know I have to steer the conversation to her husband. A part of me wants to blurt out the truth about Tempe and the apartment, but I sense that's not the way to convince her.

Alison has been talking.

"I'm sorry. I was miles away," I say.

"I asked what you did . . . your job?"

"Oh, right, yes, I guess you could call me a counselor. Domestic abuse mostly."

Her body language changes. "That must be challenging."

"Yes, but also rewarding. I meet women who are trapped in abusive relationships and I give them the strength and the tools to get out, to save themselves . . . and their children."

Alison doesn't reply, and I keep going.

"Often it's about convincing them that they're not to blame. There is no shame or guilt in having an abusive partner. Nobody likes to admit that a relationship is failing, but it's not their fault."

"What if they decide to stay?" she whispers.

"That's their choice. Some women take time to decide. Others get defensive or deny the abuse is happening or believe they can change the man they love."

"Can they—change him, I mean?"

"What do you think?"

She looks surprised. "Me?"

"You must have an opinion."

"Not really."

"Do you know anyone in an abusive relationship?"

"I mind my own business."

"You could help her, you know, your friend—"

"I don't have a friend."

"Some women hold on for the sake of the kids or because they fear being destitute or alone, or there are family expectations. I can't make that decision for them. I can only urge them to make a plan."

"What sort of plan?"

"It might mean packing some important things in a suitcase or having a safe word—some agreed signal to let a friend know they're in trouble and need help. They should have nominated a meeting place and found somewhere safe they can hide."

Alison is staring past me. "Who are you?" she whispers.

"A friend."

Her features harden and she picks up her shoulder bag and wrestles the stroller between chairs, knocking one of them over. I try to help her, while apologizing to the other patrons. I borrow a pen from the barista and jot down my phone number on a paper napkin.

Alison is outside, pushing the stroller along the footpath. Jogging to catch up to her, I press the napkin into her hand.

"Take this please."

Alison balls it up and throws it away.

I retrieve the paper and push it into her shoulder bag. She keeps walking. I yell after her.

"A suitcase. A code word. A friend."

8

My Tuesday karate class is mixed, full of men and women, mostly in their twenties and thirties. Some have been with me for two years and have moved through the levels, from white to orange to blue. Ricardo is the highest with a brown belt.

We're just finishing up our session, wiping down the impact bags and stacking the mats, when I hear them planning a quick drink in the local pub.

"Care to join us?" asks Ricardo, who is Spanish, with a sexy accent and hangdog face.

"You ask me that every week and I always say no."

"I'm an eternal optimist."

"And I'm happily engaged."

"Maybe next week," he says, giving me his rakish grin, which looks creepy rather than charming.

I change out of my Keikogi, pulling on jeans and a light sweater. I'm locking up when I sense someone behind me, standing in the shadows.

"Hello," says Tempe, stepping into the light. "I hope you don't mind."

I almost don't recognize her because her face is no longer swollen and her lip has healed.

"How did you find me?"

"You told me about your karate lessons."

"Did I?"

"At the hospital . . ."

I vaguely remember the conversation.

"There aren't that many studios in South London," says Tempe.

"You phoned them?"

She nods.

"Did you send me flowers?"

"Yes."

"You didn't have to do that."

"I wanted to apologize—for what happened."

We lapse into silence for a beat too long.

"Your face looks better," I say.

"Less Frankenstein, more Igor."

"Hardly."

Tempe glances through the glass doors into the studio. "I was hoping . . . I thought I might . . ."

"What?"

"Sign up. I want to be able to protect myself. I saw what you did to Darren. You sat him on his backside. The look on his face was priceless . . ." She stops and starts again. "Could you teach me to do that?"

"There are classes."

"I want you."

"I'm not sure that's wise. It might be seen as a conflict of interest."

"Why? I didn't make a statement."

She has a point, but I'm still wary of getting involved.

I change the subject. "I went looking for you, but you'd left the shelter. When I went to the apartment, I found blood everywhere."

"I cut myself."

"You trashed the place."

"He trashed my face." She spits the words, but the brief flash of defiance quickly fades and she lowers her eyes. "I was angry. I wanted to punish him."

"Why leave your phone?"

"To stop him finding me."

"Is he looking?"

She shrugs. "I won't risk it."

Unlocking the door of the academy, I grab a business card. "You can enroll online. I don't normally teach private lessons because I'm working shifts, but you can join one of my classes and we'll take it from there."

Tempe looks at the card and asks, "Where are you going now?"

"Home."

"Do you fancy a drink? There's a pub on the corner."

I'm about to say no, but change my mind. Henry is working tonight and there's nothing at home except leftovers and a basket of ironing. As we're leaving, Tempe retrieves a small pull-along suitcase from a hiding place beneath the stairs. Extending the handle of the case, she drags it along the footpath, where it bounces over the cracks with a clackety-clack sound.

The pub is mock old with fake timber beams dotted with horseshoes and hung with riding paraphernalia. My class has taken a large table in the corner. They wave for me to join them, but I signal that I'm with someone. Ricardo squeezes out from behind the table and approaches, but I hold up crossed fingers as if warding off a vampire. He smiles sadly and retreats.

Tempe puts her suitcase against the bar and takes a high stool, crossing her legs and displaying a glossy knee beneath her black suede skirt.

"I'm having a gin and tonic. You?"

"The same." I glance at her suitcase. "Where are you staying?"

"I had an Airbnb in Brixton for a while, but it was too expensive."

"And now?"

"I'm looking for somewhere."

"You're living out of a suitcase."

"I'm between places." She sips her drink.

"Darren Goodall claimed you were a sex worker and one of his informants."

"That's a lie." Her eyes meet mine. "I'm not . . . I don't sell my body."

"When I went back to your apartment, I found a broken camera on the floor."

Tempe screws up her face. "He liked to film us having sex."

"With a hidden camera?"

"I didn't know at first."

"It's illegal to record sex acts without a person's consent."

She shrugs ambivalently. "He filmed other things."

"Like what?"

"Sometimes he put the camera in the sitting room, sometimes in the bedroom. I thought he was spying on me, but he mostly wanted to film his meetings with people."

"What people?"

Tempe's shoulders rise and fall. "I was never allowed to stay." She reaches into the side pocket of her suitcase. "Look what I found."

It's a school yearbook from St. Ursula's. Pages have been marked with torn pieces of paper. One of them has a photograph from a swimming carnival. All of the girls are in house colors, with banners and flags, cheering from the grandstand behind the pool. Tempe points to herself in the crowd. She's with a group on the higher seats, older girls, who have painted their faces and tied streamers in their hair.

"And this is you," she says, pointing to the junior girls, who are seated lower in the stands.

She turns a page to the year photographs and picks me out from my peers.

"I look so young," I say.

"You were only fourteen," she replies.

Tempe was seventeen but looked completely grown-up even then. She was tall and athletic and graceful. In her group photograph she is standing in the back row, next to her year-eleven coordinator. If not for her school uniform, she could have been the teacher.

"I remember when you left. It was quite sudden."

"We moved to Belfast."

"But there was some story that—"

"It was only gossip." She closes the yearbook and puts it away. "Another drink?"

"Not for me."

"Please. Just one more."

Tempe signals the barman. I notice her counting out change from her purse and coming up short.

"Let me get these," I say.

"No, I can—"

"I insist."

I tap my debit card on the machine.

Tempe sips her gin and tonic.

"Are you working?" I ask.

"I have jobs coming up."

"What do you do?"

"Event planning. Festivals. Product launches. Premieres."

She has to shout because three women sitting nearby are hooting with laughter. They are dressed for a night out, with big hair and troweled-on makeup, and they've grown louder as the evening has gone on.

Tempe gets up and walks to their table. For a moment, I expect an argument, but she returns a few minutes later and takes her seat. Meanwhile, the women get up and quietly leave.

"What did you say?" I ask.

"I told them you were an off-duty police officer who was concerned that they were intoxicated and might try to drive home."

"How did you know they were driving?"

"One of them has her car keys hanging from her purse."

I marvel at how quickly Tempe had picked up on a detail like that. "You're very good. What else have you noticed?"

"That you're engaged." She points to my left hand, the ring. "Where? When?"

"September. Maybe."

"What do you mean, maybe?"

"We don't have a venue. The best places are booked out years in advance. Who plans that far ahead?"

"Most people," says Tempe. "Maybe I can help."

"How?"

"Weddings are my speciality."

"I can't afford a wedding planner."

"I'll do it for nothing. It's my gift to you for saving my life."

"I hardly did that."

Tempe begins listing what she can do, giving examples of how to save money on catering and flowers.

"How about this?" she says finally. "You give me your dates and what you're looking for and I'll make some calls. If I can't find you the perfect venue in a fortnight, I'll give up. You can get married in a shoebox in the middle of the road."

"Cardboard box?"

"Aye."

We begin riffing on the famous Monty Python sketch, putting on Yorkshire accents and talking about eating crusts of stale bread and being thrashed asleep with broken bottles.

"My dad is a huge Python fan," I say.

"Mine too," says Tempe. "He had all the DVDs."

"Where are your parents now?"

"Still in Belfast."

I remember the letter addressed to Tempe that was put in the wrong mailbox.

"I have something for you—a letter."

"Burn it."

"Why?"

"I don't talk to my parents. It's a long, boring story."

I want to hear it, because it might give us something else in common. My parents aren't boring, of course. I wish they were. I wish my father sold insurance or plumbing supplies or worked as a civil engineer. Instead, he's spent his career outwitting the police and fooling the Inland Revenue.

"How about another drink?" asks Tempe.

"This time I definitely have to go."

Her disappointment is palpable.

"I have a new phone number." She waits for me to unlock my handset and takes it from me, typing her details into my contacts.

"About this wedding. Can I give you a call tomorrow? I need numbers and budgets."

"OK."

I'm almost at the door when I spy her suitcase against the bar. A part of me wants to keep walking, but a different voice urges me to turn back.

"Where are you staying tonight?"

"I'll find somewhere."

"Do you have money?"

"I'm fine, really."

I watch her for a moment, wishing I could read her mind.

"Don't go anywhere," I say. "I have to make a call."

Stepping outside the pub, I press speed dial. My mother answers before her phone even rings. How does she do that? She must sit at home, staring at her mobile, waiting for me to call.

"What a pleasant surprise!" she says brightly. Considering that I call her twice a day, it can hardly be *that* surprising, but I let it go.

She fumbles with her TV remote, muting the volume. For some inexplicable reason she loves reality TV shows where people get voted out of the jungle or off islands or out of the house.

"You're at home," I say.

"Why wouldn't I be?"

"I thought you might be out on a hot date."

"Very funny."

My mother didn't remarry after divorcing my father, which could be down to her Catholicism or her bloody-mindedness.

Five minutes later, I return to Tempe.

"I've found you somewhere to stay. My mother has a spare room. She'll know your entire family history by tomorrow morning, but the room is lovely."

Tempe's eyes are glistening.

"You don't have to do this."

"Come on."

9

It's after ten o'clock when I get back to the house. Henry is working tonight and won't be home until morning. As I'm crossing the road to the house, I notice a pewter-colored Jaguar XJ parked beneath a streetlight. The man behind the wheel has a hat tilted over his eyes, and a newspaper is folded on the dashboard, showing a half-finished crossword.

As I reach the sidewalk, the rear door opens and a woman emerges, one long leg at a time, each foot clad in an expensive designer shoe. My stepmother, Constance, is wearing a lightweight coat with an upturned collar and oversized sunglasses, giving off her Jackie Kennedy vibes, although she looks more bug-eyed than beautiful.

"Philomena," she says awkwardly. "I hope you don't mind."

I keep walking.

"You haven't answered my calls. I thought maybe I had the wrong number."

"With my voice on the recorded message?"

"It's been so long," she explains. "I also sent you a letter and texts."

"I must have ignored them."

"Can we talk? Please?"

I am normally not rude to people. I barely know Constance. After the divorce I spent half my holidays living with my father, but he didn't marry Constance until I had left home and gone to university. She is twenty years younger than Daddy and only twelve years older than me.

A neighboring door squeaks. Mrs. Ainsley pops her head out, eavesdropping again.

"I thought I heard the doorbell," she says.

"No. It's only me."

Blaine is barking and trying to push past her legs.

She doesn't close the door immediately. I wait. The silence grows uncomfortable. Constance is about to say something, but I hold a finger to my lips, ushering her inside.

"It's about your father's birthday," she whispers.

I take her to the kitchen, where she keeps up a constant stream of talk about the party, while I separate laundry and put a load into the machine. Powder. Softener. She follows me into the bedroom.

"It won't matter who else comes; the only person Edward will look for is you. You're the only one he *wants* to see."

"Why doesn't *he* ask me?"

"You blocked his number."

It's true.

"He's turning sixty. And he's not been well."

"What do you mean?"

"His health."

"What's wrong with him?"

"He won't tell me."

I frown at her, wondering if she's lying, but I don't think Constance has the artifice to deceive anyone. I study her more closely and notice that her makeup is not quite as perfect as usual and that gravity is working to undermine her face. She still looks like a spoiled, top-heavy socialite, but less polished and assured.

"Please say you'll come," she says.

"I think I'm working that day."

"But you'll consider it?"

I sigh and roll my eyes.

"Fine. OK. I'll think about it."

After she's gone, I heat up leftovers and sit in the garden, listening to crickets and canned TV laughter and a distant emergency siren (ambulance, not fire). I don't want to think about my father. I have no desire to see him again, and my career is more important than his birthday.

I often use words like "hate" when I refer to him, which isn't entirely fair because I loved him once. I remember the good times—the holidays in Cornwall, charades at Christmas, impromptu concerts in the garden, collecting mushrooms after rain, standing on his shoes while he danced, and seeing his face in the audience at every graduation, school play, recital, and concert. Not many fathers were there *every* time.

Perhaps if there were an unseen scale that was balancing good against bad, it would tip in my father's favor, but some memories are heavier than others. One in particular haunts me—an Easter gathering of the McCarthy clan. My uncles and aunts and twelve first cousins descended on the house, my cousins sleeping top-to-tail, filling trundle beds and inflatable mattresses. Mealtimes were a production line of corned beef sandwiches washed down with jugs of cordial and followed by scoops of ice cream pressed into cones. Something happened that weekend that changed the mood from joyful to somber in the space of a few hours. The name Stella Luff was mentioned. Stella had worked as a bookkeeper for my father since before I was born and would bring me small presents each time she visited the house, annoying my mother and enchanting me.

That night, after the children had gone to bed, my father raged through the house, bellowing at Clifton and Daragh. I crept onto the landing and peered through the spindles, watching as he upended a table and toppled the same antique sideboard that Jamie Pike would crash into when he put his hand down my pants. I witnessed his rage at first hand, hardly daring to breathe, and felt as though the world were disintegrating around me in pops, groans, and sharp cracks. My tongue wet my upper lip. My bladder tightened. Who was this man?

On Easter Tuesday, a local newspaper reported the mugging of a woman outside her home in Blackheath. Attackers had left her lying in a gutter with a ruptured spleen, a fractured jaw, and six broken bones in her face. There was a photograph, but I didn't recognize Stella at first because her face was so swollen. I didn't see her again. She didn't bring me presents or turn up to family gatherings. I don't know how much she stole, but I hope it was worth it.

10

Saturday night in London. The South Bank is crowded with diners, clubbers, drinkers, and theater patrons. I am back on patrol and my current partner, PC Chris Dawson, has informed me he doesn't like working with female officers.

"Call me old-fashioned, but there are certain aspects of this job that I don't think women should have to do," he says, "such as grappling on the ground with pissheads. I wouldn't want my girlfriend doing that."

I don't respond.

"I'm not saying women coppers don't have their uses, you know. They're good at dealing with rape victims and grieving families, know wha' I mean? But in my experience most of them are too eager or are sticklers for the rules. Either that or they're crazy. I hope you're not a psycho."

"I don't know. I haven't been tested," I reply curtly.

He gives me a sidelong glance. "No offense."

Your face offends me, I want to say. *And your crooked teeth and your flat nose and your narrow mind and the incy-wincy penis that I'm sure you have.* But I say nothing.

We spend the first half of our shift patrolling the entertainment precinct on the South Bank, which is quite fun because most of the patrons are in a good mood and appreciate seeing coppers on the beat. A few drunken ratbags spoil the party, but that's why we're here.

On balance, I've learned that most people who come in contact with the police are either poor, uneducated, low-skilled, mentally ill, unemployed, drug-addicted, or simply unlucky. But since the murder of George Floyd and the Black Lives Matter protests, I've noticed a subtle difference in the way ordinary people look at me, with less trust and more doubt.

I haven't changed. I am the same compassionate, caring person that fought so hard to get this job. I have given a homeless person my gloves because he was freezing. I have stopped a woman being arrested for stealing a loaf of bread to feed her children. I have lent money to people to buy train tickets and resuscitated a drunk who was choking on his own vomit. But I know colleagues who have grown jaded and lost faith in the fundamental goodness of human beings. Either that or they get tired of dealing with the red tape and regulations and the thankless routines.

For the past few hours, radio chatter has been dominated by an operation on the river. The Marine Policing Unit has put boats in the area looking for a body and discovered a deceased male wedged against a pylon on Bankside Pier. Floaters aren't uncommon. We pull at least one a week from the Thames, mostly suicides or accidents whose bodies get snagged in barge lines or fishing nets or washed down the river to the Isle of Dogs. This one must be different because the serious crime squad has been called.

"I fancy a piece of that," says Dawson as we get back to the patrol car. "I'm sick of getting puke on my shoes."

"You'd rather have blood on your shoes?"

"You know what I mean."

He pulls into traffic and we make our way to Bankside Pier, pulling up behind three other patrol cars on the eastern side of the Globe Theatre. Crime scene tape is threaded between bollards, and theater patrons are being kept to one side of the street by security guards in high-vis vests.

Dawson ducks under the tape and disappears between vehicles, heading towards the pier.

"Are you here to relieve us?" asks a constable on crowd control.

"No. Sorry. What happened?"

"Floater."

"Must be more than that."

"Weighted down with chains and concrete."

I follow the bright lights and walk across the cobblestones to the edge of the river, where a police launch is tethered to the pier while another is using engines to hold itself against the current. Water churns beneath the propellers, creating foam that slides away on the tide. Police divers, encased in black, are standing on the deck or treading water as a crane hauls a weight from beneath the surface. The water stirs and a body emerges, cradled in a net. The arm of the crane swings over the pier where screens have been erected to shield the operation from onlookers. A TV crew has sneaked past the cordon and the dock is suddenly bathed in a spotlight that illuminates the netted body, showing a pale face and dripping hair hanging like a weed across his eyes. I push forward, shouldering people aside. Ignoring protests.

A uniformed officer tries to stop me but I duck under his outstretched arm.

"Do you know who it is?" I ask, feeling as though I have floated out of myself and that it's not me asking the question.

"You got to sign in," he says.

"I think I recognize him."

My voice is amplified by a sudden moment of quiet. People are staring at me. A detective emerges from the huddle of watchers. He's in his late thirties, tall and loose-limbed, with ginger hair and mayonnaise-colored skin. Summers must have been horrible for him as a child, having to be slathered with sunscreen and forced to wear long sleeves and hats. He introduces himself as DI Martyn Fairbairn.

"What's your name?"

"PC McCarthy. I'm stationed at Southwark."

"Wait here."

The detective goes away. I watch as technicians begin setting up lights and carrying silver boxes behind the screens. I can see the figures merging and separating like shadow puppets projected against the white canvas.

Dawson pops up beside me. "We're wanted back at the station."

"You go. I'm staying."

"We're not supposed to be here."

The detective signals to me. I'm to follow him. Dawson looks on, gormless, as I'm escorted down a set of worn wooden steps to a floating dock that can rise and fall on the tide. I'm given a pair of latex gloves and a plastic net for my hair.

Fairbairn pulls back the canvas curtain and I edge forward into a circle of light. I see the lower half of the body first. A chain is wrapped around his waist and crisscrosses the torso. Each end loops through the center holes of two concrete breeze-blocks.

A technician steps back and I get a proper look at the face. Unshaven. Shaggy brown hair. Crooked nose.

"Are you going to be sick?" asks Fairbairn.

"No, sir."

"Who is it?"

"His name is Dylan Holstein. He works for the *Guardian*."

"A journalist?"

I nod.

"Come with me."

This time I'm taken to an unmarked police car and told to sit in the backseat. Fairbairn fetches a bottle of water and cracks open the lid for me.

"How do you know this guy?"

"I don't . . . not really. I met him once. He approached me on my way to work."

"Why?"

I hesitate, unsure of how much to say.

"He asked me about an arrest that I made a few weeks ago. It was a domestic dispute. A woman was beaten."

"Why was he interested?"

I sip the water. Fairbairn senses that I'm holding out. He waits.

"I arrested a police officer, Darren Goodall."

The name doesn't seem to mean anything to Fairbairn.

"He's the hero cop. He stopped the knifeman at Camden Market."

"I remember. Why did you arrest him?"

"He took a swing at me."

I can almost see Fairbairn's mind working. He's picturing the mine-field I've asked him to walk across.

"Why would a journalist from the *Guardian* be interested in a garden-variety domestic? It sounds more like tabloid fodder?"

"I don't know. I didn't talk to him."

"He must have said something."

"Apparently, Goodall had a fiancée who died in East Sussex eight years ago. Imogen Croker's family believes she was murdered."

I can't believe I remember her name.

"Why did Holstein approach you?"

"I have no idea. Maybe he thought I might help him."

"But you didn't?"

"No."

My shoulder radio is humming. The control room is asking for my location. They'll be worried about overtime. Across the waterfront, forensic teams are still moving behind the white canvas, and a drone hovers above the pier, taking aerial footage for the investigators.

Fairbairn has left me alone in the car while he makes a call. He returns.

"Dylan Holstein didn't show up at his office today, but we won't be releasing the name until after a formal identification."

"Is he married?"

"Is that important?"

"It makes it sadder."

He tilts his head to the side, as though baffled by my reaction.

"Was he alive when he went into the water?" I ask.

"We believe so."

I picture the chains wrapped around his chest and over his shoulders. They were padlocked behind him. He would have fought for air, kicking his legs, trying to keep his head above the surface until exhaustion dragged him under.

"You're free to go," says Fairbairn, "but you're not to talk to anybody about this. Do you understand?"

"Yes, sir."

11

It is past midnight when I get back to the station, and the patrol room is emptier than at any other time of day. Sitting at a desk, I stare at the blinking cursor, which seems to be sending me a message in code.

I type in a Google search for Dylan Holstein. The first four pages have dozens of stories with his byline, mostly investigative pieces about miscarriages of justice, political infighting, corruption, and organized crime. His biography refers to him as a "freelance writer and author" who has worked for the *Guardian* for more than fifteen years as an investigative reporter. He has written two nonfiction books, one about gangland London during the sixties, and the other a history of crime reporting called *If It Bleeds It Leads*.

Next I type in the name Imogen Croker. The first pages are media reports about the death of a young woman near Eastbourne eight years ago.

I begin reading:

A London fashion model has plunged to her death from cliffs at Beachy Head in East Sussex, despite her boyfriend's desperate attempts to save her.

Imogen Croker, 19, and Darren Goodall, 30, were on a footpath above the famous chalk cliffs when a strong gust of wind blew Imogen off her feet and over the edge. Goodall, a police constable, climbed down the treacherous rock face but became trapped and had to be winched to safety.

Coastguard and police were called to Beachy Head shortly after 4:00 p.m. yesterday, where they recovered the body at the base of the cliff. PC Goodall was taken to hospital and treated for hypothermia.

The couple, who had known each other for eight months, were engaged to be married later this year. They had lunch yesterday at the nearby Birling Gap café and police said that

alcohol may have played a role in the tragedy. A report is being prepared for the coroner.

There are more stories, along with photographs. Some are modeling shots and others are taken from Imogen's Facebook page. In one she is sitting on the back of a motorbike in jeans and a leather jacket. A younger version of Goodall is leaning forward over the handlebars.

I notice the similarities between Tempe and Imogen Croker. Both are tall and slim with upturned noses and wide mouths. Perhaps Goodall has a type, although his wife doesn't match the template.

Most of Imogen's modeling work was for clothing catalogues and trade magazines. She was also studying to be a schoolteacher.

The inquest was opened and adjourned at Eastbourne Court. I search for the outcome.

A British model fell to her death at Beachy Head after being blown from a footpath by high winds, a coroner said today.

Imogen Croker fell 250 feet while walking along a well-worn tourist trail at the top of the cliffs. A toxicology report showed Miss Croker had consumed a substantial amount of alcohol, but was described by witnesses as being "merry rather than drunk."

In a statement tendered to the court, her fiancé, Darren Goodall, said the couple was taking photographs only moments before the tragedy, which happened in an area where signs warn tourists to stay away from the cliff edge.

"I told her not to get too close, but she was holding out her arms, saying she could feel the wind beneath her wings. One minute she was there and the next she had gone."

Goodall, a police constable, used a lower path to reach her body, sustaining hand injuries and suffering from hypothermia. He stayed with Miss Croker until coastguard and lifeboat crews arrived.

In a statement read out at the inquest, Miss Croker's mother, Lydia, described her daughter as someone who lived life to the fullest. "She was my beautiful, thoughtful, kindhearted firstborn, and I miss her every day."

Coroner Ressler concluded, "This is a very sad and tragic case. My heart goes out to the Croker family, who have lost a loving daughter in a terrible accident."

I read a dozen more articles. None of them calls into question the findings of the inquest, yet Dylan Holstein said that her family had doubts. He came to me looking for dirt on Goodall and now he's dead, which is either a terrible coincidence or a warning that I should leave this alone.

I'm about to close the page down when I type another search. Holstein knew that I was Edward McCarthy's daughter, something I've worked hard to keep secret. The page refreshes and I begin reading a newspaper feature written eight months ago. It focuses on the Hope Island Development, my father's latest property venture. Three local councillors have been accused of taking more than a million pounds in bribes to approve the rezoning of the former industrial site near Canning Town. One of the men, the chair of the local development committee, was found dead in the garage of his home when detectives arrived to question him.

My father is quoted in the article, pledging to cooperate fully with any investigation and denying any wrongdoing. A sidebar, published beside the main feature, details the potted history of Edward McCarthy, mentioning his two marriages and only daughter, but not my name.

It is two in the morning and my coffee has grown cold. I rub my eyes and turn off the computer.

My father's birthday is tomorrow—by which I mean today. Now I have a reason to go.

12

"We should have hired a limo," says Henry.

"Or at least had your car washed," I reply, peering through the smeared windscreen. A fallen leaf, trapped beneath the wiper blades, has been there since last autumn.

We are waiting in a procession of prestige cars that is lined up at the pillared gates, where security guards are checking registration numbers and IDs. Bulked up with shaven heads, they look like ex-boxers or ex-cons. Nearby a camera crew has set up beside a broadcast van and a pretty TV reporter is doing a piece to the camera, touching her hair when the wind blows it across her face. And farther down the lane, a coterie of freelance photographers are perched on stepladders, aiming long lenses over the wall into the estate. Paparazzi.

"Are you sure you want to do this?" asks Henry.

"You didn't have to come."

"Are you kidding me! I wouldn't miss this for the world—a chance to meet the famous Edward McCarthy, the enigma, the riddle, the gangster."

"Don't call him a gangster."

"That's what *you* call him."

"I'm allowed. And I'm really only here to see my uncles."

"Who are known criminals."

"They spent time in prison. That doesn't mean they're—"

"Old lags?"

I give him a dirty look.

"I'm joking, OK?"

Someone raps hard on my window, startling me. I think it's going to be a security guard, but it's Martyn Fairbairn, the detective I met at Bankside Pier.

I lower the window.

Fairbairn looks bemused rather than annoyed. "We meet again. Mind telling me what you're doing here?"

"I've been invited."

His eyes squint and then widen again as the penny drops.

"You're related," he says, sounding surprised. "A niece?"

"Daughter."

"Wow! I wouldn't have picked that."

I want to explain that I haven't spoken to my father in years, but that's going to sound disingenuous when I'm showing up to his birthday party.

Fairbairn crosses his arms and cups his cheek in the attitude of a man nursing a toothache. I notice the police cars parked opposite the gates. A photographer is taking pictures of number plates. They will trace the vehicles and put names to faces.

"Does this have anything to do with Dylan Holstein's murder?" I ask.

"You tell me."

The queue is moving ahead of us. A security guard spots Fairbairn and comes swaggering towards us. The detective steps back and raises his hands, saying, "It's cool. We're old friends." And then to me: "Enjoy the party."

I hand over my license and the guard consults a tablet, flicking at the screen. He's wearing an earpiece and has a microphone attached to his wrist.

"How very James Bond," says Henry, who is enjoying this.

We are waved through and follow the car ahead along the crushed-gravel driveway, where men with glow sticks are directing drivers into parking spots. Ahead of us, a rambling house with a steepled outline is visible above the treetops. Once the car has stopped, I zip up my boots and check my makeup in the mirror. Henry is waiting for me, admiring the whitewashed seventeenth-century manor house, which has nine chimneys and a porte cochere covered in ivy. Although I never lived here, I know the house once belonged to Robert Baldlock, one of the wealthiest men in England, who started his career as a smuggler before moving into brewing and gambling and finally property speculation. My father likes that story because it parallels his own career.

The garden stretches all the way to the River Darent, past a tennis court, croquet green, swimming pool, and summerhouse. Two huge canvas marquees, joined by a covered walkway, have been erected on the grass near the pond. Unlit torches line the path and waiters and waitresses dressed in black and white are serving champagne.

I'm wearing my emerald jumpsuit with my ankle boots and a short black blazer. Semi-casual. Flattering.

"You didn't say it was formal dress," whispers Henry, who has spotted what other men are wearing.

"It was optional."

"I feel like a seagull among the penguins."

"You look fine." I hook my arm into his and we match our strides.

We are approaching the main house from the river side. The guests ahead of us are carrying gifts.

"And you said no presents," whispers Henry.

"That's what the invitation said."

"Well, nobody else read it."

"I'm his gift," I say, which makes Henry laugh.

I pick up a glass of bubbly from the first tray within reach and swallow it in two gulps before grabbing another.

"Are you self-medicating?"

"No."

"Well, slow down. You might have to rescue me."

"Why?"

"I'm marrying Edward McCarthy's only daughter. If he doesn't like me I could be sleeping with the fishes." He's doing his Marlon Brando impersonation from *The Godfather*.

"Not funny."

We are walking down a flower-bedecked tunnel that leads to the main marquee. Another corner of the garden has been transformed into a funfair, with a merry-go-round, a bouncy castle, and dodgem cars. There are kids everywhere, having their faces painted or queuing for a balloon animal.

The swell of voices is rising and washing over the lawn. I can feel eyes upon me. I'm like a butterfly caught in a glass jar, fluttering and tinkling against the sides.

"That's the Lord Mayor," whispers Henry. "And that guy hosts that TV show—the one about cars."

"Jeremy Clarkson?"

"No, not him. The short, gobby one."

We're standing under a huge oak tree, watching the other guests. Some of them I recognize from my childhood. Family friends. Business acquaintances. Others are perhaps from Constance's side of the family. The "chinless toffs" is what Uncle Finbar calls them. Altogether, it makes for a strange gathering—a melting pot of East End publicans, footballers, and bookmakers, mixing with B-list celebrities and minor aristocrats.

I'm on my fourth glass of champagne when someone yells my name. I turn to see a man charging towards me. Uncle Clifton is built like a rugby prop, with short legs and a barrel-shaped chest. I remember being carried to Highbury stadium on his broad shoulders and singing "We Are the Arsenal Boys" at the top of our lungs.

Now he picks me up and swings me around like I'm five years old again.

"Put me down. You're giving me a wedgie," I say.

"Oops. Sorry."

He plants me on my feet but doesn't let go of my hand. He's wearing a black cashmere overcoat with a brilliant scarlet lining and grinning like a Cheshire cat with yellow teeth from too many cigars and glasses of port.

"What a sight you are," he says in a thick cockney accent. "We figured you were persona non gratis, you know . . ."

"I'm a birthday surprise."

"Eddie will have an 'eart attack."

"This is my fiancé. Henry, this is my uncle Clifton."

He grabs Henry in a crushing handshake and pulls him nose to nose.

"I got questions. You vote Labour?"

Henry glances at me nervously. "Mostly."

"You good to yer dear old mum?"

"Yeah."

"You a Gooner?"

"A what?"

"A Gunners fan—the mighty Arsenal. Tell me you're not a Spud."

He means a Tottenham supporter.

"Chelsea," says Henry.

"Weak as piss!" says Clifton, pushing him away and turning to me. "Sure he's not a Doris Day fan?"

"Definitely not."

"Yeah, OK," Clifton concedes. "What's he do?"

"He fights fires."

"A water fairy."

Henry looks completely lost.

Meanwhile, Clifton bellows across the lawn so loudly that the string quartet stops playing and every head turns towards us.

"Hey, Daragh! Look what the cat dragged in!"

Uncle Daragh squints into the bright sunshine, holding up his hand to shield his eyes. He waves uncertainly.

"Come here, ya blind cunt," yells Clifton. "It's the girl."

Daragh leaves the conversation and begins making his way between shoulders. The music has started again. He is halfway across the lawn when he recognizes me and does a leap to the side, clicking the heels of his polished shoes. He's wearing an expensive suit but makes it look like a sack because of his strange body shape and Popeye-sized forearms.

I feel such a surge of joy that I skip into his arms and bury my face against his chest, feeling a button press into my cheek.

Daragh has always been my favorite. Growing up, I saw more of him than the others because he and my father are the closest in age and were inseparable until Daragh went to prison. According to the stories—the legends, the myths—Daragh was always the family enforcer, a violent, vindictive, boozing sociopath whose fists answered for him. I've never seen this side of him, not firsthand. Around children, Daragh has a lightness of spirit that defies his reputation. He played Santa Claus every Christmas and is an amateur magician who can conjure coins and sweets from behind ears and below ponytails and inside pockets.

He waltzes me around, holding my feet off the ground.

"You've made my day," he says before holding me at arm's length. "Give us a twirl."

"I'm not a performing monkey."

"Cheeky as one."

I introduce him to Henry. Daragh steps closer and lifts each of Henry's arms and does a slow circuit. I half expect him to kick his tires or ask to see the logbook.

"Bit of mileage on the clock," he says. "Is he secondhand?"

"He's new enough for me," I say.

I can see Henry getting annoyed.

Clifton interrupts. "Eddie doesn't know she's 'ere."

"Where is the flash cunty? He's the only one missing."

"The duchess wants to make an entrance."

I look around and ask about Finbar, the third of my uncles.

"Poppy will still be deciding what to wear," says Daragh. "Or she's herding grandkids."

"How many does he have?"

"Seven, with another on the way."

"Who is pregnant?"

"Katie."

"But she's only, what?"

"Nineteen. Pretty as a rose."

"I used to babysit her."

"That's what you buggers do, grow up," says Clifton. "And some of you become rozzers."

"You heard."

"Course we 'eard."

"I hope you won't hold it against me."

"Why would we? Some of my best mates are coppers."

"And worst enemies," adds Daragh. "Good and bad in any profession."

"Bent and straight," I say.

"That too." He grins. "How is your mother?"

"She doesn't know I'm here."

"That's very wise. I've been banged up with some of the most dangerous fucking criminals in this green and pleasant land, but your old lady frightens me more than any of 'em."

"She likes you."

"Yeah, well, I'm very likable."

My mother's relationship with my uncles has never been an issue—she loved them and they loved her, but their loyalties will always lie with my father.

More people have arrived and the noise level has risen. A few guests approach me, knowing my name. Every conversation seems to begin with, "I remember when you were . . ."

Suddenly, the music stops and a different tune strikes up, a string-led version of "Happy Birthday." People turn and face the house, where my father emerges from the French doors. His oiled hair is darker than I remember and he's dressed in a white suit that makes him look like Colonel Sanders. Constance is beside him in a matching white dress with a swooping neckline and elbow-length white gloves. They descend the steps arm in arm and walk along the flower-lined path to the marquee. Everybody is singing the song, belting out the final lines, before launching into "For He's a Jolly Good Fellow." When the cheers have faded, Edward McCarthy is swamped by guests and I lose sight of him.

"Wait 'ere," says Daragh. "I'll go get him."

"Let him enjoy his moment."

"Bollocks! This will make his fuckin' day."

He disappears into the throng, who are all recharging their glasses and lining up for food at the buffet. Clifton is deep in conversation with Henry, discussing firefighting and famous London buildings that have burned down, deciding which ones were accidents or insurance jobs. Clifton seems to have a suspiciously good knowledge.

Clifton's accent makes Henry sound like an Eton old boy, but he's not some illiterate wide boy. His nickname is "the bookkeeper" because of his head for dates and numbers. Each of my uncles has a particular skill set they have brought to the business. Daragh is the muscle, Clifton handles the books, and Finbar can talk the language of engines and "can hot-wire any motor from a Maserati to a mobile crane," according to my father.

Amid the general hubbub, I hear Constance complaining.

"You can't just drag him away—he was talking to the Lord Mayor . . . Let go of his arm. You're creasing his suit."

The crowd parts. My father scans the faces, wondering who he's supposed to be looking for. Finally his eyes come to rest on mine. Despite the sunbed sessions, the steam rooms, and his dye-darkened hair, he looks older. He *is* older.

He reaches out and touches my cheek as if wanting proof that I'm real.

"Hello," I say.

Then his knees buckle. Clifton catches him before he lands, and Daragh takes his other arm, holding him upright.

"Eddie, are you all right?" he asks.

"I'm fine."

He tries to shrug away the helpers, but wobbles again. They won't let him go.

"I think you should sit down," says Daragh.

Constance's hand has fluttered to her mouth and she keeps repeating, "What's wrong?"

"Get him a chair," Clifton shouts, telling everyone to stand back.

Daddy ignores the fuss and reaches out to me, wanting to keep me close.

"Too much excitement," he says.

"Too much sun," I add. "He should be wearing a hat."

"You're right. Let's get him inside," says Daragh.

A man with a gray cloud of hair forces his way between shoulders. Another face from my childhood—Dr. Carmichael, our family GP, who gave me every injection and inoculation and prescription.

He pushes Daragh to one side and puts his ear to my father's chest, asking for quiet. His hands are wrinkled and blotchy but still steady.

"OK, let's get him inside."

Daragh and Clifton take his arms. He protests, threatening to "deck both of you." Eventually they let him walk unassisted across the rose garden and up the steps to the French doors. He waves to guests as he goes, shaking hands and blowing kisses.

"Won't be long. Don't drink all the bloody bubbles before I get back."

Constance is suddenly next to me.

"This is your fault."

"What?"

"Why didn't you say you were coming . . . give us some warning?"

"You spent weeks badgering me."

"Yes, but I didn't think . . ."

We go to the library, where a couch is cleared of cushions and his white coat is removed. Dr. Carmichael tells everybody to leave.

"Not Philomena." Daddy tries to take my hand but I pull away.

The room has an upright piano littered with musical scores, old portraits on the walls, shelves lined with books, and a fireplace with an enormous grate. Above the mantelpiece, the propeller from an old-fashioned biplane has been polished and put on display.

Constance doesn't know what to do with herself. She lights a cigarette. Dr. Carmichael tells her to put it out. She looks at him angrily, but
her shiny forehead refuses to buckle.

"Where are his pills?" asks the doctor.

"I'll get them," says Constance.

"What pills?" I ask.

Dr. Carmichael is taking his pulse and temperature and listening
more closely to his heart. He is firing off questions about chest pains and
dizziness and nausea.

"What pills?" I ask again.

The doctor is about to speak, but Daddy stops him. "It's nothing."

"What's wrong with you?"

"I'm fine."

"Stop saying that," I snap.

Constance returns, clutching a small brown glass bottle. Dr. Carmichael shakes two pills into my father's hand, and I fill a water glass, but
Constance takes the jug from me, using her hip to nudge me aside. I'm
the visitor. She's the queen.

The pills are swallowed. Color returns to his cheeks.

"Let me look at you," he says, motioning me closer. "You're the spitting image of your mum. Did I ever tell you the story about—"

Before he can finish, the library door bangs open and Finbar charges
into the room as though he's rescuing a hostage. Daragh and Clifton are
trying to hold him back.

Finbar is the youngest and tallest of my uncles, with a shaved and
oiled scalp and a bushranger beard.

"Where is he?" he bellows.

"I'm 'ere, Fin," says my father. "Keep your pants on."

Finbar isn't satisfied until he has hugged my father and taken an
inventory. Daddy humors him and then tells everyone to get out and
"leave me alone with my daughter."

Finbar does a cartoon double take when he recognizes me. A
moment later, I'm hoisted off the ground and crushed in his arms,
smelling his aftershave and breath mints and something metallic like
Brasso.

My feet scrabble on the floor. Why do these men keep picking me up
like a ragdoll?

"Put me down."

"You'll have to arrest me first."

"I can arrange that."

Daddy looks at my uncles and sighs tiredly. "There's a free bar outside—what are you tossers doing 'ere?"

13

I am alone with my father for the first time since I was seventeen. He pours himself a drink from a varnished wooden cabinet with rows of elegantly shaped bottles. Single malts mainly with descriptors that sound like fairy-tale dwarfs. Creamy. Peaty. Grassy. Woody. Smoky.

"Should you be drinking?" I ask.

"It's my birthday."

He swallows and pours another. His pale face is puffy and strangely weather-beaten, with wrinkles that branch out from his eyes like tiny river deltas on a floodplain. He has always been a strong man, hardened by exercise and ambition, with a deep rumbling voice that makes everyone around him sound like they're inhaling helium.

"So, what's new?" he asks.

"Is that the best you can do?"

"I'm glad you came."

"What's wrong with you?"

"I'm getting old."

"Is there something wrong with your heart?"

"You broke it. Now it's fixed."

"Don't you *dare* guilt me."

The harshness in my voice seems to shock him. I take a seat on the sofa. He wants to sit next to me, but I point to a different chair.

"How is your mum?" he asks.

"Hating you is keeping her young."

He smiles wryly. "I have angina. Sounds like Angelina, doesn't it? I had a girlfriend called Angelina, lovely, she was. I used to take her to the pictures at the Hackney Empire. Double bill. Back row. She had really soft—"

"Daddy!"

"Hands," he says, grinning. "What did you think I was gonna say?"

"I *am* your daughter."

"I thought you'd resigned that commission."

"I tried. What's wrong with your heart?"

"Too many fags and full English breakfasts. My arteries are clogged. Should have seen it coming. Your granddad had a heart attack at fifty-two. It's in my whatsits, you know."

"Genes."

"Yeah, but you won't have to worry until you hit menopause."

"Thanks for the heads-up. When is the surgery?"

He gives me a noncommittal shrug.

"You are having the surgery?"

"Right now I'm busier than a one-legged arse kicker. This COVID-whatsit has put us months behind, plus the banks are up to their usual fuckery."

"You have three brothers. Delegate."

"They're not project managers. And if the banks get word of my condition, they could pull their loans." He takes the bottle of pills from the table and rattles them. "These things are the dog's bollocks: nitroglycerin. It's the same shit they use to blow stuff up, but in small doses it widens the arteries and nourishes the ticker. Know who discovered it?"

I shake my head.

"Alfred Nobel. Same geezer who gives out them prizes for science and medicine and world peace."

"How long can you delay the surgery?" I ask.

"Few months." He glances at the door. "Constance doesn't know. None of them do."

"Why are you telling me?"

"I've never been able to lie to you."

"That's a crock of shit."

He smiles sheepishly. "Constance would drive me crazy, and the boys would do something stupid." He is close to me now. He reaches out and tries to take my hand. This time I don't pull away. "This has to be our secret, OK? You can't tell anyone."

"Only if you promise to have the surgery."

"I will."

"And I need something else. A place to stay. Somewhere off the grid."

"What have you done?"

"Not for me. A friend."

"Doesn't Scotland Yard have safe houses?"

"She's not a witness. She's a victim of domestic abuse. The man who beat her up is a police officer who might still be looking for her."

"What's his name?"

"That's not important."

"If I'm going to help this woman . . ."

"Darren Goodall."

Recognition seems to flare in his eyes.

"Do you know him?" I ask.

He doesn't answer. "How long do you need a place?"

"Until he loses interest."

I feel a dull throbbing in my head—the beginnings of a hangover that can be curtailed by more champagne or a big glass of water or maybe food.

"Have the police spoken to you?" I ask.

"About what?"

"Dylan Holstein."

He looks at me blankly.

"Don't play dumb."

A sigh. A dismissive shrug. "He wrote a few bullshit stories about me."

"You dumped a truckload of building waste outside his house."

A smile. "I thought that was rather creative."

"He was found dead last night. Someone wrapped chains around his chest and weighted him down with breeze-blocks before throwing him in the river."

I am studying his face. It's like watching comedy and tragedy masks in Greek theater.

"What are you suggesting, Philomena?"

"The detective in charge of the investigation is outside your gate."

Daddy's eyebrows almost knit together, but just as quickly equanimity returns and his features soften.

"I know what people say about me, Phil, but most of the stories are apocryphal. This country is obsessed with gangsters, geezers, and guns. I blame Guy Ritchie."

"The director."

"He keeps making these violent fantasies about trigger-happy spivs with stupid names like Headlock Harry or Get Rich Raymond. They don't exist, Phil. They're make-believe. Some gangster films are half-decent. I quite liked *The Long Good Friday* and *Get Carter*, but the rest are no more realistic than watching those westerns where cowboys shoot Indians off horses from a hundred feet away or gunfighters out-draw each other in the street. These are fantasies, just like most of the stories they tell about this family. Yeah, we hijacked a few lorries. Stole the merch. Flogged stuff at markets—"

"You ran a protection racket. Extorted money from transport companies. Orchestrated industrial action. Sabotaged building sites."

"Yeah, yeah, OK, OK, but we never sold drugs or guns or desperate people. And we didn't take from those who couldn't afford to pay."

"Just like Robin Hood," I say sarcastically.

"Fair point."

He picks up his white suit jacket and gazes sorrowfully out the window at his party. "You never got to meet your great-gran. She raised me after my mum died when Dad was still in prison. She was a girl during the Great Depression. Years later, in her eighties, she was living in this lovely little terrace and had plenty of good nosh, but she still washed out empty margarine containers and kept scraps of soap, because she remembered what it was like to be poor and to be hungry." He is still at the window. "This sort of extravagance doesn't sit well with me."

"You could have fooled me."

"Constance organized this. It makes her happy."

I want to ask him why he didn't try harder to keep my mother happy, but that's a rabbit hole I don't want to disappear down.

"Did you bribe the local councillors?" I ask.

"What do you want from me—a confession?"

"An answer."

I get a look of reproach, followed by a sad smile. "Maybe you should stay out of this one, Phil. The police will sort it out."

"I *am* the police."

He gives a soft huff. Outside, the party is getting louder and guests are starting to dance.

"Do you wish I hadn't joined the Met?" I ask.

"I couldn't be prouder."

I make a scoffing sound.

"Cross my dodgy heart. I watched you graduate."

"What?"

"A mate snuck me into Hendon."

"When you say a mate . . . ?"

"I do have friends among the police."

"On your payroll?"

"Not all of your colleagues are bent."

"Only some of them."

He smiles, clearly enjoying the banter.

"I saw you marching in the front row. They gave you a special commendation for topping your class."

"I was equal top."

"Same, same." He waves his hand airily.

"Why didn't you make yourself known?" I ask.

"I didn't want to embarrass you."

I'm trying to work out how I feel. Conflicted. Annoyed. Gratified. Why should I care what he thinks? I haven't needed him for the last third of my life.

"Have the surgery," I say.

"I will."

"No, promise me. Don't delay. I'm getting married in September and you being dead would upset my seating plans."

His face lights up. "Married! Is he here?"

Suddenly I remember Henry. I left him outside. Alone. He probably thinks I've been kidnapped or that my family has staged an intervention. Daddy is marching towards the door.

"I want to meet him. Where are you hiding him?"

It's all an act, of course, but I make him wait while I knot his tie and smooth down his jacket.

"What do you think of this suit?" he asks.

"It makes me want to eat fried chicken."

"Yeah, that's what I told Constance."

I find Henry standing in the shrubbery, cupping his hands against a window as he peers inside. He has mud on his shoes and a leaf stuck in his hair.

"Are you trying to break in or escape?"

My voice startles him, but he looks relieved and a little flushed.

"Don't disappear like that," he says. "I thought your aunts were going to eat me."

"Did you get between them and the buffet?" I stand on tiptoes to kiss him. "Daddy wants to meet you."

"Why? What did you tell him? Is he angry?"

"Relax. He's not going to bite."

"It's not his bite I'm worried about."

Taking his hand, I pull him through the crowd, smiling and saying hello to people whose faces are familiar, but I have no idea of their names. There is something stilted and artificial about all this warmth and bonhomie. Eventually we're standing alongside Daddy, who is chatting to someone who looks like a soap actor.

I tap him on the shoulder. He turns. Beams.

Henry holds out his hand. "It's a pleasure to meet you, Mr. McCarthy."

Daddy ignores the outstretched palm and puts his arm around Henry's shoulder, pulling him closer. It looks like a wrestling hold.

"This is my future son-in-law," he announces to those within earshot. "He didn't ask my permission, of course, but I'll forgive him that."

A bottle of champagne is grabbed from a passing tray. Glasses are filled.

"Another toast," says Daddy. "To youth and beauty and love."

The words are repeated. Glasses are raised. Daddy still has his hand on Henry's shoulder, stopping him leaving. He leans closer and whispers, "A quiet word," into his ear. And then to everybody, "I need a few moments alone with Henry."

I follow them. Daddy turns. "Not you."

"But he's . . ."

"A big lad. He can speak for himself."

They fight their way to the edge of the crowd. I keep them in sight, watching from a distance as they circle to the far side of the pond and take a seat on a painted wooden bench, away from the music and the squeals of children on the funfair rides. Their lips are moving. I wish I knew what they were saying. Henry laughs. A good sign. He nods. Tilts his head. Gestures to the sky. Nods again. This is torture.

Later, when I ask Henry about the conversation, he is remarkably reticent and dismissive. We're in bed. We've made love. I roll on top of him, pin his arms, and demand that he tell me what was discussed.

"He talked about you."

"What did he say?"

"He said that you expected too much of people and you were destined to be disappointed, because nobody could live up to your ideals."

"Is that all?"

"He said he was scared of me."

"Why?"

"Because I'm going to become the most important person in your life—and if I fuck this up, if I make you sad, or if I crush your spirit, if I hold you back, I'll be making a huge mistake."

"He threatened you."

"No. He said I had to keep up with you, or you'd grow bored with me. He said that you were difficult and that you didn't take kindly to being corrected."

"That's not true!"

Henry smiles, his point proven.

"What else?"

"That's enough."

I squeeze his wrists. "I want to know what he said."

"He said you were ticklish and giggled like a four-year-old."

"I do not."

Henry suddenly lifts me up and spins me over on the bed, blowing a raspberry into my belly button, making me laugh so hard that I threaten to pee my pants.

14

Tempe seems different today. Brighter. Less burdened. She's wearing worn jeans and a simple white blouse with her hair spilling over her shoulders.

"You look happy."

"I am," she replies, sliding into the bench seat opposite me.

The café is full of Monday-morning customers, mothers and nannies, some pushing prams, others in gym gear. She has something to tell me but makes me wait until we've ordered. Instead, we talk about my mother and her foibles. How persnickety she is about hanging washing so that she doesn't leave peg marks on the fabric. And how she arranges her bills in order of the due date and doesn't pay them until the last possible moment.

"She joined Instagram and I'm the only person she follows," I say. "And her handbag contains absolutely everything—wet wipes, painkillers, sachets of sugar, spare batteries."

"And a lint roller," laughs Tempe. "Who uses a lint roller?"

"Well, it won't be for much longer. I've found you somewhere to stay."

I describe the one-bedroom flat in Wandsworth, which is due to be renovated but perfectly livable, according to my father.

"You'll need furniture."

"And I insist on paying rent."

"Whatever you can afford."

Tempe reaches across the table and takes my hand. It's unexpected and intimate. "I also have news."

She pauses, heightening the suspense. "I've found you a wedding venue. It's not far from St. Mary's and is available on September the fourth. A Saturday."

"Where?"

"Milford Barn?"

"But that place is booked out until sometime next century. I checked."

"Not any longer."

"What happened?"

"A cancelation."

"But we're not on any waiting list."

"You are now. And you're first. The place is yours, but they need a deposit by Thursday. Two thousand pounds. Is that too much?" She looks at me hopefully. "Did I do well?"

I'm grinning. "You're amazing. I can't believe you managed to get Milford Barn. The manager almost laughed at me when I called her."

"It can seat two hundred guests, but you can have less. The church is only half a mile away."

"St. Mary's. How did you know?"

"You told me."

"Right. Yes. I forgot."

My mind is racing ahead. I have less than three months to prepare. I should send out save-the-date cards and arrange a photographer and a florist.

"I took the liberty of booking Robbie Honey to do the flowers," says Tempe. "And I'm putting out feelers to see if Matthew Voss can take the wedding pictures. I was hoping to get Alexi, but he's busy."

"Alexi?"

"Lubomirski. He did Harry and Meghan's wedding photographs."

"How do you know these people?"

"It's my job."

"But the cost—we can't afford . . ."

"It won't be expensive, I promise. They'll do it for me."

"When you said you could help . . . I didn't think . . . or expect."

Tempe laughs and reaches into her shoulder bag for her laptop. Shifting our coffee cups to one side, she opens it on the table.

"Here are some sample invitations."

We go through the options, choosing colors and typefaces. It's like we've been planning this all our lives, yet a small doubt snags on my happiness. The cost. I don't want to ask my father for help, because he will try to take over and arrange something ridiculously grand like his birthday party.

"What's wrong?" asks Tempe.

"Nothing."

"Are you having second thoughts?"

"Not about the wedding. I have to talk to Henry. This is happening so quickly."

"I can slow down."

"No, no, you keep going." I glance at my phone. "I promised Henry we'd take Archie to the park."

"Archie?"

"His little boy. A previous marriage."

"You're going to be a stepmum?"

"I know. Instant family."

Tempe puts her laptop away and gets ready to leave.

"I haven't even asked about you," I say. "How are you?"

"Another time," she replies. "This was nice."

"Better than nice. You should come to dinner. Meet Henry. He's a great cook."

"I'd like that."

We are standing outside the café. Tempe checks her phone.

"Did Darren Goodall ever talk about his former girlfriends?" I ask.

"Not really."

"One of them died in some sort of accident. She fell from a cliff."

Tempe doesn't react. I want to ask her if she thinks Goodall is capable of killing someone, but I don't want to hear the answer.

"He's looking for me, you know," she says absentmindedly.

"How do you know?"

"He doesn't let people go . . . not unless he's finished with them."

She glances past me, as though expecting Goodall to be watching us.

"Let's talk later," I say, moving to kiss her cheek. At the last moment, she turns her face and our lips meet. The contact is only brief, but it surprises me and I pull away.

"I'm sorry," says Tempe. "That's something we do in our family—kiss on the lips. Did it shock you?"

"I wasn't prepared, that's all."

"Some people kiss on one cheek, some on two cheeks; I kiss on the lips. Only friends. I won't do it again, if you . . ."

"No, it's fine."

"Call me when you've talked to Henry."

"I will."

15

"Are you allowed to be friends with this woman?" asks Henry as he pushes Archie on a swing.

"What do you mean?"

"Isn't she a witness or a victim or something like that?"

"She didn't give a statement. No charges were laid."

"It still seems odd—befriending someone you rescued."

We're on the west side of Clapham Common in a playground that has colorful wooden tunnels and slides. I'm sitting on the adjoining swing to Archie, who has made it a competition about who can go highest.

"I'm winning. I'm winning," he cries breathlessly.

"You're too good for me."

"Are you trying?"

"My hardest."

Henry has gone quiet about the wedding news. I thought he'd share my excitement but his first question was about the cost.

"We don't have to invite many people," I say defensively.

He makes a humming sound. Henry thinks I'm terrible with money, which isn't true. I spend almost nothing on clothes compared to Roxanne. Yes, we have a big mortgage, but interest rates are low and we're both working. If his child support payments weren't so generous compared to most fathers—and if he didn't spoil Archie rotten because he feels guilty. I know I shouldn't think things like this, but Roxanne manipulates him and Henry refuses to stand up to her.

The silence has gone on too long.

"Maybe it doesn't mean as much to you this time," I say.

"What do you mean?"

"The wedding, the reception, the honeymoon. You've been there, done that, bought the souvenir. It's not so important."

"That's not fair."

"You don't seem very excited."

"I am excited."

"Wow, that sounded really enthusiastic," I say sarcastically.

"It just seems so . . ."

"What?"

"Roxanne and I had this huge wedding, with classic cars and hundreds of guests who gave us presents. I feel guilty about making them go through it all again."

"We won't ask for gifts."

"People will bring them anyway."

"Which is not our fault."

"Yes, but we'll be pledging to love each other till death do us part—and my friends will be watching, thinking, 'Yeah, that's what he said last time.'"

"Is it the same as last time?" I ask, raising an eyebrow.

"No, of course not. I'm marrying *you*. And it's forever."

"Good answer."

Archie interrupts. "Higher, Daddy, higher."

Henry does as instructed, but I have stopped swinging. A little girl is standing to the side, waiting her turn. I hold the swing steady as she slides onto the seat.

"Do you need a push?"

"No, I'm a big girl," she says, kicking her legs.

Archie immediately wants to copy her, because he won't be beaten by a girl, but he doesn't have the coordination and immediately falls behind.

"Time for a snack," says Henry, who offers Archie a piggyback to our picnic blanket, which is set out on the grass. I open a Tupperware container with pieces of cut-up apple and grapes, most of which Henry will eat.

My phone pings. It's a message from Tempe.

Have you told him? What did he say?

I ignore her.

"It's the first time for me," I say to Henry.

"Pardon?"

"Getting married. I'm only doing it once."

16

On Wednesday morning I take the train to Camden Town to visit my mother. I'm on the Northern line pulling out of Goodge Street station when a man in a woolen hat steps into the carriage and takes a seat next to me.

I glance at the empty seats opposite, annoyed that he's chosen to sit so close. Then I realize who it is.

"Relax," says Darren Goodall. "I only want to talk."

The composition of his face surprises me—his thin lips, pale cheeks, and darkly oiled hair. I try to move away, but he grips my forearm. I want to backhand him with my fist, but I've made that mistake before.

The train doors close. Goodall takes a toothpick from his jacket pocket and sucks on one end. An old smoker's trick. I can smell his sweat through his deodorant.

"Where is she?"

I feign ignorance.

"I know you're in touch with her."

"With all due respect, sir, you should leave her alone."

"She took something of mine—I want it back."

"What did she take?"

"It's personal."

A vein seems to be pulsing in his temple. He takes a breath. Sighs. Rubs his eyes.

"I can make things very difficult for you."

"I've done nothing wrong."

"That won't matter."

He smiles and spreads his knees, touching mine. I want to move farther away.

"She was a lousy fuck, you know."

I don't respond.

"You look like you know your way around a bedroom." He cups his genitals. "I'd fuck you if you asked me nicely."

"I'm not sure your wife would approve."

"You don't need to bring her into this."

"Why? Does she count for so little?"

I stand and walk down the carriage, where three young men in England shirts are lounging, wide-kneed, shoulders hunched, studying their phones. The train jerks as it slows and I stumble into one of them, apologizing. I can hear Goodall laughing.

As soon as the doors open, I step off and duck between shoulders of people waiting on the platform. Without looking, I know that Goodall is behind me. He follows me up the escalator and through the ticket gate. I'm hoping there's a cab outside.

He's close. "Tell her she's getting nothing more from me."

"What does that mean?"

"She's a parasite."

I want to ask another question, but he's turned away. My phone vibrates. It's a message from Tempe. I suddenly wish I'd had the presence of mind to record the conversation with Goodall so I'd have proof, but the moment has passed.

My mother, Rosina, was born, baptized, confirmed, educated, and married within a mile of here, and only escaped when she and Daddy moved to Ilford before I was born. After the divorce, she returned to Camden like a migratory bird, and has been here ever since.

Her father, my grandfather Leonardo, had a barbershop overlooking Camden Lock for thirty years. When he retired, he gave it to Mum, who turned it into Belle Curls, a beauty salon squeezed between a liquor store and an Afghani grocer, in a brightly painted parade of shops. The front window is plastered with posters advertising facials, peels, lash lifts, and henna brows.

Normally I love visiting the salon, but my stomach is still churning over my meeting with Goodall. I should warn Tempe that he's looking for her. If he can find me, he can find her. I stop at a flower barrow at the markets and choose six stems from the riot of carnations, daffodils, tulips, roses, and dahlias that are crammed into zinc buckets. The aging florist wraps the bouquet in cellophane and sends his regards to Rosina, mentioning her name almost wistfully. She could have any number of suitors if she made herself available.

The bell rings above me as I enter and every head turns in my direction. Three gowned women are sitting on pink chairs having their hair washed, tinted, or blow-dried.

"Look who it is," yells Mercedes, a large West Indian stylist, who is my mother's business partner. She has a musical laugh and the softest breasts in the world.

"Come say hello, baby," she says, pressing me to her chest.

"Is mum here?"

"Having a fag."

"I thought she'd given up."

"Another false alarm."

I put the flowers on the counter near the cash register.

"Are they for us?"

"Of course."

The other employee is Lauren, the colorist, who is about my age but dresses like she's fifteen and dancing in the mosh pit of a Justin Bieber concert. Every time I see her she has a new hairstyle that she's copied from TikTok or YouTube.

The salon has a small kitchen and storeroom that leads to a rear courtyard, where my mother is seated on a low brick wall with a cigarette in her lips and a phone to her ear.

"Just two more weeks," she says. "The end of the month."

Seeing me, she drops the cigarette, crushing it under her pumps, and rapidly ends the phone call.

"Hello, gorgeous girl," she says, smiting my cheekbones with glancing blows from her own. We are roughly the same height, with the same heart-shaped face and wavy hair, although hers has been tinted so many different colors that I doubt she remembers the natural one.

I take a seat next to her. "Who was on the phone?"

She makes a dismissive sound and runs her fingers through my hair. "Who cut this?"

"You did."

"Not recently."

"It's fine."

"Nothing but split ends and flyaways. I can squeeze you in."

"Next time. Who was on the phone?"

She makes a clicking sound, as though scolding me. "We're behind on the rent. The landlord wants us to settle up now."

"How much?"

"It's not your problem?"

"How much do you owe?"

"Seven thousand pounds."

The amount shocks me into silence. "What will happen if you don't pay?"

"We'll lose the salon."

"But you've been here for . . ."

"Thirty-eight years if you count the barbershop."

"I could ask—"

"It's not Henry's concern."

"I was going to say Daddy."

Her features rush to the center of her face.

"I won't take a penny from that man."

"He didn't give you enough in the divorce."

"I got what I wanted."

"He can afford to—"

"How would you know?" She doesn't wait for me to answer. "Have you seen him?"

I contemplate lying, but she'll know when I send out my wedding invitations.

"I went to his birthday party. He was turning sixty."

Her head is shaking from side to side. "You're a police officer. You can't afford to get involved with him. He and his brothers are . . . are."

"Criminals?"

"Gangsters."

"Those things happened a long time ago."

Her whole body seems to vibrate with rage. "Your father is a cheat, a liar, and a womanizer."

"You loved him once."

"I hate him now."

"Other divorced parents learn to get along."

"Bully for them. Let me tell you something. A mother's heart is like her womb—it will stretch to make room for you. But a man's heart is made of stone. He may say he loves you. He may say that you're welcome in his house. But he is a blasphemer and a cheat."

"I want him to be at my wedding."

"God will strike him down if he ever sets foot in a church."

"I don't think the Anglicans mind so much about divorce."

Now she's even angrier. It's bad enough that Henry isn't a Catholic, but if Edward McCarthy walks me down the aisle, I'll be making a mockery of my faith.

"I won't go," she says adamantly. "I'm not going to sit in a church with that man or sit at the bridal table or listen to him make a wedding speech."

"In which case, I won't get married. I'll keep living in sin. Would that make you happy? And when I have babies they'll be bastards."

"Don't use that language around me," she says, annoyed at being wedged between her faith and her stubbornness.

"You do realize that I'm marrying a divorcé," I say.

"I'm not happy about that either."

"But you like Henry."

She stands and brushes dust from her bottom, refusing to argue with me. In *her* perfect world, I would have married some childhood sweetheart, a good Catholic boy, who kept me pure until the honeymoon and kept me pregnant until my womb fell out. And if I did have to work, I'd be a schoolteacher or a nurse or a beautician, not a police officer. That's why I don't talk about my job. She doesn't need to hear how I "blue light" around London, knocking on strange doors and grappling with criminals and drunks.

Although she missed the Second World War by a generation, she possesses exactly the kind of long-suffering spirit and stoicism that would have served her well. Keeping calm and carrying on is what my mother does best. She complains, of course—most stoics do—about the weather, graffiti, speed cameras, parking wardens, traffic, and the price of eggs, but mostly about my father.

"How is Tempe?" I ask, wanting to change the subject.

"She's trying very hard to be liked."

"In what way?"

"If I make her a cup of tea or give her a biscuit, it's the *best* tea and the *best* biscuit ever. The room is perfect. Her bed is perfect. You're perfect."

"Me?"

"She's always asking questions—wanting to know everything about you."

"Well, I've found her somewhere to stay. She'll be moving out in a few days."

I don't mention my father for fear of setting her off again. Hate gets her up in the morning and gives her energy and is so deeply ingrained, she would set fire to her own happiness if she could burn him as well. It's like Socrates said: from the deepest desire comes the deadliest hate.

17

Tempe checks through the peephole and undoes the deadlock and security chain, which my mother never bothers to latch. She ushers me inside and quickly shuts the door, hooking the chain into place.

"Are you OK?"

"Fine."

"Did something happen?"

"No."

We talk in the sitting room, which my mother refers to as "the parlor," making the place sound grander than a two-bedroom flat overlooking the railway lines that lead north from Euston station.

On the coffee table I notice an open sketchbook with a half-finished drawing done in charcoal. A portrait.

"That looks like me," I say, moving closer.

Tempe quickly closes the sketchbook.

"Can I see it?"

"No."

"Is it me?"

"Sort of."

"What does that mean?"

"I was doing it from memory."

"Please let me see."

She is holding the sketchbook against her chest but lets me prize it free. I open the page. The portrait is stunning. The eyes and ears and mouth are done, but the hair isn't finished. I'm amazed at how few lines or smudges she has needed to capture me.

I turn another page and find another partially finished drawing. My eyes seem to stare back at me in monochrome.

"Don't look at those," she says. "I had a few false starts."

These aren't portraits but fragments. My eyes. My ears. My nose. It's as though Tempe has broken down my face into separate parts and practiced each one before putting them together.

"I wanted to give you something . . . for the wedding . . . if it's good enough," she says anxiously.

"These are beautiful," I whisper.

"I was going to ask you to sit for me, but I thought you might say no, and people never sit still enough. They fidget and talk."

"How many hours does it take?"

"Depends on how quickly I draw." She laughs nervously and takes the book from me. "It's a hobby."

"It should be more. You're very good."

"Did you want to talk about the wedding?" she asks.

"No. Something else."

For a moment all is still, and Tempe looks at me so expectantly that I contemplate not telling her.

"I saw Darren Goodall today."

I expect to see fear in her eyes, but instead I see acceptance or inevitability.

"Was he angry?"

"He says you took something from him."

"Nothing I wasn't owed."

"What does that mean?"

She shakes her head.

"If you took something—"

"I took what belonged to me," she says again, more adamantly. Her eyebrows lift. "You didn't tell him where I am."

"No, of course not. And he'd be stupid to approach you." I'm trying to sound confident. "But we have to be careful."

"I am," she says confidently. "And you'll teach me how to protect myself."

If only that were enough.

We talk about the flat in Wandsworth. Uncle Clifton is arranging to put the gas and electricity under a company name so the bills can't be traced back to Tempe.

"You should avoid registering for anything. Don't take out a phone plan or change the address on your driver's license. Do you have a car?"

"No."

"Good. Be careful of Uber accounts and delivery services. Pay cash where possible, and avoid withdrawing money from the same ATM."

"Why?"

"It creates patterns that can be traced."

We're now in the kitchen drinking tea from mugs and sitting on high stools, our knees almost touching. With her hair pinned up and her head tilted at an arrogant angle, she looks almost like a boy, but the roundness of her bosom and long dark eyelashes are unmistakably womanly.

"Why won't he let you go?" I ask. "Is he in love with you?"

"He thinks he owns me."

Tempe is toying with the tag of a teabag, which is solidifying on a saucer between us.

"Were you in love with him?" I ask.

She crinkles her nose. "How can you tell?"

I laugh. "Oh, you know."

"How?" she asks, and I realize she's being serious.

"Surely you've been in love."

"Me? No. I'm a sucker for romantic movies. I'm a Richard Curtis junkie. *Love Actually. Notting Hill. Four Weddings and a Funeral.* But stuff like that doesn't happen in real life—not to me."

"One day it will," I say, but it sounds too easy and neat. "He abuses her too," I say. "His wife, I mean. She's been treated in hospital."

Tempe shrugs. "Pain gets him off."

"And you accepted that?"

"Not really, but he seemed to enjoy it."

She must see the look of horror on my face.

"I could have stopped him," she says defensively. "But he seemed to like those things, and I wanted to make him happy."

"Women shouldn't have to be subjugated or brutalized to make men happy."

"We all make sacrifices."

"I don't."

"Really?" Her eyebrow is raised. "Who makes the most important decisions, you or Henry?"

"We make them together."

"Who compromises the most? Who apologizes the quickest? Who does most of the housework? Who gets to have the most fun? Whose career is more important?"

"Don't make this about me," I say, annoyed that she's twisted the conversation to avoid answering my questions.

I can't be friends with someone who willingly chooses to be a victim. At the same time, Tempe isn't looking for sympathy or complaining that life has failed her. She is like an animate riddle, a bundle of contradictions that has to be untangled and rewrapped onto a spool, but it's not my job to make her whole.

18

Imogen Croker's parents live in a small village on the outskirts of Cambridge that appears to be surrendering field by field and farm by farm to the encroaching city. A woman answers the door. She is dressed in a simple skirt and blouse with a navy cardigan buttoned once. She opens the door widely and smiles, asking about my journey. I follow her along a hallway into an interior that feels closed up and claustrophobic despite the high ceilings.

"Are you a detective?" she asks.

"No."

"But you're with the police."

"I'm in uniform, but not today."

She tells me her name is Lydia and calls me Constable McCarthy even when I suggest first names.

We have reached a sitting room, where the sunlight from the window is so bright it creates a shaft that feels solid where it hits a faded woven rug. I notice a figure in a chair, watching TV, almost unseen. He has white-gray hair and arthritic hands and seems to be dissolving into his armchair or growing out of it.

The volume is turned down on a wildlife documentary where penguins are marching across an icy wasteland.

"That's my father. He has dementia. Are you all right, Pop?"

The old man stirs, fixing me with his rheumy eyes. "There are no polar bears in Antarctica."

"But they have penguins," I reply.

He nods sagely, as though we have settled an argument.

Lydia takes me to a darkly varnished dining table, where scrapbooks and photo albums are set out for my inspection. She had insisted I come at two o'clock, because her husband would be out, she said.

"Richard gets upset when I talk about Imogen. He thinks we should move on, but I can't forget." She has a box of tissues at her right elbow, but I see no sign of tears. "Imogen was his favorite, you see—our only daughter. I know a parent shouldn't have favorites, but she was very easy to love. That's why he won't talk about her. It hurts too much."

Without prompting she begins telling me about Imogen, describing her childhood, her personality, her foibles, using photographs to illustrate her stories. I want to get to her death, but I can see how much pride she takes in telling me about her daughter.

Gently, I nudge her forward, asking her how Imogen met Darren Goodall.

"She was barely out of school. A babe in the woods. He was a police officer—a grown man. He was working on the door of a nightclub, moonlighting as a bouncer. He took down Imogen's phone number and called her later. She thought it was romantic—a 'meet-cute' story like you see in the movies."

It sounds creepy, I think, but say nothing.

"Did you like him?" I ask.

"I thought he was too old for her."

"Is that all?"

"He seemed charming. Ambitious. Polite. Imogen was a bit of a wild child and we thought he might settle her down, but he was always quite controlling. I think she found it appealing at first, having a man who wanted to choose her clothes and who treated her like a princess. But after a while he began complaining about her friends and isolating her from us. He decided where she went and who she saw. Slowly, he undermined her confidence and crushed her spirit. He stole her spark."

"The journalist Dylan Holstein was looking into her death," I say.

"Such a lovely man. So sad what happened."

"Have the police been to see you?"

She nods. "A Detective Fairbairn. He took some letters and papers away."

"What papers?"

"From the inquest."

"The coroner found that Imogen's death was an accident."

"He was wrong," she says defiantly.

"I read his findings. According to witnesses she slipped and fell."

"*One* witness, you mean. The same witness who came to the inquest with a barrister and refused to answer questions about his statement."

"Darren Goodall."

"We don't use his name in this house."

She tugs a tissue from the box and bunches it in her fist. Her knuckles are white.

"Do you know how many times we've heard from him since Imogen died?" She forms a zero with her thumb and forefinger. "All our communications are through his lawyer. We are sent warning letters, threatening us, if we keep talking about her death to the media or attempting to have it reinvestigated. Either that, or he claims we owe him money."

"What money?"

"Imogen had a life insurance policy as part of our family trust. My father set it up years ago." She motions to the old man watching TV. "I know he doesn't look like much, but he created the biggest frozen-food company in Europe."

"How much was the insurance policy worth?"

"Half a million pounds. And there were trust payments that were due on her twenty-first birthday."

"But she and Goodall weren't married."

"He produced a will, claiming that she left everything to him, but I talked to Imogen two days before she died. She wanted to break off their engagement, but she was frightened of telling him."

"What do you think happened?"

"I think he killed her."

"Based on what evidence?"

"His own words."

"Are you saying he confessed?"

"No. He lied."

Lydia opens a photo album and shows me a picture of her daughter and Darren Goodall, side by side at a restaurant table. Each has a glass of champagne and they are resting their heads together as Goodall takes the selfie, holding the camera above their heads.

She points to Imogen's right hand, which sports a sapphire ring.

"It belonged to my great-grandmother," says Lydia. "She passed it on to her eldest daughter when she came of age, and my mother gave it to me, and I gave it to Imogen on her eighteenth birthday. She wore it everywhere."

"I still don't understand."

"She was wearing the ring on the day she died. But when they found her body at the base of the cliffs, it was gone."

"Could it have fallen off?"

Lydia rocks her head from side to side. "Imogen was so stressed that she'd started binge eating and purging. Her fingers were swollen. She was planning to give back Darren's engagement ring but couldn't get it off her finger."

"Are you suggesting that Darren Goodall pushed her off Beachy Head and stole the sapphire ring?"

"They said that Imogen's finger was broken in the fall, but he almost ripped it off. Everything that followed was pure theater—him sobbing over her body, playing the grieving fiancé."

"He suffered hypothermia."

"My daughter died."

"Was Goodall asked about the sapphire ring?"

"He said she lost it days earlier, but she was wearing it that morning when she left the house."

"Is it valuable?"

Lydia opens a folder. Inside is an insurance valuation with a photograph attached. The ring is described as a Ceylon sapphire—swimming-pool blue—surrounded by fourteen rose-cut diamonds on a silver band. It was valued at eighteen thousand pounds.

When Goodall followed me onto the Northern line train, he said that Tempe had taken something from him. Could this be what he meant? It wouldn't prove that Goodall murdered Imogen, but it would expose him as a liar and undermine his story about how she died.

"Did Goodall get any money from Imogen's trust?" I ask.

"Richard negotiated a settlement rather than lose it all in legal fees."

"How much?"

Lydia hesitates, uncomfortable talking about money.

"Fifty thousand pounds."

The front door opens. Keys are dropped on a table. A young man walks past us into the kitchen. Mid-twenties with a shock of black hair and eyes the same blue as Imogen's, he doesn't acknowledge me. He takes a jug of orange juice from the fridge and drinks from the spout, wiping his mouth with the back of his sleeve.

Lydia Croker doesn't admonish him. He's in the doorway staring at me.

"Who are you?"

"Be polite, Jared," says Lydia.

"I'm a police officer," I explain.

He rolls his eyes at his mother. "Don't you get tired of talking about her?"

She doesn't answer. He grunts and shakes his head before walking past us, along the hallway, and out the front door again.

"Where are you going?" she shouts.

"Out."

"Will you be home for dinner?"

"I don't know."

The door closes.

Lydia gazes at me sadly. "My son."

19

An hour later, I pull up at the large electric gates and press the intercom at my father's house. There are no queues today or security guards or waiting paparazzi.

"Whatever you're selling, we're not buying," brays Constance, irritated at the interruption.

"It's me. Philomena."

"Oh!" she squeaks. "I didn't recognize your car."

"Is he home?" I ask.

"No, he's on-site today."

There is a long pause. I can picture Constance weighing up her options, unsure if I'm family or police. There's a metallic click and the gates begin to slide open. I follow the single-lane asphalt driveway to the main house, which looks very different today without the crowds and fairground rides. The marquees have been taken down, but I can see the discolored turf and muddy pathways left behind. Two gardeners are pruning the hedges and replanting a damaged flower bed.

Constance opens the door as my finger hovers over the bell. She looks immaculate, as always, her clothes casual yet expensive. Breathless with enthusiasm, she brushes her cheeks against mine and trails her hand down my arm, loosely holding my wrist like we're girlfriends.

"If I tell him you're here, he might come home early," she says, taking a mobile from the pocket of her jeans.

I wander into the library, half listening to her whispered conversation. My father has a large antique desk with a leather insert. A laptop is open. The screen dark. I press the space bar. The screen lights up and asks me for a password. How do I make it go dark again? I close the lid.

Footsteps. Constance appears in the doorway.

"He wants to show you Hope Island."

I glance at my phone. It will take me forty minutes in traffic at this hour, but I'm here to ask for favors. Constance walks me to my car and tucks both hands into the back pockets of her jeans.

"I wanted to thank you," she says.

"What for?"

"Convincing Edward to have the surgery."

"I don't think it was my doing."

"You coming to his birthday—and the wedding—it's given him a new lease on life. He's almost his old self again."

The word "almost" carries more weight than I want to bear. Maybe he's better this way—a changed man. Constance stands and waves as I navigate the driveway, staying in my mirrors until I reach the main gate.

On the drive through Dartford and Greenwich, I calculate the extra numbers involved if I invite the McCarthy clan. It can't just be my father. My uncles and aunts and cousins will expect invitations. I take the Blackwall Tunnel beneath the Thames and turn east toward Canning Town. Hope Island is visible from a mile away—a forest of cranes and newly constructed buildings, rising above the old wharfs and rows of tenements and soot-blackened warehouses. It's not actually an island but an isthmus that hangs from the northern bank of the Thames like a teardrop earring.

The site office is a prefabricated building with muddy metal stairs and rows of hard hats and high-vis vests hanging on hooks. I sign a register and am escorted by a foreman in a red vest, whose heavy leather work boots are permanently curled at the toes and stained with dirt. He drives a golf cart, pointing out various projects as we weave between machinery and piles of metal formwork, girders, and pipes. Some of the office blocks have already been bought or leased by major companies or arts organizations who are advertising their new premises on billboards.

We reach one of the finished buildings, which has tape crisscrossing the large plateglass windows on the lower floor. The surrounding garden is being landscaped with sandstone blocks and rolls of turf. Somebody wolf whistles and a dozen workmen turn to look at me.

"Really?" I want to ask. "Is that still a thing?"

I know what my mother would say: "Enjoy the attention, Philomena, because one day they stop whistling."

"Top floor," says the foreman, pointing to a lift.

I should have known the slum-dog millionaire would take the penthouse. I press the top button. The doors close and I'm shot upwards at stomach-dropping speed. When they open again, I'm looking at an empty reception desk and chairs still wrapped in plastic. I follow the sound of voices until I reach an office. A receptionist is seated outside.

"He won't be long."

She shows me to a conference room that has a long table and a dozen chairs, with notepads and jugs of water and glasses set out for a meeting. The walls are covered with artists' impressions of the finished development, and at the end of the room a large table has a scaled model of Hope Island. The detail is astonishing, showing all the buildings and open spaces, right down to tiny plastic figures of joggers and cyclists on the river path and diners sitting at outdoor cafés.

I pick up and replace a tree that has fallen over.

"You always did like playing with dolls' houses," says my father. He's standing in the doorway. "Remember you had that wooden one? It took up 'alf your bedroom."

"You spoiled me."

"I can see that."

He steps closer. I'm unsure if I should hug him. Are we there yet? Avoiding the decision, I walk to the far side of the boardroom table, where floor-to-ceiling windows provide spectacular views along the Thames. We're almost at the same height as a passenger jet making its final approach to London City Airport. I can see two pilots in the cockpit. Farther west, the towers of Canary Wharf are silhouetted against the afternoon sun, and directly across the river, the O2 arena looks like a half-buried naval mine.

"What do you think?" he asks.

"Does it matter?"

"I lie awake at night wondering if this is the right thing."

"Why?"

He points below us. "You see all those apartment buildings, next to the water?"

I nod.

"That's the Royal Docks. The Luftwaffe tried to bomb it out of existence during the war. I grew up about 'alf a mile from 'ere. We had this two-up, two-down terrace with an outside privy and a lane at the back for the night soil cart. I shared a bed with Daragh for most of my childhood. Finbar and Clifton slept in an annex that Dad built."

I've heard this story before, his creation myth.

"Sometimes I look at all these new developments and think that we're burying the past."

"You said they were slums."

"Yeah, but they were our slums." His fingers touch the glass. "The people I grew up with can't afford to live in the places I build. I'm helping push proper Londoners out of London."

"What does Daragh say?"

"He thinks I'm soft in the head. He says that we didn't change London. It changed by itself. People have always complained about development. They whinged about South Bank and the Barbican and Canary Wharf."

"Why don't you build more social housing? You could give something back."

"The wealthy don't want to live next to the poor."

"That's not an excuse."

"I know."

Below us, a crane swings a girder across the skeletal framework of a building, lowering it into the outstretched arms of a dozen men, who are making sure it slots into place.

"The flat in Wandsworth will be ready by Tuesday. There won't be a name on the lease."

We walk back to his office where the keys are waiting on his desk.

I thank him. Pausing. Faltering.

"The other day—at your birthday party—you recognized the name Darren Goodall."

Dismissively. "He was all over the news."

"Is that the only reason?"

He makes a clucking noise.

"If he was bent, would you tell me?"

"No."

I want to argue. He smiles sadly. "It's safer that way."

"I need another favor," I say.

His eyebrows almost meet. "Two in one decade."

"It's not for me," I say. "Mum is going to lose the salon. She owes money to the landlord."

"How much?"

"Seven thousand pounds."

He takes a checkbook from the same drawer.

"She won't take it from you," I say, and immediately recognize the hurt in his eyes.

"How, then?" he asks.

"We have to think of another way."

"I could have it delivered in a brown paper bag."

I almost say, "Could you?" but realize that he's joking.

"That's not how things are done these days," he says.

"Perhaps you could wire transfer it from your Swiss bank account."

Now I'm the one who's joking, but not entirely.

"I'll work something out," he says.

"Is that a promise?"

He holds up his little finger and I flash back to being four years old and making pinkie promises in our back garden, where he would squeeze himself into my Wendy house and drink pretend tea made from grass clippings and water from the hose.

He's such a charming old bugger. He's like one of those animals that looks harmless, even cuddly—a polar bear or an elephant seal or an owl—but behind those big, intelligent eyes and wide, welcoming face, there will always be the mind of a predator.

20

Henry has three days off, and we've driven north to visit his parents in Hertfordshire. Henry's father is an Anglican vicar, who is married to the perfect vicar's wife, and they both regard Roxanne as the perfect daughter-in-law who gave them the perfect grandchild. I, therefore, am chopped liver.

When I first met Reverend Chapman, he terrified me because I expected Bible studies questions or a virginity test.

"He knows you're not a virgin," said Henry, laughing.

"You told him I was religious."

"I said you went to a Catholic school."

"Now you're splitting hairs."

On that first meeting, we spent the weekend at the vicarage, sleeping in separate bedrooms, of course. Pastor Bill asked me to say grace. I told him that I'd prefer not to. Later, he tried to engage me in a theological discussion, arguing that God had to be real because so many people believe in His existence. I told him we could say the same about Allah, Shiva, Vishnu, and Krishna. Finally, he gave me a pitying look and said it was sad to see someone so young going through life always demanding proof that something exists.

"How do you know love is real?" he asked. "You can't see it or hold it."

"I can hold Henry and I love him."

This triggered a smug smile. "That sounds like faith, not proof."

"Not at all. In the police we call love without evidence something else."

"What's that?"

"Stalking."

Henry laughed so hard he snorted wine out his nose.

Reverend Bill and Janet hear us arriving. They are standing side by side outside the vicarage, as though re-creating *American Gothic* without the pitchfork or the gloomy looks. The vicar is a string bean of a man wearing a black short-sleeved clergy shirt with a white tab collar. Janet is in her normal floral dress with her hair pulled back so severely that her eyebrows lift in perpetual surprise. There are hugs and kisses, and questions about the drive, which only took us an hour, but they seem to think London is in a different time zone. The weather is also covered, as well as the traffic. Boxes ticked. This could be a long three days.

We carry our bags inside and are shown to our rooms—yes, plural. Since we're not married, we can't share a bedroom, let alone a bed. On my first visit, Henry managed to sneak up to my attic room and surprise me in the middle of the night. He might have gotten away with it if not for a particularly noisy brass bedhead. At breakfast Janet looked like she'd sucked on a lemon, or at least half a grapefruit, and was beating eggs as though trying to punish them. Why do I keep surrounding myself with religious parents?

Now Janet is making tea with ritual precision, warming the pot first, spooning in the loose-leafed tea—one for each person and one for the pot. The knitted tea cozy looks like an owl. China cups and saucers are set out—her best ones, which she probably reserves for the bishop when he visits.

Standing at the French doors, I look into a neighboring yard, where two teenagers are erecting a makeshift badminton net, which keeps sagging in the middle. Janet slices an orange tea cake. The black seeds on the top look like insect droppings. She's talking about the wedding.

"Since neither of you live in the parish or regularly attend worship, we can still go ahead, because Henry was baptized here. We thought it might be nice if Rector Nicholas did the honors. He's known you since you were little."

Henry nods in agreement and puts his arm around my waist.

"We should arrange a get-to-know-you session," says Janet.

"But I already know him," says Henry.

They're all looking at me. Clearly I don't appear keen.

"It's only a chat," explains Reverend Bill. "He'll ask how you and Henry came to be together and why you've decided to get married in the church."

Because of you, I want to say, but hold my tongue.

"He'll want to talk to you frankly about your past, your hopes for the future, and your understanding of marriage. Do you want to raise your children in the Christian faith—that sort of thing."

"They're more for Henry because he's divorced," says Janet, who sounds disappointed. "He'll have to provide the decree absolute and explain what went wrong first time around."

"That was a false start," I say, trying to lighten the mood.

"And we don't want him to make another mistake," says Janet.

Ouch!

Reverend Bill suggests we talk about the order of the service.

"We have a local printer who does a lovely booklet," says Janet, who produces a folder full of examples. "You can have a photograph on the front, or a quote."

"You'll have to choose a Bible reading and what hymns you'd like people to sing," says Reverend Bill.

"Do we have to have hymns?" I ask.

"There's a wide choice and I'm sure you'll find something you like." He adds, "You can choose different music for your entrance and exit."

"As long as it's not too wacky," says Janet.

I glance at Henry. "We thought we might have a gospel choir."

Janet is nodding, but her smile is frozen.

"They'll sing 'All You Need Is Love' as I come into the church and 'Oh Happy Day' as we're leaving."

"Everybody can sing along," adds Henry.

Janet seems to be ticking like a time bomb.

Reverend Bill cuts in. "Have you decided who will be walking you down the aisle? It's entirely optional, of course. You're not anyone's property to be given away. Not in this day and age."

"My father," I say quickly.

There is no sharp intake of breath or cry of alarm. Instead there is silence. Even the ticking has stopped.

Janet lets out a laugh like a hiccup, thinking I'm being droll. At that moment, an overweight tan-colored Labrador wanders into the room and sniffs at my shoes. He raises his nose towards my crotch and I push his head away.

"He's looking for crumbs," says Reverend Bill. "On your lap."

"Oh."

He steeples his fingers. "I thought you were estranged from your father."

"I want him to be at my wedding—along with my uncles."

There is another long silence. *Come on, Henry, say something. Support me.*

Janet begins packing up the tea things, wanting to busy herself, spilling a lump of sugar, which the Labrador hoovers up and swallows without chewing.

"You can't," Janet says suddenly, as though that is the end of that.

"Pardon?"

"We don't want Edward McCarthy in our church."

"My father is a businessman."

"Yes, but . . ."

"What?"

She glances at the reverend, expecting him to agree with her, but the vicar has lowered his eyes, as though searching his conscience or praying for guidance. After a long pause, he clears his throat. "Everybody is welcome in our church."

Janet is about to protest, but Bill continues. "We all have weaknesses and we have all sinned, which is why we must keep our hearts open."

"Mr. McCarthy is very nice," says Henry, finally showing some gumption, which is a real Janet word.

My phone chirrups. It's a message from Tempe. She's catching the train from London and we're going to visit Milford Barn to discuss the catering and seating plan.

"I have to go," I say, pleased to escape. "Can I borrow your car?"

Henry fetches his keys and whispers, "Coward."

I make a chick noise and squeeze his bum. "Your family. Your problem."

Tempe is waiting for me outside the Hitchin station. She looks like a young executive in a pencil skirt and matching jacket. We laugh about my future in-laws as the satnav directs us to Milford Barn. We've been meeting up once a week to discuss the wedding or to go shopping or to galleries or to the cinema in Leicester Square. The National Gallery is a favorite because Tempe loves to look at the pencil and charcoal sketches.

We rarely talk about St. Ursula's. Back then Tempe had been a distant, unattainable figure who was part of the "cool group." Nobody was surprised when she was voted vice captain in the annual ballot for leadership positions. Usually the teachers had the final say, regardless of how the students voted, but the best candidates were obvious to everyone. I can't remember if I circled Tempe's name on the ballot, but I hope I did.

I wish I had known her back then. I wish we'd caught the same train or been cast alongside each other in the school musical. Instead, I had Sara as a best friend, who was fickle and judgmental and prone to careless cruelty. One moment she'd be mapping out our careers, boyfriends, weddings, and children; and the next she'd be ghosting me for some perceived slight. She is much nicer now, but I'm still wary of her moods.

One of the things I like about Tempe is that she admits that she's not particularly well-read or up-to-date on current affairs. "I think I peaked too early," she says in a self-deprecating way. "I hit my limits." She has an interesting way of looking at the world, often sharing homespun observations that contain an innate truthfulness. One time she said, "Two wrongs don't make a right, but they make a good excuse." And another time, "The grass isn't greener on the other side. It's greener where you water it."

In my karate classes, she has become my star student. Her technique is excellent, but whenever she's in a sparring session with a classmate, she hesitates when given an opening, as though frightened that she might go too far or not be able to stop herself. In the changing room afterwards, she often walks naked between the shower and the lockers, not bothering to wrap herself in a towel. Sometimes she pauses in front of me, finishing a story, unconcerned about her nudity. I'm definitely not a prude, but neither am I comfortable flashing my bits, which is why I scramble to get dressed with all the grace of a collapsing deck chair.

Pulling through the stone gates, we arrive at a parking area surrounded by trees that give us glimpses of the seventeenth-century oak barn. We follow signs along a tunnel of greenery to a reception area, which is located in a farmhouse adjacent to the barn. From the windows, I can see cart horses in a field and a family of ducks waddling towards a pond.

Someone somewhere is playing "What a Wonderful World" by Louis Armstrong.

"It feels like a Disney movie," I whisper to Tempe as we wait for the manager.

"Is that OK?"

"Perfect."

The manager is a hale-and-hearty, red-faced woman who curtsies when she meets me, as though I'm royalty. Her name is Marjolein, and she enthuses about the choice we've made and how thrilled she is to be hosting my wedding.

"I'm surprised we could get a vacancy," I say. "When I first called, you were booked out."

"Oh, we can always shift things around when necessary," she explains. "And when Ms. Brown explained your circumstances . . ."

"Circumstances?" I'm looking at Tempe.

She shrugs and we let Marjolein carry on.

"On the day, the wedding cars will pull up here," she explains, taking us through double doors to a turning circle. "The guests will have entered through a different door and be waiting to welcome you."

With great fanfare, she pulls aside the barn door, revealing a cavernous room with exposed beams that crisscross a sloping roof. It feels rustic and charming, with high windows that angle light into the upper corners. Workers are setting up tables, unfurling the white linen tablecloths, and arranging chairs. Marjolein acknowledges some of them as we take the tour and pauses to adjust a centerpiece on one of the tables.

"This area is often set aside for a dance floor, and the band normally sets up in that corner. We don't have any nearby neighbors, so there are no complaints about the noise."

From the reception room we move to the kitchens and the restrooms, before finishing up on the patio, where we're offered a glass of champagne and a plate of nibbles as we discuss the finer details of the feasting platters and what alcohol package we'd like to include.

Marjolein asks if we have any particular security concerns. "If you're worried about gate-crashers and paparazzi, we only have limited guards and the place is rather open. It is still a working farm, after all."

"Why would we be worried about paparazzi?" I ask.

Tempe touches my arm. "I'm taking precautions."

I hadn't even considered the possibility that my father's presence would draw attention to the wedding and to me. Henry's words come back to me. *Have you thought this through?*

BOOK TWO

I would like to be the air that inhabits you for a moment only.
I would like to be that unnoticed and that necessary.

Margaret Atwood

21

My friends are over: Margot, Phoebe, Sara, Brianna, Georgia, and Carmen. Tempe has met a few of them before but never the whole group. Phoebe is the beauty. She studied to be a print journalist, but there aren't many jobs these days. Newspapers and magazines are going the way of DVD shops and VCRs. We keep saying she should work on TV because she has that girl-next-door look—big hair, wide smile, white teeth—but Phoebe is terrified she'll finish up working on a lifestyle program, telling people how to renovate their kitchens or repurpose junk.

Brianna works in social media. She has an older boyfriend, a highflier at a merchant bank or an investment bank. (I don't know the difference.) Carmen is the most self-assured. She's already married to Paolo and is pregnant with her first and manages a bookshop in Barnes. My oldest friend, Sara, teaches at a language school in Hammersmith and has been boy crazy since puberty. Margot is creative director at an advertising agency in Soho Square, and she and Phoebe have been dating since college. That's what we've become—sensible twenty-somethings with sensible boyfriends (or girlfriends) (or husbands) and sensible jobs—but we occasionally go a little nuts.

Since school or university, we have shared houses and holidays and internet memes. We have backpacked through Europe and protested for climate action and set each other up on dates when required.

I've known Sara since primary school and we went through St. Ursula's together, doing most of the same subjects. As soon as I mention Tempe, her eyes begin dancing.

"Are you talking about Maggie Brown?"

"Her family moved to Belfast."

"She left in her final year."

"Yes."

Sara laughs wickedly. "You don't remember the stories! How she was caught making out with Caitlin Penney in the changing rooms."

"I don't believe that," I say, although it lacks conviction.

"It's true," she says earnestly. "And afterwards we had that lecture, remember? A nun came to the school and gave a talk, warning girls about having 'special friends.'" Sara creates quotation marks with her fingers.

The memory does resurface but straightaway gets lost in a flurry of other rumors that used to swirl around St. Ursula's like scraps of paper on a gusty day. Girls who fell pregnant or had abortions, or swallowed pills and had their stomachs pumped, or the senior who reportedly slept with Mr. Piccolo, our married science teacher.

I can see Sara loitering around Tempe, desperate to ask her about Caitlin Penney, but I've made her promise to stay away from the subject and give Tempe a chance to make new friends.

We're using the blender to make fruit daiquiris, mango or strawberry, which are dangerously alcoholic and addictive. I try not to drink too much and to make sure everybody is having a nice time.

The pizzas arrive. Carmen and Tempe are in the kitchen making up another batch of cocktails when I overhear them talking. Carmen asks her how the two of us met and Tempe doesn't mention our time at school or that I rescued her from Darren Goodall. I can understand why she wants to keep certain things secret, particularly being the mistress of a married man.

Instead, she recounts a story of how her bag was snatched by a guy on a scooter and how she was dragged along the road, grazing her face. I was the first police officer who arrived at the scene and I drove her to the hospital. It's a version of the story that Tempe told me about meeting Darren Goodall but with a different victim and outcome. It sounds plausible and Carmen makes all the right noises, expressing shock and sympathy.

Later, Tempe tells Georgia that she's Henry's second or third cousin on his mother's side and that she and Henry knew each other as kids and used to share baths together. It's another good story, which gets a laugh, but I can't understand why she has to lie to people. It's like a game.

Alone with Tempe in the kitchen, I finally get a chance to ask her, but she laughs it off, saying it "makes life more interesting."

"Telling lies."

"Haven't you ever wanted to pretend? I used to do it all the time in Belfast. I'd go out with friends and we'd invent cover stories. We'd be flight attendants or professional mud wrestlers or hand models."

"But these are my friends."

"I'm sorry. I'll stop."

For the rest of the evening I watch her closely and notice how she manages to look like she's drinking and getting tipsy like everybody else, but she hardly sips a cocktail. She listens and nods, soaking up information without offering an opinion.

We're outside in the garden, talking about wedding dresses and what my bridesmaids will wear. Sara, Brianna, and Phoebe are going to be my bridesmaids. Carmen will be too pregnant by then and Georgia thinks marriage is a "social and legal construct that devalues women and makes them property and objects." She still expects an invitation, of course.

"You promised not to dress me in taffeta," says Sara. "Or in orange or yellow."

"If I look like a meringue I'll never speak to you again," echoes Brianna.

They grow louder and cruder. The night wears on. Moths begin fluttering around the garden lights. At ten o'clock, I shepherd them inside, worried about complaints from the neighbors. Georgia begins rolling a joint, which I choose to ignore.

I'm in the kitchen and can hear Sara talking about her trip to Paris over Easter.

"I can see you nodding," says Georgia. "Do you like Paris?"

"Very much so," answers Tempe. "I lived there for two years."

"Where?"

"On the West Bank."

"You mean the Left Bank?" says Sara.

"Or maybe the right bank," Brianna says, and giggles.

They are making fun of her.

"You must speak French," says Georgia.

"Only a little."

"Je ne pense pas que tu parles français du tout."

Tempe mumbles, "Not that much."

There is more laughter, which draws me into the room. Tempe understands that she's being mocked and goes quiet. Sara can spot a weakness.

"Hey, Tempe, you lived in Northern Ireland. Have you heard the Irish knock-knock joke?"

"No."

"It's great, you start."

"Knock, knock," says Tempe.

Silence. Tempe's eager face slowly changes as the realization dawns on her that *she* is the Irish joke. The others burst out laughing. I want to defend her but say nothing, which makes me feel worse. I wish they'd all go home now. I'm tired and they've become drunk and annoying. Tempe isn't blameless. She's been trying too hard to be liked, instead of being herself.

They leave well after midnight, all except for Georgia, who is crashing in our spare room. She fills a jug with water, spilling some on the countertop. I wipe it down.

I'm hand washing the glasses and rinsing them in cold water.

"Why don't you use the dishwasher?" she asks, elongating the sound *dishhhh*.

"It's broken."

She perches on a stool, almost sliding off.

"Why were you so mean to Tempe?" I ask.

"Sara started it."

"That's no excuse."

"I know. I'm sorry. I fell for that knock-knock joke. Somebody always does." Georgia takes a sip of water. "Can I ask you something?"

"Sure."

"Is Tempe gay?"

"What makes you think that?"

"The way she looks at you."

I can tell that she's drunk.

"Phoebe thought you two might be, you know . . ."

"You can't be serious!"

She holds up her hands. "Don't look at me like that. You went to an all-girls school. That sort of stuff goes on in the dormitories, late at night, when the lights are off."

"I wasn't a boarder and that sounds like something Henry would say. Tempe is not gay."

"If you say so," says Georgia, giggling.

"I'm going to bed."

"What time it is?"

"Two in the morning."

"Oh God. I'll feel like shit tomorrow."

"You mean today. I've put some paracetamol beside your bed."

She gives me a hug, slurring, "You are going to make someone a wonderful wife one day."

"Yes, and I know exactly the man."

22

Tempe and I are shopping in the West End. I normally avoid this sort of thing, but buying clothes is a different experience with Tempe, who is like a personal stylist and a life coach rolled into one, encouraging me to try on outfits and mix colors that I wouldn't normally consider. Today we've bought cashmere sweaters at Uniqlo and matching white trainers at the Asics store.

When we walk along the street, she sometimes puts her arm through mine and we stay in step like we're in a Hollywood musical and about to burst into song.

My mother once told me that we make very few new friends once we reach a certain age. I don't know why that is. Perhaps we become set in our ways and want to surround ourselves with people who share a common history. I have old friends who I disagreed with over Brexit and voting for Boris and the Scottish independence referendum, but I'm less likely to make the same allowances for someone new. They have to earn a place in my heart.

We're in Carnaby Street, walking towards Covent Garden, looking for a café for lunch. We sit outside and a waitress takes our order. While I have Tempe talking, I keep asking questions. Normally, it is the other way around. Sometimes when she speaks, an extraordinary stillness comes over her body, as if she's hearing her own voice being played back to her and she's trying to moderate her tone and pitch to make it more agreeable.

She reveals that she was partially deaf until the age of four because of meningitis and that she grew up with three sisters. Her father was a soldier and was away from home a lot, fighting in Afghanistan and Iraq. He was transferred to Belfast, which is why they moved. I want to ask her about the rumors at St. Ursula's, but I figure that she'll tell me if she wants to, and it hardly matters anymore.

Tempe's two older sisters left school early and worked to support the family. Tempe stayed at school with Elizabeth, the youngest, who had asthma and "succumbed" during the first wave of the pandemic.

"When you say succumbed . . . ?"

"She died."

I'm shocked. "How old was she?"

"Twenty-seven."

"That's my age."

I'm surprised at how unmoved Tempe seems to be. Not cold, but accepting, as though bad luck is inevitable and there's no point in complaining.

"Were you close?"

"She was my sister," says Tempe, as though that says it all.

"Your parents must have been devastated. It's so rare . . . someone so young, dying of COVID."

Our food arrives and we decide to share, cutting sandwiches and sliding them between plates. Tempe keeps talking about her older sisters, who are both married. She doesn't mention her father, and I sense they didn't get on. She reaches across the table and wipes mayonnaise from my cheek.

"I'm such a messy eater. Mum says I eat like a hungry hippo."

"A what?"

"That game. Hungry Hungry Hippos. Didn't you ever play it?"

Tempe shakes her head.

"That's one of the reasons I always wanted a sister—so we could play board games on rainy days and swap clothes and play dress-up."

Tempe is picking grated carrot off her sandwich. "I wished I was an only child."

"Really. Why?"

She shrugs. "Kids get forgotten in big families."

"That's better than being lonely," I say. "Every Christmas, we made a special trip into Hamleys, the toy shop, and I'd sit on Santa's knee. I'd tell him I'd been a good girl and ask him to bring me a baby sister for Christmas."

Tempe laughs. "What did he say?"

"He would look at my mother and then suggest he bring me a doll instead. I stopped doing it when I realized how sad it made her."

"Did she try for more?"

"For years. There were false alarms and miscarriages."

"What about IVF?"

"The Catholic Church believes babies should be conceived by the beautiful sexual union of a husband and a wife, rather than in a test tube."

"That's archaic."

"Don't get me started on contraception."

Tempe glances over my shoulder, scanning the square. I turn and see a man watching from the edge of a crowd that has gathered around a busker.

"Do you know him?" I ask.

"I think I've seen him before."

"Is he following you?"

"I don't know."

When we leave the café, I notice the man again. We lose sight of him for a while, but he reappears when we cross at the next set of traffic lights.

"Wait here."

"Please don't go," says Tempe.

"I want to find out who he is."

I turn quickly and jog back, confronting the man, who is in his mid-fifties and wearing old-fashioned baggy jeans and a blazer.

"Are you following us?"

"Pardon?"

"I keep seeing you."

"I don't know what you're talking about."

He's carrying shopping bags. "I'm waiting for my wife," he says. "She's having her hair done."

He points along the street.

"Why are you staring at my friend?"

"Who?"

I point towards Tempe.

"I'm sorry." He reaches into the inside pocket of his jacket and finds his glasses. After fumbling with the case, he unfolds them and puts them on his nose. "Can you show me again?" he asks. "I'm blind as a bat."

My cheeks grow hot. "I'm sorry. My mistake."

I turn away and glance over my shoulder as I leave. I imagine that he's going to tell his wife that he was accosted in the street by a woman who accused him of being a stalker.

"What did he say?" asks Tempe.

"False alarm."

"Are you sure?"

"He's nobody," I say, and then correct myself. "I didn't mean nobody, but he's harmless."

Tempe is looking at her phone. "I took a picture of someone standing outside my flat. Later, I saw him at the supermarket."

"Show me."

I try to enlarge the blurry image, but the face isn't clear. At that moment, a message pops up on her screen. *You know how to make this stop.*

She tries to take the phone back.

"What is this? Are you getting messages?"

"A few."

I begin scrolling. There are dozens of text messages. The sender's number is hidden. The first one I read is a verse:

Forget the future,
Forget the past.
Life is over:
Breathe your last.

Others are written in capital letters:

LATE AT NIGHT, WHEN YOU'RE ALONE, I AM THE KNOCK ON THE DOOR.
TICK TOCK, TICK TOCK, TIME IS RUNNING OUT.
HAVE YOU LEARNED ANYTHING YET?

I look up at Tempe, who is biting her bottom lip.

"You have to tell the police."

"And what will they do?"

"They can trace the source."

"He's not that stupid. And he won't let them."

"How did he find you?" I ask.

She shrugs and I begin thinking out loud. If Goodall has used the police database to search for Tempe, he has broken the law.

"He's harassing you," I say.

"And I'm ignoring him," she replies.

"You have to change your number."

"I have a business to run."

"Does he know where you live?"

"I don't think so."

"What about the man outside your flat?"

"It wasn't Darren. It could have been anyone."

"This is wrong," I say. "There are laws . . ."

"Please, don't do anything. You saw what happened last time."

Inside I'm silently fuming.

"What does he want?" I ask, not expecting her to answer.

"What he's always wanted. Me."

23

Unpacking our new purchases, we spread them on Tempe's bed and begin mixing and matching outfits. The flat is on the second floor of a redbrick block that was built between the wars. It has a bedroom, kitchen, bathroom, and sitting room with a large bay window looking out on the branches of a plane tree with a mottled gray trunk.

"They should rename this place Divorcé Hall," says Tempe. "It's full of separated husbands. I keep bumping into them in the basement."

"Why the basement?"

"A shared laundry. They're always asking my advice about what they can tumble dry and when to use a cold wash."

"They're chatting you up."

"Maybe. Just a little." She smiles.

Tempe doesn't have much in the way of furniture, but I'm slowly helping her pick up things, like the flat-packed shelves and two bedside tables that we struggled to put together. Slot A went into Slot B, using a hex key and half a bottle of white wine. She has a laptop computer and a small printer and a wireless speaker to play music.

I'm still worried about the text messages. Despite Tempe's efforts, Goodall is getting closer. How long before he finds her address?

"Come to our place for dinner."

"Won't Henry mind?"

"No. Why?"

She gives a noncommittal shrug. "I think he resents how much time we spend together."

"Nonsense."

Tempe has woven herself into my life over the past month. She has a brilliant memory for completely unrelated things like birthdays and doctor's appointments and dry-cleaning pickups. I can make an observation or mention something in passing like the name of a restaurant or how much I like a particular song or a show that I watched on Netflix, and Tempe will file it away.

She seems fascinated by my relationship with Henry, wanting to know how we met, our first date, our first kiss, our first everything. Occasionally I've caught her watching us when Henry drags me onto his lap or comes up behind me in the kitchen and nuzzles my neck. She's not embarrassed by these shows of affection but seems to be studying them, as though wanting to learn.

Back at the house, I begin cooking a vegetarian pasta sauce, while Tempe looks through Henry's vinyl collection in the sitting room.

She shouts, "What music do you want?"

"You choose."

"How about *Abbey Road*?"

"A classic."

"Is it?"

"You've never heard of *Abbey Road*?"

"Music isn't my thing."

"But you've heard of the Beatles?"

"Of course."

Before she can explain, my phone begins to vibrate. Henry's name comes up on the screen. I put him on speakerphone while I'm stirring the sauce.

"I'm running late, babe. I'll be half an hour."

"That's OK. Tempe is staying for dinner."

He groans and I hit the mute button, hoping Tempe didn't hear. I pick up the handset, whispering, "What's wrong?"

"I was looking forward to spending the evening with you."

"Did you have anything in particular in mind?"

"Something extremely energetic that involves little clothing and lots of room."

"Will we have to move the furniture?"

"Yes, I will definitely require a run-up."

I giggle and tell him to hurry.

Tempe appears next to me. "Who was that?"

"Henry. He'll be home soon."

"Why do you have to move the furniture?"

"It's a private joke."

She looks a little hurt but shrugs it off.

When I hear the front door open, I set the water boiling for the pasta and pour a glass of wine. Henry wants to take a shower first. I hear the pipes rattling as he turns on the water. When he emerges, he has changed into track pants and a rugby sweater. His hair is damp. His feet are bare.

"I've poured you wine," I say.

"I'd prefer a beer." He takes one from the fridge and slumps on the sofa, toying with his phone.

"How was work?" asks Tempe.

"Good."

"Any fires?"

"No."

"What do you do when there aren't any fires?"

"We sit on our arses."

"He's joking," I say, annoyed at him.

"We test equipment. We clean trucks. We do training exercises."

Tempe makes further attempts at conversation, but Henry isn't interested. Clearly he's in a mood. Finally the silence seems to play on his mind and he says, "Tell me about yourself."

"I'm boring," says Tempe, sipping her wine.

"Phil told me how you met. You were having an affair with a married man."

"Does that shock you?"

"No."

"I didn't know he was married—not at first."

"And when you did know . . . ?"

"He told me he had an open relationship with his wife."

"Phil says that open relationships are like Communism—good in theory."

Tempe laughs and Henry seems to warm up.

I have to check on the pasta and make a salad dressing. I leave them for a few minutes. When I come back, I pause in the doorway.

"Really?" says Henry, leaning forward on the sofa. "Have you . . . ? I mean . . . are you?"

"Am I bisexual?" Tempe shrugs. "Maybe people fall in love with the person, not the gender."

"Are you saying that you've slept with men and women?" he asks.

"Sometimes both at once."

Henry is picking at the label of his beer bottle with his thumbnail, peeling it off in sticky clumps.

"Do you feel threatened by that?" asks Tempe.

"No."

"It's what men fantasize about, isn't it? Two women at the same time?"

"Some do, I guess."

"Wouldn't you like to see Phil and me getting it on?"

"No!" he says, too abruptly. "She'd never . . ."

"Are you sure? Maybe you're afraid she might like it."

Henry begins to stammer. "I think we should stop . . . I don't think . . . it's not something . . ."

Tempe laughs, rocking back in her chair. "I'm joking. The look on your face is priceless."

Henry finally joins her, but not fully, not genuinely.

"What are you two laughing about?"

"Threesomes," says Tempe. "I was teasing Henry. He thought I was being serious."

"No, I didn't," he protests. "I knew it was a joke."

We eat supper at the dining table, making small talk about politics and Brexit and how much people drink at weddings and whether we should order more champagne. Tempe leaves soon afterwards. I arrange the Uber on my account.

"Has he sent any more messages?" I ask.

"I'm ignoring them."

She wants to say goodbye to Henry, who is in the kitchen, drying dishes.

"I'm sorry if I embarrassed you," she says. "But you look like a little boy when you blush."

His face reddens.

"There it is. So cute."

24

"She's weird," says Henry as I slip into bed beside him. "That stuff she said about threesomes."

He is propped on two pillows, flicking through wedding magazines but not paying any attention to the pages.

"She says things to shock people or to prompt a reaction," I say.

"Don't you find her creepy?"

"Not at all. She's a little socially awkward."

"I would have said überconfident."

"I think she's clever the way she puts people off their stride. She makes them think."

"About what?"

"Everything."

"Well, I find it unnerving. The way she looks at you and hangs on your every word."

"Oh, rubbish." I laugh.

"And she's always doing stuff for you," says Henry. "Picking up your dry cleaning and texting you reminders."

"She's helping plan our wedding."

"OK, but it's completely one-sided. She never wants anything in return."

"I found her the flat. I'm teaching her karate."

Henry puts down the magazine and wraps his arms around me. "I just wonder how much we really know about her."

I tell him about Tempe's family—her two married sisters and the youngest, who died in the first wave of the pandemic. Her father is a soldier. Her mother is quite sick.

"*Little Women*," says Henry.

"What?"

"You just described the plot of *Little Women*. The book. The movie. It's almost the same story. The sisters, the father, the mother . . ."

"That's just a coincidence," I say as I turn off the bedside light and lie awake, wondering if Tempe would lie to me.

An hour later, I'm still awake . . . still thinking. I slip out of bed and pad across the floor and down the stairs to the kitchen, where I begin searching drawers and cupboards, looking for the letter that Tempe told me to destroy. It was addressed to Margaret Brown and put in the wrong mailbox at the apartment she shared with Darren Goodall. I couldn't bring myself to throw it away. I don't know why. When something is written on paper, it somehow has greater importance or permanence than an email or a text message. Destroying a letter is like ripping the pages from a book or defacing a photograph. It feels like vandalism.

I find the letter wedged inside the diary that my mother gives me every Christmas and never gets used apart from jotting down shopping lists or reminder notes. The envelope is postmarked from Belfast and was addressed and re-addressed at least twice before it reached Tempe.

I take a knife from the block and make a neat slit along the top edge, aware that I'm breaking the law. Inside is a single handwritten page. The sender's address is in the top left corner and the date is October 12 last year.

Dear Maggie,

I hope this letter reaches you, wherever you are. So many of my letters have bounced back to me that I'm never sure if I found you or not. Maybe this will arrive at the right address at the right time. So much depends upon timing, doesn't it?

There are things I've been longing to tell you. But more than that, I've been praying that you might come home. I know you are disappointed in me. We both said things that were unkind and hurtful, and I wish I could take my words back, because I miss you so much.

In a world of coincidence and chance encounters, I always think I might bump into you one day, that you might be walking along the street or wandering through the supermarket. There's the theory about six degrees of separation, but we are much less than six degrees apart. We are one degree. We are as close as blood allows—mother and daughter.

It is so hard to think of how things have turned out for us, and I often fixate on the "what ifs," even though they make me feel defi-cient as a mother. I know it might be hard to believe, but once there was a time when you would not dream of leaving my side, when you chose me, without question, as the person you would always love. I was a lioness. You were my cub. Now you're gone.

What news of home? I am still working at the pharmacy with Auntie Heather. She and your uncle George are fighting like the old married couple they are. Your cousin Patrick is engaged to be mar-ried to a girl from Derry whose accent is so broad, I can't under-stand half of what she says, but she's very sweet.

I have some news about Bumble, who died in February. Feline cancer, the vet said, but he had a pretty good life. Even after you left, he would sleep on the end of your bed, and we buried him in his favorite sunny spot in the garden and put up a little plaque engraved with his name.

Apart from that, we're all well. Your dad is still talking about retir-ing from the shipyard, but I don't want him at home, following me around.

We both miss you so much. Every time I think of you, I feel an ache in my chest and my stomach, as though chains are tightening. A mother and her daughter should not be estranged, and if I let myself think too long and too deeply about you leaving me, I am sure my heart will break completely.

I hope this letter finds you well. I live for you and always will.

Mum xxx

I fold the letter and place it back into the envelope, feeling both guilty and intrigued by what caused such a profound breakdown. There is no mention of Tempe's sisters, and her father appears to work for a shipyard, not the military.

Opening my laptop, I type the return address into a search engine and come across a property report. The house was last sold in 2008, which is probably when Tempe's parents arrived in Belfast. Another page shows a planning application for a rear roof extension, submitted in 2014. The applicant was a Mr. William Brown.

I have a name. I search for a phone number. Nothing. The letter mentioned a pharmacy, run by George and Heather. I do a different search, using Google Maps, and come up with eleven possible businesses.

I hear the stairs creak. Henry appears in the doorway.

"I woke up and you weren't in bed."

"I couldn't sleep."

"What are you doing?"

"Nothing important."

I close down the laptop and follow him upstairs to bed, where I continue to lie awake, listening to his gentle snores. Tempe is like a condensed drop of color that has landed in my world of water, spreading and outlining things, creating contrast and vividness. More than one drop might be too much.

25

Morning after a restless night. Up early, I dress in my running gear and borrow Henry's bike, which he keeps in the front hallway rather than chained up outside the house because the back wheel has been stolen twice. Now I bark my shins on the pedals every time I hang clothes from the radiator.

Lowering the saddle a few notches, I test the height, making sure my toes can touch the ground. The bike has drop handlebars, solid tires, and a narrow wedge-shaped seat that would cut me in half if I rode it for too long. Setting off slowly, the wheels almost floating over the ground, I cross Battersea Bridge and cut through Ranelagh Gardens before joining the cycleway and heading north through Chelsea, South Kensington, and Bayswater.

After fifty minutes, I reach Kensal Green, where I lean the bicycle against a railing fence and unclip my helmet. Taking a seat on a low brick wall, I catch my breath and wait for Darren Goodall to emerge. He doesn't get a wifely kiss on the doorstep this morning or a traveling mug of coffee for the journey.

He's almost at his car when he looks up and notices me standing opposite him. I'm too far away to see the look on his face, but glances over his shoulder, making sure that Alison isn't watching.

He crosses the road and his eyes seem to sweep the entirety of me, noting the loops of sweat beneath my arms and the curve of my breasts.

"What do you want?" he asks.

"Stay away from Tempe Brown."

"I wouldn't touch that crazy bitch with a bargepole."

"I've seen the messages . . . the threats."

"I don't make threats."

"I'm going to have them traced. I'll prove it was you."

He steps closer, crowding my space. "Make sure you get a warrant. I'd hate to see you break any more rules."

I glance towards the house. "Perhaps we could talk about this inside."

The suggestion seems to light a touch paper. He grabs at my arm, wanting to drag me farther away.

"I don't know why you're here or what you want from me, but I haven't gone near Tempe Brown. Tell her she's not getting another penny from me. She is a fucking psycho and if she or you comes near my family, I will bury you both."

"I know about Imogen Croker," I say.

A damp flurry wind seems to burst around us, and there is a moment of confusion in his eyes. His fingers curl into fists.

"I've talked to her mother and read the transcripts from her inquest. Dylan Holstein was investigating you."

Goodall raises his voice, talking over me. "Is this some kind of vendetta? Or maybe you're obsessed with me."

"You're disgusting."

"And you're the daughter of a scumbag criminal."

The swapping of insults feels childish, like I'm back in the playground at my primary school.

Under his breath, but still audible, he mutters, "You seem to have forgotten your place in the food chain. You are a doe-eyed Bambi in a forest full of wolves, and when I come for you, not even your daddy will be able to protect you."

"Is that a threat?"

"Oh no, I'm simply explaining the great circle of life, which is more like a daisy chain than a food chain."

I hear a child's voice, yelling, "Daddy!"

On the far side of the road, Alison Goodall has emerged from the house. Her little boy is waving and Alison raises her hand to shield her eyes from the glare, unsure of who I am. Any moment now she'll recognize me from our yoga class.

Goodall turns to me. "Don't come near my family again."

"Leave Tempe alone and I won't have to."

I clip on my bike helmet. Goodall wraps his fingers around the handlebars. He raises the front tire a few inches and drops it.

"Is everything all right?" asks Alison, still on the far side of the road.

"Fine," he yells back. "See you tonight."

I pull the bike from his grip and quickly spin away, pushing it along the footpath. At the next intersection, I climb into the saddle and begin riding home, replaying the conversation in my head. Up on the pedals, I push hard, driven by anger and frustration. I'm annoyed with myself and Tempe and my father, although I don't know how he comes into this.

Having crossed the Thames, I'm almost home, riding along a narrow street with cars parked on either side, when I sense a vehicle behind me. Getting closer. Too close. I risk a look over my shoulder and see a flash of dark blue, but not the driver's face. Out of my seat, I push on the pedals, looking for a gap between the parked cars. The driver is periodically flooring the clutch and revving the accelerator, making the engine growl impatiently.

Suddenly, I see a space and swerve left but can't stop. I hit the gutter, and the handlebars are wrenched from my hands. I am thrown forwards, head over heels, airborne. Tumbling. At the last moment, I roll onto my shoulder, protecting my head, which still smacks into the sidewalk, leaving me stunned. I am lying on my back, looking up at rags of white cloud in the clear blue sky.

The Saab has stopped. The passenger window glides down. Goodall leans nearer. "See how easy it would be? I wouldn't have to waste a bullet."

Sitting on the sofa, I flinch each time Henry dabs disinfectant on my grazed elbow.

"Ow!"

"Sorry." He grabs another cotton ball. "You should file a complaint."

"With whom, exactly?"

"His boss. Internal Affairs. He ran you off the road."

"Technically, I ran off the road. He didn't touch me."

"He threatened you."

"It will be his word against mine. He's a decorated detective. I'm Edward McCarthy's daughter."

"Well, I'll thump the bastard. What's his address?"

Henry gets to his feet and looks for his shoes.

"You're not going around there."

"I don't care if he's a copper. He can't get away with running you off the road."

"Don't you dare leave this house."

"I have to do something."

"Why?"

"Because he hurt you and because I love you and because he wrecked my bloody bike."

Wincing as I straighten my knees, I take his face in my hands, pulling him closer and kissing his lips.

"I don't need a knight in shining armor. I have this under control."

Henry doesn't answer, but I want to make him promise to let this go.

"I'm not scared of him," he shouts from the bathroom.

"I know."

"You should tell your father."

"Are you kidding? He'd go to war."

26

"He said that you're not getting another penny from him. What did he mean?"

"I have no idea," says Tempe.

"And when he followed me on the train, he called you a parasite. Are you blackmailing him?"

"No."

"Did you threaten to tell his wife?"

"Never."

We're at the Chestnut Grove Academy, getting changed after a class. Curtains are breathing air and light into the changing rooms, swelling from the breeze and dropping again against the louvred windows.

"When Goodall was arrested he claimed that you were his informant and a sex worker."

"He was lying to cover his arse. I'm not a call girl. I would never sleep with anyone for money."

"I'm not saying you took money, but I saw the broken camera in the living room."

"He filmed us, that's all."

I search the ceiling for a new question. "The other night you were teasing Henry about threesomes. Is that something you did . . . with Goodall?"

"It was a joke."

"Did he ever introduce you to anyone?"

"What do you mean?"

I soften my voice. "Did anyone ever visit the apartment—other police officers, business contacts?"

"He had meetings, but he made me go out. I had to phone him before I came back."

"How long did you stay away?"

"A few hours—maybe longer if they were playing poker."

"Would you recognize these men?"

"Some of them."

"Did any of them have tattoos?"

"I didn't see them naked," she snaps. "Just because he paid for the apartment and bought me nice clothes, it doesn't make me a prostitute."

"That's not what I'm saying." I point to the inside of my wrist. "Three letters. MDM."

"Darren had a tattoo like that. What does it mean?"

"It's a gang marking."

"You mean like a street gang?"

"Not quite the same."

I have to stop myself asking the same questions again. Despite her masochistic attraction to difficult men, Tempe is a victim, not a perpetrator. She shouldn't be blamed for making bad choices.

"When you went out to dinner or he bought you clothes, did he pay by card or with cash?" I ask.

"Usually with cash."

"Did he ever go to the casinos?"

"He liked the races. Is that important?"

"I'm just wondering how a detective sergeant with a wife and two kids and London-sized mortgage can afford a luxury apartment on the river."

Another shrug of her shoulders, and I get the impression she's keeping something from me.

"Goodall said you stole from him. What did he mean?"

"You've asked me that."

"Yes, and you said you were owed—but not *what* you took."

"Maybe I took away his pride. Maybe I stole his heart."

"I'm being serious."

"No. You're doing what everybody does—and making me feel guilty, as though it's my fault that he beat me, and he raped me."

"Did he rape you?"

"All the time."

"Then make a statement. Help me stop him."

"If you have to ask—you don't understand."

When I get home, I go to the office upstairs, which will one day become the nursery. Now it looks more like a junk room, full of boxes and exercise equipment that we purchased with good intentions and stopped using within a month.

Opening my laptop, I continue my search for Tempe's parents. Her mother's letter mentioned a pharmacy run by her aunt and uncle. I've come up with eleven possible businesses. I call them one by one. My script is always the same. I ask for Heather or George.

On my fifth call, I get a hit. A woman answers, "Heather isn't here today, and George is busy with a customer."

I hesitate, unsure of how to proceed.

"I'm actually looking for Mrs. Brown. She has a daughter called Margaret."

"Oh, you mean Elsa. Who shall I say is calling?"

"You mean, she's there?"

"Yes."

I didn't expect to find her so quickly. "Oh, right. Tell her it's Constable McCarthy of Southwark Police . . . in London."

She laughs. "I know where Southwark is." She lowers the phone to the counter. I hear muffled voices. The phone is picked up. A nervous voice says hello.

"Is that Mrs. Brown?"

"Yes."

"You have a daughter called Maggie?"

There is an intake of breath, followed by a flurry of words. "Is she all right? Has something happened to her?"

"No. Nothing is wrong."

"Oh, thank God. Where is she?"

"Living in London. She doesn't know I'm calling."

"Is she in trouble?"

"No. It's nothing like that. I'm a friend of hers. You sent her a letter. I know I shouldn't have opened it. I tried to give it to Tempe but she—"

"Tempe?"

"She said that was her middle name."

"No."

Her voice is shaking. It takes me a moment to realize that she's crying.

"Mrs. Brown?"

"Call me Elsa." She blows her nose. "I can't tell you what this means to me. I've been praying . . . and writing. So many letters—I've lost count. Most have been returned unopened. I didn't know if any reached her. What is she doing? Is she happy?"

"She's been helping me plan my wedding."

"Oh, that's lovely." There is an edge to her voice. "Are you her friend?"

"I guess I am. We were at school together—at St. Ursula's. I was a few years below her. Tempe, I mean Maggie, doesn't talk much about her past. She's very private."

There is a long silence. I can hear her breathing.

"She has three sisters," I say, trying not to make it sound like a question.

"No, just the one—Agnes."

"What about Elizabeth?"

"I don't know who you mean."

The silence is mine. I have so many questions I want to ask but I'm now frightened of the answers.

"What does Mr. Brown do?" I ask.

"He's an engineer. He works at the Belfast Docks."

"Was he ever a soldier?"

"No, dear. Maggie has been telling you stories. She can be terrible that way."

"Why does she make stuff up?"

"That's a good question. She's always liked to pretend. Even as a little girl she'd dress up and we'd all have to play along. One day she'd be Amelia Earhart and the next she'd be Buffy or Britney Spears or Sporty Spice. We always thought it was quite harmless, until her attachment issues."

"What issues?"

"Has she mentioned Mallory Hopper?"

"No, who is she?"

"Someone Maggie used to know."

Elsa quickly changes the subject, asking where Tempe is living and what she's doing. How did we meet up again? Does she have other friends? I feel like I'm being squeezed for every last drop of information, by someone who has been thirsting for details for too long.

"Can you tell me where she's living? Her phone number?"

"I don't feel comfortable doing that," I say. "Not without her permission."

"I understand. What if I came to London? Would you take me to her?"

"I can't make that promise. Perhaps if you told me more about what happened . . . why she left Belfast."

"I can't, I'm sorry. Maggie can tell you. Ask her about Mallory."

Elsa makes me wait while she gets a piece of paper to jot down my contact details—a phone number and an email address.

"I need to sort a few things out. I'll call you in a few days," says Elsa. "In the meantime, can I ask you for a favor, Constable McCarthy?"

"You can call me Phil."

"Don't tell Maggie that you called me."

"Why not?"

"I don't want her running away again."

It's only later, when I'm recounting the conversation to Henry, that I realize how odd it is for a mother to talk about a grown-up daughter "running away." She used the word "again," as though it had happened before. Who was Tempe running from?

27

We lost a fifteen-year-old schoolboy today. Bashir Khan was attacked outside a fish-and-chip shop on Tower Bridge Road by a gang of five youths, wearing masks, who dragged him off a number 42 bus and stabbed him to death in front of horrified passengers. We had emergency response teams swarming over the area within minutes, but the attackers had melted away.

Bashir died at the scene—another victim of knife crime in London, which is an epidemic rather than a pandemic. Machetes, box cutters, scalpels, razors, flick knives—widow-makers and child-takers. Bashir worked part-time at a small post office run by his parents, who emigrated from Pakistan twenty years ago. The store has been robbed three times in the past year.

Female officers are considered better at delivering bad news, which is why I get so many death knocks, but I had no answers for Bashir's family. His mother collapsed when I broke the news to her. She sobbed and beat her fists against her husband's chest, as though blaming him for bringing her to such a cruel and lawless country.

Now I am back at my desk, typing up notes. Nish is sitting opposite me, searching the footage from traffic cameras and CCTV from the bus. Two suspects have been identified using the gangs violence matrix database, which gives suspected gang members a rating of either red, amber, or green, depending on their level of risk.

It is four days since my run-in with Darren Goodall, and the grazes have all but healed. I haven't made an official complaint or followed up on the text messages being sent to Tempe.

I glance up at Nish.

"If you suspected a fellow officer of illegally accessing databases, would you inform on him?"

"That depends."

"On what?"

"The reasons, maybe. I mean, they could be harmless."

"What if you suspected this officer was stalking his former girl-friend?"

"Leave it alone, Phil."

"Are you advising me or answering my question?"

"Both," he says, glancing over his shoulder, worried we might be overheard. "This is about Goodall."

"It's a hypothetical."

Nish doesn't believe me. I swivel my chair away and go back to the screen.

The radio chatter from the control room has increased in volume. Heavy boots echo in the corridor outside. The shift sergeant is at the door, yelling across the room.

"We have an address. We're moving."

I feel my adrenaline spike

"Can I go, Sarge?"

He takes a moment, rolling his shoulders. "Briefing in five."

I dash upstairs and grab my stab vest and helmet before joining the others. The officer in charge is a chief inspector, Jack Horgan, who I haven't met before. He's shaven-headed with a rumbling voice and is dressed entirely in black, bulked up by a bullet-proof vest.

"We have identified two suspects, Aldous Fisher and Darnel Red-mond," says Horgan.

Mug shots appear on the TV screen behind him. The men are young, with tight curls and neck tattoos. "Fisher has priors for drug possession and property crimes. Redmond was convicted of a knife attack three years ago and is out on parole. His brother, Arlo Redmond, is serving a life sentence for murdering a shopkeeper in Brixton."

The image changes to a map of South London

"Redmond has an aunt who lives on the Brandon Estate. That's the address he gave when he was treated in hospital two weeks ago for a stab wound to his thigh. He and a second man, believed to be Fisher, were seen near the Brandon Estate less than an hour ago."

We are divided into two teams of five, each with a call sign and a team commander. The briefing ends and we're moving. Ten of us are crammed into the minivan, shoulder to shoulder, thigh to thigh, sweat-ing in our heavy gear. There are eight men and two women. Some are making jokes to relieve the tension. Gallows humor. It doesn't mean they're uncaring or making light of the task, merely finding a way to calm their nerves.

The windows are fogging up, but I can recognize the streets as we drive towards Kennington Park. The Brandon Estate was built in the 1950s as social housing. The six eighteen-story towers were labeled slums in the seventies and the "estate from hell" in the nineties. Periodically, attempts are made to clean them up, but some stains are too hard to wash out.

Redmond's aunt lives on the second floor of Cornish House, which is in darkness except for a haphazard checkerboard of lighted windows, some softened by curtains or blinds. Washing hangs from balconies, along with the occasional Union Jack flag or BLM banner. We park out of sight and move quickly towards the tower. Boots echo in the stairwell. Horgan raises his fist. We pause. He wants two officers at each end of the corridor and two more guarding the stairs. Two more will swing the "big red key," a handheld battering ram. Others will guard the stairwells.

"Where do you want me, sir?" I ask.

Horgan ignores the question. I glance at my colleagues, but nobody is looking at me.

They are taking up positions.

"What about the balcony?" I ask.

"We're on the third floor."

"Second floor," I say. "It's jumpable."

Horgan doesn't like being contradicted. "If you'd prefer to wait outside, Constable McCarthy, be my guest."

I'm surprised he knows my name.

I haven't moved.

"Are you disobeying a direct order?"

"I didn't realize it was an order, sir."

I descend the stairs and walk towards the parking area. A footpath cuts across the lawn, dotted with lampposts that are throwing patches of light onto the grass and bitumen.

I hear the first call of "Police, open up!" and the sound of the battering ram, splintering the door. At that moment, from the corner of my eye, I spot a dark shadow swing from one balcony to the lower one. A second figure is climbing over the railing. I start to run as the two men make the final drop.

"It's Aldous, right?"

Surprise in his eyes. He didn't expect me to know his name.

"Can I sit down?" I ask. "I'm knackered. You should try running in all this kit."

The woman is in her early thirties, dressed in smart casual wear, as though she works in an office. She has quieted down, but her little boy is still clinging to her leg.

"I can't breathe," she croaks.

Fisher loosens his hold, giving her more air.

"What's your name?" I ask.

"Lucinda."

"And your little boy?"

"Oliver."

"Can you send Oliver over to me?" I ask.

My shoulder radio crackles with static.

"Turn it off," says Fisher.

I turn down the volume, but it's still relaying our conversation.

"Hey, Oliver, how about you come over to me," I say, leaning forward and holding out my arms.

His wet brown eyes look impossibly large as he shakes his head. He's dressed in a Thomas the Tank Engine T-shirt and oversized shorts. His red trainers have little lights that blink when he walks.

"My name is Phil," I say. "Can I see your trainers? They're very cool."

Oliver shakes his head, unwilling to let go of his mother.

"The police will be outside by now. You can't get away," I say.

Fisher's eyes jitter back and forth.

"If you put down the knife and let her go, I'll put that in my report. I'll say you cooperated."

He motions to my Taser. "Give it to me."

"I can't do that."

He tightens the grip on Lucinda's neck. She gives a squeal of alarm.

"OK. I'm putting it down."

I lay the Taser on the slate-gray floor and slide it towards him, but only halfway. If he bends to pick it up, he'll have to let Lucinda go or lower the knife. I might get an opening.

"Let's make a trade," I say. "Release Lucinda and take me instead."

He doesn't move.

"I'll take off my vest and my belt. You can use me as a hostage."

Fisher is too agitated to think clearly. He glances at the door behind me and the window at his back, desperately looking for a way out.

"Or you could leave," I say. "Through the garden. You could jump the back fence."

Horgan will be covering both entrances. Fisher won't get more than fifty yards before they bring him down.

"But you have to go now," I say. "Time is running out."

Suddenly, he releases Lucinda and shoves her across the kitchen. She stumbles over Oliver, and I catch her before she falls on him. In that moment, Fisher crouches and picks up the Taser, which he points at my chest. Lucinda and Oliver scramble past me.

"Unlock it," he says, motioning towards the patio door, which leads to the garden. I do as he asks. He waves the Taser and tells me to back away. I take a step.

"Further."

If I could get closer, I could kick out his legs or knock the Taser from his hand. But a moment later he's gone, racing across the garden, leaping at the back fence, and scrambling over the top.

I yell into the radio. "He's running. The road behind eighty-seven."

Lucinda and Oliver are outside on the pavement being comforted by neighbors. I expect to find police cars, but the road is empty.

I radio, "This is Delta four. Where is my backup?"

"They're at the address."

"No."

Confusion. Corrections. Accusations. A few minutes later, the van appears and skids to a halt. Horgan has a face like thunder.

"Where is he?"

"He went over the back fence. I thought you had it covered."

"You gave us the wrong address. You said Cleaver Street."

"No, sir. I said Cleaver Square."

"Are you calling me a liar?"

"No. I just . . . I don't . . . I'm sure . . ."

Horgan turns his back on me, barking orders, organizing a search of the surrounding streets. Officers take off on foot, while the minivan circles the block, but Fisher will be gone by now.

Could I have made a mistake? It was dark. I was running.

Horgan comes back to me and demands to know what happened. I give him the bullet points.

"You handed over your weapon?"

"He was holding her at knifepoint."

"You allowed him to get away."

"I negotiated the release of a hostage."

He doesn't believe me. He thinks I've fucked up. I want to argue that he failed to cover the balcony at Cornish House, but it's not my place to question a senior officer. A gust of wind cuts through my sweat-soaked clothes, making me shiver.

"Go back to the station, Constable. Write up your report."

"Yes, sir."

I move towards the building.

"Where are you going?"

"I wanted to check on the mother and her son."

"She is a witness. You are not allowed to speak to her."

A witness! Am I on trial here?

I have to wait for a car to become available. In the meantime, I stand on the far side of the road, where neighbors have gathered to watch and speculate, taking photographs and posting on social media.

More personnel arrive. Paramedics check on Lucinda and Oliver. Forensics officers. Detectives in rumpled suits. Nish volunteers to drive me back to Southwark. He's the only officer who has asked about my welfare. The others treat me like I've cost them the game in the dying minutes of extra time.

"What game?" I want to scream. I chased him. I cornered him. I confronted him.

Staring straight ahead, I watch the world slip by outside the car—the pedestrians, diners, dog walkers, and joggers, the people coming home late from work or heading off to late shifts.

"Did I make a mistake?" I ask.

"No. You gave us the right address."

"But Horgan said—"

"He misheard you."

The silence seems to hum. Nish sucks in a breath, expanding his chest and holding it for a good ten seconds before he exhales.

"When we got to the address and it was obvious that you weren't there, Horgan could have called the dispatcher and confirmed your location, but he insisted that we check out the other address first."

"Why?"

There is another long pause.

"You think he wanted to leave me exposed?" I ask.

Nish doesn't answer.

My eyes are flat and my hands motionless, but I feel like I've stepped from a fairground ride and the ground is buckling and dipping beneath me.

"You should have stayed outside," says Nish. "You should have waited for backup."

"Which wasn't coming," I say bitterly.

He glances in the side mirror and indicates before changing lanes.

"I haven't known you long, Phil, but it's obvious that you're trying to prove yourself. I used to think it was because of your gender or your size, but I think you're trying to prove that you're nothing like your father."

A bubble of emotion is caught in my throat. It hurts when I swallow.

"I am a *good* police officer."

"You don't have to convince me, but they are trying to drive you out. And you can't afford to make any mistakes."

28

Sunday afternoon and I'm watching Henry play rugby at a sports ground in Chiswick. It's the last game of the season and Archie is more interested in jumping into puddles and poking sticks into muddy holes. I used to enjoy watching these games, but now I worry every time Henry gets tackled, or charges into a ruck as though he's still nineteen and indestructible.

This is supposed to be a social league, but they take it very seriously, huffing and puffing as they pack down into scrums. They grunt and shove and grunt some more. It's like watching a reverse tug-of-war, because they're pushing instead of pulling. Henry's team is losing. The opposition has some huge Maori players, who effortlessly break tackles or bring opponents to a shuddering halt.

When the final whistle blows, the teams shake hands and embrace, suddenly best mates after ninety minutes of crashing into each other. Archie runs onto the field to greet Henry, asking if they won and if Henry scored any points. No on both counts.

Henry hoists him onto his shoulders, spreading the mud around. Archie will have to change his clothes before we go out to an early dinner.

The crowd disperses. Henry showers and changes, while I wait in the car, putting on a story-time CD for Archie. He says he's too grown-up for Thomas the Tank Engine, but listens to the stories anyway.

Our favorite Chinese restaurant in Wandsworth serves yum cha on weekends. It's full of families at this hour. Henry has missed a smudge of mud on his earlobe, which I wipe away. As we wait to be seated, Archie slips from his side and peers at the fish in an aquarium. He taps the glass and talks to them, rocking back and forth on his heels.

A waitress shows us to the table. Henry inventories his aches and pains, showing me his grazed elbow and saying he might have tweaked his hammie. He seems different lately. Stressed. Normally his eyes are so warm and welcoming, but I've noticed a hardness in them, particularly when I mention Tempe or talk about the wedding. It's as though he holds her responsible for my troubles at work, which I think is unfair. Whenever a man's finger seeks someone to blame, it always seems to find a woman.

I've been off work since the hostage incident and will face a panel of inquiry into my surrendering of my weapon. The bodycam footage will exonerate me, as well as Lucinda's statement, but I can't take anything for granted because I have no allies in this fight.

This is one of the reasons that Henry is struggling—the politics. Why aren't my colleagues leaping to my defense? Why isn't the Police Federation doing more to support me?

"What is going to happen at the hearing?" he asks, toying with Archie's box of crayons.

"I will tell them exactly what happened."

"You're not going to mention Goodall, are you?"

"I have no proof."

"People are taking advantage of you," he mutters.

"What people?"

"Goodall. Your mother. Your friends."

He won't say Tempe's name.

The waitress arrives, a skinny thing with a high ponytail and heavy mascara. Henry is much nicer to her than he has been to me. He negotiates sweetly with Archie, who only wants prawn crackers but agrees to have some egg fried rice.

Our drinks are delivered, and then the food. Henry orders another beer, then another. Looks like I'll be driving home. Meanwhile, the restaurant buzzes around us and I feel captive rather than loved.

When our meals have been eaten, I excuse myself and visit the ladies'. I'm on my way back to the table when I hear Tempe's voice.

"Great minds," she says. "Are you here with Henry?"

"And Archie. How about you?"

She holds up a laminated menu. "Picking up takeaway."

"Do people still do that?" I ask, teasing her. "Why not get it delivered?"

"I'm old-fashioned," she says. "And I feel sorry for those cyclists."

"But you don't have a car."

"I borrowed one from a friend."

I want to ask her which friend, but she'd realize that I'm prying.

"How did you know about this place?"

"You mentioned it. You said it was the best yum cha in London."

"Did I?"

I glance back at Henry, who is indicating to the waitress that he wants another beer.

"We've finished eating; otherwise I'd ask you to join us," I say.

"I could have a quick drink," she says brightly.

"Look who I found," I say as we reach the table. Henry nods a greeting but doesn't get to his feet. Tempe has to find a chair. She doesn't seem to notice his chilliness, so she makes a fuss over Archie, letting him show her his Matchbox toys and the racetrack he's drawn on the paper tablecloth.

Our waitress arrives at the table with another beer for Henry, but he's changed his mind and asks for the bill. Tempe doesn't seem put out, but I'm embarrassed for both of us. My fairy-tale prince is acting like a toad, which is so unlike him. He lost a rugby game. I bumped into a friend. Ungrateful sod!

29

I make a point of visiting Tempe the next day to apologize. I pick up a bunch of carnations at a florist near the station, a Bulgarian who calls me "pretty lady" and says that a boy should be buying me flowers. After a short drive and a lucky parking spot, I jog up the steps of Tempe's building. As I reach for the buzzer, I jerk my arm away. Someone has defaced the front door with red paint. The word "WHORE" is written in leaking capital letters that reach to the edges of the door frame. More paint has spilled onto the front step and splattered the handrail.

Tempe answers the intercom, saying, "I'm sorry about the door."

"Was it him?"

"I don't know."

She meets me at the top of the stairs. We hug. She seems more fragile today. Her hair is unbrushed and her eyes hollowed out.

"I'll get Henry to clean it off," I say.

"That's OK. I'll clean it up. And Mr. Swingler upstairs says we have spare paint in the basement."

She takes the flowers. "What are these for?"

"Yesterday. I'm sorry about Henry. He was being a dickhead."

"Don't apologize. I'm used to it."

"Why?"

"People don't like me very much."

"I'm sure that's not true."

"Oh, I don't mind. My grandma used to say birds always peck at the best fruit."

Tempe's eyes begin shining. "I've never had a friend like you. You're always so happy to see me. You don't push me away. When I'm with you, I feel complete."

I'm embarrassed by her tears. "Please stop crying."

"Sorry. I'm being silly."

"Don't apologize."

She squeezes my hand. "If anything ever happens to me . . ."

"Nothing is going to happen."

"But if it does, I want you to know that I love you."

I'm embarrassed by the depths of her feelings and look for a way to change the subject. I want to ask her about her mother in Belfast and see if she openly lies to me again about her three sisters and her soldier father. I know she makes up stories, but I thought it was different with me. She didn't need to exaggerate or to fabricate to win my friendship.

We all tell little white lies. When Sara asks me whether I like her new boyfriend, I always say he's lovely. Every new dress or hairstyle is "really nice" even when it's not. I wouldn't let a friend make a complete fashion faux pas, but I can accept that our tastes are different.

Henry lies to me all the time. He says he had only the one beer or that he's just leaving the pub or that training ran late. And I tell him that I bought a dress in the sales and that my occasional let's-get-this-over-with orgasms are real. What does it matter if Tempe makes up stories? I'm sure she has a reason.

"We should talk about the graffiti," I say.

"I don't want to think about it."

"You can't ignore this."

"I'm not ignoring it. I'm surviving it."

The flat has more furniture now but she still seems to haunt the place like an anxious ghost. She has a squishy sofa that people struggle to get out of and a mismatched armchair and a mosaic-tiled coffee table. Apart from her sketches, she doesn't surround herself with mementos or souvenirs that might give clues about her past. No photographs or books or postcards. She hasn't even bothered getting a television.

"What do you do of an evening?" I ask.

"I draw."

"Can I see some more of them?"

"I'm still working on your wedding present."

"You must have others."

"You're my muse. Don't laugh. You are."

"Please show me some other drawings."

"They're rubbish."

"Please. I want to see them."

Reluctantly, she goes to the bedroom and retrieves her small wheel-on suitcase. Thumbing the latches, she opens the lid. Inside there are dozens of sketchbooks. She chooses one. I sit on the edge of the bed and open it. The drawings are similar to others she's done, but this time her model is a teenage girl with large, luminous eyes and long, straight hair that falls to the small of her back.

"Who is she?" I ask.

"A friend."

"What's her name?"

"Mallory."

I remember Mrs. Brown mentioning Mallory Hopper and asking if Tempe had ever spoken about her.

"Where did you meet?"

"At school in Belfast."

I am turning the pages. There are dozens of drawings of Mallory, some half-done or revealing small parts of her, such as hands or her feet or her ears or her eyes. As with her sketches of me, Tempe seems to have practiced drawing particular features, before putting the pieces together.

"These are beautiful," I say.

"They're rubbish," Tempe replies. "I could never get her eyes right. I tried too hard, but something was always missing. It was so frustrating."

I turn another page and this time come across a series of nudes with Mallory as the model. She isn't sexualized or idealized. There is nothing salacious or erotic about the sketches. Mallory has been captured in a series of casual poses, drying herself with a towel or pulling a dress over her head.

"Did she pose for you?"

"Yes."

"How old was she?"

"Eighteen."

The answer is quick and defensive. Tempe tries to explain. "Some people think a nude drawing has a sexual message, but that's not true, not in this case. When you take away clothes, you take away the context. It could be the past or the present. Anywhere in the world."

"They're beautiful."

"Exactly. There's nothing bad or dirty or evil about them."

"Did someone think that?"

Tempe doesn't answer, but I sense that I'm right.

"Tell me about Mallory."

Tempe sits next to me on the bed. The sketchbook is open across our thighs.

"She wasn't the prettiest or the most popular girl at our school, but she was definitely the saddest."

"Why was she sad?"

"Her twin brothers both drowned on a holiday to Ballycastle. One of them got into trouble and the other tried to save him. In one terrible afternoon, Mallory became an only child."

"Did that really happen?" I ask, concerned that she might be lying to me again.

"You can look it up. There were stories in the newspapers. Her parents were devastated. They turned the house into a shrine to the twins. Masses were said for them. Scholarships were named after them. Fundraisers were held for them. Our parish priest said that Conner and Davie were not dead because they lived in our hearts. I remember looking at Mallory as he said this and wondering how she felt.

"I followed her home from the church on the day of the funerals. Hundreds of people came back for the reception, but Mallory seemed to be invisible. She was sitting alone in the garden. I sat down next to her. We talked about our recent English exam. I liked the way she tied her hair, pulling the sides up and keeping the back long and straight.

"I invited her to my place after school. She came. We chilled out, watching videos. That's how it began. A friendship. Later, people tried to give it other names, but they didn't understand."

"What other names?"

"It doesn't matter. People were cruel to Mallory. They would tease her about her thick-soled shoes and her unshaven legs and her un-plucked eyebrows and dowdy clothes. Mrs. Hopper took me aside one day and asked me, 'What's your story?' What a stupid question! Why did I have to have a story? Couldn't I have more than one?

"'Mallory says you're very smart,' Mrs. Hopper said.

"'She's the smart one,' I said.

"'But you work harder, Mallory said, and you're better at art.'

"I offered to draw Mallory's portrait for Mrs. Hopper. I arranged her on a window seat with the sun behind her, creating a soft halo of light around her head. It wasn't the first time I had drawn her, but until then

I'd done it from memory. This time my hands were shaking and I felt like I was touching her skin with my fingertips as the pencil moved across the page.

"When I finished the drawing, I still wasn't happy, but Mrs. Hopper thought it was beautiful and wanted to get it framed. She said I should start a business, drawing people for money at St. George's Market, but I wasn't interested in drawing anyone else."

"Were you in love with her?" I whisper.

"Maybe. Yes. But not in the way you think."

"Where is Mallory now?"

Tempe shrugs. "She went off to university and found new friends."

"You didn't stay in touch?"

"No."

"That's a shame."

Tempe closes the sketchbook and returns it to the suitcase. I want to tell her that I've talked to her mother and ask her why she ran away from Belfast, but my phone is vibrating. I don't recognize the number. Normally I'd let it go through to voicemail. I pick up.

"Hi, who is this?"

There is a long silence and a muffled "Sorry" before the call suddenly ends.

"Wrong number?" asks Tempe.

"I don't know. She sounded upset."

I wait for her to call again. When nothing happens, I search my call history and find the number. It's not in my contacts list.

I call. It rings and goes to a voicemail message.

"Hello, I can't come to the phone right now—probably because of the children—but if you leave me a message I might get back to you when they're in bed or they turn eighteen."

I recognize Alison Goodall's voice from our yoga class. I'm about to leave a message for her but stop myself, aware that Goodall might have access to her voicemail or could be listening. Instead I hang up and call again. This time she picks up and says nothing. I can hear her breathing.

"It's Philomena. Are you OK?"

Silence.

"Are you hurt?"

"No."

"Is he listening?"

"No."

"Where are you?"

"At home." She stifles a sob. "I packed my bags, but he found them. I thought he was going to kill me."

"Get out! Leave now!"

"I can't. He deadlocked the doors. I'm locked in the house."

"Where are the children?"

"Nathan is at a summer holiday camp. Chloe is with me. Sleeping. It took me ages to settle her."

"Call the police."

"I can't. He'll find out."

"He can't keep you locked up."

"I'm sorry. I shouldn't have called you." She is about to hang up.

"No! Wait. Where is he now?"

"I don't know. At work."

"I'm coming over."

I grab my car keys and Tempe follows me down the stairs, asking questions. "Is she OK? Is she hurt?" She begins to tell me a story about a friend of hers who was locked in a house, but I don't have time to listen. As I pull away, she shouts the words, "Be careful."

30

The weather gives a lie to the day. Sunny. Warm. High clouds like smoky smudges on the upper atmosphere. I keep replaying the phone call in my head, wondering what pushed Alison to fight back. I should call the police. I *am* the police. But how would it look if the call came from me?

When I reach Kempe Road, I have to circle the block to find a parking spot. Pulling over near the school, I park the car and jog back towards the house. A rubbish truck rumbles past me and I catch the scent of rotting food and diesel fumes. A different wind brings the smell of the river.

The curtains are drawn. I ring the doorbell. Nobody answers. I kneel and push open the mail flap, which pivots on a hinge.

"Alison? It's me."

I see the lower half of her body as she approaches along the hallway, barefoot in frayed and faded jeans.

"Where is the key?" I ask.

"He took it with him."

"What about the back door?"

"The same."

She leans against the wall and slides down to my eye level, sitting on her ankles. Her hair falls down to cover her face.

"I thought he was going to kill her," she says.

"Who?"

Alison's chest heaves and a sob starts so deep inside her that it emerges as a long moan.

"Where is Chloe?" I ask anxiously.

"Asleep." She sniffles. "He held her over the banister by her ankles. He threatened to . . ." She can't finish. "I packed a suitcase, like you said. And I've been saving money. Hiding it. He gives me an allowance every month, but I've saved bits and pieces. My escape fund."

"Where were you planning to go?"

"My sister lives in Brighton. But Darren has threatened to have her arrested. She's scared."

"I can take you to a shelter."

"He'll find me."

"What about your parents?"

"That's the first place he'll look."

"But you'll be safe there. You can take out a restraining order."

"He'll kill me. He'll kill all of us."

"I won't let that happen."

Alison raises her head. Her hair drops away from her eyes.

"You helped that other woman. I don't know her name."

She means Tempe. "How did you know about her?"

"I found messages on his phone. Darren denied it, of course. He thinks you're hiding her. Is she safe?"

"Yes," I say hopefully.

"Can you do the same for me?"

I lower the mail flap and step back from the door. The bay window is double glazed or triple glazed. It won't break easily. The upper windows are too high to reach without a ladder. I can hear Henry's voice, telling me that I can't save every battered wife and abused girlfriend. But this woman, this mother, needs me and this is why I became a police officer. The system has betrayed Alison, my system, the one I swore an oath to uphold. What good are laws to protect the vulnerable if nobody will enforce them?

The house has a side gate leading to the rear garden. I tell Alison to meet me round the back. Following the side path, past rubbish bins and recycling tubs and a bicycle with a baby seat, I reach the rear garden, which is long and narrow with paving stones forming a barbecue area flanked by shrubs. The back door has small glass panels on the upper half and an old-style deadlock. I could smash the glass, but I couldn't break the door open without an ax or sledgehammer.

Alison appears at the kitchen window, watching me as I search for some means of forcing the door open. I point to an upstairs window, shouting, "Is that the bedroom?"

She nods.

The sash window is directly above the kitchen extension, which has a flat asphalt roof and a row of skylights. The drop is only about seven feet.

I point upstairs and shout, "Meet me at the window."

The garden has a decorative wheelbarrow, painted white and filled with potted plants. I drag it closer to the wall and push pots aside. Stepping onto the barrow, I wedge one foot into the space between the downpipe and the brick wall and reach higher, grabbing the gutter and pulling myself onto the flat bitumen roof.

Alison is at the window. She has Chloe in her arms. She undoes the keylocks and slides the sash window to the top of the frame.

"Pass her to me."

Chloe clings more tightly to her neck.

"It's OK, sweet pea. It's an adventure."

"We don't have much time."

Chloe squirms and complains but allows herself to be lowered into my arms. I feel the padding of her nappy and the softness of her hair against my cheek. It's only when I smile at her that I notice the bruise on her cheek.

Alison looks at the drop and hesitates. "Do you have your wallet and car keys?" I ask.

"I'll get them."

"Also your passport and birth certificates for the kids."

"Why?"

"Proof of identity."

She disappears and I bounce Chloe on my hip. She puts her thumb into her mouth and studies me as though she's considering crying but hasn't made up her mind.

Alison reappears. This time she pushes a small suitcase through the window and lowers it down to me. There is a second case, but it's too big to fit through the window. She leaves it behind and climbs out, one leg at a time, turning onto her stomach as she scrabbles blindly with her toes, searching for a foothold. I help direct her feet and hold her steady until we're all standing together on the flat roof, looking across neighboring gardens.

"Everything all right?" asks a female voice.

An elderly neighbor is peering up at us. She's holding a watering can in both hands and is blinking over the top of her sunglasses.

"Fine, thank you, Mrs. Purnell," says Alison.

"What you are doing up there?"

"We're considering an extension. This is my . . . my . . ."

"Architect," I say.

The old woman's face folds into creases. "You'll need planning permission. Paul will most likely complain."

"How is Mr. Purnell?"

"He only has the one setting: grumpy."

Mrs. Purnell seems keen to chat. "People want such big houses nowadays—a room for every child. When I was growing up, I shared a room with my sister. Did me no harm. Made us closer."

"You don't talk to your sister," says Alison.

"That's because she stole my Christmas pudding recipe."

"We have to go," I whisper.

I jump down from the roof and Alison lowers Chloe into my outstretched hands. The toddler is less nervous, and her arms go immediately around my neck, clinging to me.

"Where is your car?" I ask.

"I don't drive. Darren doesn't let me."

"We'll take my car. Where do your parents live?"

"In Highgate."

"Call them. Tell them you need somewhere to stay."

With every step we take away from the house, Alison seems to be losing confidence, glancing backwards, wanting to retreat.

"Nathan," she squeaks. "He's still at holiday camp."

"Where?"

"His school. He finishes at three."

"Who is supposed to pick him up?"

"Me most days." She turns back towards the house. "I can't leave. I have to stay."

I glance at my phone.

"We have time. Call the school and say there's been a family emergency. Tell them a friend is picking up Nathan. Give them my name." I open my phone and book an Uber, which is three minutes away. I give Alison the details of the car and driver.

"I'll get Nathan," I say. "I'll bring him to your parents' house."

Moments later, I'm jogging along Kempe Road towards the primary school. As I turn the second corner, I see mothers gathering at the school gates and cars queuing in the kiss-and-drop zone.

At the school office the staff are wearing fancy dress, each a different fairy-tale character. I flash my warrant card to the cheerful receptionist, who is dressed as Cinderella. Her smile fades as quickly as it formed.

"Is everything all right?"

A colleague, Snow White, answers. "Mrs. Goodall just called. We need to get Nathan from class."

Cinderella glances at the clock. "It's almost pickup time."

"I need him now," I say.

Huffing in annoyance, she looks for her shoes, which are not glass slippers and are hiding somewhere beneath her desk. After finding them, she struggles to squeeze her feet inside, seeming to relish making me wait.

I follow her across the asphalt playground where groups of children are playing tag or riding scooters around an obstacle course of traffic cones. We enter a separate building where every window is plastered with drawings and paintings and collages. I wait in the corridor where a notice board has out-of-date flyers about secondhand uniforms and a school choir recital at a local church.

Cinderella reappears with Nathan, who is weighed down by an oversized bag that makes him look like a tortoise.

"Where's Mummy?" he asks with a slight lisp. His foppish fringe falls across one eyebrow and he's missing a front tooth.

"She had to take Chloe to your grandparents' house. We're going to meet her there."

"You mean Nan and Pop."

"Right."

"I'm not supposed to talk to strangers."

"That's very good advice, but I'm not a stranger. I'm Phil."

"Phil is a boy's name."

"It's short for Philomena. Can I carry that for you?" I swing his schoolbag over my shoulder.

In that instant the bell rings. Classrooms empty and the corridors fill with small bodies and loud voices.

"Is there another entrance?" I ask.

"Is there a problem?" asks the assistant.

"My car is parked on the other side of the school."

"I suppose you could use the south gate."

"That's for seniors," says Nathan, who is clearly not a rule breaker.

"Today you are a big boy."

We cross the asphalt playground, which has painted lines for a netball court and hopscotch grids. More parents are waiting at the gate. I take Nathan's hand as we weave between shoulders. Children are chatting breathlessly or complaining about being hot or hungry or exhausted.

My Fiat is parked under the trees, where it's collected fresh splatters of bird shit on the bonnet.

"Where is my booster seat?" he asks.

"I don't have one."

"Is that allowed?"

He's six years old and sounds like a barrister.

"I'm a police officer. I can make exceptions."

"Can I sit in the front seat?"

"No."

"But you're a police officer."

"And you have to do what I say."

He sits in the back and clips up his seat belt but soon changes the subject, talking about how he has to make a shoebox diorama for his dream bedroom, and how his Nan and Pop have a dog called Betsy.

I pull out of the parking spot, but traffic is backed up in either direction because we're so close to the school.

"Hey, there's Daddy," says Nathan, waving out the window.

I tell him to duck down but it's too late. Darren Goodall is walking towards the school. He chooses that moment to glance up and his eyes meet mine. He can't immediately put a name to my face because I'm so out of place. He smiles and raises his hand, ready to wave, but the penny drops. He looks again. This time he sees Nathan in the backseat.

"Daddy! Daddy!"

Goodall has stepped between cars and is running towards me. He's fifty yards away, picking up speed. I hammer my horn, but the driver in front of me raises her hands in frustration. She has nowhere to go.

Suddenly, a gap clears on the opposite side of the road. I swerve into the oncoming traffic as Goodall reaches the driver's-side window and hammers on the glass, yelling, but I can't hear his words. He tries to open my door. I floor the accelerator. Goodall hangs on.

The driver ahead of me looks aghast, convinced I'm going to crash into her, but I swerve again and shake Goodall loose as I straighten and find the correct lane. Now he's in my rearview mirror, still running, hoping he might catch me at the next set of lights, but I accelerate through the changing red.

Nathan has gone quiet.

"Why didn't you stop for Daddy?" he lisps.

"I'm taking you to your mummy."

"You made him angry."

"Does he get angry a lot?"

"Sometimes."

"Does he ever hit your mummy?"

"I'm not supposed to say."

"Why not?"

"It makes Daddy cross."

31

Alison Goodall's parents live in a rambling house with slate-covered gable rooftops that are dotted with chimney pots. The dwelling looks pieced together, as though each new addition and extension has been an afterthought. The front garden is dominated by a large oak tree that has a rope swing hanging from the lower branches.

Keith, a short man with a softness of body and voice, is the more welcoming of the two. His wife, Jenny, is a nervous creature with a face full of sharp angles that could have been drawn with a maths set. Although happy to see her grandchildren, she treats me coolly, as though I am somehow responsible for Alison's marital difficulties. I want to show her the photographs of Alison's bruises and play her the emergency call from Nathan. Maybe then she'll change her mind about Darren Goodall.

Both grandparents are fussing over Nathan and Chloe, feeding them buttered tea cake and orange cordial in the kitchen. Alison pulls back the curtains of the sitting room, waiting for her husband to come. She has turned off her mobile phone, but periodically the landline begins ringing, echoing from a phone table in the entrance hall.

The house is full of antique furniture, or French provincial knockoffs that don't particularly match or suggest an overarching theme. It is the same with the decor, which looks dated rather than traditional.

"Maybe he'll come to apologize," says Jenny, who has brought us tea on a tray.

"Not this time," says Alison.

"But he's your husband."

"Nobody should hit a child."

"I'm sure it was an accident."

"Did Daddy ever hit you?"

Jenny looks aghast. "No, but that's . . . I mean, they're different men. Keith is a teacher."

I have to swallow a laugh. Jenny isn't impressed.

Alison argues. "Are you suggesting that police officers should be given a free pass? Beat your wife and get out of jail free?"

"No. You're taking it the wrong way."

"He threatened to kill me. He locked me in the house."

"You should try marriage counseling again," says Jenny.

"Darren lasted one session. He accused the counselor of picking on him."

Jenny looks at me, hoping for support, but I'm with Alison on this one, although I'd rather not be making enemies of people who can destroy my career.

Keith comes in for a cup of tea. He adds sugar and stirs, focusing his attention on me. "You'll stop him, won't you? If he tries to throw his weight around."

"I shouldn't be involved."

"Why not?"

"We have something of a history."

Jenny squeaks in alarm. "Are you sleeping with him?"

"Not that sort of history."

Nathan appears in the doorway. He has a cordial mustache. "Are we having a sleepover?"

"Absolutely," says Alison.

He runs back to tell his sister.

Alison turns back to the window and peeks through the curtains as a car pulls up outside. Her whole body stiffens. Together, we watch Goodall get out of his car and walk towards the house. Alison tells her mother to take the children upstairs.

"I'll talk to him," says Keith.

"No! Don't go out," says Alison.

"I'll tell him you're not here."

"He won't believe you."

The doorbell has a *bing-bong* chime. Goodall holds his finger on the button and hammers a fist on the outer glass door. Keith opens the inner door and tries to sound jovial.

"Darren. How are things?"

"Where is she?"

Alison is curled up on an armchair, hugging her knees and holding the sleeves of her cardigan in her fists.

"Alison isn't here."

"Don't bullshit me. I want to see her."

"She doesn't want to see you."

A loud bang echoes through the house. Goodall has launched a kick, trying to break the door down.

"Call the police," I whisper to Alison.

"But they won't—"

"They'll come. Call them."

I step into the entrance hall. I can hear Jenny upstairs with the children. They're singing along to a nursery rhyme recording. Alison talks to the operator, giving her address. I catch some of the words: "husband," "violent," "children."

Goodall has moved from the path to the bay window, where he begins yelling Alison's name, sensing that she's inside, listening.

"Hey, Al, we don't need this drama. Not in front of the kids. Come home and we'll sort this out."

Keith goes outside, stepping onto the grass. "You're trespassing, Darren. We've called the police."

Goodall ignores him, yelling at the window. "You can't leave me, Alison. I've already called child services. I told them I found a bruise on Chloe's face and that you must have hit her."

Alison's entire body jackknifes out of the chair and fear fills her eyes. She is shaking her head.

"I told them it wasn't the first time," he yells. "I said that you had tried to blame me before."

Alison runs for the door. I pull her back, wrapping my arms around her.

"He's bluffing. I've heard the tape."

Goodall is still talking. "Who are the police going to believe? You or me? We both know the answer. Come home."

Alison breaks free, but doesn't try to reach the door. Instead she climbs the stairs. On the landing, she throws her arms around Nathan and Chloe, pulling them into a hug. Protecting them. Guarding them.

"I'll tell them about your drinking," yells Goodall. "And the drugs."

Jenny looks over the banister. "What drugs?"

"I'll show them where you hide your pills," he yells.

Alison's head swings from side to side. "I don't, I swear. They're antidepressants. That's all."

I hear a short blast from a police siren and draw back the curtains far enough to see the patrol car pull up and two uniformed officers emerge. Goodall turns to greet them, opening his arms and smiling like he's catching up with old friends. His booming voice travels as he introduces himself, emphasizing his rank.

"I'm sorry about this, boys. It's a misunderstanding. My wife is upset. She lost her temper and hit one of our children. This is her parents' house. The kids are inside. I'm worried about them."

"He's lying," says Keith, who has joined them at the gate.

"Stay out of this," says Goodall.

Keith ignores him. "My daughter has left him and taken the children. She wants a divorce."

Goodall laughs. "Nobody has said anything about a divorce. This is a storm in a teacup. I want to see my children."

The officers have quieter voices and I catch only snippets of the conversation. Alison seems to have lost the power of speech. Jenny is trying to talk to her but getting no responses.

I sit on the step below her and touch her knee, trying to break through whatever negative thought loop has hijacked her mind and pushed aside all logic.

"The police will need to talk to you. If they ask you about Chloe's bruises, tell them exactly what happened. Say he's done it before. Tell them you're frightened. Do you understand? Ask for a DAP notice."

"A what?"

"Domestic Abuse Protection Notice. Say you need to get away from him, until he cools down."

"They won't charge him."

"Maybe not, but a protection notice means he can't approach you for forty-eight hours. In that time the police will apply to a magistrate for a prevention order, which protects you for up to twenty-eight days."

"That's not long enough."

"You can get an extension."

"What about child services?"

"They will want to talk to you."

"It will be his word against mine."

"You have hospital records. Recordings. His only hope is to bully you into silence."

"I'm not going back to him."

"Good."

Nathan is tugging at her sleeve. "Why is Daddy so cross? Did we do something wrong?"

"No, sweetheart," says Alison, brushing hair from his eyes.

The front door opens. Keith enters with a constable, who looks about my age, with wide-set eyes and a narrow face. I don't know him. This is a different command area to mine. Camden instead of Southwark.

Jenny takes the children as Alison stands and descends the stairs, pausing at the hallway mirror to check on her appearance. She follows the constable into the sitting room, where introductions are made and notes are taken. I hover in the background, looking for a chance to leave.

The second officer is talking to Goodall outside, suggesting that he leave until things cool down. They are following procedure, de-escalating the situation. I wait until Goodall has reluctantly driven away before I say goodbye to Alison.

"I'm sorry, but who are you?" asks the first constable, who is perched on the edge of the sofa, recording the information on an electronic tablet.

"A friend," I say.

"She helped me escape from the house," says Alison, who seems calmer now and more confident.

"And what's your name?"

"Philomena McCarthy."

He glances at his screen. "You picked Nathan up from his school."

I nod.

"Have you ever seen Mr. Goodall attack his wife?"

"No, but he has a history."

"How do you know that?"

"I'm a police officer stationed at Southwark. I've had dealings with Sergeant Goodall before."

"Dealings?"

"Yes."

At that moment I wonder about whether I've made a mistake. If I could turn back the clock, would I take Tempe to hospital or arrest Goodall or look for any history of domestic abuse? My chest tightens and I swallow hard on my panic, which lasts only a moment.

The officer is watching me sidelong, waiting to see what I might say next. He takes down my details and says he may need a statement from me later. In the meantime, I'm free to go.

Darren Goodall's car is no longer on the verge, but I keep glancing in my mirrors on the drive home, expecting him to be there, following me. Watching. I have poked the bear and there will be consequences.

32

It's Archie's birthday tomorrow and I promised to bake him a pirate cake, which is far beyond my *Great British Bake Off* skills. I've given up on the idea of a ship and opted for a Jolly Roger with a pink bandanna and an eye patch.

"What do you think?" I ask Henry, showing him the cake.

"It looks like Finbar without a beard. And a lopsided smile."

He's right, but that's OK. Henry helps me clean up and begins stacking the dishwasher.

"It's broken, remember?"

"But you got it fixed."

"When?"

"I came home and there was an invoice on the bench." Henry shows me the piece of paper. Ninety quid for the callout and labor.

"It must have been Tempe," I say, regretting it immediately.

"Did you give her a key?"

"No, not exactly."

Tempe knows that we leave a spare with Mrs. Ainsley in case we get locked out.

"She can't just waltz in here without permission," says Henry.

"She had my permission," I say, unsure of why I'm lying, but equally sure it's not such a big deal. "She offered to help."

"So, you're OK with her being here by herself—going through our things."

"She didn't go through our things."

"How do you know? The other day she picked up our dry cleaning. How did she even know that it needed to be collected? And what about the tires on my car? I mentioned they needed rotating and next thing she's arranged it all."

"Is that a bad thing? We're both so busy."

"She's taking over our lives."

"By collecting our dry cleaning." I laugh.

"OK, explain this." He leads me to the walk-in pantry. "Notice any-thing different?"

Shelves on three sides reach as high as the ceiling and are filled with cans and dry goods and condiments. Normally the panty is a mess, but someone has tidied the shelves, putting like with like, the sauces, tinned vegetables, pastas, pulses, rice, baking products, spices, and herbs. There are handwritten labels on each container, showing the contents and use-by dates. This is Tempe's doing.

Henry is at my shoulder. "She's a stage-five clinger."

"A what?"

"In the movie *Wedding Crashers*, Vince Vaughn called a girl a stage-five clinger because she talked about marriage after one hookup. That's Tempe. She followed you home and now she won't leave. Every time she's over here, she stays for dinner."

"Your mates drink all your beer and crash on our sofa, but I don't complain."

"That's different."

"Because they're your friends, not mine?"

"No."

"Why don't you like her?"

"I don't trust her. For all we know she could have sabotaged the dish-washer."

"Oh, come on."

"I'm serious. Read the note from the repairman: 'Replaced burned-out motor. Someone must have disconnected the waterline.' I didn't dis-connect the waterline, did you?"

"Of course not, but neither did Tempe."

Henry scoffs. "If she's such a hotshot wedding planner, why doesn't she have a website and testimonials? I've looked her up. There's not a single story or photograph. Nobody has ever heard of her."

"How many wedding planners can you name?"

His eyes have a malignant gleam. "How many times has she called you today?"

"Hardly at all," I say, but silently count.

"How many times did she text?"

"If it bothers you that much, I'll tell her that she can't come over because you think she's creepy."

"That's right—make me the bad guy."

"What do you want, Henry?"

"Get her to stop smothering us."

"I'm not being smothered."

"Well, I am."

He's about to say something else, but the doorbell sounds. Disappointed at being interrupted in mid-argument, he goes to the door, but a moment later he calls my name. I join him in the hallway. There are two police officers on the doorstep, the same constables who were at Alison's parents' house today. This time I learn their names. Noonan has a narrow face and Payne looks like one of Henry's overweight rugby mates, destined to be popping statins by the time he's fifty.

I invite them inside, but they decline.

"We would like you to accompany us to Holborn Police Station," says Noonan, addressing me as Constable McCarthy.

"Why?"

"A complaint has been made against you."

"What complaint?"

"Detective Sergeant Darren Goodall has accused you of kidnapping his son."

"That's ridiculous. You know the story—"

Payne interrupts. "We're following orders. Our boss has been fielding calls for the past hour. Chain-of-command stuff. He wants this sorted out."

I know what this means. Goodall has been calling in favors. Pulling strings. If he complains first, he might manage to fend off an investigation. He becomes the victim. I'm the perpetrator.

"Let me get my jacket," I say, going back into the house.

Henry is waiting in the kitchen. "What happened?"

"I'll explain later."

"Are you being arrested?"

"No. It's complicated."

"Is this about Tempe?"

"Not everything is about her," I say, harshly, and wish immediately that I could take it back.

In the police car, as I'm driven away, I think back to the pantry and the labels on the jars and containers. Something has been bugging me about them and it's not the fact that Tempe let herself into the house or that she secretly organized my messy shelves. I keep picturing the labels on the jars, each written in a neat cursive script. She had copied *my* handwriting.

33

Holborn Police Station looks like two buildings that have been cobbled together, one at street level made of low Portland stone and the other a tower rising from within like the stamen of a flower or a mushroom cloud.

Noonan and Payne had been chatty on the journey, pumping me for details, wanting the skinny on Goodall and his wife. They grow annoyed when I don't give them anything. By now the whole station will be talking about the hero cop whose child was kidnapped by a constable.

I'm taken to an office rather than an interview suite, which is a good sign. Waiting alone, I glance out the window, which overlooks Camden Lock. I can't see my mother's salon from here, but the painted canal boats are visible between buildings that have a faint yellow glow from the setting sun.

The door opens and I stand to attention. The first officer to enter is Chief Superintendent Drysdale, who had me suspended for arresting Goodall. I still don't know exactly what position he holds, but I remember the tattoo on his wrist. The second officer is dressed in smart casual clothes and looks like a detective or a budding politician. He introduces himself as Lawrence Pickering of the Police Federation. I didn't ask for a union rep, but I'm glad that he's here.

Pickering waits until I'm seated before he takes a chair, sitting apart from me. Drysdale is behind the lone desk, leaning forward with his hands clasped and his forearms resting on a manila folder.

"Thank you for coming," he says.

I didn't think it was optional, I want to reply, but politely nod. Don't offend. Don't provoke.

"Do you remember what I said to you when we last spoke, Constable McCarthy?"

"You said a number of things, sir."

"I expressly instructed you to let this issue go."

"What issue is that, sir?"

"This vendetta against Sergeant Goodall."

"I have no vendetta against him."

"He has accused you of kidnapping his child."

"I picked Nathan up from school."

"On whose authority?"

"His wife, Alison?"

"How do you know Mrs. Goodall?"

"I met her a few months ago."

"After you arrested her husband?" There is an arch tone to his voice.

"Yes, sir."

"You sought her out?"

"I was concerned for her safety."

"On what evidence?"

"I didn't believe that Tempe Brown was the first woman that Darren Goodall had assaulted."

"Was that your womanly intuition at work?"

Is that your misogyny asking?

"I followed the procedure for domestic abuse incidents by looking for any history of earlier complaints."

"You were told to leave the matter to others."

"I was concerned that we might be accused of covering up the incident. My bodycam footage wasn't uploaded and no paperwork was filed."

I can feel the ice beginning to crack beneath me.

"You accessed a police database for personal reasons," says Drysdale.

"I followed procedure and investigated a domestic violence callout."

"Which you were told to drop."

"You told me it was being handed over, not dropped."

There it is—the spark. Drysdale disliked me before, but now his hatred is a spluttering fuse. Pickering touches my forearm and whispers. "Word to the wise—don't antagonize him."

Drysdale is on his feet, anger radiating from him. "Are you questioning my authority, Constable?"

"That's not my intention . . . sir."

"Why did you go to the Goodalls' house today?" asks Drysdale.

"I had a phone call asking for help. Alison had been locked in the house by her husband."

"He denies that."

"Ask her."

"She hasn't given a statement to the police."

The answer shakes me. Drysdale opens the folder.

"When you went to the primary school, did you see Sergeant Goodall outside?"

"Yes, sir."

"He tried to stop you leaving, but you deliberately drove your vehicle at him."

"That's not what happened."

"He says that you're obsessed with him. You've been watching his house. Following his wife."

"He ran my bicycle off the road with his car."

"Did you make an official complaint?"

I don't answer.

Drysdale sighs in frustration and pushes back his chair. "You have maligned the reputation of a decorated police officer and disobeyed direct orders. You have used unreasonable force in making an arrest and illegally accessed a police database and used that information unlawfully. I am charging you with gross misconduct and recommending you be dismissed without notice from the Metropolitan Police Service."

I feel a scream building up in my chest, but my throat has closed and the only sound that escapes is a strangled moan.

"You will hand over your warrant card and badge and surrender any equipment that belongs to the Met."

My shoulders are shaking.

"I'm going to fight this. I will sue for wrongful dismissal."

Drysdale ignores me and gets to his feet, tucking the folder beneath his arm. As he reaches the door, he turns to me, his mouth curling in disgust. "How anybody ever let you join the Met is beyond me. Thankfully, that mistake is about to be rectified."

I expect the door to slam, but it closes with a gentle click that echoes in the silence of the room. Pickering hasn't moved or uttered a word.

"Where were you?" I ask. "You're supposed to be on my side."

He feigns surprise. "I'm afraid you are mistaken. I'm here on behalf of Sergeant Goodall."

"What?"

"He wanted to make sure that his actions and statements were correctly represented."

Pickering tugs at the sleeves of his jacket, making sure it's sitting properly on his shoulders. He's a show pony, or as my uncle Clifton likes to say, "all lace curtains and kippers for dinner."

"I did try to warn you," he says, "but your mouth doesn't know when to quit."

"Women should be seen and not heard."

"You're putting words in my mouth."

"I'm sure they'll wash down with a beer. I hear Goodall is buying."

I grab at his wrist and pull up his coat sleeve, looking for the three-letter tattoo. There isn't one.

Pickering shakes his arm loose and steps back looking at me as though I'm crazy. I can smell his aftershave and something malodorous on his breath.

"Ever heard the phrase 'all things being equal'? It's bullshit. They never are. Enjoy civilian life, Miss McCarthy."

34

Outside, angry beyond reason, I walk aimlessly through the rain-slimed streets, staying in the shadows because I don't want to see my reflection in shopwindows. I duck my head, avoiding people's eyes, crossing blindly at intersections, grieving for my future and mourning my past. I have been defined by this ambition since I was eleven. It was my purpose, my path. Now that map has been ripped up and scattered to the wind.

Replaying the meeting in my mind, I try to think what I could have said or done, swinging wildly between rebellion and febrile calm, addressing a phantom version of myself that stands over me, arms folded, lips pursed tightly, accusing me of failing. I want to blame others. Alison Goodall should have made a statement. This might be her way of placating her husband, but it won't work. Goodall won't compromise.

A car horn blares. A vehicle swerves. I'm halfway across a road, blinded by headlights. I glance up at the walk sign and see a red man akimbo. Waving an apology, I hear the driver shout, "Drunk!" as he accelerates away.

What an unforgiving city. There are no honest mistakes anymore. No unfortunate accidents. No mitigating circumstances. Everybody gets what they deserve. The poor. The sick. The unemployed. The inattentive.

I look at my phone and realize that I turned it to silent when I went into the meeting. The screen is full of messages and missed calls. Henry. Tempe. Constance. My uncles. Before I can read any of them, the phone vibrates.

"Where have you been?" asks Tempe.

"Busy. I can't talk. Henry is trying—"

"He's with me. Your father had a heart attack. We've been looking for you."

"Is he . . . ?"

"Alive. In intensive care."

I hear Henry in the background, wanting to talk. Tempe reluctantly hands him the phone.

"What are you doing there?" I ask.

"Looking for you."

"What happened?"

"He collapsed at home. Constance kept him alive until the paramedics arrived. They stabilized him on the way to hospital."

"Where?"

"The Royal Brompton. I can pick you up."

"No. I'll meet you there."

I'm already scanning the street, looking for a cab. Two pass me, but both are occupied. I start to run. Traffic is backed up along High Holborn.

A black cab is coming towards me, but somebody has stepped onto the road to flag it down. I start sprinting towards them, arriving as the cab comes to a halt. My fingers are first to the door handle.

"I'm sorry. It's an emergency."

I scramble into the backseat. The man protests.

"Royal Brompton Hospital," I tell the driver, who is young and Asian. He is about to take sides, but my urgency and destination seem to make up his mind. The man on the footpath hammers his hand on the roof of the cab as we pull away.

"What's happened?" asks the driver.

"My father had a heart attack."

Reacting instantly, he swings into a side street, taking a shortcut that misses two sets of lights. Accelerating between intersections, he talks about how his grandad had a stroke in India, but he couldn't get back in time to say goodbye. I'm only half listening. Instead I am picturing my father—how frail he looked at his birthday party. He'll be a terrible patient. He'll ignore instructions and be rude to the doctors and flirt with the nurses and try to organize a mass escape of patients to the nearest pub.

I have spent ten years avoiding this man and trying to deny his existence, but I have never escaped his shadow. That was made clear to me by Drysdale. This should make me angry, but instead I'm clutching my phone and quietly praying to a God that I don't believe in. Whispering, "Please don't die. Please don't die."

A receptionist directs me to the ICU, on level 3 of the Sydney Wing. Leaving the lift, I follow the signs along a brightly lit corridor. The counter at the ICU is unoccupied. I press the buzzer and a nursing sister appears, pulling a mask away from her face.

"My father is here. Edward McCarthy."

"Only two people are allowed by his bedside," she explains. "The rest of your family is in the lounge." She points along the corridor. "The whole village."

Two dozen people are crammed inside a space meant for half that number. My uncles and their wives, cousins, and second cousins. There aren't enough seats for everyone, so some are leaning against walls or sitting on windowsills. Four teenagers are kneeling around a jigsaw puzzle on a coffee table.

"She's here!" says Daragh, who lumbers towards me, almost tripping over a pair of outstretched legs in his eagerness to reach me first.

Heads turn but I glimpse them only briefly before Daragh smothers me in his arms.

"How is he?" I ask as his chest hairs tickle my nose through the undone buttons of his shirt.

"Poorly," says Daragh, stroking my hair. "But I'll kill the fucker if he dies."

"He's not going to die," says Finbar.

"I know that," says Daragh. "I'm trying to lighten the mood."

"You're a right comedian."

Finbar has a grandchild sitting on his shoulders, a little boy, who has to duck his head to avoid hitting the ceiling.

I notice Henry, who is surrounded by my aunts. No doubt they are quizzing him on his religion, politics, parents, and employment status.

"What did the doctors say?" I ask.

"They're going to operate in the morning," says Daragh.

"If he's strong enough," says Aunt Mary, his wife.

"What sort of operation?"

"A heart bypass."

"I knew something was wrong," says Daragh. "He had that turn at his party."

"Doc Carmichael is fuckin' useless," says Finbar. "We should pay him a visit."

"You'll do no such thing," I say.

His wife, Poppy, is hovering. "Constance did a wonderful thing. She gave Eddie CPR until the paramedics arrived. She was breathing into him and pumping his chest. She saved his life."

"Who knew she had it in her?" says Daragh, speaking with a new respect.

"Hid that light under a bushel," says Finbar.

"What's a bushel?" asks Daragh.

"Fuck knows," says Finbar. "Maybe it's like the two birds?"

"Nah, that's a bush, not a bushel."

Poppy ignores them. "I'll tell Constance that you're here."

"You don't have to bother her."

"Eddie has been asking for you."

As she moves towards the door, I notice Tempe, who is standing alone between the wall and a vending machine. She waves briefly, then pushes her hand down again, as though not wanting to attract attention.

"You didn't have to come," I say.

"I wanted to . . . but I didn't think it would be so . . ."

"Busy?"

"Hectic."

Tempe isn't good in crowded rooms. It's not the number of people that bothers her—she's fine in busy galleries and museums and on packed tube trains. She has a problem when everybody else seems to know each other and she is the odd one out. Her normal bravado and confidence seem to desert her when there are too many potential conversations. With small gatherings, she can make eye contact and remember people's names.

"I didn't realize you had such a large family," she says.

"They're a clan."

"I'm sorry about your father."

"He's going to be fine, apparently."

She glances at Henry, who seems to be purposely avoiding her.

"What happened to Mrs. Goodall?"

"She's safe."

"Did you see him?"

"Yes."

"Did he see you?"

I nod and glance at the door, waiting for Mary to return. "I can't talk about it now."

"Right. Sure. I'll go."

Her coat is lying across the back of a sofa. One of my cousins has to lean forward for her to retrieve it.

"How did you get here?" I ask.

"Henry drove me."

"I'll ask him to drop you home."

"No. That's OK. I can take a bus."

"Are you sure?"

"Uh-huh."

She slips out so quietly that nobody else notices or will remember her being here.

35

"He's in the last bay," says the nurse.

She is leading me between beds that are bathed in a soft light and partitioned by machines and curtains. Most have visitors sitting in semi-darkness, heads bowed and talking in whispers, saying prayers, making promises. All except for Edward McCarthy, whose laugh is like an empty barrel rolling down a hill.

I find him propped up by pillows, entertaining his audience of two. Constance is half sitting on the bed, stroking his hand. Clifton is slouched in an armchair, his legs spread wide, glancing at a TV on the ceiling, which is showing football with the sound turned down.

I watch them for a moment, hiding in the shadows, taking a mental inventory.

"Hello, Daddy."

His face breaks into a grin and he spreads his arms. "Man has to have a heart attack to see his own daughter."

"It usually takes something dramatic," I say, accepting his embrace.

Constance doesn't quite know how to greet me. Her right wrist is in a brace.

"What happened?"

"I think I overdid the CPR."

"Yeah, my ribs feel broken. Go easy next time."

"There won't be a next time," she says, punching his shoulder. He overreacts and she is suddenly all over him, apologizing. He winks at me. I scowl at him. Why am I pandering to his ego?

"Only two visitors allowed," says the intensive care nurse, who is sitting on a stool, almost hidden by the machines.

"I'll go," says Clifton. "I need to medicate."

"You're going for a smoke," says Daddy. "Don't let Finbar have one or Poppy will gut you like a fish."

I take the chair, which is still warm from his body.

"What happened?"

"My heart stopped for twelve minutes. I should have been a goner."
He glances at Constance, and I see the love. I don't feel jealous or resent-
ful. Everybody deserves to be loved like that.

An orderly arrives, wheeling a trolley bed. He's wearing earbuds and
has tattooed arms that poke from the sleeves of his tunic top.

"Edward McCarthy?"

"That's me."

"We're moving you to the York Ward."

After checking his full name and date of birth, the orderly lines up
the beds, and Daddy shimmies from one to the other, trying to hide the
pain involved. Pillows are arranged and the sides of the bed are raised.

"I should tell the others," says Constance. Immediately I have visions
of a McCarthy convoy escorting the transfer, making it look like a Mafia
funeral.

We're moving along the corridor to the service lift. As the doors
open, we're joined by a tall, slim woman in dark blue surgical scrubs. A
set of glasses hangs around her neck, and honey-blond hair peeks from
beneath a cloth cap that is tied around her head. Her eyes are expressive,
but her demeanor is very no-nonsense, like a private-school head girl
or one of those high achievers who wears her success like a crown. She
picks up a clipboard from the end of the trolley bed.

"Mr. McCarthy. How are you feeling?"

"Much better, thank you," he replies, unsure of who she is.

"Good. Most people don't survive a heart attack as serious as yours."
She scribbles a note on the clipboard.

"I'm taking you into surgery tomorrow at ten o'clock."

"And you are?"

"Your surgeon. Emily Granger."

"But you're a . . ."

She arches an eyebrow and waits for him to finish the statement. He
hesitates, and she does it for him.

"A woman?"

"You're so young," he says, recovering.

Dr. Granger smiles knowingly. "That's very flattering, but I'm
forty-one."

"You look younger."

She hooks the clipboard onto the frame of the bed.

"Who would you rather hold your heart in their hands?" she asks, showing him her long, delicate fingers. "A guy who swings a golf club like an ax, or a woman who can micro-suture wings onto a butterfly?"

It's not a question she expects to be answered. Instead she begins talking him through the operation, how she will take veins from his thighs to use for the bypasses.

"Has my heart been badly damaged?" he asks.

"I won't know until I take a look."

"But you can make it right?"

"I can widen arteries and bypass blockages, but I can't restore dead heart tissue."

"How many years?" he asks, fixing her with his gaze.

"I don't talk in terms of longevity, but if you eat well, exercise, avoid stress . . ."

"How long?" he asks again.

"Long enough."

The wheels of the trolley bed rattle as it is pushed from the lift and along a wide corridor to the York Ward. My uncles have arrived already and are arguing with a receptionist about securing the "best room in the place . . . no expense spared . . ."

"This is a hospital, not the Marriott," she replies.

Dr. Granger says goodbye. Daragh seems particularly taken by her, admiring her figure as she walks away.

"Stop ogling my surgeon," says Daddy.

"What?"

"But she's a woman!" says Finbar.

"So?" I ask.

"She can sew wings onto a butterfly," says Daddy.

"Great, I'll get my net," says Daragh. "Is she really the best?"

"Yes," I say. "Now you can all go home."

After a long, drawn-out goodbye, Daddy is wheeled to a private room and hooked up to a different heart machine that feeds information to the nursing station. A handful of other patients are out of bed, shuffling along the corridor. All of them wear the same monitors as they test their mended hearts.

"I'll talk to you tomorrow," I say, kissing his cheek. He holds out his arms, wanting a hug. I lean down and he grips me tightly.

"If anything happens to me—you and your mother are going to be looked after."

"You're going to be OK."

"Yeah, I know. I'm just saying . . ." He hesitates. "Do you think the surgeon knows?"

"Knows what?"

"Who I am?"

"Does that matter?"

"Mmmmm."

36

Dreams, then waking; it is sometimes hard to tell the difference. Henry's side of the bed is cold and smooth. He worked last night. I used to be quite comfortable being alone, keeping my own company, but the house feels empty without Henry, and my heart gives a little contraction of sorrow at his absence.

Out of bed, I press my nose to the bedroom window and peer down at the garden, which is overgrown and needs mowing. The wind swoops. Sunlight flickers. There are unanswered messages on my phone. One of them is from Alison Goodall. A half apology, or a fraction of the whole, delivered in a tremulous voice.

"I'm sorry I didn't make a statement to the police. I was frightened. You heard him—he threatened to take the kids away from me. He told the police that I hurt Chloe."

I don't blame her for being scared. In her shoes, I might have done the same. Although I'd like to think that I would never be in her shoes, that I'd never let a man control my existence or raise his hand to me, I know that's naive. Strong women can be abused. Rich women. Poor women. Old. Young. Victim blamers, often men, claim that women enable their violent husbands by being somehow codependent or enjoying their victimhood, but none of that is true. There is only one person who can control domestic abuse, and that's the abuser.

When a woman has been traumatized again and again by a partner who claims to love her, it starts to warp her reality. She begins to doubt herself, to mistrust her perceptions. And believes she is worthless and deserves to be punished. It's not Imogen Croker's fault that she fell for Darren Goodall. It's not Alison's fault for marrying him, or Tempe's fault for beginning the affair. All of them chose someone who appeared kind, caring, and compassionate at the outset. They fell in love. They invested in the false narrative, and only when they were in too deep did the mask start to slip and the true monster show his face.

It's still early when I call Alison back. She answers as though she's been holding the phone.

"I'm sorry. I'm sorry," she says. "I heard what happened. Please forgive me."

"No. You did nothing wrong," I say, only half meaning it. "Did the police issue a protection notice?"

"No. Darren convinced them it wasn't necessary."

"You can take out a private injunction. Apply directly to the family court."

"How long would that take?"

"A week, maybe longer. You have to find a lawyer."

"I don't want to antagonize Darren."

"Do you want to be free of this marriage?"

"Yes."

"This is your chance."

Alison goes quiet. I hear her mother in the background, telling Nathan that his pancakes are ready.

"I don't have any proof," says Alison.

"There are hospital records. Recordings."

"But I don't have them."

"A lawyer will do that."

"Will you come?"

"I'm not a witness."

"You saw what he did . . ." She pauses and sucks in a breath. "I don't have anybody else. Darren didn't like me getting close to people. He pushed my friends away."

There is another long pause.

"Get a court date. I'll see what I can do."

I hang up as the doorbell sounds. Mrs. Ainsley is on the steps holding a dog leash but no dog.

"Sorry, dear, but have you seen Blaine?"

"No."

She's still wearing her slippers and pajama bottoms under a knee-length padded jacket.

"I let him out into the garden last night, but he didn't come back. I must have left the gate unlocked, but I never do. I'm very careful."

She's talking about the side gate where she keeps her rubbish bins.

"I've looked everywhere. Have you seen him?"

"No. Normally, I hear him barking."

"Does he bark?"

Only all the time.

There is a tremor in her voice and I can see the worry etched across her forehead.

"I was wondering if I should call the police?" she asks.

"They don't look for missing dogs."

"What if he's been dognapped? People do that, you know. They steal dogs to use them in dogfights."

"Blaine wouldn't be much of a fighter." *More like an entrée.* "I'll put on my sneakers and help you look," I say. "You should get changed."

She looks down at her clothing and reacts with surprise.

Five minutes later, I meet her outside and we walk as far as the dog park and the supermarket—the usual places she takes Blaine. We also visit the Golden Pie on Lavender Hill, because Blaine is partial to a chunky beef pie as a weekend treat.

Mrs. Ainsley talks constantly, veering wildly between various conspiracy theories that could explain Blaine's disappearance.

"I never leave the gate open. I was only saying that last night to your friend."

"What friend?"

"The pretty one with the Irish accent."

"Tempe?"

"That's her."

"What did she want?"

"To borrow your keys. She wanted to drop something off. She said you were at the hospital with your father."

Tempe didn't mention dropping anything off.

"What time was this?" I ask.

The old woman purses her lips. "In the evening. I was watching *Vera.* I do like those police shows. That Brenda Blethyn might look like a bag lady, which is why everybody underestimates her, but she's a very fine detective."

"Are you all right to get home?" I ask. "I'm going to visit Tempe and ask her if she's seen Blaine."

"That's a good idea," says Mrs. Ainsley.

"And when I get back, I'll print out a flyer. We'll put it on lampposts and in shopwindows. You look for a photograph."

"Oh, I have so many. There's a nice one of him wearing his tartan winter jacket . . . but maybe one of him in the garden."

I leave her on the corner. She looks incomplete without her Jack Russell, like she has lost her shadow on a sunny day.

As I near Tempe's flat, I feel myself growing more annoyed. I'm tired of making excuses for her and giving her the benefit of the doubt. She has fabricated stories and embellished the truth and kept secrets from me. She has invaded my home and created tensions where none existed before.

Her front door has been freshly repainted. I press the intercom. Nobody answers. I call her number. It goes to her voicemail. I'm about to leave a message when she unlocks the door remotely and I begin climbing the stairs. Tempe is waiting on the landing.

"I'm sorry." She yawns. "I was still in bed. I had a terrible night's sleep. I was worried about you. How is your dad?"

"He goes into surgery at ten." I check the time. "You dropped by the house last night."

"Huh?"

"Mrs. Ainsley saw you."

"Oh. Yeah."

There is a long pause, the smile forgotten on her face. She is barefoot, still in her pajamas. Her toenails are painted pink.

"What were you doing . . . at the house?" I ask.

"I returned your blue blazer . . . the one I borrowed. I had it dry-cleaned."

"You could have given it to me anytime."

"I thought you might need it. Is something wrong?"

"Henry doesn't want you letting yourself into the house."

"Oh."

"He doesn't like you being there when we're not home."

"And how do you feel?"

"Maybe you shouldn't come around anymore," I say. "I appreciate all the wedding stuff, but I can pick up my own dry cleaning and get a dishwasher repaired."

"If that's how you want things," she says, with no hint of antipathy.

She does that sometimes—her face becomes swathed in blankness, and I can't guess what's going on behind her eyes.

"Do you still have the keys you borrowed from Mrs. Ainsley?"

"Yes."

"I'll need them back."

"Oh. Sure."

She turns on the landing and goes into her flat. When I fail to follow her, she returns.

"Are you coming in? I'll make you a coffee."

This is her olive branch. Either I grasp it, or things could be difficult for the wedding, which is less than a month way. She has the names, the numbers, the details. I wouldn't know where to start.

I join her in the kitchen, taking a stool at the breakfast bar. I notice a green rubbish bag on the floor near the sink. The top is wrung tightly and tied off in a knot. It looks like the scrawny neck of an old man.

"What are you doing up so early?" Tempe asks as she puts water in the coffee machine.

"I've been looking for Blaine."

"Who?"

"My neighbor's dog. The Jack Russell."

"You hate that dog."

"I don't hate him."

"You're always complaining about how he barks and keeps you awake."

"I didn't want him to go missing. Did you see him?"

"Me?"

"Mrs. Ainsley thinks somebody left the side gate open."

"And she's blaming me."

"No, of course not."

Tempe makes an "mmmmph" sound and puts a pod in the machine. I notice a gauze bandage on her hand, dotted with blood. It has been clumsily wrapped.

"What did you do?" I ask.

She looks at the bandage and frowns, as though she's forgotten.

"Oh, I scratched myself on a wire coat hanger . . . the dry cleaning."

"Do you want me to bandage it properly? I've done a first-aid course."

"Don't bother."

"It's still bleeding."

"I'm fine."

The coffee machine gurgles and spits, producing a dark sludge that smells wonderful. She adds frothy milk and hands me a mug. I glance at the rubbish bag. Tempe changes the subject and talks about my wedding dress. I was due to have the final fitting today, but I want to be at the hospital when Daddy wakes up.

"I'll reschedule," says Tempe. "We should also talk about the table arrangements."

"I thought we decided on orchids."

"Yes, but if you wanted to be a little more daring, you could choose lisianthus. They have pretty layers like roses and come in white, purple, and pink bouquets."

"I'm happy with orchids," I say, feeling as though Tempe is again trying to change my mind.

We're sitting opposite each other. Our knees touch. I move away. She asks about Alison Goodall. I tell her what happened and watch her react with a mixture of anxiety and anger.

"He'll come for you now."

"Why? He got what he wanted. I've lost my job."

"He'll want more. I remember when he thought Alison had learned about me. Darren accused me of telling her. He threatened to kill me if he found out I was lying. I had to prove that I loved him."

"In what way?"

"It doesn't matter."

"Did he want you to sleep with other men?"

"Don't keep asking me that. You're blaming me, just like he did."

"No, that's not—"

"He used to say I was nobody. I was shit on his shoes. I was a bug on the windscreen . . . a miserable, pathetic piece of garbage that he could toss away and nobody would miss me. Nobody would care." Tempe is looking at me seriously. "Somebody has to stop him, Phil. He can't keep doing this. He's relentless. He's like the Terminator. He never gives up." Her bandaged hand is beating at the air like she's hitting a drum. "Someone has to kill him."

Her solemnity makes me laugh. "Now you're being melodramatic."

"How would you do it?" she asks.

"What?"

"Kill him."

"I wouldn't."

"With your karate, you could do it so easily." She makes a chopping motion with the same hand.

"Karate is for self-defense."

"Yeah, but if you could crush his windpipe or drive his nose into his brain, I bet you could do it and nobody would ever know it was you. The perfect crime."

"There is no such thing," I say.

"But if you get away with it?"

"It's still a crime."

"What if you make it look like an accident?"

"That doesn't make it perfect."

"Bad people get away with things all the time. Why can't good people do the same?"

"Good people don't commit murder."

"When is it our turn?"

Her earnestness reminds me of my younger self, when I would argue with my mother about life being unfair because I couldn't go to a party or sleep over at a friend's house. It was never my "turn." Back then I had no real concept of fairness. After three years as a police officer, I'm still not sure. Justice and fairness are like rain that falls more heavily on some people than others. People with umbrellas tend to stay dry. People on high ground avoid the flood. Rich people. Connected people.

Tempe is frowning at me, unhappy with the analogy. I laugh and she shakes her head before a shy smile breaks across her face.

As I'm leaving, I pick up the bag of rubbish, saying I'll drop it at the bins. Tempe takes it from me and grimaces, swapping the bag to her good hand.

"My bin is full."

"We have room in ours. I'll take it home."

"No. That's OK."

We stand for a moment, holding the bag between us. Almost by default, I'm second-guessing Tempe, imagining all sorts of dark motives and twisted acts. Surely she wouldn't have killed a dog. She's not a monster.

"I'll be praying for your father," she says as I descend the stairs.

"You don't believe in God."

"I believe in prayer."

"Who do you pray to?"

"My heart speaks to the universe."

37

I remember the first time I realized that my family was different. In year eight at St. Ursula's, the head teacher called a full-school assembly and warned students about a local drug dealer. All of us knew who she meant. He wore jeans and an army jacket and normally sat on the low brick wall opposite the Greenwich Theatre, where he'd smoke cigarettes and chat to people who were walking to the ferry or the tube station.

Whenever a transaction took place, the dealer would whistle to a young boy, who took the customer into a side street where money and pills were exchanged. The boy was only eight or nine and looked like the dealer's younger brother.

I went home and told my mother about the assembly and she told my father. A few days later, as I walked to the station, I noticed Uncle Daragh talking to the drug dealer. I was going to wave, but they seemed to be having a grown-up conversation. Later, when I asked Daragh, he looked confused, saying I must have mistaken him for someone else, but nobody looks like Daragh, with his block-shaped head and his pale protruding eyes. I didn't see the drug dealer or his brother again.

There are many stories like this one. Some are apocryphal or exaggerated, but others I know to be true. Finbar has a crescent-shaped scar on his left side, below his ribs. He was stabbed twice in the stomach by a sharpened toothbrush in the prison exercise yard, but he took down three men before the guards arrived. When I asked him about the scar, he said, "Shark attack. Bondi Beach. 1985."

One of Henry's rugby mates told him a story about Uncle Clifton being charged with tax evasion. Two days before the hearing, the main prosecution witness, a customs officer, disappeared from his house. Sixteen hours later, he walked into a police station three hundred miles away, looking pale and shaken and suffering from complete memory loss. The case collapsed. Clifton walked free.

These are the reasons I have avoided my family, but there are other reasons for embracing them. Morality isn't a rule, or a plumb line that swings back and forth. It is something that is part of each of us, like a gene that evolves over time, but unlike other genes, it is affected and altered by the decisions we make and don't make, by compassion, empathy, forgiveness.

Late afternoon and I'm crossing Battersea Bridge, heading to Royal Brompton Hospital. As I turn into King's Road I hear the blast of a siren behind me and see flashing lights in my mirrors. I pull over, expecting the patrol car to pass me, but it angles to a stop in front of the Fiat. Was I driving too quickly? Did I fail to indicate? I know I'm distracted, but I'm a careful driver.

Two uniformed officers emerge from the car. Hitching trousers. Straightening hats. The driver approaches my lowered window. He smiles pleasantly, showing small teeth and wide pink gums. Maybe early thirties. A razor burn glows on his neck.

"Can I see your driver's license?"

"Of course." I reach into my jacket pocket. "Is there a problem?"

"Is this your vehicle?"

"Yes."

"And what's your name?"

"Philomena McCarthy. I'm a police constable."

"Is that right."

I get a sinking feeling in the pit of my stomach.

"This vehicle was reported stolen last night."

"No. There's been a mistake. If you run the number—"

"Please get out of the car."

"Why?"

"I need you to step out of the vehicle."

His hand is resting on his baton. His partner is at the passenger-side window, cupping his hand against the glass. I step out of the car. The driver walks around the vehicle and I lose sight of him. A moment later, I hear a dull thud and the sound of something breaking.

"You have a broken taillight," he yells.

I walk to the back of my Fiat and discover the broken casing and the shards of plastic lying on the asphalt.

"This is bullshit," I mutter.

"What did you say?" asks the driver.

I take a deep breath and tell myself to relax and not make things worse.

"Step away from the vehicle."

I do as he asks, moving to the sidewalk, where a handful of people have gathered to watch. One of them has a mobile phone. A teenager. Unkempt hair. Bum fluff on his chin.

"Can you film this for me, please?" I ask. The teenager lowers his phone for a moment, unsure of what to do. "Please," I say again.

The first officer pushes me against a wall, ordering me to brace my hands and spread my legs. He kicks my legs wider apart and roughly pats me down, touching me in places that should be private. His colleague is searching my car, lifting the floor mats and looking under the spare wheel. I keep turning my head, watching him, worried he might plant evidence. The teenager is still filming.

"This is an illegal search," I say.

No reply.

"I assume those bodycams have been turned off."

Again nothing.

"You are driving an unroadworthy vehicle," says the second officer. "You will be issued with a vehicle defect rectification notice. You must rectify the defect and submit your vehicle for inspection by an approved garage. You must return to the police with a completed inspection form within fourteen days, or you will face prosecution. Do you understand?"

I don't answer. He hands me a defect notice and I get back behind the wheel. The officers are talking to the teenager, who glances nervously at his phone. The footage will be deleted. Evidence erased.

I pull into traffic and leave the crowd behind me. Tears are prickling in my eyes, making the road blur and shimmer. I wipe them away with my sleeve. I feel soiled and degraded. The bastards! The absolute bastards!

The Royal Brompton has no visitor parking. I circle the surrounding roads until I find a rare parking spot in a side street. As I reverse, another car does a U-turn and darts into the space.

"Hey, that was mine," I yell, getting out of the Fiat and leaving it double-parked with the engine running.

"Didn't see you," replies the driver blithely. He's in his early forties, wearing stovepipe jeans and a tight-fitting T-shirt. He grabs a man-bag from the passenger seat of his gleaming new Audi.

"Can you see me now?" I ask.

"Pardon?"

"You stole my spot."

"I got it first."

A red mist now blurs my vision. Almost out of body, I watch myself shoving him hard in the chest, demanding that he move his car. It's not just the names I call him or my aggression that frightens me. I want to hurt him. I want to break his bones. I want to cause him pain.

White-faced and shaken, he gets back into his car and pulls out of the space, gunning the engine as he departs in a token attempt to restore his male pride. I take the spot and turn off the engine, resting my head against the steering wheel as the adrenaline leaks away.

38

The nurse in the recovery ward has one of those warm, plump faces that makes her look like a kindergarten teacher or a librarian. She gives me a mask and gown to wear.

"Don't be shocked by his appearance. This is major surgery."

"Did it go well?"

"Three bypass grafts. He was four hours on the table."

"How was his heart?"

"There was some damage, but he should be fine."

My father's bed is empty. For a moment I fear something terrible has happened, but the nurse pulls back a curtain and I glimpse a pale figure with wispy hair sitting in a chair beside the bed. Both his thighs are bandaged, and there are multiple tubes taped to his arms, chest, and groin. He looks like a puppet held upright by strings, and when he raises his right hand, I wonder if someone has operated a pulley.

"You're looking well," I say.

"I look like shit," he replies. "I want to go home."

"Seven days if you're lucky," says the nurse, who is checking one of the drips.

A black male orderly arrives with a walking frame. He and the nurse help Daddy onto his feet and urge him to grip the handles of the frame that takes his weight.

"OK, big mon," says the orderly. "Once around the dance floor."

"I don't like this song," Daddy moans and I watch the pain force his eyes closed.

He slides his right foot forward a few inches, props for a moment, then his left foot. The drips come with him, wheeled on a trolley. When he reaches the end of the bed, he pauses, breathing hard. It's like watching a stop-motion puppet being painstakingly moved between frames. Shuffle. Pause. Click.

"That's enough for today," says the orderly.

"I can make it back."

Daddy tries to turn but overbalances. Hands reach out. He brushes them away. Stubborn old bastard.

When he finally reaches his chair, I feel as though I've walked every step with him, twenty-six miles, uphill, into a raging headwind. He is lifted back into bed. Exhausted, he mumbles something to me, which is too slurred to be coherent. I lean closer and kiss his bristled cheek before whispering in his ear, "It's official."

One eyebrow lifts quizzically.

"You have a heart."

As I'm leaving the recovery ward, I bump into Daragh and Finbar, who are deep in conversation outside the lifts. They stop talking abruptly and Finbar smiles so widely it must hurt his face.

"How's the guvnor?" he asks.

"Fine. He wants to go home."

"Can he?"

"No. What are you two talking about?"

"Nuffin," replies Daragh.

"Do you often talk about 'nuffin'?"

The lift opens and two suits emerge wearing name tags. Middle-aged white men, at the top of their career ladders. One is the hospital administrator and the other the head of security.

"You had something to discuss," says the administrator, who introduces himself.

Daragh glances at me, clearly not expecting an audience. "Could we go somewhere more private?"

Finbar reads the signals.

"Let's get a coffee," he announces, hooking his arm through mine.

"Why? What are you discussing?"

Before I can stop Daragh, the lift door closes and we're heading downstairs. Finbar tries to change the subject, asking me about the wedding, but I won't be fobbed off.

"Why does it involve the head of security?"

Finbar shrugs, playing dumb. I pinch the skin on his wrist, like I did when I was a child and demanding that he produce the tickling spider from his pocket.

"Ow!" He rubs the redness.

"Tell me or I'm going straight back upstairs."

"We're concerned that Eddie might be vulnerable."

"How?"

"There are people—cunties, all of them—who may use this time to make a move against our whatnots . . ."

"Businesses?"

"Yeah."

"Other property developers?"

"Yeah. Right. Law of the whatsit, you know."

"Jungle?"

"Exactly."

"Are you saying he's in danger?"

"No, no, no, yeah, maybe. Better to be safe than sorry, as our dear old dad used to say."

"He died in prison."

"That's what I mean—you can't trust anyone these days."

"Are you talking about a turf war?"

He shrugs noncommittally. "No harm in taking precautions, eh?"

We are downstairs in the foyer. Finbar points to a café. The tables are set far enough apart for our conversation to be private, but he makes sure to sit with his back to the wall, where he can keep an eye on the main doors. Force of habit.

"What's the real reason?" I ask.

He sighs and leans forward.

"Some Grub Street hack took a swim in the Thames using bricks as floaties. They're trying to pin it on us."

"Dylan Holstein?"

Finbar's eyes are no longer hooded.

"You know him?"

"I was there when the police found his body."

There is a beat of confusion as Finbar remembers what I used to do as a day job—and a night job.

"Maybe we should—leave this be," he says, less certain now.

"No. Talk to me. Did you ever meet Dylan Holstein?"

"Nah. Never."

"But you know his name?"

"He'd been stirring up trouble about Hope Island, how Eddie got the planning whatsit through council."

"By bribing three councillors."

Finbar looks at me blankly. "Not my area."

"Who does the bribing in the family?"

"Gimme a break, Phil." He sighs, wishing we hadn't started.

"Go on."

"Holstein was writing these stories, but Eddie wasn't concerned. Fake news, you know. Lot of that around these days. But then Holstein turns up dead and the rozzers start pointing the finger at us. Tapping our phones. Following our cars. They dragged Eddie out of bed the morning after his birthday and searched the place."

"Did they find anything?"

"Nuffin to find," he snaps. "But the OIC is the ambitious type, you know. Trying to make a name for hisself."

"Are you suggesting he might fabricate evidence?"

"Been known to happen."

It's a throwaway line, which might have annoyed me once, until the breaking of a light on my Fiat and the wiping of footage on my body camera.

"Who killed Dylan Holstein?"

"How would I fuckin' know?"

"Was it Daddy?"

"Get off!"

"Would you tell me?"

Finbar lumbers to his feet, his face twisted in misery. "I know you think you're one of 'em, Phil, and that you're better than the rest of us, but we never closed the door. Eddie kept a light burning in his window, hoping you'd come home."

He turns to leave.

"I have a question, I say, girding myself.

"I'm done talkin'."

"If I needed some legal advice, where should I go?"

He pauses. Turns. "Are you in trouble?"

"I'm asking for a friend."

Finbar pulls out his wallet and jots down the name of a legal chambers and a phone number on a torn beer coaster.

"Tell them you're Eddie McCarthy's daughter."

39

An appointment is arranged for the following day in a pub at Spitalfields, which is hardly a good sign. I am picturing some overweight port-sodden solicitor in a crumpled suit, whose expertise is drawing up dodgy insurance claims or postdating wills.

When I arrive at the Ten Bells, Uncle Clifton jumps to his feet and bows slightly from the waist. I kiss his unshaven cheeks and am instantly a little girl again, saying good night to my uncles before going off to bed. Poker night was every Wednesday: four men around our kitchen table, smoking cigars and drinking Scotch. I would fall asleep listening to them laughing and my mother telling them to be quiet.

"What are you doing here?" I ask.

"Making the introductions."

"But I arranged the meeting."

"And I'm not going to interfere."

Clifton is wearing his usual attire, baggy jeans and a Gunners shirt. He has a cowlick that makes parting his hair an impossible task. The clockwise whorl lies in the opposite direction to whichever way he wants to comb it, unless he puts the parting so close to his right ear that he looks like Adolf Hitler.

He pulls out a chair for me and begins telling me the history of the pub, which has a Ripper connection. Two of Jack's victims, Annie Chapman and Mary Kelly, were either regulars or local prostitutes who plied for trade on the pavement outside.

"It used to be called the Eight Bells Alehouse because the church on the corner had eight bells, but when they changed the bells, they changed the name."

"Who am I meeting?" I ask.

"David Helgarde."

"The mob lawyer!"

"He's a criminal barrister."

"Who represents dodgy Russian oligarchs and gangsters."

"He's been the family lawyer for twenty years."

"Enough said."

We're sitting near a window, where the bright August sunshine is blasting onto the table, highlighting the condensation rings. Clifton has bought a Guinness, and I've opted for a lemon squash, which makes me feel underage.

He wipes foam from his top lip. "So why do you need a Tom Sawyer?"

"I'd rather not make it family business."

"Yeah, I get that, but if you're in trouble . . ."

"I'm not!"

Helgarde pushes through the pub door. He could be forty, or he could be sixty, with the lean, emaciated look of an obsessed amateur triathlete. Dressed in chinos and an open-neck shirt, he ducks as he enters the pub, as though frightened the ceiling might be too low.

"Sorry about my hair. I drove back from the country. The convertible," he says, as though it should be obvious.

He examines the waiting chair and recoils. I half expect him to pull out a handkerchief and flap it clean of germs before he takes a seat.

"You must be Philomena," he says in a plummy voice. "You can call me David." He turns to my uncle. "Dry white wine."

Clifton leaps to his feet and would doff a cap if he were wearing one. While he goes to the bar, Helgarde makes small talk about his house in the Cotswolds. I'm picturing gin and tonics on the lawn and the *thwock, thwock* of tennis balls.

Our drinks are delivered.

"I'll head out for a fag," says Clifton.

"I thought you'd given up," says Helgarde.

"I did, but I find smokers are more interesting than nonsmokers. They don't take life as seriously."

We're alone. "I'm not sure that I need a barrister," I say.

Helgarde gives me a noncommittal shrug. "I'm here now."

"Charging how much an hour?"

"More than you can afford, but I'll be billing your father."

Grudgingly, I set out the details, telling him about Goodall and my misconduct charges. It's like I'm knitting a sweater and Helgarde is looking for every dropped stitch and loose end. Finally, he leans back and crosses his legs.

"It seems you have two major problems, Philomena. The allegation of using unreasonable force, if proven, may amount to the equivalent of assault occasioning actual bodily harm, which is a criminal level of offending."

"He swung at me first."

Helgarde holds up his hand, acknowledging the point. "I'm more concerned about the charge of accessing data illegally. The police have become very strict about data protection. There is a public expectation and legal requirement that information will be treated in strictest confidence and only used for legitimate policing purposes."

"I was attempting to expose a cover-up."

"By the very people who want you removed."

"You're telling me it's hopeless."

"I'm giving you my professional opinion."

I take a moment to quietly seethe, disliking Helgarde's arrogance or maybe just his answers.

He grows pensive. "There might be another way, although it is a rather blunt approach. Crash through or crash in flames."

"Which is?"

"The whistleblower defense."

"I'm not a whistleblower."

"Not yet."

I am already shaking my head. "You want me to go public."

"Expose them. Shame them."

"My name would be mud. They would never take me back."

"They could be forced to."

"And I'd be treated like a pariah. Whistleblowers are worse than corrupt cops. I'd never get a promotion or a decent posting or a positive performance review. I'd be a traitor in their eyes."

"Is that what you think of whistleblowers?"

"No. I think they're incredibly brave and stupid. Mostly brave, but I'm neither of those things."

Helgarde doesn't respond. We look past each other, marinating in the silence.

40

My father is out of hospital. When he first arrived home, he could barely climb the front steps. Now he can circumnavigate the garden twice, and his shuffle has become a stride. He's wearing a Panama hat and a loose-fitting cotton shirt, below which is a simple heart monitor strapped to his chest, which relays information to his phone, giving him his heart rate and how far he's walked.

"Is there a finish line?" I ask as we pass the pond for the second time.

"An hour of moderate exercise a day."

"After that the English Channel?"

"I was thinking Everest."

He has lost weight. He blames the hospital food, but I think his brush with his own mortality has made him conscious of his diet. He is also more philosophical. Maybe he's found God, which would please my mother if nobody else.

When he grows tired, we rest on a rusted swing set, rocking together to the rhythm of groaning springs. We chat about birds and flowers, which is odd because I never regarded him as a nature lover. Again, it might have something to do with his heart attack.

"Can you accompany me on a trip?" he asks as I help him unlace his walking boots on a bench near the sunroom.

"Are you allowed to go out?"

"It won't take long."

The Range Rover is summoned. I recognize the driver, Tony, who chauffeured Constance to my house when she pleaded with me to attend the birthday party.

Holding the car door, he calls me "miss." I slide onto the backseat, tugging down my shortish skirt. Tony's eyes don't stray from the horizon, which could be professionalism or self-preservation. After all, I'm the boss's daughter.

We drive with the windows open, because Daddy likes to smell the air, which is thick and muggy and hazy with pollen. As we near Wool-

"You're telling me that I have no choice. If I go quietly, they win. If I go public, they win."

"But it costs them. You sue for wrongful termination. They'll settle out of court."

"To keep me quiet."

"You'll have the money."

"But no career."

Smiling sadly, he brushes imaginary lint from the thigh of his trousers. "I think that ship has already sailed."

wich, we join a queue of trucks and cars waiting for the ferry to arrive from the opposite bank. Men in yellow vests direct vehicles into lanes, nudging them nose to tail. The journey across the Thames takes only a few minutes before the ferry bumps up against the far dock and ramps are lowered.

Fifteen minutes later, Tony parks the Range Rover alongside a construction hoarding on Barking Road. A woman is waiting for us. She's in her fifties with short-cropped hair and blotchy skin. Crushing out a cigarette, she kisses my father on both cheeks.

"Emily, this is my daughter, Philomena."

"I remember you," she says. "You were only this big."

She holds her hand at waist height.

"Emily used to be my secretary," says Daddy.

She makes a dismissive sound. "I cleaned your office."

"You answered the phone."

"I told lies for you." She puts on a posh voice. "Mr. McCarthy has just stepped out. Mr. McCarthy is in a meeting. Mr. McCarthy posted that check this morning."

They both chuckle and look misty-eyed.

"What is this place?" I ask, trying to peer through a gap in the hoardings.

"The old Royal Picture Palace. It was built in 1911," says Daddy.

Emily gives him a set of keys and a padlock clicks open. He unhooks the chain, and the wooden door swings inwards. We squeeze between two builders' skips and pallets of plasterboard wrapped in plastic.

The cinema has an Art Deco facade with colonnades flanking large double doors and a fanlight window made of colored lead glass. A side door is unlocked and opens on stiff hinges. I peer into the gloom, smelling mildew and decay.

As we step inside, I wonder if the floor can hold our weight or will collapse into the basement. I follow my father, stepping where he steps, until we reach the entrance foyer, where carpets have been ripped up and dumped in piles. Broken light fittings dangle from the ceiling, and wires poke from wall sockets. A confectionary counter is covered in crumbling plaster and debris, and the old box office has a shattered glass screen.

"They used to call it an 'electric theater,'" says Daddy. "People would queue around the block to watch silent movies where somebody played the piano in accompaniment."

"You're not that old."

"I was told the stories. My parents, your grandparents, met on the footpath outside. She was a Jewish seamstress from Finchley. My dad was chaperoning his sister, my auntie Beryl, who was sixteen and considered to be boy crazy. He came across my mother waiting in the queue and they sat in the same row and watched Frank Sinatra in *Some Came Running*. A year later they were married."

I can hear a thickness in his voice.

"I used to walk past this place on my way to school. And I got my first part-time job working at an ironmonger's factory which was two streets away."

"How long has it been boarded up?"

"In the nineties they turned the foyer into a bingo hall and later it became a snooker club, but the auditorium has been empty for twenty years."

"Who owns it?"

"I do."

We enter the main cinema, a cavernous room where the floor slopes down towards a stage with a torn screen. Most of the seats are still in place, but occasional ones are missing like rotting teeth. High above us, the decorative moldings are stained with mold that blooms like bacteria in a petri dish. Two pigeons flutter through a hole in the ceiling.

"What do you want with a cinema?" I ask.

"The plan was to build luxury flats, but now I've changed my mind."

"You're going to knock it down."

"No. I'm going to bring it back to life. It makes no sense financially. Small independent cinemas are dying, but not everything has to be about money."

"If you build it, they will come."

"*Field of Dreams.*"

I glance around the auditorium, looking at peeling wallpaper and rusting power boxes and the remnants of a green copper dome on the ceiling, stripped by scavengers for scrap metal.

"Why have you brought me here?"

"I thought you might like to help."

"Me!"

"You could manage the restoration. Talk to the experts."

"I have no experience."

"You could learn on the job."

I'm about to say, "I have a job," when I realize what he's doing.

"Conversations with lawyers are supposed to be privileged," I say through clenched teeth.

"It wasn't Helgarde."

I want to argue, but I realize that my father's reach is so great that he could have heard the news from any number of people, possibly even within the police force. At the same time, I wonder if his influence reaches high enough to save my career. Before the thought even finishes, I dismiss it. Neither of us could risk the fallout if it ever became public.

"I don't need help finding a job," I say, trying to sound calm.

"They don't deserve you," he says.

"Some of them maybe. Most are good people."

We make our way to the projection room, where snippets of celluloid are curling on the floor and a shelf contains diaries that recorded every film shown at the cinema over seventy years. They should be valuable. They're probably not.

I peer through the projection window, looking down to the screen, imagining how the cinema used to be, when it echoed with laughter or shocked oohs and aahs.

"Is Darren Goodall a bent copper?" I ask.

My father's shoulders lift and fall. "There are rumors."

"Surely you'd know."

"Why? Because you think I bribe people like him?"

"Yes."

The bluntness of the answer seems to offend his sensibilities. He sways back on his heels, looking pained and breathless. I grip his elbow to steady him. When I pull up a chair, wanting him to sit down, he refuses.

"Things were so much simpler in the old days. We hijacked trucks. We flogged the merch. We bribed fair-trading officers to look the other way."

"You were breaking the law."

"OK, but we knew which side of the law we were on."

"Your brothers spent ten years in prison."

"I wish I could change that."

I take his arm and we walk back to the car.

"I want to do something for you," he says, explaining the excursion.

"I don't need anything."

"We all need something, Phil. You just don't know what it is yet."

41

A letter arrived this morning listing the date of my misconduct hearing. Normally, proceedings are held in public, but this one will be behind closed doors, without witnesses, because the Met wants to limit any negative publicity.

Maybe Helgarde is right and I should go public about Goodall and his history of domestic abuse. I'm sure that Drysdale will be prepared for that. He'll leak the story of my family connections and the tabloids will have a field day writing about the poacher turned gamekeeper—a gangster's daughter who deceived the Met. Truth will be the first casualty.

Henry would be happier if I walked away from the job. It's OK for him to charge into burning buildings and to rescue cats from trees, but he doesn't want me wearing a stab vest and putting myself in danger— not if this is what gratitude looks like.

We still have the wedding to look forward to, which means practicing our wedding waltz. Each time we clear the furniture and take a spin, we finish up giggling, which is a sure-fire way of getting me into bed. We're there now, lying in each other's arms.

"I've been thinking—why don't we go traveling?" says Henry.

"When?"

"Now."

"We're getting married in two weeks."

"We could elope. You've always talked about taking a year off and doing something adventurous. We could ride motorbikes across America or go to Australia. You have that friend of yours in Melbourne. Jacinta. You're always saying we should visit her. Now is our chance."

"We will. One day."

He goes quiet.

"What's wrong?"

"Nothing."

"Is this about my family?"

"No."

"Are you having doubts?"

"Not about you," he says. "Never that."

"What, then?"

"If we left now, you could avoid having the hearing. You could resign. Walk away."

"Give up, you mean."

"The Met doesn't want you, Phil. They've made that clear."

I swallow a mouthful of air that gets trapped in my throat, making it hard to breathe.

"I've done nothing wrong," I whisper.

"I know, but even if you get reinstated, they'll make your life a misery. That's what happens."

It's exactly what I said to Helgarde, but it's hard hearing it from Henry. I need him in my corner, telling me I can still win.

"I want a proper wedding," I whisper. "I want my father to walk me down the aisle and my mother to call a truce for a day and Archie to carry the ring."

"OK, but after that, we can go."

"What about the house?"

"We'll rent it out."

"My passport might be out-of-date."

"Apply for a new one."

He has a vaguely enigmatic smile on his face.

"What are you hiding?"

He leans over and opens the bedside drawer, producing an envelope. Inside are two British Airways ticket vouchers.

"Booked and paid for," he says.

"For when?"

"Whenever you're ready."

My phone pings. Carmen has sent me a message, asking where I am. We had arranged to meet for coffee. Another appointment missed. I'm letting things slip.

She won't take no for an answer. We meet at a café in Barnes, not far from the bookshop she manages. In the park across the road, mothers are rocking prams, toddlers are feeding ducks, and old people are doing tai chi beneath the trees. This part of London feels like a village rather than a piece of the urban jigsaw.

She wobbles to her feet and we hug. Her pregnancy presses against my stomach.

"I feel like a whale."

"Are you nervous?"

"Not really."

"This is what you always wanted—a husband, a nice house, a family."

"Does that make me weird? Some women think that choosing a family over a career is conforming to the patriarchy. Surrendering my independence."

"Stop listening to Georgia."

"It's not just her. I was at a prenatal class the other day and I heard some of the other women talking about how quickly they wanted to get back to work. When I said I was going to stay at home, they looked at me like I was a Stepford Wife. How are women supposed to win? Either we feel guilty about going back to work and missing milestones or guilty about staying at home and betraying the sisterhood."

"You're overthinking this."

"You wouldn't give up your career."

What career?

We change the subject. Georgia is arranging a girls' night out, which I'm refusing to call a hen night, because I want something classy, not debauched, and I will withdraw wedding invitations if anyone asks me to wear fairy wings or matching T-shirts or a stupid hat.

"Is it all right if we don't invite Tempe?" asks Carmen, looking at me sheepishly. "It's just that . . . she's not really an old friend or part of . . ."

"The gang?" I suggest.

"Yeah." She takes a deeper breath. "The other girls think she's a bit of a Karen."

"She's not entitled or shrill."

"No, but she seems rather fake. The stories she tells. Her comments. They're always a little bit off."

"She's trying hard to be liked."

"Maybe that's the problem. Remember the other week when Sara had her hair cut and dyed and everyone was saying how good she looked? Tempe went out and had her hair cut and colored exactly the same way."

"She used the same stylist."

"But don't you think that's odd?"

"OK, yes, I accept that she isn't everybody's cup of tea—but Tempe has done so much for me."

"I think we should have a rule about inviting new people into our group."

"What sort of rule?"

"We can vote them out."

"We're not playing *Survivor*." I laugh. "And I can't tell Tempe to leave—not until after the wedding."

"OK, but we don't have to tell her about our night out. We won't put anything on social media. No photographs. No tweets. What she doesn't know can't hurt her."

I'm not hard to convince, but I still feel a pang of guilt. It's like I'm nine years old and discovering that I'm the only girl in my dance class who hasn't been invited to Erica Horner's ice-skating party. I still don't know what I did to upset Erica, but that's why I withdrew from dancing and took up karate instead.

Years later I bumped into Erica at Victoria Station, waiting for a Circle line train. My heart began to race and I was a child again, desperate to be accepted. She smiled warmly and gave me a hug. The train arrived. We sat side by side, making small talk about university and families. I desperately wanted to ask her why she didn't invite me to the party, but it seemed childish, like holding a grudge that should have been discarded. As the train came into Blackfriars station, we quickly swapped phone numbers and talked about getting a coffee, but as I ascended the escalator towards daylight, I looked at her contact details and hit delete.

I have been avoiding Tempe since the dishwasher incident. It's true what Carmen said. There's something not quite right about Tempe. The way she seems to "lean in" to bad news, making all the usual sympathetic noises, but never sounding completely genuine. At other times she goes out of her way to be nice about my girlfriends, but there is often a slight barb to her comments, or a double meaning, that borders on passive-aggressive behavior.

Tempe has noticed my retreat. She keeps leaving messages, asking me if something is wrong. I've told her that I'm distracted and that I need some space. I feel like saying, "It's not you, it's me," but on the list of pathetic excuses, that always comes near the top.

It's difficult because the wedding is a week from Saturday and we still have to finalize the seating plan and the dress rehearsal, and a hundred different particulars, each a fraction of a whole.

Another complication is that Tempe's mother is arriving tomorrow. Elsa has been calling me every few days, asking about "my Maggie," always cheerful and chatty. I can hear the relief in her voice when I tell her that Tempe is fine and living at the same address. She used the word "we," which makes me think that Mr. Brown is coming too.

"Why did Maggie run away?" I asked her on her last call.

"It was a misunderstanding."

"An argument?"

"Something like that. Does she ever talk about me?"

"Not really."

"Is she taking her medication?"

"What medication?"

There was another pause. "For her anxiety."

"Why is she anxious?"

"I shouldn't really talk about it. I'll explain when we meet."

42

The flight is twenty minutes late. Chauffeurs and taxi drivers are gathered at either end of the barriers, holding up clipboards and handwritten signs with passenger names and company logos. I borrow a piece of paper and a marker pen from one of them, writing the name "Elsa Brown" in capital letters. I'm holding the sign above my head when a man steps in front of me. He's so big that I lean sideways to make sure Mrs. Brown isn't hiding behind him.

"Philomena McCarthy?"

"Yes. Are you Mr. Brown?"

"No. I'm Dr. Thomas Coyle."

"I don't understand."

"Elsa thought it best if I came instead. I'm a psychiatrist. I was looking after Maggie in Belfast."

He is so tall that I have to tilt my head to look at his face. "Why? What was wrong with her?"

"Let's talk somewhere more private."

An awkward silence follows. I toy with my car keys.

"Why didn't Elsa tell me?"

"We were concerned that you might alert Maggie and we'd lose her again."

There's that word again.

"Do you often *lose* her?"

"A poor choice of words, perhaps."

He's in his early forties, with salt-and-pepper hair and a body assembled from odds and ends, bulging where it should taper, except for his eyes, which are large and brown and full of intelligence. He's wearing a cotton business shirt, folded to his elbows, tan trousers, baggy around the bottom, and lace-up loafers. A crumpled linen jacket hangs over his arm.

My Fiat is on the second level of the car park. It feels smaller because Dr. Coyle's knees are touching the dashboard and his head is brushing the roof.

"Are we going to the address?" he asks as we pass through the boom gate.

"I want some answers first. I told Elsa I wouldn't reveal Tempe's address without getting her permission or unless I felt it was in her best interests."

"It is," he says adamantly.

"Why didn't Elsa come?"

"Maggie has a fractious relationship with her parents. She blames them for having her sectioned."

"Is Tempe dangerous?"

Coyle treats the question with interest rather than surprise. "Why do you ask?"

"People are usually sectioned when they pose a risk to themselves or to others."

He considers this for a moment and pats his stomach.

"Do we have time for breakfast?" he asks. "I'm famished."

I take him to a café in Richmond overlooking the river. The outside tables have umbrellas and wooden boxes with cutlery and condiments. The serviettes are pinned beneath painted rocks.

Dr. Coyle has a strange way of sucking his teeth while he's studying the menu, as though he's imagining how each dish will taste before deciding what he should order. Our coffees arrive. He opens a sugar satchel but only adds a few granules. The silence is filled with the clack and bang of crockery and hiss of steaming milk.

Coyle takes a small notebook from the pocket of his linen jacket and begins scribbling something on a page.

"Are you going to be taking notes?" I ask.

"Does that bother you?"

"I'd rather you answer my questions."

He puts the notebook away.

"I first met Maggie Brown at the Rathlin Ward in Belfast, a twenty-four-bed acute facility for people with serious mental health issues. Maggie was nineteen when she was first admitted and had three subsequent stays over the next eight years."

"What's wrong with her?"

"I can't discuss the specifics of her case."

"What can you tell me?"

"Eighteen months ago, Maggie left the clinic unexpectedly. We were close to making a breakthrough, but sometimes that's when a patient is most vulnerable, because they're more exposed. She signed herself out of the hospital and left Belfast. We know she caught a ferry across the Irish Sea to Liverpool and a train to London. After that we lost her."

"Were the police involved?"

"No. But her parents hired a private detective with only limited success. Until you called, Elsa had begun to worry that she might never find Maggie. Or worse, that her daughter might be dead."

"Why are you so keen to get her back?"

Coyle has been folding and unfolding his serviette. "You call her Tempe, correct?"

I nod.

"Has Tempe ever mentioned Mallory Hopper?"

"They were friends."

"For a while, yes. Mallory's mother called their relationship a 'friendship for the ages,' but it didn't last longer than a year. In that time, Tempe became the most important person in Mallory's life. She protected her. She cocooned her. But eventually Mallory grew tired of Tempe's attentions, because they were so all-consuming. Tempe didn't make friends, she *owned* them. She took them hostage."

Coyle is watching me as he speaks, reading my reactions.

"Tempe could sense Mallory losing interest in her. The light didn't go out, it simply dimmed, and she grew jealous. She felt as though she had given Mallory confidence, had made her brighter and shinier, until others began to notice her and compete for her attention.

"A Facebook page appeared with some nasty things about Mallory. Tempe helped get it taken down. Mallory was appreciative. And when someone broke into her school locker and scrawled horrible lies about her brothers, Tempe cleaned up the graffiti before Mallory saw the worst of it."

Our meals have arrived. Coyle has chosen the full English breakfast. My fruit toast looks paltry in comparison. He pauses and cuts up his sausage and bacon and grilled tomato, working right to left across the plate before turning it forty-five degrees and repeating the process. He then dots the meal with brown sauce and eats with a fork in his right hand.

"One day, Mallory was left alone in Tempe's room. She found sketches—hundreds of them, mostly drawn from memory, but some from life. The ones of her sleeping bothered Mallory the most. The idea that Tempe had been awake during those hours, sitting beside her bed."

As he utters these words, I feel as though someone has run a cube of ice down my spine, slowly rolling it over each vertebra.

"Mallory accused Tempe of trying to steal her soul, like she was some native tribeswoman frightened that a tourist's camera might capture more than a likeness. Tempe tried to defend herself. She did it out of love. She didn't mean to hurt anyone. Mrs. Hopper called the police.

"For the rest of that summer, Tempe watched Mallory from a distance, following her to and from her part-time job at a supermarket. She would also hide in shrubs on a railway siding, where she had a view of Mallory's bedroom, or she rode her bike up and down the road outside her house.

"In September they both went to university in Belfast, but Mallory changed courses after the first semester, because Tempe kept showing up at her lectures and tutorials. Mallory moved out of her home, but Tempe found her and broke into her shared house one night, leaving a drawing on her pillow. Other sketches were posted around the university. Some had the eyes missing, or the ears, or the nose. Mallory left the college before the end of her first year and went into hiding."

Coyle has been eating and talking between mouthfuls of food, dabbing egg yolk from the corners of his lips with a folded serviette.

"Tempe suffers from something known as white knight syndrome. She bases her self worth on her ability to fix other people's problems, which is why she became fixated on Mallory Hopper. This compulsive need to be the rescuer in an intimate relationship is often used to avoid the rescuer's own problems. By prescribing her difficulties to others, Tempe is trying to save herself through a proxy.

"This syndrome usually originates from early life experiences that have left the white knight feeling damaged or guilty. The person often has a history of loss or abandonment. Tempe is emotionally sensitive and empathetic, which means she's very good at putting herself into another person's shoes. It also means she can use this ability to control and to hurt them."

"You said she was sectioned."

"She was arrested for setting fire to Mallory Hopper's house."

"Was anyone hurt?"

"The family escaped. Tempe denied it at first, but the police had CCTV footage of her filling a plastic container at a petrol station, and traces of accelerant were found on her clothing.

"Tempe spent the next two years at the Rathlin Ward. She suffered psychotic episodes, but these were brought under control by medication. Since then, her admissions have been voluntary."

"Why did she run away?"

"Mallory Hopper took her own life eighteen months ago. She jumped off a road bridge onto Belfast's Westlink."

My breath catches in my throat. "Surely you can't blame Tempe for that."

"Mallory left a suicide note that set out what had happened to her. Even when Tempe was at Rathlin, she was still finding ways to send messages to Mallory; to smuggle out drawings and notes, saying they'd be together one day."

I pause, considering the story and comparing it to my own situation. Tempe didn't save me from sadness, but something drew her to me and now she refuses to let go.

"What happens now?" I ask.

"Hopefully you'll take me to her."

"I was tricked."

"You were depressed. Suicidal."

"You made me that way," says Tempe, wrung out with self-pity. "You were trying to control me—to tell me what to think and do—but I'm happy now."

"Why are you happy?"

"I have friends." She looks at me hopefully.

"What else makes you happy?"

It's a simple enough question but almost impossible to answer. Happiness isn't objective or measurable and cannot be plotted on a scale or a graph.

Tempe has taken a seat, perching on the edge of an armchair with her eyes closed. She is breathing in short gulps, as though fighting pain. I feel like a voyeur who is intruding on her grief, but at the same time, I want to stay and learn more. I notice the fine hairs on her arms, the scarp of dried skin on the edge of her foot, the loose weave of her jumper, the smudge of misapplied mascara. Everything about her seems clearer now, the troubled girl who became a troubled woman. No longer a figment, but still a mystery.

"I think I'll go," I say.

Tempe's eyes flash open and she reaches out towards me. "Please. Stay. Whatever he's told you, it's not true—not anymore. I'm better now. You've helped me."

She starts to cry. Genuine tears. I ask Coyle if I can talk to him for a moment in private. He follows me to the kitchen.

"I'm concerned about what happens next," I whisper.

Coyle glances through the open door. "I can't make her come back to Belfast with me, and I don't have enough information to have her sectioned under the Mental Health Act, but if she were to return as a voluntary patient, I could make sure she was safe."

"What do you mean, safe?"

"In a secure environment. Close to her family."

"You talked about medication. What was she taking?"

"She was on a regime of neuroleptics."

"What is that in layman's terms?"

"Risperidone is an antipsychotic."

He must recognize the look on my face.

43

I ring the intercom. Tempe answers.

"It's me," I say. "Can we talk?"

The automatic lock releases and I glance up the stairs, expecting to see Tempe waiting on the landing. We climb. Knock. The door opens with a flourish. Tempe's smile evaporates when she sees Coyle standing behind me.

"Hello, Maggie," he says.

I expect to see surprise or anger. Instead I see fear. She steps back, shaking her head.

"No. No. I'm not going back. You can't make me."

"Can I come in?" he asks gently.

"How did you find me?"

Her gaze turns to me, and she doesn't need an answer.

We are all in the sitting room, which has suddenly become very small and Tempe looks ready to tear down the walls to escape.

"I'm not going back. You can't make me."

"I only want to talk," says Coyle. He turns to me. "You can leave us now

"Please don't go," says Tempe. "Protect me."

Coyle looks aggrieved. "You can't keep making up stories, Maggie

"Don't call me Maggie!"

"You don't like it?"

"It makes me want to puke. It's my mother's name for me."

"The one on your birth certificate."

I'm still hovering in the doorway, unsure of what to do.

"Are you taking your medication?" he asks.

"No. It poisons my mind. You're trying to control me—tell m
to think and do."

"I'm trying to make you better."

"Is that why you zapped my brain?"

Dr. Coyle opens his palms. "You were given electroconvuls
apy. You gave us permission."

"She is more likely to harm herself than anyone else. The medication controls her obsessive behavior and stops any negative thought loops."

"I think she's become fixated on me."

Coyle doesn't answer immediately. "Clearly, you're a stronger personality than Mallory Hopper."

You hardly know me.

"What if I walk away?" I ask.

There is a beat of silence. The tip of Coyle's tongue emerges to wet his lips.

"Maggie could find someone else to rescue, or she could try to win you back."

44

Willesden County Court is a squat redbrick building in Acton Lane in the shadows of a Catholic church that is far grander and more imposing than the humble courthouse, which begs the question, what judgment should people fear most—the earthly or the heavenly? Metal shutters protect the twin front doors, flanking a life-sized coat of arms with an English lion and Scottish unicorn who are supporting a quartered shield. Below is the motto: Dieu et mon droit (God and my right).

People are milling on the paved forecourt, waiting for their cases to be called. This is where divorces and child custody applications are decided: marriages ended, possessions divided, and lives uncoupled. The end of the line. All change.

Alison Goodall is waiting for me, looking anxiously up and down the street, as though afraid that I've changed my mind and decided not to come. I don't want to be here, but she begged and I promised. She is applying for a Domestic Abuse Protection Order, which would prohibit Goodall having any contact with her or the children for twenty-eight days. The police should have done this for her, but Alison has had to make a private application.

As I draw nearer, I realize that her mother has come along with her. Jenny looks even more birdlike and nervous than usual, holding her handbag against her chest as though expecting a bag snatcher to accost her.

Alison smiles in relief.

"Where is your lawyer?" I ask.

"I couldn't find one. I mean, I tried. I called a dozen of them. When I told them the details they said I should find someone else, but they were all—"

"Busy?"

She recognizes my sarcasm and nods.

"One of them said I didn't need a lawyer."

"You don't," I say, "but it would have been helpful."

"Can you represent me?"

"I shouldn't even be here. Your husband blames me for this." I wave my hand towards the courthouse as though I'm responsible for this whole pageant.

Deep into August, today is bright and cloudless with that slight haze that blurs anything distant. I'm scanning the crowd, looking for Goodall.

"Will he come?" she asks.

"Most likely, yes."

"What do I say?"

"You tell the judge what happened and that you need a protection order."

At that moment, I spot Goodall standing beneath a tree on the far side of the road. He is dressed in a charcoal-gray suit, white shirt, and blue tie. He has a lawyer with him, and the two of them are laughing like old friends.

A court usher calls Alison's case number. For a moment she looks panic-stricken. I take her arm and we walk into the building together. I give her last-minute instructions. "Stay polite and calm. Speak in a loud voice. Don't interrupt. If you want to say something, raise your hand."

The courtroom is empty except for the judge and his clerk. Alison is told to take a seat at the bar table. I sit in the public gallery, only a few rows behind her. Jenny chooses to sit apart from me.

Goodall enters and I can feel his eyes on me, on my skin, inside my head. When I risk a glance in his direction, he has a strange smile on his face. It's like watching a cobra uncoil and begin to sway.

The judge, a woman in her sixties, is a tall, spare figure with fine features and an explosion of ash-colored hair. Her dark eyes are magnified behind black-framed glasses that slide up and down her nose when she nods her head.

"Are you represented here today?" she asks Alison.

"No, Your Honor, Your Worship, My Lordship . . ."

The judge smiles. "I'm Justice Rees. You can call me Your Honor."

"My mother is here, Your Honor, as well as a friend."

Goodall makes a mocking sound, which the judge doesn't seem to hear.

Judge Rees glances at her paperwork. "You're making a private application for a DAP notice. Why aren't the police seeking the order?"

"I don't know," says Alison. "I asked them to . . ."

Goodall's lawyer is still standing. "If Your Honor pleases, my name is Bernard Dardenne. I represent Mr. Goodall. This matter should never have been listed. It is a vexatious application designed to deny my client access to his children."

Rees raises a thin hand. "You'll get your chance, Mr. Dardenne."

She addresses Alison. "Are you frightened of your husband?"

Alison nods.

"You'll have to speak up."

"Yes," she murmurs.

"Has he threatened you or your children?"

"Yes, ma'am."

"OK. Let's hear what you have to say."

She motions to the witness box. Alison makes her way to the front of the court, stepping onto a raised platform with a single high-backed chair. Having sworn the oath, she takes a seat and produces a piece of paper that looks tattered and damp from perspiration. She tries to read but falters.

"Maybe if you use your own words," suggests the judge.

Alison begins describing the breakdown of her marriage, outlining her husband's controlling and coercive behavior: How he would read her text messages and block her friends from calling her. How he refused to let her drive and gave her a weekly allowance to buy shopping, making her justify how much she spent on every purchase.

"He wasn't always like that. I loved him once," she whispers. "When I put on weight after Chloe was born, he wouldn't let me eat. But when I tried to look good for him, he accused me of dressing up for other men . . . of flirting with them." She starts and stops and starts again, struggling to get the words out. I think I hear the word "ruffles."

The judge interrupts her. "Excuse me, but who or what is ruffles?"

"Our dog. Darren said she was dangerous, but Ruffles would only bite when she was frightened."

"What happened to Ruffles?"

"I came home and she was gone. Darren said she ran away. Nathan was inconsolable. He's my little boy."

Alison wipes her eyes. A box of tissues is found for her.

"Has your husband ever been physically violent towards you?" asks the judge.

Alison is about to respond, but she catches sight of Goodall and swallows the words.

Judge Rees asks her again. "Do you have any medical evidence? Doctor's reports. Hospital admissions."

Alison nods, less certain now. "I was taken to hospital by the police, but I don't have the photographs."

"Why not?"

"The hospital couldn't find them."

"This is bullshit!" mutters Goodall. Dardenne puts a hand on his shoulder, urging him to be quiet.

The outburst unnerves Alison, who loses her focus. She begins speaking too quickly jumbling her words.

"He chokes me until I think I'm going to die, and then he lets me breathe and starts again."

"That's a lie!" says Goodall.

Dardenne is on his feet. "My client strenuously denies that he has ever been physically violent towards his wife."

"Each time he whispers to me that I'm going to die this time, and when I'm dead, he will kill the children."

"More lies," says Goodall.

The judge points a finger. "One more word and I'll have you removed." She turns back to Alison. "Have you reported his behavior?"

"Nathan did—my little boy made an emergency call."

"And you gave the police a statement."

Alison shakes her head, looking miserable. "I was too scared. I mean—he's one of them—a police officer."

The last statement is delivered with rancor and also a strength that I haven't recognized in Alison until now.

"Do you have any corroborating evidence? A police report. A recording of the call?"

"No."

"Where are you living now?" asks Judge Rees.

"With my parents. My children have nightmares. They don't want to see their father."

"How old are your children?"

"Six and two."

"That's very young to have made up their minds."

"Old enough to be frightened of him."

Judge Rees thanks Alison and asks her to step down. She glances to the opposite end of the bar table, where Dardenne gets slowly to his feet and slips his hands into his pockets.

"My client is a decorated police officer who was badly wounded in the line of duty. He is a hero in anyone's language, who has suffered from PTSD as a result of his bravery and has been undergoing counseling for the past ten months. He concedes that there have been problems in the marriage, but he categorically denies the allegations that he was violent or abusive towards his wife and children. Rather than being the perpetrator here, Mr. Goodall is the victim. His wife's behavior has become increasingly irrational, unlocking his phone, reading his text messages, accusing him of having an affair."

"He *was* having an affair," says Alison, her voice shaking.

"You've had your turn, Mrs. Goodall," says Rees.

Dardenne picks up a document.

"A week ago, my client went to his local police station and reported that he and his wife were having marital difficulties. Sergeant Goodall feared that his wife would make false accusations against him, and he wanted his concerns to be documented to protect himself. This is a copy of the notes taken by the desk sergeant."

A court clerk collects the paper and delivers it to the judge.

Dardenne picks up a second document.

"This is a report from the social care team at Brent Council. Five days ago, Sergeant Goodall noticed bruises on his daughter's arms that appear to be the result of the child being violently gripped and shaken. When he asked his wife about the bruises she lost her temper and threatened to blame him. Although reluctant to make a complaint against his wife, Sergeant Goodall contacted the social care team at Brent Council and registered his concerns."

Alison lets out a squeak of protest, and I glance at the judge to see if she's buying any of this. Hard to tell.

"Mrs. Goodall is on antidepressants, which have been prescribed by a Harley Street psychiatrist, a Dr. Helen Krause. I had hoped to persuade Dr. Kraus to attend today's hearing, but patient-doctor privilege prevents her from discussing details. There is, however, another witness in court today. Mrs. Jennifer Hammond, my client's mother-in-law. She can testify to her daughter's fragile state of mind."

The look on Alison's face is one of numbness rather than disbelief. She is staring at her mother, who has turned pale, clearly ambushed by the request.

Judge Rees seems to take pity on both women.

"I don't think that will be necessary."

Dardenne continues. "There is no medical evidence to support Mrs. Goodall's allegations. No photographs. No doctor's reports. No record of the police ever being called to their address."

"But the ambulance came," says Alison, sounding defeated.

"Paramedics attended the address because Mrs. Goodall had threatened to harm herself."

"That's not true," she says plaintively. "He threatened my baby. He hit my little boy."

Goodall shouts, "They're *my* children too."

Without realizing it, I'm on my feet. "I've heard the recording."

Everybody stops and turns. Judge Rees peers at me over the top rim of her glasses. "And you are?"

"Constable Philomena McCarthy. I'm with the Metropolitan Police."

Goodall interrupts. "She's not a serving police officer. She's been suspended."

Judge Rees sighs in irritation, waving her hand up and down, wanting him to sit down. She glances at her watch. Then she points to me.

"I'm going to hear from Constable McCarthy."

Goodall begins to protest.

"My previous warning stands," says the judge. "I will have you removed."

I begin to speak, but she points to the witness box. "You'll swear an oath like everybody else. The truth and the whole truth." There is a tiredness in her tone which makes it sound like a pointless exercise because she's heard too many lies masquerading as the truth.

I walk to the front of the courtroom, suddenly aware of how I'm dressed in faded jeans and a blouse with a middle button hanging by a loose thread. Normally I'm wearing my uniform when I give evidence in court. My mother would be mortified. She's the sort of woman whose worst nightmare is being cut from the wreckage of a car and taken to hospital wearing tattered knickers.

I take the oath and give my name and address.

"How do you know Mrs. Goodall?" asks the judge.

"I helped her escape from her house when her husband locked her inside."

Dardenne objects. "Calls for speculation."

"We're not in front of a jury," says Rees, who is twirling a pen across her knuckles. "Carry on, Constable McCarthy."

I tell her about the phone call from Alison and how I picked up Nathan from school.

"Why did she call you? Are you friends?"

"Acquaintances."

"Do you also know Detective Sergeant Goodall?"

"Yes."

"How do you know him?"

"I arrested him when he beat up his mistress."

Dardenne has been whispering furiously to Goodall. He stands suddenly and interrupts her next question.

"Your Honor, we request an adjournment. I wasn't aware this witness would be called, and I need to take instructions from my client."

"How long do you need?"

"Two weeks."

"I was thinking more like fifteen minutes."

"I need longer."

"Are you suggesting I postpone granting an injunction for two weeks?"

"Bear with me," says Dardenne, returning to his seat and whispering to Goodall. After a few minutes, he gets to his feet again.

"My client maintains that he has done nothing wrong and is determined to fight for full custody of his children. He agrees to abide by any court ruling made today but is asking that the children be placed in the care of the relevant authorities for their own protection."

"No!" yells Alison. "Not my children!"

Judge Rees's twirling pen drops from her knuckles and rattles to the floor. She demands silence, staring us down.

"I am not Judge Judy and this is not some reality TV show where people get to grandstand."

She turns to me.

"Have you heard a recording, yes or no?"

"Yes, Your Honor. The little boy made a triple nine call to the police. He said his daddy was hitting the baby."

Dardenne interrupts again. "My client is willing to abide by any DAP notice until a full hearing is arranged."

Judge Rees looks at him with a skeptical air before addressing Goodall.

"You will not be able to approach, follow, or communicate with your wife or her friends or her family for the next twenty-eight days."

"What about my kids?" he asks.

"They will stay with their mother and you are denied access without supervision."

He starts to complain, but Judge Rees talks over him.

"Any breach of this order will be punishable by up to two months' imprisonment or a substantial fine. I will relist this matter for a month from today. At that time, I will either extend the order or let it lapse. In that time, get your ducks in a row, people, and have your evidence ready."

Judge Rees pauses and looks at Alison. "Do yourself a favor, Mrs. Goodall. Get a lawyer."

45

Alison spends fifteen minutes in the bathroom, sitting fully clothed in a cubicle, with her fists sunk into the sagging pockets of her jacket.

"Those things he said about me . . . I would never hit a child. I'm not a terrible mother." She tears off a length of toilet paper and blows her nose. "I take Prozac. And he encouraged me to see a psychiatrist. How could he say those things?"

"He doesn't like to lose," I reply, leaning against the sink opposite and talking to her through the open door. "You have to fight back."

"How?"

"Make a statement."

"They won't charge him."

"You need to put something on the record, or he'll keep doing this."

The outer door opens and Alison's eyes shoot to mine. A woman enters the bathroom. She smiles nervously, self-conscious about urinating with an audience. Changing her mind, she washes her hands and leaves.

Alison is rocking back and forth in a rhythmic motion. It's a coping mechanism, a primal reaction from a brain seeking comfort, which is why we rock newborns and babies and sick children. I wonder if Alison has always been this vulnerable, or if Goodall has chipped away at her self-esteem. Coercive controllers will often look for women who are already damaged, like a predator singling out the weakest in the herd. They will gaslight and demean, isolate and undermine, stripping away any last vestiges of self or worth.

"We should go," I say.

"Has he gone?"

"I'll check."

I walk outside and study the faces in the hallway, then search the forecourt, but I can't see any sign of Darren Goodall. Returning to the bathroom, I tell her that it's safe.

"I didn't see Jenny," I say.

"She'll have gone home."

"Without you?"

Sadly. "We're not on the same page at the moment." Alison flushes the tissues away.

I offer to drive her home. My car is parked two streets away. As I get nearer, I notice a crowd of people has gathered on the footpath. I have to push between shoulders, holding on to Alison's hand. My lovely red Fiat is barely recognizable. The paintwork is blistered and blackened by acid or some other caustic substance that has been splashed over the bonnet and roof.

"Did anyone see what happened?" I ask.

Nobody answers.

Alison is next to me. "I'm so sorry," she whispers.

"We don't know it was him."

The words sound hollow.

"Are you going to call someone?" she asks.

"Yes. But first I'll take you home."

I carefully open the doors, trying not to get acid on my hands or clothes. Then I peer beneath the chassis and examine the wheel nuts, making sure that nothing else has been tampered with or vandalized. Satisfied, I start the engine and pull into traffic, checking the mirrors to make sure nobody is following us.

Alison has her knees drawn up and is peering nervously through the side window.

"How did you meet Darren?" I ask.

"You're going to think it's creepy."

"Try me."

"He came to my school to give us a talk about staying safe online, you know, not sending naked photographs or befriending strangers."

"How old were you?"

"Seventeen." She winces. "Me and my girlfriends were chatting to Darren afterwards. I guess we were flirting with him. He started flirting back and asked me if I ever did any babysitting. I asked him if he had a baby and he said he'd like to make a few. Corny, I know."

"Are you saying . . . ?"

"No, not then," she says, half laughing. "I didn't meet him again until three years later. He asked to friend me on Facebook."

"How did he remember your name?"

"He said it stuck with him because I was so cheeky. We started messaging each other. And he asked me on a date."

"He's quite a bit older."

"Eleven years, but he's always looked younger."

We are caught in traffic on Finchley Road.

"When we first hooked up, it was like being love bombed. He was so thoughtful. Flowers. Messages. Presents. Romantic dinners. I was besotted. We moved in together within a month and got married that summer. Darren wanted me to get pregnant straightaway. He didn't really like me working."

"When did the problems start?"

She is toying with a loose thread on the cuff of her blouse. "I don't know. A year maybe." She half turns to face me. "What I thought was cute—the clothes he bought me, the hourly phone calls and messages—after a while they seemed . . ." She struggles for the word.

"Suffocating?"

"Mmmmm.

"He doesn't like any of my friends. I used to think he did, but then he started to bad-mouth them or make up stories. He told me one of my girlfriends had a drug conviction, but it made me wonder why he looked that up. She was eighteen and at Glastonbury and got caught with a few pills.

"Darren used to get angry if I mentioned that I'd taken drugs." She laughs and glances at me. "It was only ecstasy—two times, well, maybe five. I'm hardly Amy Winehouse."

"I'm not judging you."

"Another of my girlfriends left her husband and filed for divorce. Darren wouldn't let me see her. He blocked her calls. That's how I discovered that he could access my phone and read my texts. When I say it out loud like this, it all seems so clear, but when it was happening, I didn't realize. It was like . . . like . . ."

"Boiling a frog?"

"Yeah. After Darren was stabbed, I tried to blame it all on PTSD. I thought counseling would change him—make him the man he used to be. But things only got worse."

Traffic is moving again. Alison asks about Tempe. "He hit her, too, didn't he?"

"Yes."

"Is that why she left him?"

"Yes."

"She must be stronger than me."

"No."

"Would she help me now? Would she make a statement? They might believe us if we both . . ."

"I can ask her," I say, but I already know the answer.

Fifteen minutes later, we pull up outside her parents' house. Keith is in the front garden, watching over the children, who are playing under a sprinkler. A French bulldog is keeping a safe distance.

"Betsy doesn't like water," explains Alison, giving them a melancholy smile.

Chloe tries to aim the water at Nathan, who keeps dodging out of the way. "I won't spray you," she says sweetly, hoping to lure him within range.

"Did Darren ever talk about Imogen Croker?" I ask.

"I know they were engaged. I looked her up online and found a photograph. She was very beautiful."

Opening my phone, I pull up the image of Imogen's sapphire ring.

Alison gasps softly. "That's my ring. Darren gave it to me."

"When?"

"Years ago. It was after an argument. He could be very sweet sometimes."

"Where is the ring now?"

"I stopped wearing it when Chloe was born because my fingers swelled up and I didn't want to scratch her. To be honest, it's too blingy for me." She shows me her simple wedding band. "Why do you have a picture?"

"Imogen Croker was wearing that ring on the day she died. It was given to her on her eighteenth birthday."

Alison takes a moment for the information to register, and then her entire body shudders. "Are you saying he gave me a secondhand ring?"

"When they found Imogen's body at the bottom of the cliff—the ring was missing."

She blinks at me, still struggling to comprehend what I'm saying.

"Where is the ring now?" I ask.

"In my jewelry pouch. The suitcase was too big to fit through the window. Remember? I put it under Nathan's bed."

"If we could get that ring . . ." I say, but before I can finish the statement, Alison is shaking her head.

"I'm not going back to the house."

"You're right. Stupid idea."

"It must be a different one," she says tentatively. "He wouldn't give me a dead woman's jewelry." The statement is almost a question.

Mentally, I'm considering my options, holding them up to the light, as though looking for the flaws in a glass. Even if I could convince the police to investigate, there isn't enough evidence for a search warrant. And if Goodall gets wind of this, he'll destroy the ring or hide it until people stop looking.

"Darren keeps a spare set of keys in his car," says Alison, trying to be helpful. "He locked himself out one day and I wasn't home. God, he was angry. He broke the downstairs window and then complained about the cost."

She steps out of the car and the children run to her, clinging to her legs. I feel something tug and almost break inside me. Nothing crucial or vital. A single thread, attached to my heart.

"That's what happens when you take away handguns," he says.

"I don't see the connection."

"Well, your general, garden-variety scumbag and gangbanger will always look for another weapon. That's why they're all carrying knives or throwing acid."

"You'd prefer guns."

"Not necessarily, but mankind has been making weapons for sixty-four thousand years—Stone Age, Bronze Age, Iron Age, Nuclear Age. You ban one weapon and they'll find another."

"Finbar and the Art of War."

"I read books," he says, sounding affronted. "I know your dad thinks he's the only pseud in this family, but you don't need a diploma from a whatnot to know things."

"A university?"

"Yeah. How many Shakespeares have you read?"

"You mean the plays?"

"Plays. Sonnets. Tragedies. Comedies."

"Three, maybe. Four. I studied them at school."

Finbar taps his chest. "All of 'em." He begins to recite a sonnet. "'Shall I compare thee to a summer's day? / Thou art more lovely and more temperate. / Rough winds do shake the darling buds of May, / And summer's lease hath all too short a date.'" He adds, "OK, I'm not sure what 'temperate' means, but I know he's talking about love and the weather and how the two are pretty similar."

"When did you read those?"

"In prison. Fuck all else to do. Pardon my French."

He laughs and I am transported back into my childhood, when my favorite moments were making my uncles laugh, particularly Finbar, who had a smile I could fold up and carry with me all day.

"I need another favor," I say. "I wouldn't normally ask."

"In for a penny, in for a pound."

Nine o'clock. Light fading. Air turning cool. Finbar is late. I can't call him because I've turned off my phone. Maybe he lost the address or had second thoughts. I wouldn't blame him. I should be at home, curled up on the sofa with Henry, watching reruns of *Top Gear* or some Netflix

46

Finbar whistles through his teeth and slowly walks around the Fiat, examining the ruined paintwork. He's wearing overalls, work boots, and a baseball cap.

"Can you fix it?" I ask.

"It needs a respray and new seals around the windscreen."

"It's insured."

"Don't worry. A guy owes me a favor."

"What sort of favor?"

"The sort that you don't ask about."

We're at a garage in Shoreditch, one of those places built beneath railway arches where trains rumble overhead every few minutes, shaking the walls.

"What color?"

"The same red."

"It'll fade."

"I don't care."

"Is this why you needed a lawyer?"

"No."

Finbar makes a note. "I'm gonna need it for a few days. In the meantime, you can borrow the bug." He points to a VW Beetle which is just visible beneath a tarpaulin. "Hope you can drive a stick shift."

He is walking around the Fiat again. "Did you report this to the police?"

"I'm going to."

"You'd better take some photographs. What about the brake light?"

"Fix that as well. I have a defect notice."

He looks surprised. "You got pulled over?"

"It's a long story."

I take some pictures with my phone while Finbar fills out the paperwork. He starts talking about the number of acid attacks in London, most of them gang related.

series about impossibly beautiful teenagers with superpowers. Instead I'm waiting in the shadows, looking at an empty house, preparing to commit a crime. London never gets fully dark, not with the ambient light from a billion globes and TV sets. My collar is turned up, and I lower my white face from the streetlight, trying to be less conspicuous. I stand at ease, weight on both feet, legs straight, balance slightly on my heels. It's the way I was taught to stand at Hendon when we were on parade.

The dark blue Saab is parked nearby, beneath the branches of a tree. Pigeons have deposited splatter marks on the bonnet, which will annoy Goodall but provides me with a fleeting moment of perverse joy.

Farther along the road, I see headlights, a van moving slowly. I step from behind a tree and wave to Finbar, showing him where to pull over. The engine idles and dies as he shoulders open the door.

"Are you nicking this motor?"

"I'm retrieving a set of keys."

"To the motor?"

"To a house."

"You're breaking into a house."

"I'm using the keys."

"With or without permission?"

"I'm a police officer."

Finbar isn't convinced. He knows that I need a warrant to search a car or a house and that the Met has approved locksmiths for a job like this one.

"Are you sure you want to do this?" he asks.

"Yes."

"And you're not going to tell me why."

"No."

I glance up and down the street, hoping the neighbors aren't the sort who twitch curtains or take note of number plates. I asked Nish to check Goodall's work roster and he shouldn't be home for another few hours.

Finbar takes a box of tools from the van. He chooses a long metal rod with a hook on one end. Then he takes two small rubber wedges and inserts them at the top corner of the driver's-side window. Using the palm of his hand, he hammers each wedge deeper, forcing the door to slightly bend outward, creating a gap that is wide enough for the metal rod to enter. He slides the thin rod into the car and maneuvers the hook until it reaches the internal button that triggers the door mechanism. The car opens with a telltale click. The entire operation has taken less than thirty seconds.

Finbar offers to bypass the electrics and "take it somewhere else" if I need more time.

"That won't be necessary. You can go now. Thank you."

"You sure?"

"Yes."

The house keys are in a small compartment between the seats, amid a handful of petrol receipts, sweet wrappers, and a coffee club discount card. The key chain is a faux rabbit's foot. How retro.

Finbar has gone by the time I climb out of the car. A part of me wishes that he'd stayed. He would have helped me if I'd asked him to, and I feel guilty about that. Our argument at the hospital café still haunts me. My accusations. His hurt. I won't risk getting him into trouble. This is my decision, not his, and I have weighed up the possible outcomes. If I don't find Imogen's ring, then it's likely Goodall has destroyed it or hidden it permanently or had it broken up and fashioned into a new design. And if I do recover the ring, I'll have to convince Alison Goodall to say she took the ring with her when she fled from her husband. Nobody can know of my involvement without tainting the evidence or incriminating myself. These are the ifs and buts and maybes that have brought me here, to this road, and to this house.

When I reach the front door, a security light triggers on. Immediately I feel the pressure of the houses behind me, the inquisitive neighbors who might be watching from the windows. There are two keys on the key chain—one for a lower deadlock, which I open first. Once inside, I shut the door immediately and hear the warning beeps of an alarm. *Shit! Shit! Shit!*

For a split second I want to run. The control box will be nearby, but I have only thirty seconds to deactivate the device. Last summer I disabled our alarm system when it shorted during a thunderstorm. The code didn't work, so I found the main control panel and uncoupled it from the power source. That's what I look for now, searching the usual places, beneath the stairs and in the laundry. I find the gray metal box tucked behind a rack of winter coats in a cupboard near the kitchen.

I search for a knife or a screwdriver, something that can force open the flimsy metal lock. The beeping stops and a moment later the alarm explodes. My heart somersaults. I open another drawer and find a small chisel. Jamming the sharpened tip into the slot, I pop it open. The leads are screwed into place. I don't have time to be delicate. I wrench them out of the transformer and backup battery, red and black.

The alarm stops so suddenly, it feels as though the oxygen has been sucked out of the room, along with the noise. I listen to the silence until my chest hurts. Then I realize that I've been holding my breath. I exhale and inhale, slowing my heart rate and taking a moment to study the console. A lot of modern security systems are linked to mobile phones. Goodall could have already received a message and be on his way home.

Quickly climbing the stairs, navigating by the soft glow of a children's night-light, I reach the landing. Alison said she slid her suitcase beneath Nathan's bed. The little boy's room overlooks the garden. It has racing car wallpaper and a shelf full of dinosaurs. Kneeling on the floor, I lift a corner of the duvet and reach underneath the bed, feeling with my fingertips. There is no suitcase. Goodall must have found it. What would he do? Put it somewhere, expecting Alison to come home with her tail between her legs.

The door to the main bedroom is ajar. I imagine Goodall standing behind it. Listening. Waiting. With one finger, I push open the door and step inside. The curtains are drawn but I can't risk turning on the light.

I take the night-light from the landing and find a wall socket in the bedroom. It casts a soft glow over the room. The iron-framed bed is messy, and a pillow bears a head-shaped hollow. Discarded clothes are lying on the floor. The man is a slob when he doesn't have someone to clean up after him.

I check under the bed and open the drawers of a dressing table. His and hers. Alison's are mostly empty. I find a picture frame lying face-down. Holding it closer to the light, I discover it's a wedding photograph. He looks smug. She looks like a teenager playing dress-up.

There is a large walk-in wardrobe between the bedroom and the en suite, with shelves and hanging spaces on either side. Goodall has arranged his sweaters and jeans on different shelves. As I turn back to the bedroom, I notice a large suitcase standing upright in a hanging space on Alison's side of the wardrobe. Unclipping the latches, I fold it open. The main compartment is full of clothes and shoes, packed in haste. There are children's pajamas and soft toys. I search the lid compartments, sliding my hand inside the different pockets.

My fingers close around a velvet pouch and pull it free. The pouch has been rolled up like a sleeping bag and secured with a double bow. I tug at the velvet string, and it unfurls and reveals a rectangular shape, sewn with small pockets for earrings and a zippered section for necklaces. In the middle is a sausage-shaped pillow for her rings. Three of them. Even in semidarkness, I recognize the Ceylon sapphire surrounded by diamonds. It is Imogen Croker's ring. Her mother's ring. Her grandmother's ring. It is proof that Goodall lied about Imogen's death.

Downstairs, I hear the sound of a key entering a lock and feel the air pressure change as the front door opens. I feel the tremor of feet. The ring slips from my grasp and falls into the suitcase. I gently feel for it, searching the clothes, growing more desperate as the seconds tick by. Another sound, closer at hand. A light switch. The strip of light beneath the door glows brighter than before.

"Wait here. I have to turn off the alarm," says Goodall.

A woman answers. I can't make out the words.

I am pulling at clothes, shaking them, hoping the ring might fall loose.

"It's not working," yells Goodall. "There must have been a power outage. Make yourself at home."

I can't stay here. I can't be found. I cannot even count the laws I'm breaking. I shove the jewelry case back into the suitcase and force it closed, only managing to secure one latch. I push it behind the door of the wardrobe and step into the bedroom. Listening. They're in the kitchen. Laughing. I hear the muffled pop of a champagne cork and the clink of glasses. He's supposed to be working, but he's brought a woman home. Not his wife. A date.

Ahead of me are the stairs. If I stay close to the wall, I might be able to reach the front door without being seen. The other option is to hide. I choose Nathan's room, squeezing myself between his bed and the wall, pulling the duvet partially across my body to hide myself.

I am lying on my stomach, with my head turned to one side, listening to the music playing downstairs. Time passes. Drags. Expands. The stillness settles over me, but I feel a strange fullness in my ears, as though I'm underwater and the weight of the ocean is pressing against my eardrums.

The stairs creak. They're coming. I press my cheek to the floor and see two shadows pass across the door. They're in the bedroom. He's apologizing for the mess. I should warn her. I should run.

Crawling out from beneath the bed, I cross the room and flatten myself against a wall, poking my head out, one eye only. The main bedroom door is half-closed, offering me some protection.

The plumbing rattles. The shower. Without hesitating, I cross the landing and descend the stairs, aware of every creak from the carpeted boards. At any moment, I expect the bedroom door to open and Goodall to appear.

I turn the spring lock gently and open the front door. It will be louder when it closes. I flinch as the latch bolt clicks against the strike plate, echoing through the house. The security light triggers. I don't stop. I keep moving, walking down the short path and turning left, where I will disappear quickly behind the neighbor's front hedge.

I return the keys to Goodall's Saab and make sure that it's locked before making my way along the road. A woman emerges from a front gate, taking her dog for a walk. For a moment I get tangled in the leash and she apologizes, smiling and wishing me good night.

I mumble a reply and keep moving. My hands are shaking when I reach the VW. I struggle to find the ignition, then first gear, second, third . . . accelerating. Too fast. Slow down. Stay calm.

I'm furious with myself. What a pointless, ridiculous exercise—to risk so much and gain so little. I don't have the ring, which means I can't use it against Goodall or return it to Imogen's family. All I have is a secret that I can never share with anyone.

BOOK THREE

I want her to melt into me, like butter on toast.
I want to absorb her
and walk around for the rest of my days
with her encased in my skin.

Sara Gruen,
Water for Elephants

47

This is our third nightclub, and each one has been louder than the last, with darker corners, brighter flashing lights, and more bodies on the dance floor. I can't remember how long it's been since I went out dancing, but nothing much has changed, particularly the cost of drinks and the chat-up lines.

I went through a clubbing phase in my late teens, wearing clingy dresses and high heels, sweet-talking bouncers, and getting free entry because girls bring in guys. Usually, we couldn't afford to buy more than one cocktail, but there were always stockbrokers and traders who kept us supplied. Today's suitors don't have the same sort of cash or cache. They're younger and braver, strutting around like playboys, hoping to hook up with a "bit of posh" but happy to fight with a jealous boyfriend if that's how the night unfolds.

A group of young guys has been doing their best to get us to dance with them. They barely look eighteen, although it's hard to tell in this lighting. One guy in particular seems to have taken a shine to me. I explain that this is my hen night, but I don't think he understands, or he doesn't hear me. His name is Jasper and he has a Russian accent and looks like he should be in a boy band, with his gelled hair and on-trend shirt.

Jasper keeps asking me to dance, but my feet are sore because I listened to Margot and wore high heels, which are giving me blisters. I'm also quite drunk because Brianna keeps buying me cocktails, which I've taken to pouring into a potted plant when she's not looking. I hope it's plastic.

Yelling over the music, I try to explain to Jasper that I'm getting married. He wants to know why my fiancé let me come out on my own.

"I'm not on my own," I shout. My lips brush his ear and I pull away, embarrassed, and point to my friends.

"Are they single?" he asks.

"Some of them, but I think you should look for someone younger."

"How old do you think I am?"

"Forty-five," I say jokingly.

He looks aggrieved.

"Are you allowed to be here?" I ask.

"Of course. I have proof." He shows me a UK driver's license.

"Well, that's fake. I hope you didn't pay a lot."

"How do you know?"

"I'm a police officer."

He laughs, thinking I'm joking, but then looks concerned that he's been caught out. He makes an excuse and disappears, looking for someone else to chat up.

I'm sitting on my own again, watching the others dance. Carmen has joined them, clearly and proudly pregnant, and high on life rather than alcohol or drugs.

Sara has her arms around a boy, who is thrusting his pelvis into hers, but she seems amused rather than annoyed.

I hear Tempe's voice before I realize that she's sitting beside me.

"You're not dancing," she says, putting a drink in front of me.

"My feet are hurting."

I try not to look surprised and wonder for a moment which one of my friends invited her. The song is ending but bleeds into the next one, which is slower. Tempe is wearing a short black dress, which rides up, exposing the top of her stockings.

"That's rather old-fashioned," I say, pointing to her suspenders. "Are they comfortable?"

"Not really, but they make me feel sexy."

Her cocktail matches mine, a strawberry daiquiri. After a long pause, she asks, "Why didn't you invite me?"

"Sara arranged it. It was a surprise."

"You're lying."

I can't match her gaze. I take a sip, then another, trying to delay the conversation. I have to say something.

"Please don't be upset."

"I'm not," she says blithely. "It's not my fault if your friends don't like me."

"Can we talk about this tomorrow? I can barely hear myself think."

Tempe is sitting close. I can smell her perfume and her shampoo.

"I try so hard," she says, yelling in my ear, on the verge of tears. "What more can I do? I listen. I don't talk about myself. I ask questions about their work and hobbies. Nobody ever asks me questions."

"I do."

"But I wasn't invited."

"These are my oldest friends. It's like a school reunion."

"This is your hen night. I helped arrange your wedding."

"You're a new friend, not an old one."

"Don't treat me like a child," she says bitterly.

"You're here now."

"I'm not staying." She motions to where the others have left the dance floor but are avoiding us. "They're talking about me. They're always saying things behind my back."

"No, they're not."

She looks at me skeptically. And leans forward. A delicate silver pendant swings from her neck.

"Margot saw me earlier at the bar. She didn't come over. She didn't acknowledge me. I'm always the one who makes the effort. I'm the one chasing after them."

"You should back off—let people come to you."

"Fine," says Tempe, picking up her clutch bag, preparing to leave.

"Stay."

"You'll have a nicer time without me."

"I'll buy you a drink."

"No, let me buy. Then I'm going."

I watch her walk to the bar. Her hips are hugged by her dress. The men are looking. She could have any of them, but she's only interested in me. Margot appears at my shoulder. She has clearly been designated by the others to find out what's happening.

"Hey," she shouts. "What's Tempe doing here?"

"Don't worry, she's leaving."

"Any particular reason?"

I shake my head and sigh tiredly. "Go back to the others. Tell them I'm fine. I'll be over soon."

Tempe returns. She has bought cocktails for both of us. A man approaches; his top button is undone and his tie at half-mast. He asks Tempe to dance, but she smiles and declines. He turns to me, his second choice, but I shake my head, feeling drunker than before.

Tempe says something to him. His eyes widen and he bows to me, apologizing before leaving.

"What did you say to him?" I shout.

She shrugs and sips her drink.

"What happened with Dr. Coyle?"

"He's gone."

"Back to Belfast?"

Another shrug. A change of subject. "I can be a good friend, you know."

"You've done enough for me."

"But I could be better."

"You've done enough."

She reaches out and takes my hand. Her touch is cool. She brushes my palm with her fingertip.

"Promise you'll never shut me out."

48

My eyes refuse to open. Sticky. Blind for a moment. Mouth rank. Body poisoned. Head pounding. I'm awake, trying to hold the pain at bay, but it comes in waves. I imagine that I'm in my own bed, in my own house, with Henry's arms around me.

Only, it's not Henry. Tempe is behind me. Her skin against mine. I roll away, moving too quickly. Vomit in my mouth. Swallowing hard. I drag a sheet around me. Tempe stirs.

"What happened?" I ask.

"What do you mean?"

"How did I get here?"

"Don't you remember?"

"No."

It's like I fell asleep in one world and have woken up in another. I have pieces. Fragments. We were dancing. Drinking. I don't recall leaving the nightclub. How did I get to Tempe's flat? Who undressed me? An image flashes into my mind. Tempe talking to me. Saying things that I can't understand. Her dress has slipped down. She kisses me. I'm kissing her back. She smells of smoke and perfume and something sweetly dirty and I have a strange feeling this is happening to someone else. It's not unpleasant. It's interesting. An experiment.

Tempe rolls out of bed and grabs her robe from a hook behind the door.

"You were drunk. I mean really drunk," she says, lifting her hair over the collar. "I didn't think it was safe to let you go home alone, so I brought you here. I didn't want Henry seeing you like that."

"I remember being at the nightclub. We were talking to that young guy. Do you think he could have slipped something into my drink?"

Her eyes widen. "A roofie. I guess it's possible. One minute you were fine and the next you were totally wasted."

I look around the room. "Where are my clothes?"

"You vomited on your dress. It's soaking in the sink."

"I don't remember being sick."

"Not in the Uber, thank God. He pulled over just in time. He didn't want to take us after that. I had to promise him extra money."

"I'll pay you back," I say, still not remembering. I'm racking my brain.

"You were having a really good time," says Tempe. "Dancing and laughing. You were flirting with two guys who kept buying you drinks."

"Really?"

I feel the bruising on my toes and notice the blisters left by the straps.

"I need something to wear."

"Of course. Choose something from the wardrobe."

When I first try to stand, I almost fall over. I steady myself against the wall. Head hammering. I look through her things, choosing a pair of cargo pants and a baggy T-shirt. When I pull the T-shirt over my head, I feel dizzy and I can't rid myself of the sense that something dreadful has happened and that I haven't been paying attention.

In the same breath, the nausea overwhelms me. I dash to the bathroom and kneel over the toilet heaving up a caustic stew of alcohol and fruit and what's left of last night's dinner. In between the waves of retching, I prop myself against the wall, pressing my forehead against the cool tiles.

Tempe is in the shower. She turns off the water and steps out, pressing a towel against her lower belly. Drops of water glint on her shoulders and breasts. I clear my throat and avoid looking at her.

"You poor thing," she says, stroking my hair. I notice her left hand, which is no longer bandaged. There is a semicircle of puncture wounds that look like bite marks on either side of her thumb. I want to say something, but she's naked and I'm trying not to be sick.

Going back to the bedroom, I look for my phone and my wallet, lifting bedclothes and pillows, searching the dresser and windowsill.

I call out to her. "Have you seen my phone?"

"Pardon?"

"Have you seen my phone?"

"No."

"I had it last night."

"I'll call your number."

She appears and unlocks her own mobile and calls up my contact details before pressing the phone against her ear. Shaking her head.

Shit!

"Maybe you left it at the nightclub or in the Uber."

"*Shit! Shit!*"

"I'll call the club . . . and the driver."

Tempe gets dressed as I search the room again. Memories of last night are coming back to me in staccato-like flashes. I'm sitting on a bench of a bus shelter. People are around me, but I can't make sense of what they're saying. Tempe has two heads. Four eyes. It's like some form of sedated consciousness, where I'm awake and aware but unable to intervene or converse.

"I can't remember what happened," I say.

"At least you had a good time," says Tempe.

"Did I?"

She punches paracetamol from a foil packet and pours me a glass of water. Every little noise is amplified.

"Can I use your phone to call Henry?"

"I've sent him a message. I told him you were here."

"Why?"

"Because he was looking for you." She makes it sound so obvious

I contemplate calling Henry but decide to leave that conversati
when Tempe isn't in the room.

"I have to go."

"I'll make you a coffee."

"No time."

Tempe insists on driving me. I get into the front se
immediately lower the window in case I feel sick. Pr
the dashboard, I tie the laces of her white sneakers
of red on the toe cap and tongue. She must hav
was cleaning the front door. I have a matching
them together at a two-for-one sale in the W

Tempe drives with her chin held high, b
ming to herself. I want to turn on the ra
keeps going back to last night. Tempe
invited. It was more disappointment
invited herself. I was drugged an
other friends? Sara, Margot, Br

I want to ask Tempe if sh
embarrassed. What if I imagin
if I kissed her?

We've reached the western edge of Clapham Common and I tell Tempe to pull over because I think I might be sick. Out of the car, I lean over my knees, but nothing comes up. When I straighten, I have sweat dripping off my face.

"I can walk from here."

"Are you sure?"

"Yes."

I set off, grateful for the fresh air. Tempe follows me until I reach the next intersection before tooting her horn and turning left into Elspeth Road. Finally away from her, my whole body relaxes. I'm suddenly so tired that I want to curl up under a tree and fall asleep.

Nearing the house, I notice someone on the far side of the road, keeping pace with me. A police car is parked opposite. Fairbairn reaches the steps before I do and takes up a lounging position, leaning on one elbow, raising his face to the sunshine.

"I rang the doorbell. Your fiancé said you weren't home," he says breezily.

"Is something wrong?"

"Where were you?"

"I stayed with a friend."

I pause, assuming that he has something to tell me. He points to my forearm. "You've hurt yourself."

I follow his gaze and notice the long red scratches that haven't quite broken the skin. I pull down my sleeve.

"What happened?"

"I don't remember."

"Really?"

"I must have been asleep."

"It was a violent dream."

I take him upstairs and make him wait in the kitchen while I go to the bathroom and splash water on my face, trying to wake up. Henry appears.

"I got a message from Tempe. What happened?"

"I think my drink was spiked. Tempe took me back to her place and I crashed."

"She used your phone . . . to send messages."

"I know. I'm sorry."

"You should go to the hospital."

"I know. Let me deal with this first."

Fairbairn has been waiting in the kitchen.

"I took the liberty," he says, handing me a cup of tea. "Big night?"

"Something like that."

"What was the occasion?"

"I'm getting married."

"I see," he says, but I don't think he sees at all.

"My girlfriends took me out clubbing. I drank too much or my drink was spiked."

"Which one was it?" he asks.

"I don't know. What's this about?"

"Darren Goodall."

"What's he done this time?"

"He's dead."

I'm staring at Fairbairn, trying to decide if this is some sort of sick joke, but I can see he's telling the truth. My stomach cramps, and I feel another wave of nausea. I clench my teeth.

"What happened?"

"He was murdered. We're following up on anyone who had dealings with Detective Goodall. When did you last see him?"

"A few days ago. I was in court when his wife applied for a DAP order."

"You accompanied her?"

"I offered her moral support."

"As a friend."

He makes me sound compromised, as though I've been caught out in a lie. I feel myself growing annoyed.

"Do I need a lawyer?" I ask.

"I don't know. Do you?" He looks at me quizzically. After a long pause, he smiles disarmingly and finally sips his tea.

Henry is hovering in the doorway to the living room, wanting to know why a police officer is in our kitchen. I wave him away. Fairbairn slips his notebook into his jacket pocket, patting it with his hand.

"How did he die?" I ask.

"Detective Goodall burned to death."

"In his car?"

"No, his house." Fairbairn glances at his mobile. "I can show you if you'd like."

"I don't understand."

"You seem to have taken quite an interest in Sergeant Goodall—searching the police database, talking to his wife . . . Perhaps you can help me understand why someone would do this."

"He must have made enemies."

"What makes you say that?"

"Dylan Holstein was investigating him."

"You think this is payback for a dead journalist."

"I don't know."

"His fiancé fell from a cliff eight years ago. She was drunk. It was windy. The coroner decided it was a tragic accident. Goodall didn't care if some journalist was sniffing around, digging up dirt."

"How do you know?"

"Stands to reason."

Whose reason, I want to ask, but let him go on.

"The chains. The breeze-blocks. The swim in the river. That was a gang-land hit," says Fairbairn. "The sort of thing your father might arrange."

"He's a property developer."

The detective finds this funny. I wait for him to stop laughing.

"It was odd that you happened to be there when we found his body," he says.

"It was a coincidence."

"Coincidences can sometimes take a lot of planning."

I don't rise to the bait.

"How is your father?" he asks.

"Recovering from a heart attack."

"I heard. Shame. On the mend, I hope."

"Yes."

"Eddie McCarthy seems to have a foot in every camp and a finger in every pie these days. Must be handy having a daughter in the Metropolitan Police."

"I resent what you're implying."

Another smile. "What am I implying?"

I don't answer.

"Dylan Holstein was investigating the Hope Island development.

Two local councillors resigned, another is dead, yet nothing stops Eddie McCarthy—not even a heart attack."

"If you have questions, you should ask him. You know his address."

"I do. It's quite the manor." He scratches his unshaven chin. "Drugged, you say. I can take you to hospital if you'd like a toxicology test. But if it turns out you've been using recreational drugs, it will be the end of your career."

It's already over, I think, but I need more information about last night before I risk getting a drug test. Did one of my girlfriends give me something? Did I take it drunkenly, yet willingly? A blood test might implicate me rather than clear me. I ask if I can take a shower. Fairbairn waits.

In the bathroom I catch a glimpse of myself in the mirror. I have dark circles under my eyes and my lips are bloodless and cracked. I look like a zombie. I feel like a rape victim.

Henry sits on the bed as I get changed.

"You told me Tempe wasn't invited," he whispers.

"And you told her where we were."

"No, I didn't."

I'm about to argue, but he pushes back. "I didn't know where you were going."

"Tempe said she called you."

"Yes."

"You must have said something."

"I said you'd gone out with your friends."

"Because you knew it would hurt her."

Henry tries to change the subject. "Who spiked your drink?"

"I didn't think to take down his name," I reply. "Silly me."

"Was there anyone sniffing around you or buying you drinks?"

"Yes and no."

"To which question?"

I'm annoyed that I have to defend myself. "A woman should be allowed to go out without being drugged and assaulted."

His head jerks up. "Were you assaulted?"

"No. I don't . . . it's complicated . . . I let my hair down. I drank too much. I danced."

I get changed, pulling on jeans, a blouse, and a short leather jacket.

"When will you be home?" Henry asks.

"When I'm finished."

49

There are no sirens and little sense of urgency about the journey. Fairbairn has chosen the front seat of the unmarked police car but looks over his shoulder to talk to me. The driver is a uniformed constable who is roughly my age with a face like a fairground clown, all red cheeks and round mouth.

"Are you going to tell me what happened?" I ask, still unsure of what I'm doing here.

"I'd rather show you."

"Why?"

"A fresh set of eyes."

"I'm not a homicide detective."

"Tell me what you see."

I recognize the houses when we turn into Kempe Road, where temporary barricades have been erected at either end of the block. Police vehicles and forensic vans have taken up every available parking space, along with a lone fire engine with an extension ladder.

Signatures are given and names taken. I am escorted past firefighters who are rolling up hoses and securing equipment to the truck. The first thing I notice about the house is that the upper windows have been shattered by heat or water. There are sooty marks above the window frames and some of the eaves are blackened.

Crime scene tape has been set up around the house, threaded along the hedges and across the gate. The forensic teams are packing up, having finished collecting samples and dusting surfaces. Lights and cameras are slotted into silver boxes. Tripods are folded. Evidence collected. Evidence bagged. Sealed. Labeled.

Having passed an outer ring, we move to an inner one, closer to the house. More signatures are required and I am issued a set of coveralls, including a hairnet that looks like a shower cap, a face mask, and plastic booties that go over my shoes. The front door of the house is hanging by a single hinge. Fire crews must have battered it down to reach the blaze.

"Have you been here before?" asks Fairbairn.

A bubble of air gets trapped in my throat. "Why do you ask?"

"Mrs. Goodall said you helped her leave her husband."

"You've talked to her."

"I had to break the news."

"How did she take it?"

"Her mother did most of the crying."

We step into the house, where square plastic duckboards are arranged along the hallway. The smell of smoke is thick in the air, and the sodden carpet squelches each time I take a step. I glance into the sitting room, where fingerprint powder covers every smooth surface.

Three days ago, I broke into this house. I could have left behind skin cells, clothing fibers, strands of my hair. I should get out in front of this by telling Fairbairn the whole story—how I found Imogen Croker's sapphire ring, which proves that Goodall lied at her inquest. But that would mean admitting my own crimes—trespass, break and enter, attempted burglary, and criminal damage. Perhaps, if they catch the killer quickly, none of that will matter.

"How did you and Mrs. Goodall meet?" he asks.

"What did she tell you?"

"You were at the same yoga class."

"That's right."

"Was it a coincidence?"

"No," I say, deciding to stick to the truth where possible. "I followed her."

"From this house?"

"Yes."

"Why?"

"I heard a recording of an emergency call made by Nathan, her little boy, during a domestic dispute. The case was covered up."

"What business was that of yours?"

"After what happened to Tempe Brown, I suspected that Goodall had abused women before. When Holstein told me about Imogen Croker, I decided to dig a little deeper."

"You accessed the police database without permission."

"Yes."

"Did you discuss your concerns with your superiors?"

"I was told to leave it alone."

"But you didn't."

We are climbing the stairs, turning on the landing.

"When did you last speak to Alison Goodall?"

"I went to court with her on Wednesday. She applied for a DAP notice."

"You encouraged her to leave him."

"She made that decision."

We have reached the main bedroom, which reminds me of those rooms uncovered in ancient Pompeii after Mount Vesuvius buried the city in volcanic ash. Everything is covered in an oily black soot that has created a perverse shadow land. The room is devoid of color except for the duckboards and our blue coveralls and a small clear patch of fabric on a cushioned chair near the window.

Fairbairn speaks. "This is exactly as we found it. Only the body has been moved."

A new smell assaults my senses—the sweet, cloying stench of burnt flesh. It sticks to the insides of my nostrils. My stomach heaves, but I have nothing left to bring up.

Despite the damage, I recognize the room—the queen-sized iron-frame bed, the matching sets of drawers, and the antique dressing table. I have searched those drawers and seen my reflection in the mirror.

"This was the ignition point," says Fairbairn, pointing to the bed.

The mattress is so badly burned that I can see the inner springs and melted foam that has solidified into coal-black clumps.

"He was handcuffed to the bed."

"Police-issue handcuffs?"

"Yes. One wrist. His right one."

"What was the accelerant?"

"Lighter fluid."

Fairbairn steps onto the duckboards. I follow tentatively, my arms tightly folded, as though frightened of touching anything.

"A neighbor, who lives across the road, heard the sound of breaking glass and looked out her window. She saw the flames in the upstairs window."

"Did she see anyone leaving?"

"A figure dressed in dark clothing and white sports shoes."

"Male? Female?"

"She couldn't tell. Goodall had company last night. We found a half-finished bottle of wine downstairs and two glasses."

"Fingerprints?"

"Wiped clean."

"That suggests he knew his killer."

The whiff of burnt flesh catches in my throat again and my stomach spasms.

"He must have been gagged," I say, glancing at the bed.

"What makes you say that?"

"You said the neighbor heard the sound of breaking glass, but nothing about anyone screaming. Goodall would have been yelling the house down if he was burning."

"He had something stuffed in his mouth."

"What?"

Fairbairn seems reluctant to tell me. "Women's underwear. We are hoping to get DNA from them."

"That's unlikely."

"What makes you say that?"

"Anyone who went to the effort of wiping down a wineglass wouldn't make a rookie mistake like leaving her DNA on underwear." I nod towards the dressing table.

"Could have come from the drawer."

"How do you know that's where Mrs. Goodall kept her underwear?"

"It's the obvious place."

"You think it was a woman?"

"Don't you?"

Fairbairn makes a mumbling sound deep in his chest, and I silently admonish myself for offering too many thoughts.

"Where was Alison last night?" I ask.

"At her parents' house. Her little boy was awake most of the night with an ear infection. She took him to the doctor first thing."

I glance at the walk-in wardrobe, remembering the suitcase and Imogen Croker's sapphire ring.

"Has anything been removed?" I ask.

"No. It's exactly as we found it."

Stepping between duckboards, I edge closer to the wardrobe and glance inside. The door must have been closed when the fire took hold because less soot covers the shelves and hanging clothes.

"Did Alison tell you about the suitcase?" I ask.

"What suitcase?"

"When she was leaving, she packed her things in two suitcases but had to leave one of them behind."

"Is that important?"

"I showed her a photograph of a sapphire ring that Imogen Croker was wearing on the day she died. She told me Goodall had given her a similar-looking ring." I step into the walk-in wardrobe and glance behind the door. The suitcase is still there.

"It was in a jewelry pouch."

Fairbairn grunts dismissively. "Goodall wasn't murdered over a piece of jewelry that went missing eight years ago." I want to argue, but he's still talking. "This is payback for something more recent."

I think of the woman he was with three nights ago. I didn't see her face, but she sounded like someone who was new to the house. A first timer. A date.

Fairbairn is still talking. "Someone tampered with the alarm system. They forced the lock and unhooked the leads, which doesn't fit with the bottle of wine and the wineglasses."

"It could be unrelated," I say.

"Or the killer had an accomplice who broke in earlier and was waiting in the house."

"You think two people did this?"

Fairbairn rubs at his cheek as though removing his freckles. Again, I wish I'd kept my mouth shut.

"Explain to me again your relationship with Darren Goodall."

"We didn't have a *relationship*. He was stalking Tempe Brown. Sending her threatening messages. He vandalized my car with acid. He painted insults on her front door."

"Did either of you call the police?"

"I *was* the police, remember?" The comment is too glib and cursory.

"When you say vandalized . . . ?"

"With acid. I took photographs." I reach for my phone and remember. "I lost my phone last night," I say, aware of how lame that sounds.

"Where?"

"At a nightclub, I think, or maybe in an Uber on the way home."

"That's unfortunate. Perhaps we can track it down for you."

He doesn't believe me.

"Where is your car now?" he asks.

"I'm having it resprayed."

Fairbairn sighs in frustration.

I was wrong to come here. I should have refused and clammed up, told him nothing about myself or my impressions of the crime scene. Clearly, I'm a person of interest, peripheral or otherwise, and this is a fishing expedition.

Fairbairn motions to the stairs and leads me outside, where I peel off the latex gloves and step out of the coveralls. The detective tosses his into a waiting pile, but mine are kept separate. He's collecting my DNA. He opens the rear door of a patrol car that will take me home.

"I want the names and contact details for girlfriends, including Tempe Brown."

"They're on my phone," I say. "But I'll get them for you."

I need time to talk to them, to discover exactly what happened at the nightclub and afterwards.

As the police car pulls away, I glance over my shoulder at the house. The detective is standing in the middle of the road, his hands pushed into his pockets, his coat flaring over his wrists, like a lone gunfighter, waiting for high noon.

50

Henry is in the back garden clearing away vines that are threatening to engulf the rear fence. His hair has grown fairer over the summer and needs to be trimmed before the wedding.

"What happened last night?" he asks, wiping his forehead with his forearm.

"I told you. Tempe took me home."

"Did she give you that love bite?"

"Where?"

He puts his finger on my neck above my clavicle.

I touch the spot, but not his hand, which has moved away. I laugh, thinking it's a joke, but Henry doesn't join me. I want him to look at me, but his eyes keep pulling distractedly to the side.

"Nothing happened," I say.

"How can you be sure? You were drugged."

He leans down and picks up a water bottle, turning his face up to the sunshine as he drinks.

"Do they know who killed Goodall?"

"No."

"Are you a suspect?"

"I think so."

Henry blows out his cheeks and a lock of his hair rises and falls on the current of air. "Did you tell them what Goodall did to you? How he ran you off the road and attacked your car?"

"That's what makes me a suspect."

"But you have Tempe as an alibi."

I nod uncertainly. He takes a seat on the low brick wall and asks me about the fire, taking a professional interest. Henry often talks about the nature of fire and how it reacts in given circumstances. Once, seven minutes deep into a burning building, his breathing apparatus began to whistle as he ran out of air. It hadn't been filled properly. Henry survived by crawling beneath the worst of the smoke, navigating blindly, taking short breaths. He spent two days in hospital and didn't tell me all the details until months afterwards because he was worried his lungs might have been permanently damaged.

"How far did the fire spread?" he asks.

"Up the wall, but it didn't get into the ceiling."

"What about the curtains?"

"Burned."

"Were the windows smashed?"

"Yes, but it could have been the hoses. I was amazed at how much soot was left behind."

"Was it sticky or dry?"

"Why?"

"There's a difference between wet smoke and dry smoke. Wet smoke comes from burning plastics and rubber. Dry smoke comes from paper and wood. It burns at higher and faster temperatures. One leaves a pungent, almost sticky soot. The other leaves a dry soot, which is easier to wipe off."

"It was sticky."

"That was probably the mattress burning," he says.

"It turned everything black—the walls, the floor, the furniture."

I am picturing the room in my mind—completely devoid of color except for the duckboards and our coveralls and the cushioned chair near the window.

"Why would a cushion not get covered in soot?" I ask.

Henry considers the question. "Something must have been resting on it."

"The police said they took nothing from the room."

Henry pauses to think. In the silence, I can hear bees buzzing among the flowers and the distant sound of a hedge trimmer. I keep picturing the geometric design on the cushion and everything else coated in soot. There is an answer, which almost eludes me because the idea seems too horrible to countenance.

"Could someone have been sitting in the room while the bed was burning?" I ask.

"They would have left footprints," says Henry.

"Which were obliterated by water and the boots of firefighters."

"They would have needed to stay below the smoke."

"Is that possible?"

"Dangerous, but yes."

I shudder at the thought of someone watching Goodall die, hearing his gagged screams as the fire engulfed his body. That level of hatred is almost incomprehensible.

"Maybe it was your father," says Henry.

"Why would you think that?"

"You told me that he'd go to war."

"Not everything has to do with my family," I snap.

"You're right. I'm sorry."

Even as he apologizes, I feel a sudden gnawing doubt begin to spin inside my chest. My father knew that Goodall had threatened me. Maybe Finbar told him about the acid attack.

Henry has turned back to the vines. We're only a few feet apart, but it feels like a huge gulf. I want to hug him. I want to press my face to his chest and to stand motionless in the garden with his arms wrapped around me, while I shudder little sighs and let the world repair itself.

"I have to go," I say.

"Where?"

"I need to talk to Carmen. I want to know what happened last night."

"Maybe you should stay home?"

"Why?"

I wait for an explanation, but his only response is a puzzled, fleeting frown. "Every time you go charging off, you seem to make things worse. If you stopped . . . took a breath . . ." He doesn't finish.

"I didn't start this."

"You can walk away."

"It's too late for that."

His eyes have filled with a pained hope, and I realize how distant we've been. We used to talk about everything, chatting about friends and gossip and current affairs; swapping internet memes and cat videos. Binge-watching *Bob's Burgers* and *Fleabag* on TV. All that has changed. I have changed.

I'm almost back at the house when he calls my name. "Tempe found your phone. It's in the kitchen."

"Where was it?"

"She didn't say."

My phone is plugged into a charger on the island bench. The screen shows a dozen missed messages, from Tempe and Henry and from the other girls. Georgia has sent me a drunken emoji. Why do other people find hangovers so amusing? I was drugged, not drunk, although I can't be certain. My brain feels like a computer that has crashed and lost data that I can't get back. Eight hours are missing. Erased. Corrupted.

Carmen's bookshop specializes in storybooks for children and has a reading corner with tiny tables and chairs in primary colors. Her young assistant is dressed up like Alice in Wonderland, but I'm not sure if it's her normal fashion choice or a costume. Carmen is out back, "doing the returns."

She hears my voice and emerges, wiping ink from her fingers. I pull her back into her office, which is barely big enough for both of us—a storage cupboard lined with books.

"What happened last night?"

"Why?"

"I woke up this morning at Tempe's flat. I can't remember getting there."

Carmen seems ready to make a joke but stops herself. "You seemed to be having a great time, the life and soul. Drinking. Dancing."

"Who was I dancing with?"

"Loads of people."

"Who invited Tempe?"

"I thought you did."

"No."

"How did she know where we'd be?"

"I don't know."

Clearly, Carmen is telling the truth because she's not the sort of person who embellishes stories or exaggerates to make them more interesting.

"How did I seem when you last saw me?" I ask.

"A little emotional. You were telling us how much you loved us. We decided to take you home."

"Why didn't you take me?"

"Tempe offered. She lives the closest. Georgia had hooked up with some guy, who said he would take her to Madrid for the weekend. I had to rescue her. Brianna bailed early because of work."

My voice breaks. "Why can't I remember?"

Carmen realizes something is wrong. "Did something happen?"

"I think someone spiked my drink."

"No. When?"

"At the last club. I remember Tempe showing up. A guy came over and asked us to dance. Tempe went to the bar. I spoke to Georgia. That's it."

Carmen's face is a picture of concern. "But nothing happened, did it? I mean, you were always safe."

My phone chirrups. Tempe has sent another message, asking if I want to have a final fitting for my wedding dress. I'm only five minutes from the bridal shop. It's almost as though she knows where I am.

In that instant the machinery of the world seems to fall silent and I hear only the sound of my breath escaping. Tempe didn't accidentally bump into me at the Chinese restaurant in Wandsworth or at Brixton Market or when I was training at the Chestnut Grove Academy. Each time we had laughed it off. We were so simpatico that we ran errands at the same time. Pretty soon our cycles would synchronize, or we'd be finishing each other's sentences.

My mind skips through other examples, which had seemed so random at first, with no method or reason. Gradually a pattern emerges. No, nothing as definite as a pattern—a faint almost-meaning that grows clearer as I put the pieces together. It was never a coincidence. It was always by design.

51

The young guy in the computer shop is cultivating a beard that is sprouting in patches across the lower half of his face. He seems quite proud of it, stroking his chin as he studies a screen.

I put my phone on the counter and ask, "How do I find out if someone is tracking me?"

He looks up. Straightens. Adjusts his crotch. "A jealous boyfriend?"

"Something like that."

The name tag on his shirt pocket says Symon, spelled with a *y*.

"I can run an antivirus program," he says.

After attaching my phone to a computer, he taps at the keyboard. On the screen, I watch a red bar slowly filling, indicating progress. For all I know he's downloading all my images, but I don't think I need to worry. I don't have embarrassing photographs. Naked ones, I mean.

"What are you looking for?" I ask.

"Viruses. Malware. It shouldn't take long."

The computer makes a pinging sound. "OK, that looks all right. Let's look at what apps you're using."

He scrolls through my phone. "I can't see any obvious tracking apps. A lot of parents use them to keep tabs on their children. Some are pretty sophisticated. They send out alerts if a handset hasn't been used for a period of time. It stops kids leaving their phones at a mate's place and going to a party."

Still talking, he plugs the phone into a different computer and runs another program. This time a screed of script appears, looking like a foreign alphabet.

"Fuck!" he yells, quickly unplugging the phone.

"What is it?"

"Malware. I must have triggered it when I went looking for the app."

"What does that mean?"

"Your phone has a virus. And whoever wrote the coding doesn't want me interfering."

"Can you get rid of it?"

"Not without doing a factory reset. Do you have it backed up any-where? The cloud? A computer at home?"

"I don't know. Henry does that for me."

Symon plugs my phone into a new computer and holds down the volume key, opening a recovery mode screen. "You sure you want me to do this? You'll lose everything. Passwords. Emails. Contacts. Photo-graphs."

"I don't care."

"You should also wipe any computers and tablets you have at home which share the same network."

"OK. Make it safe. What does the malware do?"

"Hard to say without seeing the coding, but it could give someone access to your data and location and some control of your phone—turn-ing on the camera and microphone without you knowing."

"Eavesdropping."

"Yeah."

"How did I get infected?"

"Maybe you opened an attachment, or someone had access to your phone."

My mind is skipping ahead. Tempe is always sending me photographs and attachments, information about the wedding. And when she visits, my phone is always lying around.

Symon returns the handset. My contact list is purged. My emails, my messages, my photographs. I want to call Henry, but I only remember a few digits of his number.

I'm outside on the pavement, being jostled by passing pedestrians because I'm unsure of where I'm going and what I should do. What Tempe did is illegal—phone hacking, reading my messages . . . She could be watching me now. She could have followed me to the bookshop and the computer store. I scan the street and the churchyard over the road, looking into the shadows beneath the trees.

What does Tempe want from me? I befriended her. I found her accommodation when she was homeless. I introduced her to my friends. I treated her like a sister. But it was never enough. I don't care if she's a white knight or has a history of mental health issues or thinks I need rescuing. This has to stop.

At the bridal shop, I wait outside, still deciding what to do. The owner spies me through the window and joins me on the footpath.

"Is everything OK? You can come inside. I'll put the kettle on."

Martina is in her mid-forties, dressed in a smart skirt and coordinating jacket that sets off the blue in her eyes. She is one of those women who gushes over every bride-to-be and makes each of us feel like her most important customer.

"What have you done to yourself?" she asks, concerned. "You have bags under your eyes. That won't do. You need cold tea bags. Hydration."

"I didn't sleep well."

She takes me into the fitting room, which has a lounge set up for viewing and mirrors on three walls. Tea is poured. Chocolate biscuits arranged on a plate. I haven't eaten since yesterday. The chocolate gives me a momentary sugar hit, but I know it won't last.

A singsong chime announces Tempe's arrival. She's in jeans and a light cashmere cardigan over a white T-shirt. My cardigan. My style. She smiles and leans towards me, expecting a kiss on the cheek, but at the last moment, I pull away.

"I have a sore throat. I don't want to give you anything."

Martina lets out a squeak of alarm. "You can't be getting a cold. Not this close to the wedding. I know just the thing—you need a saltwater gargle and honey in our tea."

While Martina prattles on about how she hasn't had a head cold in seven years, I am watching Tempe.

"How did you know where I was?" I ask.

"What?"

"When you texted, I was around the corner at Carmen's bookshop."

"That was handy," she says, oblivious to the subtext.

"Have the police been to see you?"

"Why?"

"Darren Goodall was killed last night."

Tempe doesn't feign surprise or concern. The news barely causes a ripple on her serene unflustered face.

"In the line of duty?" she asks, picking up a bridal magazine.

"No. He was at home."

"Did someone . . . ?"

"He was set on fire. Early hours. It was horrible."

"You saw him?"

"I saw the crime scene."

She is casually turning the pages, pausing to look at photographs. "Do they know who did it?"

"No, but the police will want to speak to you."

"Why?"

"Because of the threats he made and the vandalism."

"I don't have any proof it was him."

"Who else could it be?"

Tempe doesn't answer. I expected more. Some sense of shock or sadness. She talked of loving him once, of hoping he might leave his wife and marry her, although she quickly changed her mind and grew to hate him.

Martina returns with my tea. She has taken the dress from its tissue-lined paper box and left it hanging in the changing room. I go inside and begin undressing. Tempe follows.

"I can handle this," I say, pulling the curtain closed. The sharp tone of my voice seems to register, which is unusual for Tempe, who misses or ignores the most blatant of clues.

I strip down to my underwear and pull the dress over my head, tugging it down over my hips. It falls to my knees. It has a figure-hugging, sixties vibe, with a tight bodice and flared skirt, and reminds me of the dress my mother wore when she married my father. I need help to do up the bodice. Martina obliges, tugging the strings and tying them into bows.

"You've lost weight," she says, making a tish-tosh sound. "I'll have to adjust the bust."

"Most brides are happy to lose weight."

"Don't lose any more."

I step into the viewing area. Tempe claps her hands gleefully. She has put our earlier conversation about Darren Goodall out of her mind. Martina has me step onto a stool while she tugs at the hem of the skirt and pinches fabric on my arms, considering what minor adjustments might be made.

"It's perfect," I say, not wanting her to make a fuss.

"I can make it better."

"No. Please. Don't bother."

I step back into the changing room and struggle to unfasten the bodice and release myself from what feels like a straitjacket. Growing frustrated, I rip it from my arms and crush it under my feet.

Martina pokes her head through the curtains and lets out a cry of alarm. She rushes past me and gathers up the dress like she's carrying an injured child. I feel embarrassed. It's not the dress's fault or Martina's.

"Pack it up, I'm taking it with me," I say.

"But I need to adjust—"

"It's fine. Thank you."

I get dressed quickly and leave the store, carrying a polished white cardboard box with my wedding dress. Tempe has to run to keep up with me, asking what happened. When I don't stop walking, she grabs at my arm, but I shrug her away and spin to face her.

"How did you find us last night?"

"What?"

"At the nightclub. How did you know we were there?"

"Henry told me."

"No. He didn't."

"I guessed. There aren't that many clubs."

"No. You followed me. You infected my phone with a virus that keeps track of me."

"That's ridiculous."

We're arguing in the middle of the pavement outside an Italian restaurant with a chalkboard menu propped near the door. Pedestrians are stepping around us. I can hear my voice getting louder.

"That's how you've been finding me for months. You know when I'm at home or at karate or at work or shopping."

Tempe is shaking her head. "You're sounding paranoid."

"The other day, you turned up at the markets in Brixton. How did you know I was there?"

"It was a coincidence."

"And when I was at the restaurant in Wandsworth?"

"The same."

"What about when I chased that knifeman in South London? You knew it happened near the Brandon Estate."

"I heard something on the news."

"The estate wasn't mentioned."

"You must have told me."

"No."

"Why would I follow you?"

"Because you're obsessed. Because you're jealous. Because you don't have any friends." Am I shouting? "Because you're toxic. You're manipulative. You're dangerous. Your mother told me the truth about you. You don't have a dead sister or a soldier father. You're a pathological liar."

Each statement should be landing like a slap, but Tempe doesn't even flinch. She tells me to calm down and reaches for me again. I slap her hands away.

"Don't touch me! Never touch me!"

"You need to calm down," she says sternly. "Let's talk about this."

"OK. Let's talk," I say accusingly. "What happened last night?"

"I told you."

"Did you spike my drink?"

"I looked after you."

"You undressed me."

"You vomited all over your dress."

"Did you try to kiss me?"

"That's not what happened. You kissed me."

"Bullshit!"

She shrugs. "Believe what you like."

"You could have put me to bed on the sofa. You didn't have to sleep with me."

"I was worried that you'd be sick again. People die that way all the time, aspirating on their own vomit."

"I think you sexually assaulted me."

She laughs incredulously. "You think I raped you?"

"I think you took advantage of me."

She is shaking her head. "I would never do that. And you can't remember what happened. Maybe it was the other way around."

"What?"

"Maybe you forced yourself on me."

"That's bullshit! And you better get your story straight because the police are going to ask you about last night."

"I'll tell them we were together," she says, as though it should be obvious.

I want to stop her. I want to edit her story and come up with a better one, to protect myself and to protect Henry.

"You need to calm down and listen to yourself," says Tempe, softening her voice.

"No. I'm going home. Don't call me again. Don't visit. Forget you even know me."

"But the wedding."

"You're not invited."

"You don't mean that. Have you eaten today?"

Ignoring her words, I step onto the road, trying to hail a passing cab, but the driver swerves and honks his horn. He has a passenger already on board. Then I remember that I drove the VW and parked near the computer shop.

I'm walking. Tempe yells after me, saying she'll call me tomorrow and suggesting that I need a good night's sleep. When will she get the message? She is not my friend. She is a parasite and a manipulator who is not welcome in my life.

52

My phone vibrates beneath my pillow. Henry and I promised long ago that we would never take technology to bed with us, but things have changed. I turn sideways and listen to his soft, steady breathing. Sometimes when he's sleeping, he looks like he's quietly solving puzzles in his mind. Henry wants certainty in his life, but I keep arguing that life makes a mockery of planning. When it's steep we have to climb. When it's downhill we can coast. And when it's messy we pick up a broom.

I have apologized for the other night, but he doesn't seem ready to forgive and forget. Each attempt at making amends is greeted with one-word answers and soundless shrugs. I think he enjoys playing the martyr, even though I'm the one who was drugged and can't remember what happened.

Fairbairn has been talking to my friends. Each of them called me afterwards. All except for Tempe, who has gone quiet. I don't regret what I said to her outside the bridal shop. I have come to loathe her smugness, her cloying neediness. The worst type of stalker is a stalker who doesn't realize that she's a stalker.

My phone vibrates again. It's a text message from Nish.

Are you watching the TV? BBC News.

I slip out of bed and go to the sitting room. Calling him. He answers.

"What am I looking for?"

"They've released footage from the night of Goodall's murder."

I turn up the volume. A stony-faced reporter is standing outside the house in Kempe Road. Why do they always sound so earnest, as if delivering news of a global catastrophe rather than a lone death? "Tragedy" is an overused word. It should be reserved for terrible events that involve no malice or wickedness. A tsunami is a tragedy, so is an earthquake, but we've come to use the word for every moral failure, or flaw in character, or everyday misfortune.

"Scotland Yard has released CCTV images of a suspect wanted for

questioning over the murder of Sergeant Darren Goodall, who died in a
house fire early on Saturday morning."

The shot changes to poor-quality footage, bleached of color by the
brightness of a home security light that was triggered by a motion sensor.

"*The camera began recording at two forty-nine a.m., and the suspect
is only in frame for a few seconds, but we can see dark clothing, a hooded
jacket, and white trainers,*" says the reporter. "*The police believe this
person either came from the house or walked past it as the fire was taking
hold and could have important information.*"

"Does it look like a woman?" I ask.

"Maybe," says Nish. "They only released part of the footage. According to my mate, there's more. A few moments after the suspect disappeared, a second figure is visible on the far side of the road. It could be
unrelated or it could be an accomplice."

"What else did your mate say?"

"Not much."

"Did he mention me?"

"No."

I feel my throat begin to close. "I'm frightened they're going to stitch
me up. You saw what happened at the Brandon Estate."

"I've heard good reports about Fairbairn," says Nish, trying to reas-
sure me, but he doesn't realize how deeply I'm involved in this. Right
now I can't see any bright side or silver lining. I have no memory of that
night, and my only alibi is someone who has lied about everything else.

Mrs. Harriet Pearl has been the admissions clerk at St. Ursula's Convent
for thirty years and has always been called Pearlie by the students. I
don't know if she's married, but all of our female teachers were called
"Mrs." and the men were "Sir."

Pearlie hasn't aged at all and still wears her trademark floral dresses
and sensible shoes, and her tightly permed hair looks like a motorcycle
helmet has been squeezed onto her head. Her face lights up when she
sees me waiting outside her office.

"If it isn't Philomena McCarthy."

"Do you remember every student?" I ask.

"Only the naughty ones," she jokes.

"I was never naughty."

"You were cheeky. I remember that prank with the business cards. That was your idea."

In my final year, on our last day before our exams, we printed our names on thousands of business cards and hid them throughout the school, under desks, in cupboards, behind panels and ceiling tiles, in pipes and musical instruments. Those cards are still turning up ten years later.

Pearlie opens her office door and invites me into a cluttered room full of filing cabinets and shelves stacked with box files. Admissions and applications. There is a desk and enough chairs for the prospective parents and a student to be interviewed.

"What have you been doing with yourself?" she asks. "No, don't tell me. You became a police officer."

"I did."

"Mr. Shem told me." My old drama teacher.

"Is he still here?"

"Of course. He's planning to donate his skull to the drama department for when they do *Hamlet*."

"Alas, poor Yorick."

"Exactly."

She has a laugh like a dolphin.

"You're too young to have a school-age daughter—what brings you here?" she asks, cleaning up her desk, moving aside a misshapen pottery coffee cup that was clearly a gift from a student.

"I wanted to ask you about an old girl, Margaret Brown. She was a few years ahead of me. A vice captain."

The change in Pearlie is immediate as her face hardens and her lips tighten into thin lines.

"Is this a police request?"

"A personal one."

"I can't talk about former students."

"Can you confirm that she was expelled?"

"She was asked to leave."

"Why?"

"My job is to protect the reputation of St. Ursula's, not to spread scuttlebutt. That was years ago. It was handled correctly and there is nothing more to be said."

"What was handled correctly?"

She gives me a watery glare. "Philomena, please don't ask me again."

"I've heard so many different stories," I say. "One is that Maggie was caught making out with Caitlin Penney in the changing rooms."

"No comment."

"Another is that she was having an affair with a male teacher and that she fell pregnant. There was talk of drugs."

Pearlie is about to interrupt, but I keep going.

"This is important," I say. "Over the past few months, I've become friends with Maggie—she calls herself Tempe now—but I'm now concerned about her. She put a tracking app on my phone and has been following me."

"Which is nothing to do with the school."

"Two days ago I woke up in Tempe's bed with no memory of getting there. I think she drugged me and . . ."

I can't finish. Pearlie's hand goes to her mouth. My voice is rising.

"I'm not asking you to reveal any privileged information. This is between us. It doesn't leave this room."

"I really can't comment on—"

"Please. I just need to know. Would you trust her?"

There is a long pause. Pearlie gets to her feet and opens her door. I feel like I'm a schoolgirl being expelled from class. As I pass her, she leans close, her breath against my ear, whispering.

"No."

53

There are two reasons why the police execute warrants in the predawn darkness. The first is the obvious one. Like the proverbial early bird, they want to catch the worm when it's still at home tucked up in bed. The second reason is the element of surprise—nabbing the worm halfway between sleep and wakefulness, giving him or her no time to hide or destroy evidence or to alert accomplices.

Right now they are hammering on the front door, shaking the entire house. I'm awake because I have barely slept. Henry takes longer to respond.

"Who is it?" he asks groggily.

"The police."

"How do you know?"

"Who else would it be?"

The knocking grows louder. Front and back now. Taking no chances.

Refusing to meet my fate wearing flannelette pajamas, I take my robe from a hook in the bathroom and slide my arms through the sleeves as I make my way downstairs. Six officers are standing on my doorstep. Fairbairn is at the front. He has his warrant card in one hand and a search warrant in the other.

"Good morning. I hope we didn't wake you."

"Not at all. Coffee? Tea?"

The officers push past me and begin searching the house.

The warrant has been signed by a magistrate and issued under Section 8 of the Police and Criminal Evidence Act. They are looking for evidence of indictable offenses.

"I will allow you to stay in the house as long as you don't interfere," says Fairbairn, following the usual script. "A police officer will accompany you while you get dressed."

Henry has appeared at the top of the stairs, dressed only in boxer shorts. He blocks a detective who tries to get past him. The officer shoves him roughly aside, saying, "Touch me again, sir, and I'll have you arrested."

Henry joins me in the hallway, asking questions, hoping for an explanation. I want him to be quiet, because I know that Fairbairn is listening, looking for any sign of a weakness or a wedge that he might use to drive us apart.

A female officer accompanies me to the bedroom and watches me get changed, checking each item of clothing that I remove from the cupboard or drawers. As I move towards the bathroom, she follows.

"Really?"

"I can't leave you alone."

At least she turns her face away as I pee and wipe.

Henry is next to change, before we are reunited in the kitchen, sitting in the center of the room on high stools, as our house and our lives are picked apart, opened, examined, and swabbed. Forensic officers are checking the sinks and washing machine, looking for any fibers or particles that might match the crime scene. Our phones have been confiscated, as well as our laptops and iPads.

They think I killed Darren Goodall. What have they found? Traces of me at the house? Fingerprints? Fibers?

Fairbairn joins us, taking a seat at the island bench.

"Do you own a pair of white sports shoes?" he asks.

"Yes."

"Where are they?"

"They're upstairs in a wardrobe."

"These ones?"

He's holding sneakers with red paint splatters.

"No. They belong to Tempe. We have matching pairs. We bought them together."

"We found only these."

I try to think. Maybe they're in a locker at the academy or in my car.

Henry interrupts. "You can't seriously believe that Phil is a suspect."

"I'm following the evidence," says Fairbairn. He turns to Henry. "Did you know Darren Goodall?"

"Me? No."

"Ever met him?"

"Leave Henry out of this," I say.

The detective sighs tiredly. "I will, if you stop pissing on my leg and blaming the dog." He nods towards Henry. "You were seen arguing with Darren Goodall outside his house two weeks ago."

I can feel my mouth drop open and want to push it closed with the palm of my hand.

"A neighbor heard you threaten him," says Fairbairn.

"I wanted to punch his lights out," says Henry.

"The truth at last. Incriminating, but honest."

I'm staring at Henry, horrified. "You went to see him?"

"I didn't kill him. I wanted him to withdraw his complaint against you. He said that half of Southwark nick had fucked you . . . and you kept coming back for more."

"And you believed him."

"No! But I took a swing."

Fairbairn interrupts him. "Where were you on the early hours of Saturday morning?"

"I was here," says Henry.

"Alone?"

"You know that."

One of the officers enters the kitchen carrying the polished paper box that is tied up with a ribbon. "What's in here?"

"My wedding dress."

"Open it."

I undo the ribbons and lift off the top. My gown is neatly folded. I tell Henry not to look. "It's bad luck."

He starts to laugh. His chuckle becomes a rumble and eventually brings tears to his eyes. Moments later I'm laughing with him, realizing how ridiculous it sounds to think luck has played a role in any of this.

Fairbairn must think we're crazy. His phone starts playing the "Ride of the Valkyries." How appropriate. He takes the call, listening and giving one-word answers. Eventually he lowers the mobile and turns to me.

"Philomena McCarthy, I am arresting you in connection with the murder of DS Darren Goodall. You do not have to say anything, but it may harm your defense if you do not mention when questioned something which you later rely on in court. Anything you do say may be given in evidence."

54

At university I did a semester of philosophy and learned about the trolley dilemma—a classic thought experiment developed by the philosopher Philippa Foot. The scenario involves a runaway tram that is hurtling down the tracks towards five workers, who cannot hear it coming. As the disaster unfolds, you see a lever connected to a railway switch. By pulling the lever, you would divert the tram down a second track, saving the five workers, but a lone worker on the sidetrack would certainly die.

The question is: Would you pull the lever? Would you sacrifice one life to save five? What if it were fifteen lives to save a hundred? What if the lone victim were your child or your mother or your fiancé? One life is meant to be the same as any other, but we all know that's not true. Some are infinitely more valuable, but it depends on who is holding the lever.

When I became a police officer, I had to swear an oath to serve the Queen and to uphold the office of constable with fairness, integrity, diligence, and impartiality. I swore to protect fundamental human rights and accord equal respect to all people and strive to keep the peace to the best of my ability. The oath said that all lives mattered equally. The good, bad, ugly, cruel, rich, and poor. I wanted to believe those words. I have tried to live by them. I was wrong.

My holding cell is six paces long and four paces wide with a polished concrete floor that is tinted green. There is a lavatory, a sink, and a bunk bed with a thin vinyl cushion. Graffiti has been scratched and gouged into every wall, although valiant attempts have been made to cover it up. Above the heavy metal door, chipped into the brickwork, is the message: *Send out a search party, I can't find my self-esteem.* Another says, *I don't have a problem with drugs. I have a problem with the police.*

I am being held at Paddington Police Station, which is the protocol when police officers are arrested. The officer is separated from former colleagues to remove any possibility of favoritism or interference.

Leaning back, I rest my head against the wall and listen to doors clanging, toilets flushing, and inmates either sobering up or kicking off along down the corridor. The custody suite has been busy all morning, processing the usual parade of drunks, drug dealers, and addicts; the homeless and the unhinged. Some don't want to leave or complain about being woken.

There are footsteps outside. The observation flap opens. Eyes peer at me. After several seconds, the hatch shuts and I go back to staring at the ceiling light. I don't know the time. They took away my mobile phone, along with my belt and shoelaces.

There are more footsteps. This time the door unlocks. A tall figure appears, half in silhouette. Detective Fairbairn.

"We are ready for you."

I am handcuffed to a uniformed officer, who grips my forearms as we leave the cell. I am led down the corridor towards the custody suite. Doors are opened by unseen hands. More officers are watching from alcoves and intersecting corridors. I can sense their hatred. One of them spits on me. The warm phlegm hits my forehead and runs down the side of my nose.

Fairbairn reacts angrily, threatening to discipline anybody who "pulls a stunt like that again." I deserve the same respect afforded to any other prisoner, he says, but he is a lone voice. Most of these officers think I'm scum, the lowest of the low—a cop killer.

We enter Interview Room 1. The handcuffs are unlocked.

"I'm sorry about that," says Fairbairn, handing me a tissue to wipe my face.

He is wearing a cheap cologne and hasn't shaved since yesterday, or maybe earlier. Another detective joins him who is younger and chubbier, with a port-colored birthmark on his neck that his collar doesn't fully hide.

Fairbairn turns on the recording device.

"This is the first part of a recorded interview with Philomena McCarthy. The date is August twenty-fourth, at Paddington Police Station. I am Detective Inspector Martyn Fairbairn. Also present is Detective Constable David Briggs. What is your full name?"

"Philomena Claire McCarthy."

"Can you confirm your date of birth for me?"

"November twelve, 1993."

"And your full address?"

"One hundred and fifteen Marney Road, Clapham Common, London."

"Can you confirm that you have been cautioned and that you understand what that means?"

"Yes."

"You are entitled to free and independent legal advice either in person or by telephone at any stage. Do you wish to speak to a legal adviser now or have one present during the interview?"

"No."

"All right, Phil, by way of background, you were born in London and educated at St. Ursula's Convent in Greenwich. You studied history and politics at Leeds University, and applied to join the London Metropolitan Police four years ago."

"Yes."

"And for the past two years, you have been stationed in South London."

"Yes."

"What is your current employment status?"

"I am suspended from duty, pending a misconduct hearing."

There is a small, square window high up on one wall. It gives me a glimpse of blue sky and a vapor trail that looks like a skywriter has forgotten what he wanted to say. Elsewhere in the room is a mirror, behind which there will be a camera videoing the interview. I will not look at the mirror. I do not want to see my reflection.

"Let's start at the beginning?" says Fairbairn, adopting his game face. "Tell us how you met Tempe Brown."

It is strange being on this side of the table, being interviewed rather than asking the questions. It feels like I'm back at the training college, doing role-playing where we practiced the various interrogation techniques and learned how to handle difficult suspects.

The key to any successful interrogation is to get as much as possible from a suspect before they demand to see a lawyer. Experienced crims will lawyer up from the outset and "no comment" every question, forcing the police to do all the work. They will stonewall and prevaricate and refuse to concede even the most obvious of facts. The sky is not blue. Water is not wet. The truth is not the truth.

In contrast, ordinary, law-abiding people get arrested because of stupid mistakes or mind-fades or anger issues. They want to talk, to explain, to make their excuses while the digital recorder is getting it all down—every inconsistency and falsehood.

Fairbairn uses open questions to begin with, followed by closed inquiries, trying to pin down exact details. He rarely repeats himself or attempts to speed me up. He is trying to establish a rapport, hoping I might accidentally reveal some detail that will prove my guilt. But the clock is ticking. He has twenty-four hours to either charge me or to seek an extension or to let me go.

Eventually he will start to introduce the physical evidence against me. This is what I've been waiting for—the smoking gun that got him warrants to search my house and seize my car. In the meantime, he spends a lot of time establishing my movements on Friday evening and Saturday morning. I tell him about my hen night and how somebody must have spiked my drink because I can't remember leaving the nightclub or going back to Tempe's place.

"Did you go to the hospital?"

"No."

"Undergo a drug test?"

"No."

"What is the last thing you remember?"

"I was sitting at a bus shelter."

"How did you get back to Tempe Brown's flat?"

"We caught an Uber."

"You remember that?"

"I was told about it afterwards. I vomited. Tempe had to wash my dress."

The detective constable is making notes. Each of these details will be checked.

"Did you leave her flat again?"

"No."

"Where was Tempe Brown?"

I hesitate. "We were together."

"You shared a bed."

"Yes."

"That's cozy," says Briggs, smirking.

"Your mobile phone stopped transmitting just after midnight," says Fairbairn. "Why was that?"

"I must have turned it off. I don't remember doing it."

"You told me the phone had been lost."

"I left it somewhere. Tempe found it."

"And today, when we arrested you, we discovered the contents had been wiped—every address, photograph, text message, email, and app."

"I had a virus."

"Your laptop and iPad were also wiped clean."

"The technician told me to do that. He said the virus might have infected every device on our home Wi-Fi network."

I expect Fairbairn to follow up, but instead he opens a file and takes out a new sheet of paper.

"Do you own a pair of white women's training shoes, size six?"

"You have asked me that already."

"Where do you normally keep them?"

"I told you—in my karate bag."

"Which we can't find. Do you own a pair of black leggings?"

"Several pairs. Most women do."

"A hooded sweatshirt?"

"Yes."

"Have you ever been inside Darren Goodall's house?"

This is the question I've been waiting for. He could be fishing, or he might know the answer already.

"I'd like to take a break," I say.

"How long do you need?"

"Until my lawyer arrives."

"You haven't asked for one."

"I've changed my mind."

Fairbairn looks at me like a disappointed father as he announces the time and turns off the recording machine. A different uniformed constable escorts me back to my holding cell. He whispers to me as we walk, calling me the c-word, knowing it can't be heard by the overhead cameras that are filming us. He digs his thumb and forefinger into the flesh of my upper arm.

"Let me go, or I'll break it," I mutter. "You know I can."

"You're in enough trouble," he whispers.

"In for a penny . . ."

We're in a staring contest. He loosens his grip.

The holding cell has been cleaned. The floor is still wet and reeks of disinfectant.

I take a tissue from my pocket and wipe down the bench seat before lying on my side, staring at the window, where a small spider is trying to rebuild a web across one of the right angles. It is a clumsy metaphor but makes me think of Tempe. Our friendship had seemed so natural and organic—one thing leading to another. She was like a puppy abandoned by the side of the road who wanted to be loved and to love someone back.

Only she's not a puppy or a stray dog. She is like the Old Man of the Sea in Arabian mythology, who tricks travelers into letting him ride on their shoulders to cross a stream but never releases his grip. His victims are forced to carry him forever, allowed no rest, until they die crushed under his weight.

55

David Helgarde is dressed like a barrister today in a Savile Row suit and polished brogues with neatly combed hair that shines under the halogen lights. He ducks as he enters the cell.

"What have you told them? Nothing, I hope."

"I'm innocent," I say, wondering how often he's heard those words and how hollow they must sound.

"But you've said nothing."

"I want to help solve a murder."

He sighs and shakes his head. "In my experience, fashioning the gallows and putting one's head in the noose is rather counterproductive."

"I'm innocent," I say again, but sound even less convincing.

Helgarde is right. I know how this works. The truth isn't absolute. Innocence isn't a guarantee. Fairbairn wants to solve a murder. One of their own, a detective, is dead. I am now their prime suspect, and everything I've told them will be checked, rechecked, and reframed in a light that will undermine my credibility and point to my guilt.

Opening a briefcase, Helgarde produces a yellow legal notebook and a Montblanc pen that is fatter than a Cuban cigar. "My first priority is to get you out of here."

He begins by asking me questions about my domestic circumstances and employment, gathering evidence for a bail application. He will need to convince a judge or magistrates that I'm not a flight risk or likely to interfere with witnesses.

Finally he turns to the murder itself.

"Did you know the victim?"

"He ran me off the road and vandalized my car."

"Do you have proof? Witnesses? Photographs?"

"Finbar saw the car."

"Did Goodall ever threaten you?"

"Yes."

"Did you ever threaten him?"

"Yes."

Helgarde brushes a speck of fluff off his suit sleeve.

"The police are going to try to break down your alibi. They have arrested Tempe Brown. She is your friend, am I right?"

"She's not my friend," I say, surprised by the vitriol in my voice.

"But you were with her that night."

"She followed me to a nightclub."

"And you went home with her."

"I was drunk. Possibly drugged."

"Did you report the incident to the police?"

"No."

"Go to the hospital?"

I shake my head.

The barrister gives me the weary look of a schoolteacher who can't see a single correct answer amid a forest of raised hands.

"Could Tempe Brown have killed Darren Goodall?"

"Yes. Maybe. I don't know. He was sending her threatening messages. Stalking her."

Helgarde screws the top onto his fountain pen and holds it between both his hands.

"Will the police find anything that links you to the crime scene?"

I hesitate and nod. Helgarde slips the pen into his pocket and stands abruptly, knocking twice on the door to signal that he's finished.

"Don't you want to know why?"

"No."

"I didn't kill anyone."

"Save your plea for the jury."

"Will it get that far?"

"It will if your alibi doesn't hold up."

Fairbairn is waiting in the interview room, picking at his fingernails with a straightened paper clip. The recording starts again and he names everyone present. Helgarde is sitting beside me and a little behind.

"Let's pick things up, shall we?" says Fairbairn with a calm, impassive gaze. "I asked you earlier if you have ever been inside Darren Goodall's house in Kempe Road."

"No comment."

"What about his car, a blue Saab?"

"No comment."

My heart is playing a military drumbeat. Fairbairn's eyes hold mine, devoid of any sentiment, indifferent to whatever discomfit he's causing.

"On Wednesday August eighteen, Darren Goodall reported to police that someone had broken into his house and disabled his alarm system by unhooking the power supply. His neighbors remember hearing the alarm trigger that night. They say it went off a few minutes later."

He waits. I don't respond.

"Detective Goodall found no evidence of forced entry, and nothing appeared to have been stolen. He did, however, keep a spare set of house keys in his car, which could have been used to obtain access."

"No comment."

"Are you denying taking the keys?"

"No comment."

"Another neighbor, walking her dog, bumped into a woman that evening at around ten o'clock. She said the woman was driving a VW Beetle."

Fairbairn produces a photograph taken by a traffic camera. The date and time are coded into the image.

"We believe this is the vehicle she saw." He quotes a number plate. "Do you recognize this car?"

"No comment."

He produces a second document, a signed statement.

"Alison Goodall told you that her husband kept a spare set of house keys in his blue Saab, which was parked outside the house that night."

"No comment."

"You stole the keys. You entered the house. You disabled the alarm. You lay in wait for Darren Goodall, intending to kill him, but he wasn't alone when he arrived home, so you aborted the plan."

"No, that's not what happened."

"Which part?"

Helgarde touches my shoulder, wanting me to be quiet.

Fairbairn continues. "You returned to the house two nights later. You drugged him. You handcuffed him to the bed. You doused him with lighter fluid. You set him on fire and watched him die."

"No."

"We have found your fingerprints and traces of your DNA at two locations within the house. We have also matched fibers found on your clothing with those from an Afghan rug in a bedroom at Goodall's house. There is a partial thumbprint on a chisel in the utility room."

"I have an alibi."

"Really?" He gives me a sad smile. "Tempe Brown is giving us a statement now, but I don't know how much good it will do you."

Fairbairn takes out a new photograph from the folder. He slides it across the table.

"How long have you and Tempe Brown been lovers?"

56

I am back in my holding cell, lying on one of the narrow bunks, with a thin blanket over the top half of me. I haven't been charged yet, but it's only a matter of time. The photograph was not doctored or faked. Perfectly framed and lit, it looked like a work of art—a Helmut Newton nude, provocative but not obscene, alluring but not salacious. It showed me lying in Tempe's arms, with my head on her shoulder and my leg draped over her body. Both of us were naked, but nothing explicit was on display.

"It is quite beautiful," Fairbairn said, running his fingers over the image, making my skin crawl.

I have no memory of it being taken. There were other images, but only one showed us together. The rest were of me lying on Tempe's bed, arranged in different poses, with a sheet moving up and down my body. I remember Dr. Coyle's story about the drawings found in Tempe's room. She had drawn Mallory Hopper as she slept, spending hours at her bedside. Is that what Tempe did to me, or was it worse? Is it rape if you don't remember? Is it murder if you don't remember?

Fairbairn believes that Tempe and I are lovers, which means our alibis will be dismissed or discredited or ignored. We are coconspirators or willing accomplices or are lying to save each other.

I have told Helgarde about breaking into Goodall's house and finding the ring that belonged to Imogen Croker. I laid out the story, hoping it might aid my defense, but each new revelation exposed my impulsive, witless stupidity. Some stories sound more plausible when uttered aloud and delivered with certainty, but this one seemed to grow more frayed and tattered even as I stitched it together.

"You found the ring?"

"Yes."

"But you left it there?"

"Yes."

"Why?"

"It was an accident. It slipped from my fingers. I was searching the suitcase when Goodall arrived home. I couldn't keep looking. I had to get away."

"Perhaps you should forget about the ring," said Helgarde.

"But it can explain my fingerprints and my DNA."

"Admitting one crime doesn't exonerate you from another. It will lessen you in the eyes of a jury. They will see a woman who was so mad with hatred that she risked her career and her liberty to smear a decorated police officer."

"That's not why I was there."

"Regardless, I can't put it in front of a jury because it confirms too much of the case against you. The police claim you were obsessed with Darren Goodall and blamed him for ruining your career. You saw him as a bent copper. A traitor to his uniform. A wife beater. His very existence seemed to goad you, so much so that you stalked his family, befriended his wife, and encouraged her to leave him. Still not satisfied, you snuck into his house, seduced him or drugged him, and set him on fire. They have the motive and evidence of premeditation but cannot put you at the house on the night of the murder."

That was twelve hours ago, give or take. I don't know the exact time because I have no phone or watch or anyone I can ask. I wonder if Tempe is also in custody and where she's being held or what she's told the police. If they track her movements, if they study the cameras, if they talk to Dr. Coyle, surely they'll realize it wasn't me.

I haven't been able to call Henry since I was arrested. Under the law, I'm allowed legal advice and medical help and regular breaks for food and to use the bathroom, but the idea of being allowed one phone call is a myth. All the police are required to do is to contact whoever I name and tell them that I've been arrested.

I hear a commotion outside the cell. A drunken woman is yelling, calling someone a pig and telling them to "keep yer fuckin' hands off me."

The lock disengages and the door opens.

"You got company," says a constable. "The place is full tonight."

The same drunken woman stumbles or falls into the cell. Along with a second woman, her friend, who spins back and spits. The ball of phlegm hits the closing door and slides down the paintwork.

I sit up, hugging my knees. Both my cell mates are dressed for a night out in tight-fitting clothes, but their makeup is smeared and one has broken skin on her knuckles.

"What are you lookin' at?" she asks accusingly.

"Nothing," I reply.

She holds up her fist. "Nobody gives me the stink eye."

"I'm sorry," I mutter, looking at the floor. She slumps on the bench seat opposite me. Her friend, who is the drunker of the two, immediately curls up on the floor and falls asleep, snoring softly.

"Does she want to lie down?" I ask, offering her my bench.

"How would I fuckin' know?" says the other woman, who has unbuckled her sandals and is rubbing her feet. She is swearing under her breath, still abusing the police. I stay as quiet as possible, looking at the floor.

Eventually she asks, "What's your story?"

"Pardon?"

"Why are you here?"

"I'd rather not talk about it."

She repeats the phrase, mimicking my accent. "You sound like a fuckin' princess. Are you too good to talk to me?"

"No. I want to sleep."

"Yeah, sure."

She launches into a rambling account of driving home and being only two minutes away from her house when the police pulled her over. She tried to reverse but hit another car, which wasn't her fault, because she "wasn't pissed" and they shouldn't have pulled her over in the first place.

She adjusts her knickers. "I'd kill for a smoke."

"They don't allow that."

"I'm not a fuckin' idiot. Do I look like an idiot?"

"No."

She gets to her feet unsteadily and takes two steps towards me.

"Please, sit down," I say.

"Make me."

"I don't want to hurt you."

"Oh, this won't hurt a bit," she says, grabbing at my hair.

I grip her wrist with both hands and pull her arm towards me, spinning and trapping it under my armpit. She tries to struggle. I add pressure. She cries out in pain. I could break her arm with very little force.

When I let her go, she reels away, rubbing at her elbow and bashing her fist on the door. An officer comes. The same one.

"What's wrong, Josephine?"

"She attacked me. Damn near broke my arm."

The constable glances at me. I'm sitting on the bench, hugging my knees.

"What happened?"

I shrug.

He turns to Josephine and tells her to be quiet. She calls him a pig. He ignores her. The door closes. The cell goes quiet.

The woman on the floor makes a gurgling sound and gets up on all fours, vomiting between her hands.

"Bloody Norah!" says Josephine, holding her nose.

"Is that her name?" I ask.

"How would I fuckin' know?"

"I thought she was with you."

"Nah."

I kneel next to the woman, rubbing her back, asking if she needs a doctor.

"I'll be fine," she says apologetically. She sits up, leaning against the wall.

"What's your name?"

"Katrina."

"I'll get you some water."

"And a cleaner," says Josephine, wrinkling her nose.

I bash on the door, calling for the constable, but he ignores me, fed up with interruptions.

"Have you taken drugs or swallowed anything?" I ask.

Katrina shakes her head. I push back her hair, revealing piercings around the shell of her ear and a small tattoo lower down. She's young.

"Are you a nurse or something?" she asks.

"No. Here. Sit up."

I help her to the bench seat, where she curls up on her side, resting her head on her hands. She shouldn't have been put in a cell in this condition. A detainee has to be able to stand and walk unaided or to say a few words; otherwise they should be transferred to hospital.

Katrina's eyes are open. "Will you tell me a story?"

"What sort of story?"

"You choose. My mum used to tell me stories when I was sick."

"Were you sick a lot?"

"Yeah."

I tell her about being on the number 30 bus at Tavistock Square when a bomb exploded and all that happened in the aftermath.

"I don't remember the bombings," she says.

"How old are you?"

"Nineteen."

Suddenly I feel old.

57

"Silence, please! All rise."

The clerk of the court has a face like a funeral director and a commanding voice. He looks around the vaulted courtroom, defying anyone to speak, as the three magistrates enter and sit side by side at a large table. Dressed in layman's clothes, the two men and one woman look more like librarians than legal officers.

I have been brought upstairs from the cells beneath Westminster Magistrates' Court, using a private staircase that emerges directly into the dock. Two court sheriffs are on either side of me. My handcuffs are removed and I rub my wrists.

The chairman tells me to stand.

"Are you Philomena Claire McCarthy?"

"Yes, sir."

"It is alleged that between August twentieth and August twenty-first you did murder Darren Charles Goodall. Do you wish to enter a plea?"

"Not guilty."

"You may sit down."

I look up at the public gallery. My mother is sitting straight-backed, as though posing for a photograph. She has a handkerchief in her hand, which flutters as she waves to me. Farther along the front row I see Clifton and Finbar and Daragh. My father is at the end, his hands resting on the bulb of a walking stick that is braced between his knees. I search the other seats, looking for Henry, but know instinctively that he hasn't come.

Helgarde introduces himself and broaches the subject of bail. The prosecutor, Mr. Summers, asks for a separate hearing, suggesting the Crown Court decide the issue next week.

"My client shouldn't have to spend another four days in custody if we can come to an agreement today," says Helgarde. "Her family is willing to put up a substantial surety. And my client is willing to abide by any reporting restrictions that are deemed appropriate."

Mr. Summers chuckles dryly.

"Is there a problem?" asks the chairman of magistrates.

"My learned friend seems to have forgotten how things are done in the lower courts. Perhaps he's spent too long under a horsehair wig."

Rather than insult Helgarde, the prosecutor seems to have annoyed the magistrate.

"Are you suggesting that we're not qualified to hear this bail application?" asks the chairman.

"No, not at all. I didn't mean to—"

"Perhaps you should be quiet, until it's your turn to speak."

"Yes, Your Worship."

Helgarde has enjoyed the exchange, but doesn't let it show.

"Your Worships, Philomena McCarthy is twenty-seven years old and is a serving police officer. She graduated equal top of her class at the Hendon Police College and has, until recently, earned glowing performance reviews for her service.

"Miss McCarthy is due to be married a week on Saturday and more than a hundred guests are coming to her wedding. Her parents are both in court today and they are committed to taking her home and ensuring that Philomena defends these charges, which she strenuously denies."

Quietly, yet passionately, Helgarde pushes back against the weight of evidence, respecting the story I told him. There are no verbal fireworks or debating flourishes, but instead he shows a practiced sincerity and a deep appreciation of the legal tenet that every defendant is innocent until proven guilty.

Summers gets to his feet, thumbs hitched to his belt and feet splayed.

"A life sentence is mandatory for murder, but there are statutory guidelines that determine how long 'life' should be. These minimum terms are set at thirty years when a police officer is killed. That is because the community regards crimes against the police as being attacks on the rule of law and against society itself."

"Spare us the grandstanding," mutters Helgarde.

Summers ignores the comment. "A man is dead. A decorated detective was handcuffed to a bed and set alight. This defendant's DNA and fingerprints were found at the scene. She had threatened Sergeant Goodall. She had stalked his family and tried to smear his name."

"My client has an alibi," says Helgarde, still on his feet.

"Her lover."

"That is a lie!" I shout.

"Please instruct your client to be quiet," says the chairman.

Summer continues. "We believe the defendant to be a flight risk. She recently applied for a new passport, and the police found two airline tickets at her address."

"For her honeymoon," says Helgarde.

"The safety of the wider community must be paramount."

"And the safety of my client shouldn't be ignored," says Helgarde. "In prison she will have to be kept in solitary, and the guards will do her no favors. Constable McCarthy doesn't dispute that her DNA was found in the house. She claims to have visited that address prior to the murder, and the prosecution cannot place her at the scene on the night in question.

"She also admits that she disliked the victim because he beat his wife and his mistress and terrorized his children. But to handcuff a man to the bed and set him on fire, to watch him die, that takes real hatred. That's primal fury. That is a crime of passion." Helgarde pauses and I half expect him to step closer to the bench or to wander around the courtroom as he makes his case, both actions which aren't allowed. Barristers are meant to stay at the bar table.

"This is a headline-grabbing case," continues Helgarde, "which will make or break careers. Enormous pressure has been placed upon the police to obtain a quick conviction because one of their own has been killed. Overtime was canceled. Emotions ran high. Corners were cut. When a suspect emerged, the investigation immediately stopped looking for anyone else because it might compromise their one shot at a conviction. That's why they have not examined the other possibilities. Philomena McCarthy is right in front of them and has become their only option. It's easy. It's simple. Let's make it stick. But that is not how the legal system should function. My client is owed the presumption of innocence. She is not a flight risk. And she is not a danger to the community. Set bail and let her go home, until a jury can decide."

The magistrates have heard enough. They confer, speaking in whispers. The chairman turns back to the court.

"Bail is set at one million pounds. The defendant will surrender her

58

Two hours later, I am escorted from the cells and handed my belongings in a plastic bag. I am not party to the signatures or the lodging of sureties or whatever other guarantees were required to secure my release. Clifton and Daragh have come to collect me, both dressed in crisp white shirts and clean jeans and shiny black shoes. It looks like a uniform. I kiss their cheeks and apologize for looking like "death warmed up."

"Where did Daddy get a million pounds in two hours?" I ask.

"Eddie would have robbed the Bank of England," replies Daragh.

Dozens of reporters and TV crews have been waiting outside the courthouse, which is why we leave through a side entrance in Seymour Place. Clifton holds open the car door. I'm about to duck inside when I hear someone shout. A photographer has found us. Moments later a phalanx of journalists and photographers come into view, scrambling to get TV cameras onto shoulders and spotlights in place.

"The bastards!" says Clifton. He pushes me onto the backseat and throws a coat over my head, which smells of nicotine and breath mints. I used to question why people covered their faces for the cameras outside courtrooms and police stations. Surely it made them look guiltier, as though they had something to hide. But now I understand. It's a fear that the camera will expose some hidden doubt or frailty or make me look like a startled deer trapped in the high beams of an advancing truck.

The braying mass has surrounded the car. I hear them shouting and swearing, demanding that I show my face and answer their questions. The car horn sounds and I feel the vehicle jerk forward before accelerating away. I peer from beneath the coat.

"Where are we going?"

"There was some debate about that," says Daragh, who is driving. "Your mother and father had a heated whatnot."

"They argued?"

"Yeah, and for a good Catholic girl, your mother knows a lot of bad words," says Clifton.

passport and report daily to the nearest police station to her residence. There will be no contact with prospective witnesses."

He addresses me directly.

"Should you decide to get married, Miss McCarthy, there will be no honeymoon, do you understand?"

"Yes, Your Worship."

I glance at my father, who is already getting to his feet. A million pounds. He doesn't look shocked by the figure. Maybe it's too ridiculous to even countenance. I want some signal or sign, but he has already turned away.

"Who won?" I ask.

"Scoreless draw," says Daragh.

"Eddie on penalties," says Clifton.

"Where is Henry?" I ask.

"I haven't seen your boy," says Daragh. "Have you called him?"

"They wouldn't let me. I have to go home."

"That's not what the court agreed."

"I need to see Henry."

"Call him."

"No. In person. I need to explain."

Daragh and Clifton glance at each other, unsure of what to do. "Maybe you should wait until tomorrow."

"Take me home, or I'm getting out of the car *right* now."

Daragh makes the final decision, circling Hyde Park Corner and driving west towards Knightsbridge.

"Headstrong," says Clifton.

"Like her mother," says Daragh.

"We should warn the poor bugger."

"Too late for that."

"I can hear you," I say.

They grin.

It's still an hour from dusk and the house is bathed in a soft twilight that makes the exterior look golden. I walk through the rooms, hoping Henry might have left a note, but find nothing. A calendar pinned to the fridge has his shifts blocked off with red crosses. He's not working tonight.

As I move between rooms, I sense that everything has undergone a subtle transformation, as though a group of intruders has come in and shifted things around before putting them back exactly as they had been.

Daragh has followed me into the house. I borrow his phone and call Henry's number. He doesn't answer. In the bedroom I discover that his overnight bag is missing and he's taken his toothbrush and shaving gear.

I have his parents' phone number in my wedding book. It rings for a long while. A woman answers. Henry's mother. I call her Mrs. Chapman, even though she's told me it's "Janet." For some people a first name seems superfluous.

"Is Henry with you?" I ask hopefully.

"Philomena?"

"Yes. Is he there?"

A pause. "He can't come to the phone."

"I need to speak to him."

"Is this your one phone call?" She thinks I'm still in custody.

"I've been released."

"But you were charged. We saw it on the news."

"I'm on bail. Can you please put Henry on the line?"

Another silence. "He doesn't want to speak to you."

"Don't be difficult. Put him on."

"I don't think you understand how much you've hurt him."

"Me?"

"Those photographs . . . on the internet."

"What photographs?"

"You and that woman. I have nothing against gay people, and I know attitudes to sex and gender have changed, but you can't expect to marry my son after something like this."

The police must have leaked Tempe's photograph.

"Nothing happened," I say.

"You were naked."

"I did nothing wrong."

"You've been charged with murder."

"Let me talk to him. It's about the wedding."

"There won't be a wedding. I'm hanging up now. Please leave Henry alone."

I'm listening to a dial tone. I call again. Nobody picks up.

"I have to go and see him," I say to Daragh.

"Not now."

"But he doesn't understand."

"Give him time. Let's get you home."

This is my home, I want to say, but it doesn't feel like that anymore. I'm torn between leaving and staying, hoping that Henry might change his mind and drive south from Hertfordshire and slide beneath the covers beside me during the night.

Daragh waits while I pack a small suitcase. Periodically he glances into the street, worried the reporters might have followed us.

"We're all a little concerned about Finbar," he says.

"Why?"

"The police found a partial palm print on Darren Goodall's car."

My heart plunges.

"What did he tell them?"

"He said a lot of cars come through the garage." Daragh takes the suitcase from me. "Finbar has to be careful. A lot of people rely on him. Kids. Grandkids. He can't afford to fuck up."

"I'm sorry," I whisper.

"No harm done."

We go back through the house, turning off the lights. I notice my wedding dress, still boxed, sitting on the dining table. I contemplate taking it with me, but I don't want to be reminded of what I might have lost.

My father is standing beneath the portico light when the Range Rover pulls up at the house. He puts his arms around me, holding me wordlessly for a long while as a moth flutters against the light casing, throwing shadows on the steps.

He sighs, as though baffled with himself, and leads me into the brightly lit hallway.

"Do you want to talk?" he asks.

"Not tonight."

"We have decisions to make."

"They can wait."

59

Morning comes with wind and showers and scudding clouds. Outside my window, seagulls fight over mitten crabs, uttering deep-throated cries. Why do they make everything sound like pandemonium? I didn't expect to sleep, but exhaustion is the best sedative. For eight hours I disappeared into unconsciousness and dreamt of nothing.

My phone has been turned off since my arrest. I risk using it now, hoping Henry might have called. Dozens of text messages and emails ping into my inbox. Some are from Tempe. I read only a few of them.

Are you OK? The police have been here. They searched the flat and took your clothes. Call me when you get this.

And another one: *The police have let me go. I just heard the news. I know you didn't kill him. You were with me. How can they be so stupid? I love you. Call me.*

There are other messages from Carmen, Georgia, and Margot. Sara mentions the photographs and I stop reading immediately. Everybody will have seen the images by now. The whole world. The internet of things. Public humiliation is a strange feeling, a fluttering sensation in my chest and an overpowering urge to put my head under the pillow and scream.

I venture downstairs. Breakfast has been set up in the sunroom: a buffet of cereals, along with fruit salad and yogurt. A young woman asks if I want coffee or tea.

"Do you work here?" I ask.

"Yes, ma'am. I'm Molly."

"Call me Phil."

"Yes, ma'am, I mean Phil."

I shouldn't be surprised that my father has staff. Constance has taught him how to spend money, but I know the poor man isn't far below the surface. Scratch him and the lacquer would come off like on the cheap nesting dolls he once flogged at market stalls before he turned the family's fortunes around.

Molly has gone. I'm eating a triangle of toast, sitting propped in the open window, when Daddy arrives, wearing chinos and a casual shirt and loafers.

"How did you sleep?" he asks.

"Fine."

He pours muesli into a bowl and cuts up a banana, adding a dollop of yogurt.

"What happened to your cooked breakfasts?" I ask.

"A triple bypass. It took away my appetite."

He pulls a wicker chair next to me. I prop my feet on the armrest. He spoons cereal into his mouth and chews slowly.

"Do you want to talk about what happened?"

"I didn't kill him if that's what you're asking."

"Never crossed my mind." He takes another mouthful. "Helgarde tells me the case is largely circumstantial, but the forensic evidence puts you at the murder scene."

"Not that night," I reply.

"You broke into his house."

"I had a key. I thought I could sneak in and out again without anyone knowing."

"Finbar knew."

"I'm sorry about that."

He leans down and places his bowl on the floor. A tortoiseshell cat languidly uncurls from a patch of sunshine and wanders across the sunroom and begins lapping up the dregs.

"Cats are lactose intolerant," I say.

"So are humans," he replies, rising from his chair and pouring himself a coffee from a glass pot.

"What about your alibi?"

"Tempe Brown."

"And the photographs."

"Those pictures were taken when I was sleeping, or drugged."

"So, you're not a whatnot?"

"A lesbian? A bisexual? No, Daddy. And two women can sleep in a bed without scissoring each other."

"What's scissoring?"

"Never mind."

"Why would she drug you?"

"She has a history of obsessive behavior, of stalking people. I talked to a psychiatrist who has been treating her for years."

"Could Tempe Brown have killed Goodall?"

"Yes. Maybe. I can't be certain."

There is more I could say, but I'm not sure of what I believe. Tempe talked about murdering Goodall and having someone else blamed. We argued about perfect and imperfect crimes and whether they exist. I also remember Dr. Coyle talking about Mallory Hopper and how far Tempe went to hold on to a friendship. Stalking her. Setting fire to her parents' house.

Daddy returns to his seat, nursing his coffee two-handed, ignoring the heat of the mug.

"Helgarde says your friend will come under pressure to change her story."

"She's not my friend."

"You need her now."

I want to change the subject. I'm sick of people treating this like a game of Clue: Who killed Professor Plum in the library with a candlestick? This is not an intellectual exercise or a parlor game or a puzzle to be solved.

"Your mother has been calling," says Daddy. "It's strange to talk to her again after so long. In a good way."

"Not shouting, you mean."

A grimace deepens the wrinkles around his eyes, but he manages to smile.

"I'll visit her," I say, "but first I have to see Henry."

"You're not allowed to talk to prospective witnesses."

"He's not a witness."

Daddy takes a mobile from his pocket and calls the garage, asking Tony to bring the car around to the front. "He'll be ready in ten minutes."

"Thank you."

He reaches for my foot, touching it with his fingertips. I have a small birthmark on the inside of my left ankle. He has an almost identical birthmark in the same place. It's another link between us.

"In my experience, Phil, the police won't stop digging on this. They're seeking justice for one of their own."

"I am one of their own," I say defensively.

"Yes, but you're also my daughter."

"An accident of birth."

"No accident. Loved and wanted."

Mrs. Chapman answers the door as though expecting someone else. Her smile fades, and her small, birdlike body begins to fluff up, trying to appear more intimidating.

"Where is Henry?"

"He doesn't want to see you."

"Let him tell me that."

Mrs. Chapman tries to brace her arm across the doorway, but I duck underneath and enter the house, glancing into the sitting room, which she calls a parlor, just like my mother. I call up the stairs. "Henry? It's me."

Ignoring her protests, I carry on into the kitchen. Surely he can't be hiding from me. I'm about to search the house when I spot a bottom-heavy hammock in the garden, suspended between two trees. Henry's bare feet are draped over the sides, and a straw hat is resting upon his face.

I'm halfway across the lawn when his mother yells a warning and Henry raises the hat. There is no elegant way of getting out of a hammock and he stumbles as he finds his balance.

"I'll call your father," says Mrs. Chapman, sounding flustered.

"I can handle this, Mum. You go back inside."

She is hovering protectively. "I think I should stay."

"How about a cup of tea?"

This adds insult to injury, the idea that she has to make me a beverage. She bustles away and Henry walks me to a different section of the garden where a wrought-iron bench seat is sitting beneath a willow tree. He looks at me with unconcealed sadness but not contempt. I guess that's something.

"I tried to call you," I say.

"I've had my phone turned off."

"Why?"

"Reporters keep calling me. Either that or my friends want to commiserate."

"About what?"

"The photographs."

"Nothing happened."

"You were naked in bed with her."

"I was drugged."

"Your eyes were open."

"I *was* drugged."

There is nothing tender about his questions. He wants to know if I loved her, if I slept with her, if I purposely set out to humiliate him. I deny everything, but he sighs and shakes his head.

"I'm a pretty normal bloke, Phil. I fight fires. I play rugby. I watch cricket. I love my little boy. But I don't think my tender heart can recover from this."

"None of it is—"

"I could cope with being second best in your life because Archie will always be first in mine, but what you've done—those photographs . . . I'm a laughingstock. There is a meme going around which says, 'It's not cheating if your fiancé watches.'"

I want to scream at his selfishness and stupid male pride. I'm the one who was drugged, arrested, and charged with murder. Instead I whisper, "What about the wedding?"

"There won't be one. The venue canceled this morning. They saw the news reports and didn't want the bad publicity."

I'm speechless.

"The manager claimed he was misled," says Henry. "Tempe told him that you were Kate Middleton's cousin and that the Duchess of Cambridge was expected at the wedding."

I half laugh, thinking it must be a joke, but now I understand how Tempe managed to secure a venue that is usually booked out years in advance. She lied. She probably lied to all of them—the florist, the photographer, the cake maker.

"You're not going to defend her?" he asks.

"Of course not."

"I warned you."

"Yes, but I didn't expect . . ."

Henry won't look at me.

"I used to think she was obsessed with you, but maybe it was the other way around," he says. "You invited this cuckoo into our nest."

"I made a mistake. I'm sorry." My voice catches. "Do you still want to get married?"

Henry won't look at me. "I think you should leave."

His mother appears from the house, walking across the spongy turf, balancing two mugs on a tin tray. Reverend Bill is three paces behind her, hands in his pockets, acting like it's a pleasant stroll around the garden.

"Philomena. Nice to see you," he says, sounding genuine.

"Hello, Reverend Bill."

"She was just leaving," says Henry.

"But Janet made tea."

"I have to go," I say, adding hollowly, "Next time."

Henry doesn't stand or try to follow me. I feel like a child being banished to my bedroom for bad behavior and told to think about what I've done. Growing up, my punishments were like that. I would have preferred to go hungry or be grounded or surrender privileges, but my mother knew that coldness and silence were the greatest penance—the withholding of affection.

Moving in a daze, I retrace my steps through the house to the entrance hall. Pastor Bill turns the latch to open the door. He leans closer. I expect him to kiss me on the cheek, but he whispers in my ear.

"You have to forgive Henry. His allegiances are torn."

"I don't understand."

"Roxanne has threatened to fight for sole custody of Archie if Henry marries you."

"But that's—"

"She doesn't want Archie exposed to . . . to . . ." He doesn't finish.

"Me?" I ask.

"Or your family," he replies.

60

My mother's voice is muffled behind the heavy painted door.

"Philomena?"

"Yes."

"Are you alone?"

"Yes."

The key turns. The lock slides back. A security chain is unhooked. The door opens a crack and she peers at me anxiously. Brown curls. Brown eyes. Satisfied, she opens it wider and wraps me in her arms, her lips pressed against my cheek and her perfume filling my nostrils.

"Why have you deadlocked the door?"

"I thought maybe you were Tempe. She's been calling. Texting. Last night she came at midnight."

"What did she want?"

"You, of course. She thinks I'm hiding you."

Pulling me into the parlor, she takes a moment to examine me, as though looking at a piece of secondhand furniture that needs restoration. Normally she complains about my hair or my skin or that I dress "like a boy." This from someone who looks like a 1950s housewife in frocks and housecoats.

"There's something wrong with that woman," she says. "She was bashing on the door, calling your name. When I threatened to call the police, she laughed and said the police had only just let her go. She called them the gestapo and said they wouldn't mess with her again."

"What did she mean?" I ask.

"I have no idea. Did she get you into trouble? I told you not to trust her."

"When?"

"Right at the beginning when she was drawing all those sketches of you."

I don't remember that. I feel as though everybody has become an expert in hindsight: my friends, Dr. Coyle, Elsa, Pearlie, and Henry. It's like when people see photographs of Ian Brady or Myra Hindley or Jeffrey Dahmer and say, "Don't they look evil," as though their crimes are written on their foreheads and should be obvious to everybody. I wasn't blind to Tempe's odd behaviors and neediness, but she was also great company and a brilliant organizer, and she made me laugh.

"How is Henry?" my mother asks. "Worried sick, I expect."

"He's called off the wedding."

Her eyes widen in surprise and narrow again.

"I've embarrassed his family," I explain.

"You or your father?"

"You can't blame this on him," I say, which might not be completely true. Right now his money is the only thing standing between me and a prison cell. The irony isn't lost on me. I've spent the past decade trying to distance myself from my father, but now I'm staying in his house, taking advice from his barrister.

We move to the kitchen, where I finally get that cup of tea. She makes me tell her the story, but I reveal only those pieces that will make her feel reassured. We are both playing a game. She is pretending to be ignorant of how the legal system works and I'm editing the facts to present a more hopeful picture.

After an hour of talking, I make my excuses, saying that I have a meeting with the lawyers.

"Where to?" asks Tony when I get back to the car.

I give him the address of the Chestnut Grove Academy. I need to practice. I need to sweat. Maybe if I hit something hard enough the answers will shake loose.

61

Classes at the studio are normally mornings and evenings, which means it is empty in the middle of the day. I get changed into my Keikogi and wrap the black belt around my middle, crossing the ends, tucking the right over the left, and pulling both strands tight before completing the knot.

I begin with movement exercises: hip drives, flat rolls, and half-circle monkey hops. I move on to shadow sparring, which is like shadowboxing, studying my reflection. From there I shift to the heavy bag, throwing actual kicks, punches, and hand strikes with such force and speed that the bag swings back towards me and I pretend that I'm being attacked.

I have sweat dripping off my nose when I hear the door open and recognize Tempe's silhouette.

"I thought I might find you here," she says brightly.

"That's what all the stalkers say."

I turn back to the mirrors, keeping her in sight.

"I've missed you," she says, oblivious to my terseness.

"I've been rather busy."

"Did you get my messages?"

"I've blocked you," I say, which is a lie because I don't know how.

"Why?"

I try to laugh, but it sounds strangled. "I'm not allowed to talk to witnesses."

"I didn't release those photographs," she says. "It must have been the police."

"You took them. You spiked my drink. You took off my clothes. You photographed me naked."

"It wasn't like that. You're making it sound—"

"Creepy?"

"I didn't mean for any of this to happen. I wanted to draw you. You look so beautiful when . . . when you're—"

"Unconscious? Comatose?"

She falls silent and moves farther into the studio. "Do you want a sparring partner?"

"No."

"You always say it's better to train with someone."

"You don't want to spar with me, Tempe, I mean that."

Ignoring my warning, she disappears into the locker rooms, and I wonder whether she's simple-minded or deliberately trying to goad me. She's either the most sanguine or most stupid person I've ever met. A few minutes later she's back in the studio, dressed as I am, with a different-colored belt.

"I don't want to spar with you," I say.

"Oh, come on, we're here now."

She bows and says, "*Shomen ni rei*," acknowledging the history of karate and the long line of instructors who have carried on the martial art until now. She bows again, this time to me, saying, "*Sensei ni rei!*" before thrusting her fists down and dropping into *kiba-dachi*, ready to defend.

I dance forward and she dances back. I feint with left and right, before spinning a kick at her head, which she blocks. I trained Tempe well, but she's not a black belt. She has a longer reach than I do, which means not letting her get too close or attacking her without a strategy. She will not come to me. She will wait and defend.

Moving smoothly, I barely seem to shift weight onto my left foot when I spin with my right, slamming a kick into her torso. She collapses on the floor, winded. I wait for her to stand.

"That was quick," she says. "Maybe we should use the pads."

"No, you'll be fine," I reply. "I barely touched you."

She gets reluctantly to her feet and readies herself. We begin again. This time she's waiting for the same move, but I use the opposite leg. And although I'm looking at her torso, I aim the kick at her head.

She lets out a cry and holds her hand across her bloody bottom lip. "Why are you being so mean?"

I am standing over her. "You put a tracking app on my phone. You followed me. You invaded my home. You lied to me about everything. Your past. Your family. Your job. The wedding . . ."

"What about the wedding?"

"The venue canceled. I won't be getting married."

"Why?"

"It could be because you told them I was someone important. Or that my photograph is all over the internet, lying naked in your bed. Or it could be that I've been charged with murdering a detective, who I met because I was trying to protect you."

"You couldn't have killed him. You were with me."

"Exactly. You're my alibi."

"I'm your friend."

"No. We're not friends."

Tempe is still sitting on the mat. She touches her finger to her bottom lip and examines the blood, wiping it between her thumb and forefinger like it's a drop of oil.

"Did you kill Blaine?" I ask.

"Who?"

"Mrs. Ainsley's dog."

Tempe shakes her head, adamantly. "I wanted to lose him, that's all—teach him a lesson for barking—but the little bastard latched onto my hand. I had to hit him with a brick to make him let go."

"You're a monster."

"It was an accident, I swear." She pushes herself upright. "I think I've had enough."

"No. Come at me. Give it your best shot."

"You're too angry."

"Oh, you haven't seen me angry."

Halfheartedly, she drops into her *kiba-dachi* and begins circling around me. Occasionally, she lunges forward as though launching a punch or a kick but skips away again, too scared to fail.

"Did you leave the flat that night?" I ask.

"No."

"Did you kill Darren Goodall?"

"Don't be ridiculous. I was frightened of him."

Angry and overconfident, I launch a punch at her chest. Tempe parries, sidesteps, and parries a second punch before ducking and spinning. Her kick connects, which surprises me. I'm off balance, trying to recover, but she grapples and we're scrabbling on the ground. She has the better position, sitting behind me. Her legs are hooked around my waist. Her right arm snakes around my throat and grabs her left bicep in a classic chokehold.

I use both my hands to pull at her forearm, keeping it off my throat, but she tightens the hold, cutting blood to my brain. I fight harder, pushing her backwards, giving her less leverage, but she is ready for every move. When I roll, she rolls. When I kneel, she kneels, never letting go.

"Tap out," she says, wanting me to concede.

I refuse.

She tightens her arm around my throat. I scratch at her wrists, growing dizzy.

"Tap out."

"No," I croak.

My grip is weakening. She leans her forehead against my head, pushing me more firmly onto her forearm. I can feel myself losing consciousness. It's like watching a picture dissolve from a TV screen, shrinking to a single white dot before the world goes dark.

Although I'm out for only a few seconds, it feels like much longer. When my eyes open, Tempe is still cradling me in her arms, more gently now. Her legs are wrapped around me like we're lovers, not opponents.

"You should have tapped out," she says.

I push her legs away and get to my feet.

"I want you to stay away from me. Stop calling my number. Stop visiting my mother."

Tempe shakes her head like I'm a problem child who won't listen to reason. Her voice changes and her eyes narrow. "Without me you have no alibi. Without me you could go to prison."

"I'll tell them you drugged me and left me sleeping while you murdered Darren Goodall."

"But that's not true."

"Prove otherwise."

"How can I prove a lie?" she asks, genuinely curious. "I don't mind if you hurt me. I'm used to being hurt. But please don't stop loving me."

"Loving you! You're delusional."

"You said we were like sisters."

"I was wrong. I hate you. I hate what you've done to me."

Tempe sighs and springs to her feet. "You should go home and get a good night's sleep. I'll call you in the morning."

"No! You won't call me. You won't text me."

"But we need to talk about how we're going to handle this."

"There is no 'we'!" Spittle shoots from my mouth. "Coyle was right—you need help. Go back to hospital, Tempe."

She brushes down her uniform and touches her hair. I see a droplet of spit drying on her cheek.

"I'll go now. Call me when you've calmed down."

"Why are you doing this to me?" I ask, pleading with her.

"What a silly question. We're best friends."

62

I'm still angry when I arrive at my father's house. I storm through the door and head straight for the library and the drinks cabinet. Tempe's cloying, irritating, girlish voice is still echoing in my head. "We're best friends," I parrot as I pour myself a Scotch that sloshes over the sides of the tumbler. I need two hands to hold it steady. She did it. She killed him. And now I'm trapped. She still has her arm across my throat, slowly choking me.

"Is everything OK?"

My father is sitting in a large leather armchair beside the window. He's not alone. David Helgarde is opposite him in a matching high-backed chair. The barrister has his legs crossed, and his trouser cuffs have ridden up, exposing a pale, veined shin above his dark socks.

"What are you doing here?" I ask. "Has something happened?"

"David has been updating me on developments. Sit down. You should hear this."

I'd rather go and drown myself in the bath, I think, as I pour another drink. A spare chair is positioned between them and I get the impression that they've been waiting for me.

Helgarde begins. "Do you know the meaning of 'disclosure' in a legal sense?"

"I'm not stupid," I reply, annoyed.

This earns me a look from my father, but Helgarde doesn't seem to notice.

"The prosecution is obliged to disclose to the defense all materials collected by the police during the course of the investigation. Usually we don't gain access this early, but I have my sources."

"You have a spy?" I suggest.

"Nothing quite so dramatic." He clears his throat. "On the positive side, two traces of your DNA have been identified at the house, both beneath the bed in a smaller upstairs bedroom. This supports your story of being in the house earlier. Finbar has also provided a statement about breaking into Darren Goodall's car, which backs up your version of the timeline. But it doesn't rule out the possibility that you returned to the house, which is why your alibi is so important."

He glances at a legal folder in his lap.

"The police are still tracking mobile phones and looking at footage from traffic cameras and private CCTV, but to date they haven't been able to place either Tempe or you in the vicinity of the house when the fire broke out. Your mobile was turned off shortly after midnight. Miss Brown's phone has been tracked from the nightclub to her flat, and it didn't leave that location until she drove you home at ten forty-two the following morning."

The more the lawyer talks, the more I dread the moment he stops. The silence that follows will signal my turn to speak, to give account, to explain, to provide the why and how and when.

"The police also appear to be hardening in their conviction that you and Tempe Brown were working together," says Helgarde. "In criminal law, the joint enterprise doctrine permits two or more defendants to be convicted of the same criminal offense, even if they had different levels of involvement in the incident."

"But I wasn't involved," I slur. "I think Tempe left the flat while I was sleeping."

A shadow seems to pass across the lawyer's eyes. "Are you saying that you can't alibi her?"

"I don't *want* to alibi her." I avert my eyes and look down at my hands.

"Why would she kill Darren Goodall?"

"He was stalking her. Sending her threatening messages."

Helgarde glances at my father. Something is wrong.

"The police have found no evidence that Goodall was stalking or harassing Miss Brown."

"I saw the messages. There were dozens of them. Hateful texts. Threats . . ."

Helgarde pauses and waits for me to fall silent. "The police did, however, discover several apps on Miss Brown's phone and home computer which allowed her to send anonymous text messages. The program could hide her caller ID and location."

It takes a moment for the information to register.

"Are you saying that she sent the messages to herself?"

"I'm simply telling you what the police have uncovered."

I feel my throat beginning to close. "But Goodall found her address. He terrorized her."

"There is no evidence of that."

"He attacked my car with acid."

"He was meeting with his lawyer when your car was vandalized."

"He painted the word 'WHORE' on Tempe's front door." Even as I make the claim, I remember the spatters of red paint on her white shoes.

"Did you speak to anyone while you were being held at the police station?" asks Helgarde.

"No."

"You didn't talk about your arrest—how Goodall had ruined your career?"

"No."

"The police have obtained a statement from someone called Katrina Forsyth, who shared a cell with you. She says you admitted to killing Goodall."

"That's a lie! I would never—" I bite off the sentence. The girl who vomited in my cell. She was a plant.

"I barely spoke to her. She was sick. I looked after her. I said nothing." Fairbairn is stitching me up. That bastard! "How damning is it?" I ask.

"Katrina Forsyth has a history of drug possession and soliciting. We can use that to discredit her statement. I'm surprised the police went down this route, and it suggests their case is weak."

"What about the sapphire ring?"

"Nothing has turned up."

"But it was in the suitcase."

"Not according to the police."

Goodall must have hidden the ring or disposed of it.

Unsteady on my feet, I reach for the bottle of Scotch.

"Perhaps you've had enough," says Daddy.

"Perhaps you should mind your own business," I say, mimicking his tone.

I know that I'm angry at the wrong person, but this fuckery has gone too far. It isn't my father's fault, but he could have chosen another career. He could have been a stockbroker or an engineer or an actuary. I don't know what an actuary does, but it has to be better than being a criminal.

"I'm sorry, David," he says, apologizing for my behavior.

"He happens to be *my* lawyer," I say. "You shouldn't even be here."

"I'm paying for him."

"There it is, ladies and gentlemen, if you can't be a proper father, throw money at the problem."

Daddy gets slowly to his feet and takes the bottle of Scotch from my hand.

"You think I'm standing between you and your future," he says softly, "but I am trying to make sure that you have one."

He turns away, but pauses at the door.

"Did Tempe Brown kill the detective?"

Our eyes meet. Mine have a cold certainty in them. I nod my head.

63

When I was a little girl, my parents bought me a fish tank for my bedroom. It was a proper aquarium with a water heater and overhead lights and an aerator that bubbled up from a shell amid water plants and a bed of white gravel. I chose the fish and went for the most colorful tetras and guppies and loaches, giving them all names. That night I fell asleep listening to the bubbles and watching my underwater Eden.

In the morning I found a tiny dead guppy on the carpeted floor beneath the tank. The aquarium had a glass lid and only the smallest of gaps where the aerator cord ran over the corner of the tank. We buried Penny in a matchbox in the garden. A day later Crystal lay stiff and glassy-eyed on the floor. One by one, each of my beautiful new friends did kamikaze-like dives, perishing on the beige carpet. I was blamed for overfeeding them or leaving the lid off, but none of those things were true.

Replacement fish arrived. The suicides continued. Eventually, only one fish remained of my original dozen. Moby was small and copper colored and had a rainbow sheen and short fins. Convinced it was my fault, I took him back to the pet shop in a plastic bag of water.

"How did she slip in there?" said the aquarium man. His face was magnified as he looked into the bag. "She's a Siamese fighting fish—very territorial and aggressive. She must have terrorized the others until they couldn't take it anymore."

He placed Moby in her own small round bowl.

"That was our fault," he said. "You can choose some new fish."

"What's going to happen to her?" I asked.

"She'll be staying by herself."

"Won't she get lonely?"

"She's happier that way."

Henry said Tempe was a cuckoo, but I think she's more like that Siamese fighting fish, who forced every other fish out of the tank except me. She sought me out. She manipulated me. And now she thinks we are tethered by a secret, bonded by another man's blood, friends for life.

I am curled up on my bed, clutching a rag doll called Hermione that I haven't played with since I was a child. I found it on a shelf in a small, unused bedroom along with a pile of books from my childhood: *Matilda. The Secret Garden. The Hobbit.* I thought my mother was the keeper of my childhood mementos, but she must have surrendered these, or Daddy took them without her knowledge.

Hermione is made of wool with beige limbs and a knobbly bald head and crosses for eyes. She has such a blank expression that I envy her ambivalence as I wallow drunkenly on the sheets and the room spins each time I close my eyes. I am grimy and sweat stained and used up and angry, but I shall strike another match tomorrow and hope it lights a new day.

64

Summer has come to pound on my eyelids because I was too drunk to close the curtains. Fumbling in a bedside drawer, I search for paracetamol, every movement a fresh assault. Pills swallowed, I cover my head with the duvet, wanting the sun to go away and the seagulls to stop fighting.

Time passes. I crawl out of bed and shower, leaning against the tiles, letting the water wash over me, wishing it could take away more than dirt. I have lost Henry. I have lost my career. I have been charged with murder. I am clinging to the wreckage.

Making my way downstairs, I find Constance mopping the parquetry floor of the library. She's wearing tailored slacks and a fitted cotton blouse.

"What happened?"

"A spillage."

"It was probably me," I say. "I'll clean it up."

"I'm here now." She dips the mop into the bucket and squeezes out the excess water.

"Don't you have Molly to do that?" I ask.

"I can mop a floor." She pushes the bucket with her foot. "I know you all call me the duchess behind my back, but whatever money my family once had was gambled away before I was born."

"Where's Daddy?"

"I thought you might know."

"Me?"

"He left late last night after you went to bed. He asked Tony to bring the car and they drove off."

"Is that unusual?"

"I guess. He left his phone behind, which is strange."

Water sloshes over her sandal.

"Bugger," she says quietly. "He's not been himself lately. I blamed his heart, but I think he's worried about you."

Her statement barely registers. My mind is putting together the pieces of last night. Snippets of conversation. Words exchanged. It's like watching fragments of a montage shift and re-form to create a new picture. He asked me if Tempe had killed Darren Goodall. I didn't say yes. I nodded. God help her.

I'm moving, searching for my mobile. I must have left it in the library last night. I find it on the drinks cabinet. I have a dozen text messages. Only one from Tempe.

I didn't mean to hurt you, but everything I did was out of love. I hope I can make things right. Remember me. Goodbye.

I try to call her, but it goes straight to her voicemail.

"Where are you going?" asks Constance as I dash up the stairs.

I search for my car keys and realize that I don't have any. My Fiat is at the garage and the police have impounded the VW. Moments later I'm running across the lawn towards the old stable block, where large sliding doors secure the garage. The Range Rover is missing. There are three other cars parked side by side, all expensive and beautifully maintained.

Tony has a small office set off to the side, behind a wall of tools. The car keys are hanging on a corkboard above the desk. I choose the Alfa Romeo, which must belong to Constance because the driver's seat is pushed forward and I can smell her perfume.

The engine rumbles rather than purrs, but I give it no time to warm up. Swinging out of the garage, I accelerate down the gravel drive, pausing as the electronic gates open. Minutes later I'm heading north along Hawley Road towards Dartford, overtaking where possible. The smell of early autumn fills the car, and strands of mist are hanging over the river like wisps of smoke. A single sculler is moving across the water, creating ripples that widen in his wake.

My phone is on my lap. I try Tempe's mobile again and get the same prerecorded greeting. I leave her a voicemail message: "It's me. If you can hear me, pick up the phone." I pause, hoping to hear her voice. I try again, yelling in frustration. "Pick up the fucking phone, Tempe. Answer me."

I keep trying her as I drive east along the A2, through Bexleyheath and Eltham and Forest Hill and Dulwich Park. Twenty miles. Fifty minutes. It feels longer. Outside her ugly, redbrick block, I double-park and run up the steps, pushing my thumb on the intercom. Tempe doesn't answer. I press all of the buzzers, hoping someone will let me inside. The door unlocks. I push it open. I'm halfway up the stairs when a woman screams. It's not coming from Tempe's flat, but lower down. The basement has a communal laundry and a utilities room. I follow the sound, letting gravity carry me down the stairs.

The screaming has stopped. A woman is covering her mouth, backing away from the laundry door. She has a little girl, a toddler, who is hiding between her legs, covering her ears from the noise. I recognize them. They live in the flat opposite Tempe.

The laundry door is partly ajar. There is a sign stuck to it with Sello-tape.

DO NOT ENTER. CALL THE POLICE.

I try to push the door open, widening the gap, but something is leaning against it. Reaching inside. My fingers touch fabric. I take hold of a leg. Hanging.

"What's your name?" I ask the neighbor, trying to sound calm.

"Alice."

"OK, Alice, I want you to go upstairs and call triple nine. Ask for an ambulance and the police. Tell them it's an emergency."

Alice doesn't move. She's in shock. I touch her shoulder. She flinches but comes back to me.

"The police and paramedics. Understand?"

She nods and leaves, taking her little girl. I take two steps back and charge at the door, slamming into it with my shoulder. Each time, I sense a body swinging on the far side like a pendulum before it crashes back against the door. I wedge myself into the gap, first my arm, then leg, my shoulder, half my chest, forcing it open. Groaning with the effort, I squeeze myself through and drop to my knees.

Tempe is hanging above me. A thin nylon clothesline is wrapped around her neck and looped over a lagged water pipe. I grab her around the thighs and lift her, taking the weight off her neck. I reach up with one hand and try to hook my fingers under the noose, but the weight of her body is making it tighter.

Her skin is still warm. Her eyes are open.

I look around the laundry. A small stepladder is lying on the floor near her feet. I need to cut her down, which means letting her go. I release her gently and begin flinging open drawers and cupboards, searching for a knife or scissors or a box cutter. I find a set of rusting garden secateurs with curved handles and short blades.

Picking up the stepladder, I climb high enough and start scissoring at the nylon cord, using both hands to force the blades open and closed, slowly fraying the rope. Her face is close to mine. Her eyes are accusing me, saying, "You did this. This is your fault."

The rope unravels and breaks. Tempe topples to the floor. I manage to catch her top half before her head hits the polished concrete.

Turning her onto her back, I check her airways are clear and begin mouth-to-mouth and heart compressions. I know where to put my hands and how hard to press down, keeping a steady rate of at least a hundred compressions a minute. After every thirty, I give her two breaths, trying to remember the CPR beat. In between the breaths, I talk to Tempe, telling her to hang on because I don't want to be responsible for this. I don't want to sit bolt upright in the night, with my heart hammering, unable to breathe, reliving this moment.

I already have my nightmare—the bus bombing at Tavistock Square. The bomber that day, Hasib Hussain, was only eighteen. He looked so ordinary and unassuming when I saw a picture of him later. I tried to remember if I'd seen him on the bus, if we'd made eye contact. Hasib was born in Leeds and grew up in Holbeck in West Yorkshire, the youngest of four. His father worked in a factory. His mother was an interpreter. Both had emigrated from Pakistan. Hasib went to Ingram Road Primary School, and later to South Leeds High School. He did his GCSEs in English language, English literature, maths, science, Urdu, and design technology. He was supposed to set off his bomb on the Underground that day, but the earlier explosions had closed down the stations, so he chose to board the number 30 bus carrying a home-made bomb in his rucksack. The explosion killed thirteen people, but it could easily have been more. The bus had changed its normal route because of a police roadblock, and fifty passengers stepped off only moments before the blast.

Hasib Hussain was among the dead. I didn't know him or see him, so I couldn't yell at him like I'm yelling at Tempe. The paramedics can hear me when they arrive. They take over the resuscitation, using drugs and a defibrillator machine, but I can tell they're going through the motions and that Tempe won't be coming back.

Eventually a police officer leads me to a car, where I'm told to wait. I don't know how long I'm there, sitting inside the patrol car, watching police and forensic officers come and go. Neighbors are being interviewed. Statements taken.

Martyn Fairbairn arrives. It must be his day off because he's wearing old jeans and a rugby jumper that hangs from his skinny frame. He barely glances in my direction before he disappears inside the flats. Each time I close my eyes, I see images of Tempe's lifeless body hanging from the pipe. I feel the weight of her body as I tried to hold her up. I search again for a blade to cut her down, frantically opening drawers and cupboards. The shelves were lined with bottles of bleach, turpentine, detergent, drain cleaner, and acid.

Everything becomes a sign. The red paint spatters on Tempe's white shoes. The half-full bottle of acid on the shelf. The threatening text messages. It was *always* Tempe. Whenever I was drifting away from her, she dragged me back by conjuring some new threat or outrage, or she became the victim of another injustice.

For the past four months, she has been at the center of my life. She was my Girl Friday and my best friend and my stalker and my Siamese fighting fish and it all happened so slowly that I didn't notice until it was too late. I understand why Mallory Hopper took her own life; why she felt trapped and unable to escape.

Fairbairn emerges from the building. He jogs across the road, and I force myself to meet his eyes as he opens the door and leans inside.

"Are you OK?"

"I don't know."

"I talked to the paramedics. They said you did everything you could."

Tears blur my vision.

"What were you doing here?" he asks.

"Tempe sent me a text message. She said goodbye. I was worried."

"I thought you hated her."

"I never wished her dead," I say, but the words sound thick in my throat.

I wipe my eyes. "Did you have someone watching her?"

"What makes you think that?"

"She was a suspect. I thought you might have set up surveillance."

Fairbairn gives me a grim smile. "Why? We weren't watching you." His face softens and he sighs. "We had a team on her yesterday, but it wasn't round-the-clock."

He motions for me to move over, and he sits down next to me.

"She left a note."

"I saw it."

"Not the one on the laundry door. Upstairs. She confessed to killing Goodall. She said you had nothing to do with it."

"Was it typed?"

"Sitting on her printer. Why do you ask?"

"No reason."

He expects me to have more questions, but I don't know where to begin.

"You should be relieved."

Is that how I should react? I wonder. I'm not sure what I feel, apart from guilt. I'm sorry that Tempe is dead. I'm less sorry about Darren Goodall. I'm not angry anymore. I guess that's something.

Fairbairn is still talking.

"I spoke to her psychiatrist yesterday, who told me about her history."

"She wasn't obsessed with Goodall," I whisper.

"She was obsessed with you. That's why she killed him. In her twisted mind, you had saved her when she needed help, and now she wanted to save you. She didn't expect you to be charged with his murder. She thought your joint alibi would be enough to save you both."

"Why would Goodall let her into the house? Why would he let himself be handcuffed to the bed?"

"Clearly, she could be very persuasive," says Fairbairn. "She photographed you naked in her bed."

I feel my cheeks color.

"We got the lab results back on the dress you wore to the nightclub, the one you vomited on. They found traces of a date rape drug called gamma hydroxybutyrate."

"GHB."

"Class C. Odorless, colorless, and tasteless. It also leaves the body within a short amount of time, making it hard to detect. We also found the Uber driver. He remembered you."

We sit in silence, watching dappled sunshine shift on the pavement as a breeze shakes branches and rustles leaves.

"You planted someone in my cell who made up lies about me."

Fairbairn exhales. "That wasn't my idea."

"Who, then?"

"You have made a lot of enemies in a very short time."

We study each other, both with questions, both with secrets.

"Am I free to go?" I ask.

"We'll need a statement, but it can wait till tomorrow."

65

My paternal grandmother has an epigraph on her gravestone, which is written in Gaelic, that translates as: *Death leaves a heartache no one can heal, love leaves a memory no one can steal.*

I have visited the grave only once—when I was eleven and we went to Ireland for the Gathering, a McCarthy clan reunion at Blarney Castle in County Cork. I remember climbing the steps and kissing the famous stone, which according to legend endows a person with the gift of the gab. Perhaps it worked on my father, who has always had a way with words. He will need them now.

I find him in the garden doing his daily walk around the pond. He has added a new leg to the journey, crossing the meadow and following the path along the river, past a pony paddock and an overgrown tennis court, almost hidden in the beech trees. He walks with more purpose now, and barely raises a sweat. I fall in step beside him and we walk in silence until we reach the blackberry bushes that are growing wild over the stone ruins of a crumbling wall.

He stops and begins eating berries.

"They're sweet this year. We should make jam."

"Did you have her killed?" I ask.

His eyes are large and clear and brown. "That's a brutal question."

"Answer me."

"I don't think I will."

He looks at me in that familiar way, lowering his chin, observing me beneath his drawn brows. "I did not create this situation."

"And what am I supposed to do?"

"Accept your good fortune. Get on with things."

"You took a life."

"I saved one."

"That's bullshit. That's wrong."

I want to be angry and disgusted, but I *made* this happen. I *let* this happen. I might as well have forced Tempe's hand as she wrote that suicide note or put the noose around her neck or kicked the steps away.

Heavy raindrops have begun falling. We turn back towards the house, arriving as a fierce summer storm blurs the landscape and gurgles in the downpipes, creating puddles on the drive.

My father is being fussed over by Constance, who is drying his hair with a towel.

I go upstairs to my bedroom and find a familiar sports bag resting on a chair beside the bed. There is a note attached from Uncle Finbar.

I've been meaning to give you this. Someone took it out of the Fiat when we were spray-painting. Hope you didn't miss it.

Unzipping the bag, I sort through my karate gear and find the missing white trainers that Fairbairn had fixated on. Their absence proved my guilt, he said, convinced that I had destroyed the shoes after fleeing from the murder scene. But I hadn't lied to him. The bag was in my Fiat, until someone unwittingly took it out.

I add more clothes and collect my other suitcase.

"Where are you going?" asks Constance as I carry the bags downstairs.

"Home."

Someone is in the house. I sense it as soon as I cross the threshold and stand motionless in the hallway. I smell food cooking. When I drop my keys onto the table, Henry pokes his head out from the kitchen. He's wearing a frilly apron and has a smudge of tomato sauce on his chin.

"What are you doing here?" I ask.

"I'm making my world-famous spaghetti Bolognese."

"It's not actually world-famous."

He gives me a hurt look.

"There are seven Bolognese sauces that are better than yours, and that's just in Italy," I say.

"So, mine makes the top ten."

"In London, in Clapham, in Marney Road, definitely top ten."

He wraps his arms around me in a bearlike hug that makes me feel safe and warm and loved, and as I press my pelvis against his, I get a sign that perhaps life can be mended or remade.

He whispers into my hair. "I'm sorry for those things I said."

"Does that mean you still love me?"

"Always."

"And you want to marry me?"

"I would marry you in a car, in a bar, on a log with a frog, with a bear on the stairs, here or there or anywhere."

"Did you know that when Dr. Seuss wrote *The Cat in the Hat* there was a specific list of only three hundred and forty eight words that he could use?"

Henry laces his fingers into mine. "I did not know that."

"And when he wrote *Green Eggs and Ham*, he won a bet with his publisher that he couldn't use fifty words or less."

"I love that book." He nuzzles my neck. "How do you know stuff like that?"

"I'm a sponge."

He leads me to the table, which is set out with Tupperware containers ready to freeze the Bolognese into portions.

"What about Archie?" I ask.

"Roxanne won't ask for full custody. She likes having me around."

"To torture?"

"Exactly."

My stomach rumbles. "Can we have some now? I haven't eaten since some time yesterday."

Henry boils water for the spaghetti and takes a block of Parmesan from the fridge, setting it on a plate next to a grater. While I'm waiting for the pasta to cook, I tell him about finding Tempe's body and the police dropping the charges against me.

I still don't feel relieved. Instead, I have a nagging sense of having escaped rather than been vindicated. Henry listens and asks questions, refusing to bad-mouth Tempe or criticize the police. He's happy and I'm grateful, but something between us is impenetrably sad and I know it won't be repaired over a bowl of Bolognese.

That night, there's no mention of Tempe's death on the TV news. Suicides are rarely publicized unless the victim is someone famous or the death is unusual. "No suspicious circumstances" is the euphemism we use. Nothing to see here. Look the other way. Move on.

"We have to let everybody know about the wedding," says Henry. "Tell them it's off."

"It doesn't have to be off."

"We don't have a venue."

"We'll think of somewhere."

66

Henry can't find his black shoes. He has a pair of oxford brogues with thick soles that he only wears to weddings and funerals. A man can't get married in brown shoes. I'm sure there is some rule or superstition about that.

The cars are due to arrive any minute. I'm not getting dressed until we reach the house, but my hair and makeup have been done by two lovely women that Carmen used when she got married.

For the first few days after Tempe's death my phone didn't stop. People I hadn't spoken to in weeks suddenly wanted to call me. Some commiserated about the suicide of a friend, while others celebrated the dropping of charges against me. Most were fishing for details. A few didn't know what to say. I accepted their good wishes but spent most of my time alone or with Henry. His love is like liquid that has poured into my life, filling every crack and hollow and empty space.

"Found them," he yells. He's perched on a chair, searching boxes at the top of his wardrobe.

The doorbell chimes. I think it might be Tony, come to pick me up, but he's early.

Instead I find a Lycra-clad courier on the doorstep. I sign for a large square package wrapped in brown paper and Bubble Wrap. A solicitor's name and address are stamped on the back.

I tear it open and find a picture frame that contains one of Tempe's portraits of me. Done in astonishing detail, it looks like a black-and-white photograph which is so lifelike and beautiful it takes my breath away. On the back she has written: *My gift to you on your wedding day. I miss those days when your smile made me real.*

I look for more. A small envelope is taped to one corner of the frame. Tearing it open, I discover a small plastic square—a memory card— which falls into the palm of my hand. Opening my laptop, I plug in a card reader and click on the files.

The screen fills with a wide-angle shot of a living room. I recognize the location—Goodall's apartment at Borough Market. The camera must be hidden in the TV cabinet or nearby because the view is partially obstructed by a potted plant. I can see a sofa and two armchairs, with balcony doors in the background.

Tempe enters the shot. She is followed by Goodall, who is shirtless, wearing a towel around his waist. He pulls at her clothes. She wants him to wait. He tears at her blouse and pushes her to her knees, bending her over the coffee table. He is staring at his reflection in the TV as he violates her, but Tempe doesn't make a sound. She tries to look away. He grabs her hair and forces her to watch.

Once the act is over, Goodall tosses the torn blouse at Tempe and tells her to "get lost" because he has mates coming over. She wants to shower.

"No time."

"When can I come back?"

"When I tell you."

Tempe leaves. The camera is still running. I fast-forward. The doorbell sounds. I hear male voices. Three men walk into the frame, but I can't see their faces because the camera cuts them off at chest height. Goodall goes to the fridge. Beers are handed out. Opened. Clinked.

"Fucking journalists," says Goodall.

"Bottom-feeders," is the reply. The voice sounds familiar.

"Trump got it right—enemies of the people."

"What did you dig up?"

"His sister spent six months in rehab—heroin addiction—but she's been clean for five years. And his old man lost his license for drunk driving, but that was last century. Apart from that, I couldn't find so much as a speeding ticket or unpaid parking fine."

"We need more than that."

"Where's the Scarlet Pimpernel?"

"Late, as usual."

The three men sit down. Goodall takes the armchair. The others take the sofa. I see their faces. Superintendent Drysdale breaks wind, earning rebukes and laughter. He's been protecting Goodall from the outset, wiping the bodycam footage and burying the investigation.

The man sitting next to him is unknown to me.

"What if we leaked classified documents to Holstein and had him charged under the Official Secrets Act?" says Drysdale.

"That'll make him a martyr for the freedom-of-speech brigade," says Goodall.

"Drugs?"

"Too obvious."

"Child porn?"

"That might work."

"Losing evidence is easier than planting it."

The doorbell sounds. Goodall grunts as he gets up from the chair. Another guest has arrived, out of frame. Drysdale is still talking.

". . . I only know what filters down."

"Well, it's too late now."

The new arrival walks in front of the camera as he crosses the room.

"Want a beer?"

"Nah."

He collects a glass of water, then he comes back to the others.

"We need a more permanent solution," says Goodall. *"Holstein has been writing stories about gangland feuds. Why not make him a victim of his own success?"*

"A gangland hit," says Drysdale.

"Yeah. And we can blame it on the Albanians or Eddie McCarthy or the Cocky Watchman for all I care."

"And we control the investigation," says the third man.

The new arrival finally takes a seat and I see his face. Pale. Freckled. The shock of red hair. Martyn Fairbairn is staring directly at his reflection in the TV. He could be looking into my eyes.

The final piece falls into place. The lead detective on Dylan Holstein's murder had helped arrange the killing. Now I understand why he was outside my father's birthday party, directing attention away from the real killers. He must have lobbied hard or called in favors to get assigned to Goodall's murder as well as the Holstein case. He wanted to control both investigations, to steer them in the right direction, blaming my father for one killing and me for the other.

I close my laptop and retrieve the memory card. This is what Tempe took from Darren Goodall when she ran from him. It was her protection, her insurance policy, her guarantee that he would never come looking for her. Tempe must have lodged it with a solicitor and given instructions that it be sent to me if anything ever happened to her.

"What are you watching?" asks Henry, arriving in the kitchen.

"Nothing important," I say, sliding the memory card into the envelope. "But I might have to visit a newspaper office before we go on our honeymoon. I want to give someone a story."

The doorbell rings again. This time it's Tony, who has come to pick me up. I grab the polished box with my wedding dress and my shoes and my going-away clothes for later.

"Wait!" says Henry, who dashes along the hallway and sweeps me into his arms. The kiss lasts an age.

"That's a down payment," he says breathlessly.

"On what?"

"Our life together."

"That's corny."

"Yeah, but you love it."

Tony is driving the Range Rover. He's wearing his best suit with a carnation in the jacket pocket but still looks more like a pallbearer than an usher.

"The place is looking good," he says as he stows my bags. "Your stepmother knows how to throw a party."

"She was born to do it," I say.

"Your in-laws arrived last night." He means Henry's parents. "They seem very nice."

"You mean uptight?"

He gives me a sideways glance and matches my smile.

We're about to pull away when someone knocks on the glass. I turn to see Lydia Croker, who looks embarrassed at intruding. I lower the window. She apologizes profusely and speaks too quickly. I'm amazed at how different she looks from when I met her. Lighter. Less troubled.

"I should have called," she says. "And then I saw the news." She glances at Tony, who has a wonderful way of appearing to be busy and deaf at the same time. Lydia begins again. "I wanted to thank you for recovering Imogen's ring."

"I'm sorry?"

"The sapphire ring."

"I don't know what you're talking about."

She reaches into the side pocket of her dress and retrieves a small, square ring box covered in velvet. She hands it to me. The hinged lid pivots and the sapphire catches the light.

"How?"

"It arrived by mail," she says. "I was sure it was you."

"No."

She grows flustered. "Who else . . . ?"

"Did it come with a note?"

"No, but I still have the envelope."

Searching in her handbag, she produces a small, padded postbag with no return address. It is postmarked the twenty-third of August. Darren Goodall was dead by then. His house was a crime scene.

Henry emerges from inside. His hair is still damp from the shower and he's carrying his suit jacket over his arm.

"Are you getting married?" asks Lydia, having noticed my makeup and the boxed wedding dress.

"A month later than planned, but today is the day."

"Isn't it considered bad luck to see the bride before the wedding?"

"Oh, we're past that." I smile. "He's going to pick up his best man from school."

"How old is his best man?"

"Almost seven."

Mrs. Ainsley waves from her doorstep, wishing me luck. She's holding a new dog, Rumpole, a pug with a frying pan face that she adopted from an animal rescue shelter in Battersea. I drove her to pick him up.

"You have to go," says Lydia. "Thank you again."

"I didn't do anything."

"You listened. And you knew the woman who finally gave us justice." She's talking about Tempe. "Do you think she sent me the ring?"

"Maybe," I say, allowing a gentle lie, to hide a darker truth.

67

Alison Goodall is waiting at the school gates to pick up Nathan. Chloe is strapped in a stroller, chewing a biscuit that is breaking up in her fist, leaving sodden lumps on her dress. Alison's freckles are showing on her nose and she's wearing makeup.

"You're back in the house," I say. She turns. Surprised to see me. Anxious for a moment. Smiling now.

"I'm putting it up for sale. Too many bad memories."

"How have you been?"

"Good. Better."

She looks away nervously, as though scared that I might see something in her eyes. Some secrets are too big for a single person to hide. It takes a family to keep them; it takes blood and history and sacrifice.

I picture this woman a month ago. Downtrodden. Subjugated. Broken. A human punching bag married to a man who belittled and demeaned her, who slowly eroded her self-esteem, using fear and abuse to control her actions and her thoughts. A woman trapped in a loveless, violent marriage who could not afford to leave and could not afford to stay.

Day after day, she dreamed of being free of him, until an idea took hold, a thought that wouldn't go away. She escaped from him but didn't run far because he had her on a leash, and he was certain that she'd come crawling back to him like a kicked dog.

He was right. She did come back. She turned up late one night and begged for forgiveness. She took him to bed. She handcuffed his wrist to the bedhead. She set him on fire. She watched him die.

She had an alibi. Her little boy was sick. Her mother and father confirmed her movements. She was home all night, nursing Nathan, sleeping next to him.

The breeze has freshened, raising goose bumps on Alison's bare arms where there used to be bruises that she had to cover up with long sleeves and excuses.

"I was wrong about you," I say. "I thought you were a mouse, but you learned how to roar."

"No, I'm the same person—boring, uninteresting, uninspiring." She smiles shyly. "Darren spent years telling me so, but he still wouldn't let me go. He didn't love me—he didn't even like me—but he wouldn't let me go."

She glances at Chloe and makes a clucking sound as she brushes soggy biscuit crumbs from the toddler's lap.

"I don't want you to think I had it all planned," she says. "When I went back to the house, he took me to bed. I could smell another woman on the sheets. Even as he was telling me how much he loved me and how he wanted us to try again, I knew that he'd already been unfaithful."

The school bell rings. Small, excited voices spill from classrooms and fill the corridors.

"I'm sorry you were arrested. I didn't mean for that to happen. I thought they'd come to arrest me, but they chose you instead."

I am silent for a long while, still putting the pieces together. Alison didn't set out to incriminate anyone. She didn't plant my DNA in the house or lie to me about Imogen Croker's sapphire ring.

"How did you know?" she asks.

"Lydia Croker came to see me. You sent her Imogen's sapphire ring."

For a moment, Alison looks puzzled.

"I know it was in the suitcase," I say. "But when the police found Darren's body, the ring had gone. It had to be the killer. Who else knew it was there and who it belonged to?"

Alison doesn't answer, but seems to accept the truth.

"Why did you stay in the room while it burned?" I ask.

"I didn't want to live."

I glance at Chloe. Alison follows my eyes. "Mum and Dad would have looked after them."

Ahead of us, children have begun streaming through the gates. Alison looks for Nathan, her face bright with expectancy. When she sees him, it is like witnessing pure joy distilled into a single smile. I wish I could bottle that sort of joy and drink from it every time I feel sad.

"Hello, Nathan, do you remember me?"

"You're the police officer."

I smile and think, yes, once, maybe again, hopefully. Chloe raises her arms and Nathan bends to hug her.

"What are you going to do?" asks Alison, terrified of what I might say.

"I'm going to get married."

She waits, expecting more. Tony is standing beside the Range Rover. He taps his wrist, which doesn't have a watch, but I know we're running late.

There is another long pause. Nathan is pulling at his mum's hand, wanting to go home. Alison is still gazing at me fretfully, aware that I hold her future in my hands.

"You have a nice life," I say as I turn to leave, walking back to the car, where Tony holds the door open.

"Everything all right?" he asks.

"Perfect."

We drive away and pass Alison and her kids as she walks along Kempe Road. Chloe is kicking her legs in the stroller and Nathan is skipping ahead of her, jumping between cracks in the pavement. They look like any other family on their way home from school. There will be baths, dinner, and bedtime stories. Prayers and kisses good night.

When I joined the London Metropolitan Police I was taught about justice and what it means. The word comes from the Latin "*jus*," meaning "right" or "law," and is defined as being the quality of being fair and reasonable. Would it be fair and reasonable for Alison Goodall to be charged with murder? Would it be fair and reasonable for her children to lose a mother, having already lost a father? Others might answer yes, but I can't agree because this family has been punished enough.

That's why I'm going to leave Alison, Nathan, and Chloe to get on with their lives. Occasionally, I'll look in on them to learn their news. I'll watch their school concerts, graduations, recitals, performances, and milestones. I will see two beautiful children grow up in a loving environment, and I will not add them to my nightmares. I have enough of those already.

Summer has ended and the air is growing cooler as the days shorten. I am not the same person I was four months ago, or even a week ago, or even this morning. An innocent woman is dead. If I could change that, if I could pull the lever and save everyone, I would, but that's not how the trolley dilemma works. An innocent has to die, and I will have to live with Tempe's death for the rest of my life.

Pushing those thoughts away, I picture my future husband, waiting at the house, straightening Archie's bow tie and leaning down to wipe a speck of dust from his shoes. I picture my uncles, uncomfortable in their suits, shepherding guests to their seats in the marquee on the lawn. I picture my mother with a fixed smile, being impossibly polite to Constance, while secretly appraising her hair and her dress and her shoes.

Finally, I see my father, standing nervously outside, waiting for me to arrive. I thought I knew this man, that I understood his motives and his instincts. I was wrong. I fear my father, and I love him. I have spent a decade denying his existence, steering away from anything that might link me to my family, but that's no longer possible. We are complicity. Bound by blood with bloody hands. Guilty but uncharged.

It is sheer vanity to believe that I can change my father, and I will not make apologies for him, but neither will I let him control my life. I will fight to hold on to my values, dented as they are, and not let him drag me down to his level, not again. Perhaps that's the best way to ward off my demons—to have one of them at home.

Acknowledgments

It is a wonderful thing, after two decades of writing fiction, to come to the blank page with all the same excitement and wonder as when I penned the first chapters of *The Suspect* in 2001. With each subsequent novel, I have always strived to push myself as a writer, using different tenses, new voices, or dual narratives. This is also one of the reasons that I write occasional standalone novels like *When You Are Mine*, because it challenges me to come up with new characters and to explore new lives.

This is a novel about domestic abuse, toxic friendships, and the baggage that all families carry with them. Three women a day are killed by an intimate partner in America. Two women a week die from domestic violence in the UK, and one woman dies every week in Australia. If this were terrorism, we would have done something by now.

I wish to thank Nick Lucas for his advice and expertise on police matters. Any procedural mistakes in this text are mine and made willfully because sometimes exact protocols slow down the story. That's one great advantage of writing fiction—I get to make stuff up.

I am indebted, as always, to my wonderful agents Mark Lucas, Richard Pine, Nicki Kennedy, and Sam Edenborough, and to my editors Lucy Malagoni, Rebecca Saunders, and Colin Harrison. Working in the background are wonderful publishing teams at Little, Brown Book Group UK, Hachette Australia, and Scribner in the US, as well as my many foreign publishers far and wide, most notably Goldmann in Germany.

This was not an easy book to write—my wife Vivien can attest to that. And she will doubtless claim credit for never wavering in her belief that I could make it work. She was right, of course. When will I ever learn? I love her to bits, along with my three beautiful and talented children, Alex, Charlotte, and Bella, who are my greatest creations.

About the Author

Michael Robotham is a former investigative journalist whose bestselling psychological thrillers have been translated into twenty-five languages. He has twice won a Ned Kelly Award for Australia's best crime novel, for *Lost* in 2005 and *Shatter* in 2008. His recent novels include *When She Was Good*, winner of the UK's Ian Fleming Steel Dagger Award for best thriller; *The Secrets She Keeps*; and *Good Girl, Bad Girl*. After living and writing all over the world, Robotham settled his family in Sydney, Australia.